JINGO

A Discworld® Novel

Terry Pratchett

JINGO

A Discworld® Novel

HarperPrism

![HarperPrism]

HarperPrism

A Division of HarperCollins*Publishers*
10 East 53rd Street, New York, NY 10022-5299

Copyright © 1997 by Terry and Lyn Pratchett
All rights reserved. No part of this book may be used or reproduced in any
manner whatsoever without written permission of the publisher, except in
the case of brief quotations embodied in critical articles and reviews. For
i   Ltd.,
Wellington F   BB Great Britain.

3 1759 00117 7009

HarperCollins®, ■ ®, and HarperPrism®
are trademarks of HarperCollins Publishers, Inc.

HarperPrism books may be purchased for educational, business,
or sales promotional use. For information, please write:
Special Markets Department, HarperCollins Publishers,
10 East 53rd Street, New York, NY 10022-5299.

A hardcover edition of this book was published
in Great Britain by Victor Gollancz Ltd.

First U.S. printing: May 1998

Printed in the United States of America

Library of Congress Cataloging-in-Publication Data

Pratchett, Terry.
    Jingo : a novel of Discworld / Terry Pratchett. — 1st U.S. ed.
        p. cm.
    ISBN 0-06-105047-4
    I. Title.
PR6066.R34J56 1998
823'.914—dc21   97-47590

Visit HarperPrism on the World Wide Web at
http://www.harperprism.com

98 99 00 01 02 ❖ 10 9 8 7 6 5 4 3 2 1

To all the fighters for peace

JINGO

*I*t was a moonless night, which was *good* for the purposes of Solid Jackson.

He fished for Curious Squid, so called because, as well as being squid, they were curious. That is to say, their curiosity was the curious thing about them.

Shortly after they got curious about the lantern that Solid had hung over the stern of his boat, they started to become curious about the way in which various of their number suddenly vanished skyward with a splash.

Some of them even became curious—very *briefly* curious—about the sharp barbed thing that was coming very quickly toward them.

The Curious Squid were extremely curious. Unfortunately, they weren't very good at making connections.

It was a very long way to this fishing ground, but for Solid the trip was usually well worth it. The Curious Squid were very small, harmless, difficult to find and reckoned by connoisseurs to have the foulest taste of any creature in the world. This made them very much in demand in a certain kind of restaurant where highly skilled chefs made, with great care, dishes containing *no trace of the squid whatsoever.*

Solid Jackson's problem was that tonight, a moonless night in the spawning season, when the squid were especially curious about everything, the chef seemed to have been at work on the sea itself.

There was not a single interested eyeball to be seen. There weren't any other fish either, and usually there were a few attracted to the light. He'd caught sight of one. It had been making through the water extremely fast in a straight line.

He laid down his trident and walked to the other end of the boat, where his son Les was also gazing intently at the torch-lit sea.

"Not a thing in half an hour," said Solid.

"You sure we're in the right spot, Dad?"

Solid squinted at the horizon. There was a faint glow in the sky that indicated the city of Al-Khali, on the Klatchian coast. He turned round. The other horizon glowed, too, with the lights of Ankh-Morpork. The boat bobbed gently halfway between the two.

"'Course we are," he said, but certainty edged away from his words.

Because there was a hush on the sea. It didn't look right. The boat rocked a little, but that was with their movement, not from any motion of the waves.

It *felt* as if there was going to be a storm. But the stars twinkled softly and there was not a cloud in the sky.

The stars twinkled on the surface of the water, too. Now *that* was something you didn't often see.

"I reckon we ought to be getting out of here," Solid said.

Les pointed at the slack sail. "What're we going to use for wind, Dad?"

It was then that they heard the splash of oars.

Solid, squinting hard, could just make out the shape of another boat, heading toward him. He grabbed his boat-hook.

"I knows that's you, you thieving foreign bastard!"

The oars stopped. A voice sang over the water.

"May you be consumed by a thousand devils, you damned person!"

The other boat glided closer. It looked foreign, with eyes painted on the prow.

"Fished 'em all out, have you? I'll take my trident to you, you bottom-feedin' scum that y'are!"

"My curvy sword at your neck, you unclean son of a dog of the female persuasion!"

Les looked over the side. Little bubbles fizzed on the surface of the sea.

"Dad?" he said.

"That's Greasy Arif out there!" snapped his father. "You take a good look at him! He's been coming out here for years, stealing *our* squid, the evil lying little devil!"

"Dad, there's—"

"You get on them oars and I'll knock his black teeth out!"

Les could hear a voice saying from the other boat, "—see, my son, how the underhanded fish thief—"

"Row!" his father shouted.

"To the oars!" shouted someone in the other boat.

"Whose squid *are* they, Dad?" said Les.

"Ours!"

"What, even before we've caught them?"

"Just you shut up and row!"

"I can't move the boat, Dad, we're stuck on something!"

"It's a hundred fathoms deep here, boy! What's there to stick on?"

Les tried to disentangle an oar from the thing rising slowly out of the fizzing sea.

"Looks like a . . . a chicken, Dad!"

There was a sound from below the surface. It sounded like some bell or gong, slowly swinging.

"Chickens can't swim!"

"It's made of iron, Dad!"

Solid scrambled to the rear of the boat.

It *was* a chicken, made of iron. Seaweed and shells covered it and water dripped off it as it rose against the stars.

It stood on a cross-shaped perch.

There seemed to be a letter on each of the four ends of the cross.

Solid held the torch closer.

"What the—"

Then he pulled the oar free and sat down beside his son.

"Row like the blazes, Les!"

"What's happening, Dad?"

"Shut up and row! Get us away from it!"

"Is it a monster, Dad?"

"It's worse than a monster, son!" shouted Solid, as the oars bit into the water.

The thing was quite high now, standing on some kind of tower . . . "What is it, Dad! *What is it?*"

"It's a damned weathercock!"

There was not, on the whole, a lot of geological excitement. The *sinking* of continents is usually accompanied by volcanoes, earthquakes and armadas of little boats containing old men anxious to build pyramids and mystic stone circles in some new land where being the possessor of genuine ancient occult wisdom might be expected to attract girls. But the rising of this one caused barely a ripple in the purely physical scheme of things. It more or less sidled back, like a cat who's been away for a few days and knows you've been worrying.

Around the shores of the Circle Sea a large wave, only five or six feet high by the time it reached them, caused some comment. And in some of the very low-lying swamp areas the water swamped some villages of people that no one else cared about very much. But in a purely geological sense, nothing very much happened.

In a purely geological sense.

"It's a *city*, Dad! Look, you can see all the windows and—"

"I told you to shut up and keep rowing!"

The seawater surged down the streets. On either side, huge, weed-encrusted buildings boiled slowly out of the surf.

Father and son fought to keep some way on the boat as it was dragged along. And, since lesson one in the art of rowing is that you do it while looking the wrong way, they didn't see the other boat . . .

"You lunatic!"

"Foolish man!"

"Don't you touch that building! This country belongs to Ankh-Morpork!"

The two boats spun in a temporary whirlpool.

"I claim this land in the name of the Seriph of Al-Khali!"

"We saw it first! Les, you tell him we saw it first!"

"We saw it first before you saw it first!"

"Les, you saw him, he tried to hit me with that oar!"

"But Dad, you're waving that trident—"

"See the untrustworthy way he attacks us, Akhan!"

There was a grinding noise from under the keel of both boats and they began to tip as they settled into the sea-bottom ooze.

"Look, Father, there is an interesting statue—"

"He has set his foot on Klatchian soil! The squid thief!"

"Get those filthy sandals off Ankh-Morporkian territory!"

"Oh, *Dad*—"

The two fishermen stopped screaming at each other, mainly in order to get their breath back. Crabs scuttled away. Water drained between the patches of weed, carving runnels in the gray silt.

"Father, look, there's still colored tiles on the—"

"Mine!"

"Mine!"

Les caught Akhan's eye. They exchanged a very brief glance which was nevertheless modulated with a considerable amount of information, beginning with the sheer galactic-sized embarrassment of having parents and working up from there.

"Dad, we don't *have* to—" Les began.

"You shut up! It's your future I'm thinking about, my lad—"

"Yes, but who *cares* who saw it first, Dad? We're both hundreds of miles from home! I mean, who's going to *know*, Dad?"

The two squid fishermen glared at one another.

The dripping buildings rose above them. There were holes that might well have been doorways, and glassless apertures that could have been windows, but all was darkness within. Now and again, Les fancied he could hear something slithering.

Solid Jackson coughed. "The lad's right," he muttered. "Daft to argue. Just the four of us."

"Indeed," said Arif.

They backed away, each man carefully watching the other. Then, so closely that it was a chorus, they both yelled: "Grab the boat!"

There was a confused couple of moments and then each pair, boat carried over their heads, ran and slithered along the muddy streets.

They had to stop and come back, with mutual cries of "A kidnapper as well, eh?" to get the right sons.

As every student of exploration knows, the prize goes not to the explorer who first sets foot upon the virgin soil but to the one who gets that foot home first. If it is still attached to his leg, this is a bonus.

The weathercocks of Ankh-Morpork creaked around in the wind.

Very few of them were in fact representations of *Avis domestica*. There were various dragons, fish and miscellaneous animals. On the roof of the Assassins' Guild a silhouette of one of the members squeaked into a new position, cloak and dagger at the ready. On the Beggars' Guild a tin beggar's hand asked the wind for a quarter. On the Butchers' Guild a copper pig sniffed the air. On the roof of the Thieves' Guild a *real* if rather deceased unlicensed thief turned gently, which shows what you are capable of if you try, or at least if you try stealing without a license.

The one on the library dome of Unseen University was running slow and wouldn't show the change for half an hour yet, but the smell of the sea drifted over the city.

There was a tradition of soap-box public speaking in Sator Square. "Speaking" was stretching a point to cover the ranters, haranguers and occasional self-absorbed mumblers that spaced themselves at intervals amongst the crowds. And, traditionally, people said whatever was on their minds and at the top of their voices. The Patrician, it was said, looked kindly on the custom. He did. And very closely, too. He probably had someone make notes.

So did the Watch.

It wasn't spying, Commander Vimes told himself. Spying was when you crept around peeking in windows. It wasn't spying when you had to stand back a bit so that you weren't deafened.

He reached out without paying attention and struck a match on Sergeant Detritus.

"Dat was me, sir," said the troll reproachfully.

"Sorry, sergeant," said Vimes, lighting his cigar.

"It not a problem."

They returned their attention to the speakers.

It's the wind, thought Vimes. It's bringing something new . . .

Usually the speakers dealt with all kinds of subjects, many of them on the cusp of sanity or somewhere in the peaceful valleys on the other side. But now they were all monomaniacs.

"—time they were taught a lesson!" screamed the nearest one. "Why don't our so-called masters listen to the voice of the people? Ankh-Morpork has had *enough* of these swaggering brigands! They steal our fish, they steal our trade and now they're stealing our land!"

It would have been better if people had cheered, Vimes thought. People generally cheered the speakers indiscriminately, to egg them on. But the crowd around this man just seemed to nod approval. He thought: they're actually *thinking* about what he said . . .

"They stole my merchandise!" shouted a speaker opposite him. "It's a pirate bloody empire! I was boarded! In Ankh-Morpork waters!"

There was a general self-righteous muttering.

"What did they steal, Mr. Jenkins?" said a voice from the crowd.

"A cargo of fine silks!"

The crowd hissed.

"Ah? Not dried fish offal and condemned meat, then? That's your normal cargo, I believe."

Mr. Jenkins strained to look for the speaker.

"Fine silks!" he said. "And what does the city care about that? Nothing!"

There were shouts of "Shame!"

"Has the city been told?" said the inquiring voice.

People started to crane their heads. And then the crowd opened a little, to reveal the figure of Commander Vimes of the City Watch.

"Well, it's . . . I . . ." Jenkins began. "Er . . . I . . ."

"*I* care," said Vimes calmly. "Shouldn't be too hard to track down a cargo of fine silks that stink of fish guts." There was laughter. Ankh-Morpork people always like some variety in their street theater.

Vimes apparently spoke to Sergeant Detritus, while keeping

his gaze locked on Jenkins. "Detritus, just you go along with Mr. Jenkins here, will you? His ship is the *Milka*, I believe. He'll show you all the lading bills and manifests and receipts and things, and then we can sort him out in jig time."

There was a clang as Detritus's huge hand came to rest against his helmet.

"Yessir!"

"Er . . . er . . . you can't," said Jenkins quickly. "They . . . er . . . stole the paperwork as well . . ."

"Really? So they can take the stuff back to the shop if it doesn't fit?"

"Er . . . anyway, the ship's sailed. Yes! Sailed! Got to try and recoup my losses, you know!"

"Sailed? Without its captain?" said Vimes. "So Mr. Scoplett is in charge? Your first officer?"

"Yes, yes—"

"Damn!" said Vimes, snapping his fingers theatrically. "That man we've got in the cells on a charge of being Naughtily Drunk last night . . . we're going to have to charge him with impersonation as well, then? I don't know, more blasted paperwork, the stuff just piles up . . ."

Mr. Jenkins tried to look away but Vimes's stare kept pulling him back. The occasional tremble of a lip suggested that he was preparing a riposte, but he was bright enough to spot that Vimes's grin was as funny as the one that moves very fast toward drowning men. And has a fin on top.

Mr. Jenkins made a wise decision, and got down. "I'll . . . er . . . I'll go and sort . . . I'd better go and . . . er . . ." he said, and pushed his way through the mob, which waited a little while to see if anything interesting was going to happen and then, disappointed, sought out other entertainment.

"You want I should go an' have a look at his boat?" said Detritus.

"No, sergeant. There won't be any silk, and there won't be any paperwork. There won't be anything except a lingering aroma of fish guts."

"Wow, dem damn Klatchians steals everything that ain't nailed down, right?"

Vimes shook his head and strolled on. "They don't have trolls in Klatch, do they?" he said.

"Nossir. It's der heat. Troll brains don't work in der heat. If I was to go to Klatch," said Detritus, his knuckles making little bink-bink noises as he dragged them over the cobbles, "I'd be really *stoopid.*"

"Detritus?"

"Yessir?"

"Never go to Klatch."

"Nossir."

Another speaker was attracting a much larger crowd. He stood in front of a large banner that proclaimed: GREASY FORANE HANDS OFF LESHP.

"Leshp," said Detritus. "Now *dere's* a name that ain't got its teef in."

"It's the land that came back up from under the sea last week," said Vimes despondently.

They listened while the speaker proclaimed that Ankh-Morpork had a duty to protect its kith and kin on the new land. Detritus looked puzzled.

"How come dere's dese kiff and kin on dere when it only just come up from under der water?" he said.

"Good question," said Vimes.

"Dey been holding dere breath?"

"I doubt it."

There was more in the air than the salt of the sea, Vimes thought. There was some other current. He could sense it. Suddenly, the problem was Klatch.

Ankh-Morpork had been at peace with Klatch, or at least in a state of non-war, for almost a century. It was, after all, the neighboring country.

Neighbors . . . hah! But what did that mean? The Watch could tell you a thing or two about neighbors. So could lawyers, especially the real rich ones to whom "neighbor" meant a man who'd sue for twenty years over a strip of garden two inches wide. People'd live for ages side by side, nodding at one another amicably on their way to work every day, and then some trivial thing would happen and someone would be having a garden fork removed from their ear.

And now some damn rock had risen up out of the sea and everyone was acting as if Klatch had let its dog bark all night.

"*Aagragaah,*" said Detritus, mournfully.

"Don't mind me, just don't spit it on my boot," said Vimes.

"It mean—" Detritus waved a huge hand, "like . . . dem things, what only comes in . . ." he paused and looked at his fingers, while his lips moved ". . . fours. Aagragaah. It mean lit'rally der time when you see dem little pebbles and you jus' *know* dere's gonna be a great big landslide on toppa you and it already too late to run. Dat moment, dat's aagragaah."

Vimes's own lips moved. *"Forebodings?"*

"Dat's der bunny."

"Where does the word come from?"

Detritus shrugged. "Maybe it named after der soun' you make just as a t'ousand ton of rock hit you."

"Forebodings . . ." Vimes rubbed his chin. "Yeah. Well, I've got plenty of them . . ."

Landslides and avalanches, he thought. All the little snow-flakes land, light as a feather—and suddenly the whole side of a mountain is moving . . .

Detritus looked at him slyly. "I know everyone say 'Dem two short planks, dey're as fick as Detritus'," he said, "but I know which way der wind is blowin'."

Vimes looked at his sergeant with a new respect.

"You can spot it, can you?"

The troll's finger tapped his helmet twice, knowingly.

"It pretty obvious," he said. "You see up on der roofs dem lit-tle chickies and dragons and stuff? And dat poor bugger on der Fieves' Guild? You just has to watch 'em. *Dey* know. Beats me how dey always pointin' der right way."

Vimes relaxed a little. Detritus's intelligence wasn't too bad for a troll, falling somewhere between a cuttlefish and a line-dancer, but you could rely on him not to let it slow him down.

Detritus winked. "An' it look to me like dat time when you go an' find a big club and listen to grandad tellin' you how he beat up all dem dwarfs when he was a boy," he said. "Somethin' in der wind, right?"

"Er . . . yes . . ." said Vimes.

10

There was a fluttering above him. He sighed. A message was coming in.

On a pigeon.

But they'd tried everything else, hadn't they? Swamp dragons tended to explode in the air, imps ate the messages and the semaphore helmets had *not* been a success, especially in high winds. And then Corporal Littlebottom had pointed out that Ankh-Morpork's pigeons were, because of many centuries of depredation by the city's gargoyle population, considerably more intelligent than most pigeons, although Vimes considered that this was not difficult because there were things growing on old damp bread that were more intelligent than most pigeons.

He took a handful of corn out of his pocket. The pigeon, obedient to its careful training, settled on his shoulder. In obedience to internal pressures, it relieved itself.

"You know, we've got to find something better," said Vimes, as he unwrapped the message. "Every time we send a message to Constable Downspout he eats it."

"Well, he *are* a gargoyle," said Detritus. "He fink it lunch arriving."

"Oh," said Vimes, "his lordship requires my attendance. How nice."

Lord Vetinari looked attentive, because he'd always found that listening keenly to people tended to put them off.

And at meetings like this, when he was advised by the leaders of the city, he listened with great care because what people said was what they wanted him to hear. He paid a lot of attention to the spaces outside the words, though. That's where the things were that they hoped he didn't know and didn't want him to find out.

Currently he was paying attention to the things that Lord Downey of the Assassins' Guild was failing to say in a lengthy exposition of the Guild's high level of training and value to the city. The voice, eventually, came to a stop in the face of Vetinari's aggressive listening.

"Thank you, Lord Downey," he said. "I'm sure we shall all be able to sleep a lot more uneasily for knowing all that. Just one minor point . . . I believe the word 'assassin' actually comes from Klatch?"

"Well . . . indeed . . ."

"And I believe also that many of your students are, as it turns out, from Klatch and its neighboring countries?"

"The unrivaled quality of our education . . ."

"Quite so. What you are telling me, in point of fact, is that their assassins have been doing it longer, know their way around our city and have had their traditional skills honed by you?"

"Er . . ."

The Patrician turned to Mr. Burleigh.

"We surely have superiority in weapons, Mr. Burleigh?"

"Oh, yes. Say what you like about dwarfs, but we've been turning out some superb stuff lately," said the President of the Guild of Armorers.

"Ah. That at least is some comfort."

"Yes," said Burleigh. He looked wretched. "However, the thing about weapons manufacture . . . the important thing . . ."

"I believe you are about to say that the important thing about the business of weaponry is that it is a business," said the Patrician.

Burleigh looked as though he'd been let off the hook on to a bigger hook.

"Er . . . yes."

"That, in fact, the weapons are for selling."

"Er . . . exactly."

"To anyone who wishes to buy them."

"Er . . . yes."

"Regardless of the use to which they are going to be put?"

The armaments manufacturer looked affronted.

"Pardon me? Of *course*. They're *weapons*."

"And I suspect that in recent years a very lucrative market has been Klatch?"

"Well, yes . . . the Seriph needs them to pacify the outlying regions . . ."

The Patrician held up his hand. Drumknott, his clerk, gave him a piece of paper.

"The 'Great Leveller' Cart-Mounted Ten-Bank 500-pound Crossbow?" he said. "And, let me see . . . the 'Meteor' Automated

Throwing Star Hurler, Decapitates at Twenty Paces, Money Back If Not Completely Decapitated?"

"Have you ever heard of the D'regs, my lord?" said Burleigh. "They say the only way to pacify one of *them* is to hit him repeatedly with an axe and bury what's left under a rock. And even then, choose a heavy rock."

The Patrician seemed to be staring at a large drawing of the "Dervish" Mk III Razor-Wire Bolas. There was a painful silence. Burleigh tried to fill it up, always a bad mistake.

"Besides, we provide much-needed jobs in Ankh-Morpork," he murmured.

"Exporting these weapons to other countries," said Lord Vetinari. He handed the paper back and fixed Burleigh with a friendly smile.

"I'm very pleased to see that the industry has done so well," he said. "I will bear this particularly in mind."

He placed his hands together carefully. "The situation is grave, gentlemen."

"Whose?" said Mr. Burleigh.

"I'm sorry?"

"What? Oh . . . I was thinking about something else, my lord . . ."

"I *was* referring to the fact that a number of our citizens have gone out to this wretched island. As have, I understand, a number of Klatchians."

"Why are our people going out there?" said Mr. Boggis of the Thieves' Guild.

"Because they are showing a brisk pioneering spirit and seeking wealth and . . . additional wealth in a new land," said Lord Vetinari.

"What's in it for the Klatchians?" said Lord Downey.

"Oh, they've gone out there because they are a bunch of unprincipled opportunists always ready to grab something for nothing," said Lord Vetinari.

"A masterly summation, if I may say so, my lord," said Mr. Burleigh, who felt he had some ground to make up.

The Patrician looked down again at his notes. "Oh, I do beg your pardon," he said, "I seem to have read those last two sentences in the wrong order . . . Mr. Slant, I believe you have something to say here?"

The president of the Guild of Lawyers cleared his throat. The sound was like a death rattle and technically it was, since the man had been a zombie for several hundred years although historical accounts suggested that the only difference dying had made to Mr. Slant was that he'd started to work through his lunch break.

"Yes, indeed," he said, opening a large legal tome. "The history of the city of Leshp and its surrounding country is a little obscure. It is known to have been above the sea almost a thousand years ago, however, when records suggest that it was considered part of the Ankh-Morpork empire—"

"What is the nature of these records and do they tell us who was doing the considering?" said the Patrician. The door opened and Vimes stepped in. "Ah, commander, do take a seat. Continue, Mr. Slant."

The zombie did not like interruptions. He coughed again. "The records relating to the lost country date back several hundred years, my lord. And they are of course *our* records."

"Only ours?"

"I hardly see how any others could apply," said Mr. Slant severely.

"Klatchian ones, for example?" said Vimes, from the far end of the table.

"Sir Samuel, the Klatchian language does not even have a word for lawyer," said Mr. Slant.

"Doesn't it?" said Vimes. "Good for them."

"It is our view," said Slant, turning his chair slightly so that he did not have to look at Vimes, "that the new land is ours by Eminent Domain, Extra-Territoriality and, most importantly, *Acquiris Quodcumque Rapis.* I am given to understand that it was one of our fishermen who first set foot on it this time."

"I hear the Klatchians claim that it was one of *their* fishermen," said Vetinari.

At the end of the table Vimes's lips were moving. *Let's see, Acquiris* . . . "'You get what you grab'?" he said aloud.

"We're not going to take their word for it, are we?" said Slant, pointedly ignoring him. "Excuse me, my lord, but I don't believe that proud Ankh-Morpork is told what to do by a bunch of thieves with towels on their heads."

"No, indeed! It's about time Johnny Klatchian was taught a lesson," said Lord Selachii. "Remember all that business last year with the cabbages? Ten damn boatloads they wouldn't accept!"

"And everyone knows caterpillars *add* to the flavor," said Vimes, more or less to himself.

The Patrician shot him a glance.

"That's right!" said Selachii. "Good honest protein! And you remember all that trouble Captain Jenkins had over that cargo of mutton? They were going to *imprison* him! In a *Klatchian* jail!"

"Surely not? Meat is at its *best* when it's going green," said Vimes.

"It's not as if it'd taste any different under all that curry," said Burleigh. "I was at a dinner in their embassy once, and do you know what they made me eat? It was a sheep's—"

"Excuse me, gentlemen," said Vimes, standing up. "There are some urgent matters I must deal with."

He nodded to the Patrician and hurried out of the room. He shut the door behind him and took a breath of fresh air, although right now he'd have happily inhaled deeply in a tannery.

Corporal Littlebottom stood up and looked at him expectantly. She had been sitting next to a box, which cooed peacefully.

"Something's up. Run down to . . . I mean, send a pigeon down to the Yard," said Vimes.

"Yes, sir?"

"All leave is cancelled as of now and I want to see every officer, and I *mean* every officer, at the Yard at, oh, let's say six o'clock."

"Right, sir. That might mean an extra pigeon unless I can write small enough."

Littlebottom hurried off.

Vimes glanced out of the window. There was always a certain amount of activity outside the palace but today there was . . . not so much a crowd as, just, rather more people than you normally saw, hanging around. As if they were waiting for something.

Klatch!

Everyone *knows* it.

Old Detritus was right. You could hear the little pebbles bouncing. It's not just a few fishermen having a scrap, it's a hundred years of . . . well, like two big men trying to fit in one small room, trying to be polite about it, and then one day one of them just *has* to stretch and pretty soon they're both smashing the furniture.

But it couldn't really happen, could it? From what he'd heard, the present Seriph was a competent man who was mostly concerned with pacifying the rowdy edges of his empire. And there were Klatchians living in Ankh-Morpork, for heaven's sake! There were Klatchians *born* in Ankh-Morpork. You saw some lad with a face that'd got camels written all over it, and when he opened his mouth it'd turn out he had an Ankhian accent so thick you could float rocks. Oh, there's all the jokes about funny food and foreigners, but surely . . .

Not very funny jokes, come to think of it.

When you hear the bang, there's no time to wonder how long the little fuse has been fizzing.

There were raised voices when he went back into the Rats Chamber.

"*Because,* Lord Selachii," the Patrician was saying, "these are *not* the old days. It is no longer considered . . . *nice* . . . to send a warship over there to, as you put it, show Johnny Foreigner the error of his ways. For one thing, we haven't had any warships since the *Mary-Jane* sank four hundred years ago. And times have changed. These days, the whole world watches. And, my lord, you are no longer allowed to say 'What're *you* lookin' at?' and black their eyes." He leaned back. "There's Chimeria, and Khanli, and Ephebe, and Tsort. And Muntab, these days, too. And Omnia. Some of these are powerful nations, gentlemen. Many of them don't like Klatch's current expansionist outlook, but they don't like us much, either."

"Whyever not?" said Lord Selachii.

"Well, because during our history those we haven't occupied we've tended to wage war on," said Lord Vetinari. "For some reason the slaughter of thousands of people tends to stick in the memory."

"Oh, *history*," said Lord Selachii. "That's all in the past!"

"A good place for history, agreed," said the Patrician solemnly.

"I meant: why don't they like us now? Do we owe them money?"

"No. Mostly they owe *us* money. Which is, of course, a far better reason for their dislike."

"How about Sto Lat and Pseudopolis and the other cities?" said Lord Downey.

"They don't like us much, either."

"Why not? I mean t'say, we do share a common heritage," said Lord Selachii.

"Yes, my lord, but that common heritage largely consists of having had wars with one another," said the Patrician. "I can't see much support there. Which is a little unfortunate because we do not, in fact, have an army. I am not, of course, a military man but I believe that one of those is generally considered vital to the successful prosecution of a war."

He looked along the table.

"The fact *is*," he went on, "that Ankh-Morpork has been violently against a standing army."

"We all know *why* people don't trust an army," said Lord Downey. "A lot of armed men, standing around with nothing to do . . . they start to get ideas . . ."

Vimes saw the heads turn toward him.

"My word," he said, with glassy brightness, "can this be a reference to 'Old Stoneface' Vimes, who led the city's militia in a revolt against the rule of a tyrannical monarch in an effort to bring some sort of freedom and justice to the place? I do believe it is! And was he Commander of the Watch at the time? Good heavens, yes, as a matter of fact he was! Was he hanged and dismembered and buried in five graves? And is he a distant ancestor of the current Commander? My word, the coincidences just *pile* up, don't they?" His voice went from manic cheerfulness to a growl. "Right! That's got *that* over with. Now—has anyone got any point they wish to make?"

There was a general shifting of position and a group clearing of throats.

"What about mercenaries?" said Boggis.

"The problem with mercenaries," said the Patrician, "is that they need to be paid to start fighting. And, unless you are very lucky, you end up paying them even more to stop—"

Selachii thumped the table.

"Very well, then, by jingo!" he snarled. "Alone!"

"We could certainly do with one," said Lord Vetinari. "We need the money. I was about to say that we cannot *afford* mercenaries."

"How can this be?" said Lord Downey. "Don't we pay our taxes?"

"Ah, I thought we might come to that," said Lord Vetinari. He raised his hand and, on cue again, his clerk placed a piece of paper in it.

"Let me see now . . . ah yes. Guild of Assassins . . . Gross earnings in the last year: AM$13,207,048. Taxes paid in the last year: forty-seven dollars, twenty-two pence and what on examination turned out to be a Hershebian half-*dong*, worth one-eighth of a penny."

"That's all perfectly legal! The Guild of Accountants—"

"Ah yes. Guild of Accountants: gross earnings AM$7,999,011. Taxes paid: nil. But, ah yes, I see they applied for a rebate of AM$200,000."

"And what we received, I may say, included a Hershebian half-*dong*," said Mr. Frostrip of the Guild of Accountants.

"What goes around comes around," said Vetinari calmly.

He tossed the paper aside. "Taxation, gentlemen, is very much like dairy farming. The task is to extract the maximum amount of milk with the minimum of moo. And I am afraid to say that these days all I get is moo."

"Are you telling us that Ankh-Morpork is *bankrupt?*" said Downey.

"Of course. While, at the same time, full of rich people. I trust they have been spending their good fortune on swords."

"And you have *allowed* this wholesale tax avoidance?" said Lord Selachii.

"Oh, the taxes haven't been avoided," said Lord Vetinari. "Or even evaded. They just haven't been paid."

"That is a disgusting state of affairs!"

The Patrician raised his eyebrows. "Commander Vimes?"

"Yes, sir?"

"Would you be so good as to assemble a squad of your most experienced men, liaise with the tax gatherers and obtain the accumulated back taxes, please? My clerk here will give you a list of the prime defaulters."

"Right, sir. And if they resist, sir?" said Vimes, smiling nastily.

"Oh, how can they resist, commander? This is the will of our civic leaders." He took the paper his clerk proffered. "Let me see, now. Top of the list—"

Lord Selachii coughed hurriedly. "Far too late for that sort of nonsense now," he said.

"Water under the bridge," said Lord Downey.

"Dead and buried," said Mr. Slant.

"I paid mine," said Vimes.

"So let me recap, then," said Vetinari. "I don't think anyone wants to see two grown nations scrapping over a piece of rock. We don't want to fight, but—"

"By jingo, if we do, we'll show those—" Lord Selachii began.

"We have no ships. We have no men. We have no money, too," said Lord Vetinari. "Of course, we have the art of diplomacy. It is amazing what you can do with the right words."

"Unfortunately, the right words are more readily listened to if you also have a sharp stick," said Lord Downey.

Lord Selachii slapped the table. "We don't have to *talk* to these people! My lords . . . gentlemen . . . it's up to us to show them we won't be pushed around! We must re-form the regiments!"

"Oh, *private* armies?" said Vimes. "Under the command of someone whose fitness for it lies in the fact that he can afford to pay for a thousand funny hats?"

Someone leaned forward, halfway along the table. Up to that moment Vimes had thought he was asleep, and when Lord Rust spoke it was, indeed, in a sort of yawn.

"Whose *fitness,* Mister Vimes, lies in a thousand years of breeding for leadership," he said.

The "Mister" twisted in Vimes's chest. He knew he was a mister, would always be a mister, was probably a blueprint for mistership, but he'd be damned if he wouldn't be Sir Samuel to someone who pronounced years as "hyahs."

"Ah, good breeding," he said. "No, sorry, don't have any of *that,* if that's what you need to get your own men killed by sheer—"

"Gentlemen, please," said the Patrician. He shook his head. "Let's have no fighting, please. This is, after all, a council of war. As for re-forming the regiments, well, this is of course your ancient right. The supplying of armed men in times of need is one of the duties of a gentleman. History is on your side. The precedents are clear enough, I can't go against them. I have to say I cannot afford to."

"You're going to let them play soldiers?" said Vimes.

"Oh, Commander Vimes," said Mr. Burleigh, smiling. "As a military man yourself, you must—"

Sometimes people can attract attention by shouting. They might opt for thumping a table, or even take a swing at someone else. But Vimes achieved the effect by freezing, by simply doing nothing. The chill radiated off him. Lines in his face locked like a statue.

"I am not a military man."

And then Burleigh made the mistake of trying to grin disarmingly.

"Well, commander, the helmet and armor and everything . . . It's really all the same in the end, isn't it?"

"No. It's not."

"Gentlemen . . ." Lord Vetinari put his hands flat on the table, a sign that the meeting had ended. "I can only repeat that tomorrow I shall be discussing the matter with Prince Khufurah—"

"I've heard good reports of him," said Lord Rust. "Strict but fair. One can only admire what he's doing in some of those backward regions. A most—"

"No, sir. You are thinking of Prince Cadram," said Lord Vetinari. "Khufurah is the younger brother. He is arriving here as his brother's special envoy."

"Him? *That* one? The man's a wastrel! A cheat! A liar! They say he takes bri—"

"Thank you for your diplomatic input, Lord Rust," said the Patrician. "We must deal with facts as they are. There is always a way. Our nations have many interests in common. And of course it says a lot for the seriousness with which Cadram is treating this matter that he is sending his own brother to deal with it. It's a nod toward the international community."

"A Klatchian bigwig is coming *here?*" said Vimes. "No one told me!"

"Strange as it may seem, Sir Samuel, I am occasionally capable of governing this city for minutes at a time without seeking your advice and guidance."

"I meant there's a lot of anti-Klatchian feeling around—"

"A really greasy piece of work—" Lord Rust whispered to Mr. Boggis, in that special aristocratic whisper that carries to the rafters. *"It's an insult to send him here!"*

"I am sure that you will see to it that the streets are safe to walk, Vimes," said the Patrician sharply. "I know you pride yourself on that sort of thing. Officially he's here because the wizards have invited him to their big award ceremony. An honorary doctorate, that sort of thing. And one of their lunches afterward. I do like negotiating with people after the faculty of Unseen University have entertained them to lunch. They tend not to move about much and they'll agree to practically anything if they think there's a chance of a stomach powder and a small glass of water. And now, gentlemen . . . if you will excuse me . . ."

The lords and leaders departed in ones and twos, talking quietly as they walked out into the hall.

The Patrician shuffled his papers into order, running a thin finger along each edge of the pile, and then looked up.

"You appear to be casting a shadow, commander."

"You're not *really* going to allow them to re-form the regiments, are you?" said Vimes.

"There is absolutely no law against it, Vimes. And it will keep them occupied. Every official gentleman is entitled, in fact I believe used to be *required,* to raise men when the city required it. And, of course, any citizen has the right to bear arms. Bear that in mind, please."

"Arms is one thing. Holding weapons in 'em and playing soldiers is another." Vimes put his knuckles on the table and leaned forward.

"You see, sir," he said, "I can't help but think that over there in Klatch a bunch of idiots are doing the same thing. They're saying to the Seriph 'It's time to sort out those devils in Ankh-Morpork, offendi.' And when a lot of people are running around with

21

weapons and talking daft stuff about war, accidents happen. Have you ever been in a pub when everyone goes armed? Oh, things are a little polite at first, I'll grant you, and then some twerp drinks out of the wrong mug or picks up someone else's change by mistake and five minutes later you're picking noses out of the beer nuts—"

The Patrician looked down at Vimes's knuckles and stared fixedly until Vimes removed them.

"Vimes, you will be at the wizards' Convivium tomorrow. I sent you a memo about it."

"I never—" A vision of the piles of unread paperwork on Vimes's desk loomed treacherously in his mind. "Ah," he said.

"The Commander of the Watch leads the procession in full dress uniform. It's an ancient custom."

"Me? Walk in front of everyone?"

"Indeed. Very . . . civic. As I'm sure you recall. It demonstrates the friendly alliance between the University and the civil government which, I may say, seems to consist of their promising to do anything we ask provided we promise not to ask them to do anything. Anyway, it is your duty. Tradition decrees it. And Lady Sybil has agreed to see to it that you are there with a crisp bright shining morning face."

Vimes took a deep breath. "You asked my *wife?*"

"Certainly. She is very proud of you. She believes you are capable of great things, Vimes. She must be a great comfort to you."

"Well, I . . . I mean, I . . . yes . . ."

"Excellent. Oh, just one other thing, Vimes. I do have the Assassins and the Thieves in agreement on this, but to cover *all* eventualities . . . I would consider it a favor if you could see to it that no one throws eggs or something at the Prince. That sort of thing always upsets people."

The two sides watched each other carefully. They were old enemies. They had tested strengths many a time, had tasted defeat and victory, had contested turf. But this time it would go all the way.

Knuckles whitened. Boots scraped impatiently.

Captain Carrot bounced the ball once or twice.

"All right, lads, one more try, eh? And this time, no horseplay. William, what are you eating?"

The Artful Nudger scowled. *No one* knew his name. Kids he'd grown up with didn't know his name. His mother, if he ever found out who she was, probably didn't know his name. But Carrot had found out somehow. If anyone else had called him "William" they'd be looking for their ear. In their mouth.

"Chewing gum, mister."

"Have you brought enough for everybody?"

"No, mister."

"Then put it away, there's a good chap. Now, let's— Gavin, what's that up your sleeve?"

The one known as Scumbag Gav didn't bother to argue.

"'s a knife, Mr. Carrot."

"And I *bet* you brought enough for everybody, eh?"

"'sright, mister." Scumbag grinned. He was ten.

"Go on, put them on the heap with the others . . ."

Constable Shoe looked over the wall in horror. There were about fifty youths in the wide alleyway. Average age in years: about eleven. Average age in cynicism and malevolent evil: about 163. Although Ankh-Morpork football doesn't usually have goals in the normal sense, two had been nevertheless made at each end of the alley using the time-honored method of piling up things to mark where the posts would be.

Two piles: one of knives, one of blunt instruments.

In the middle of the boys, who were wearing the colors of some of the nastier street gangs, Captain Carrot was bouncing an inflated pig's bladder.

Constable Shoe wondered if he ought to go and get help, but the man seemed quite at ease.

"Er, captain?" he ventured.

"Oh, hello, Reg. We were just having a friendly game of football. This is Constable Shoe, lads."

Fifty pairs of eyes said: We'll remember your face, copper.

Reg edged around the wall and the eyes noted the arrow which had gone straight through his breastplate and protruded several inches from his back.

"There's been a bit of trouble, sir," said Reg. "I thought I'd better fetch you. It's a hostage situation . . ."

"I'll come right away. Okay, lads, sorry about this. Play amongst yourselves, will you? And I hope I'll see you all on Tuesday for the sing-song and sausage sizzle."

"Yeah, mister," said the Artful Nudger.

"And Corporal Angua will see if she can teach you the camp-fire howl."

"Yeah, right," said Scumbag.

"But what do we do before we part?" said Carrot expectantly.

The bloods of the Skats and the Mohocks looked bashfully at one another. Usually they were nervous of nothing, it being a banishment matter to show fear in any circumstances. But when they'd variously drawn up the clan rules, no one had ever thought there'd be someone like Carrot.

Glaring at one another with I'll-kill-you-if-you-ever-mention-this expressions, they all raised the index fingers of both hands to the level of their ears and chorused: "Wib wib wib."

"Wob wob wob," Carrot replied heartily. "Okay, Reg, let's go."

"How'd you do that, captain?" said Constable Shoe, as the watchmen hurried off.

"Oh, you just raise both fingers like *this*," said Carrot. "But I'd be obliged if you don't tell anyone, because it's meant to be a secret sig—"

"But they're thugs, captain! Young killers! Villains!"

"Oh, they're a bit cheeky, but nice enough boys underneath, when you take the time to understand—"

"I heard they never give anyone enough *time* to understand! Does Mr. Vimes know you're doing this?"

"He sort of knows, yes. I said I'd like to start a club for the street kids and he said it was fine provided I took them camping on the edge of some really sheer cliff somewhere in a high wind. But he always says things like that. And I'm sure we wouldn't have him any other way. Now, where are these hostages?"

"It's at Vortin's again, captain. But it's . . . sort of worse than that . . ."

Behind them, the Skats and the Mohocks looked at one another warily. Then they picked up their weapons and edged away with care. It's not that we don't want to fight, their manner said. It's just that we've got better things to do right now, and so we're going to go away and find out what they are.

Unusually for the docks, there was not a great deal of shouting and general conversation. People were too busy thinking about money.

Sergeant Colon and Corporal Nobbs leaned against a stack of timber and watched a man very carefully painting the name *Pride of Ankh-Morpork* on the prow of a ship. At some point he'd realize that he'd left out the "e," and they were idly looking forward to this modest entertainment.

"You ever been to sea, sarge?" said Nobby.

"Hah, not me!" said the sergeant. "Don't go flogging the oggin, lad."

"I don't," said Nobby. "I have never flogged any oggin. Never in my entire life have I flogged oggin."

"Right."

"I've always been very clean in that respect."

"Except you don't know what flogging the oggin means, do you?"

"No, sarge."

"It means going to sea. You can't bloody trust the sea. When I was a little lad I had this book about this little kid, he turned into a mermaid, sort of thing, and he lived down the bottom of the sea—"

"—the oggin—"

"Right, and it was all nice talking fishes and pink seashells and stuff, and then I went on my holidays to Quirm and I *saw* the sea, and I thought: here goes, and if our ma hadn't been quick on her feet I don't know what would have happened. I mean, the kid in the book could breathe under the sea, so how was I to know? It's all bloody *lies* about the sea. It's just all yuk with lobsters in it."

"My mum's uncle was a sailor," said Nobby. "But after the big plague he got press-ganged. Bunch of farmers got him drunk, he woke up next morning tied to a plough."

They lounged some more.

"Looks like we're going to be in a fight, sarge," said Nobby, as the painter very carefully started on the final "k."

"Won't last long. Lot of cowards, the Klatchians," said Colon. "The moment they taste a bit of cold steel they're legging it away over the sand."

Sergeant Colon had had a broad education. He'd been to the School of My Dad Always Said, the College of It Stands to Reason, and was now a postgraduate student at the University of What Some Bloke In the Pub Told Me.

"Shouldn't be any trouble to sort out, then?" said Nobby.

"And o'course, they're not the same color as what we are," said Colon. "Well . . . as me, anyway," he added, in view of the various hues of Corporal Nobbs. There was probably no one alive who was the same color as Corporal Nobbs.

"Constable Visit's pretty brown," said Nobby. "I never seen him run away. If there's a chance of giving someone a religious pamphlet ole Washpot's after them like a terrier."

"Ah, but Omnians are more like us," said Colon. "Bit weird but, basic'ly, just the same as us underneath. No, the way you can tell a Klatchian is, you look an' see if he uses a lot of words beginning with 'al,' right? 'Cos that's a dead giveaway. They invented all the words starting with 'al.' That's how you can tell they're Klatchian. Like al-cohol, see?"

"They invented beer?"

"Yeah."

"That's clever."

"I wouldn't call it *clever*," said Sergeant Colon, realizing too late that he'd made a tactical error. "More, luck, I'd say."

"What else did they do?"

"Well, there's . . ." Colon racked his brains. "There's al-gebra. That's like sums with letters. For . . . for people whose brains aren't clever enough for numbers, see?"

"Is that a fact?"

"Right," said Colon. "In fact," he went on, a little more assertively now he could see a way ahead, "I heard this wizard down the University say that the Klatchians invented nothing. That was their great contribution to maffs, he said. I said 'What?' an' he said, they come up with zero."

"Dun't sound that clever to me," said Nobby. "Anyone could invent nothing. I ain't invented anything."

"My point exactly," said Colon. "I told him, it was people who invented numbers like four and, and—"

"—seven—"

"—right, who were the geniuses. *Nothing* didn't need inventing. It was just there. They probably just found it."

"It's having all that desert," said Nobby.

"Right! Good point. Desert. Which, as everyone knows, is basically nothing. Nothing's a natural resource to them. It stands to reason. Whereas we're more civilized, see, and we got a lot more stuff around to count, so we invented numbers. It's like . . . well, they *say* the Klatchians invented astronomy—"

"Al-tronomy," said Nobby helpfully.

"No, no . . . no, Nobby, I reckon they'd discovered esses by then, probably nicked 'em off'f us . . . anyway, they were *bound* to invent astronomy, 'cos there's bugger all else for them to look at but the sky. Anyone can look at the stars and give 'em names. 's going it a bit to call it *inventing*, in any case. We don't go around saying we've *invented* something just because we had a quick dekko at it."

"I heard where they've got a lot of odd gods," said Nobby.

"Yeah, *and* mad priests," said Colon. "Foaming at the mouth, half of 'em. Believe all kinds of loony things."

They watched the painter in silence for a moment. Colon was dreading the question that came.

"So how *exactly* are they different from ours, then?" said Nobby. "I mean, some of *our* priests are—"

"I hope you ain't being *unpatriotic,*" said Colon severely.

"No, of course not. I was just asking. I can see where they'd be a lot worse than ours, being foreign and everything."

"And of course they're all mad for fighting," said Colon. "Vicious buggers with all those curvy swords of theirs."

"You mean, like . . . they viciously attack you while cowardly running away after tasting cold steel?" said Nobby, who sometimes had a treacherously good memory for detail.

"You can't trust 'em, like I said. And they burp hugely after meals."

"Well . . . so do you, sarge."

"Yes, but I don't pretend it's *polite,* Nobby."

"Well, it's certainly a good job there's you around to explain things, sarge," said Nobby. "It's amazing the stuff you know."

"I surprise myself, sometimes," said Colon modestly.

The painter of the ship leaned back to admire his work. They heard him give a heartfelt little groan, and both of them nodded in satisfaction.

Hostage negotiations were always tricky, Carrot had learned. It paid not to rush things. Let the other man talk when he was ready.

So he was whiling away the time sitting behind the upturned cart they were using as a shield from the occasional random arrow and writing his letter home. The exercise was carried out with much frowning, sucking of the pencil and what Commander Vimes called a ballistic approach to spelling and punctuation.

Dere Mum and Dade,

I hope this letter finds you in good health as I am also. Thank you for the big parcel of dwarf bread you sent me I have sharred it with the other dwarfs on the Watch and they say it is better even than Ironcrufts ("T' Bread Wi' T' Edge") and you carn't beat the taste of a home-forged loaf, so well done mum.

Things are going well with the Wolf Pack that I have told you about but Cmdr. Vimes is not happy, I told him they were good lads at heart and it would help them to learn the ways of Natchure and the Wilderness and he said hah they know them already that is the trouble. But he gave me $5 to buy a football which proves he cares deep down.

We have more new faeces in the Watch which is just as well with this truble with Klatch, it is all looking very Grave, I feel it is the Clam before the Storm and no mistake.

I must brake off now because some robbers have broke into Vortin's Dimond Warehouse and have taken Corporal

Angua hostage. I fear there may be terrible bloodshed so,
I remain,
Yr. Loving Son,
Carrot Ironfoundersson (Captain)

ps I will write again tomorrow

Carrot folded the letter carefully and slipped it under his breastplate.

"I think they have had long enough to consider our suggestion, constable. What's next on the list?"

Constable Shoe leafed through a file of grubby paper and pulled out another sheet.

"Well, we're down to offenses of stealing pennies off blind beggars now," he said. "Oh, no, this is a good one . . ."

Carrot took the sheet in one hand and a megaphone in the other and raised his head carefully over the edge of the cart.

"Good morning again!" he said brightly. "We've found another one. Theft of jewelery from—"

"Yes! Yes! We did it!" shouted a voice from the building.

"Really? I haven't even said when it was yet," said Carrot.

"Never mind, we *did* it! Now can we come out, please?" There was another sound behind the voice. It sounded like a low, continuous growl.

"I think you ought to be able to tell me what you stole," said Carrot.

"Er . . . rings? Gold rings?"

"Sorry, no rings mentioned."

"Pearl necklace? Yes, that's what—"

"Getting warmer, but no."

"Earrings?"

"Ooo, you're so close," said Carrot encouragingly.

"A crown, was it? Maybe a coronet?"

Carrot leaned down to the constable. "Says here a tiara, Reg, can we let—?" He stood up. "We're prepared to accept 'coronet.' Well done!"

He looked down at Constable Shoe again.

"This *is* all right, isn't it, Reg? It's not coercion, is it?"

"Can't see how it can be, captain. I mean, *they* broke in, *they* took a hostage . . ."

"I suppose you're right—"

"Please! No! Good boy! Down!"

"Seems to be about it, sir," said Reg Shoe, peering around the edge of the cart. "We've got them down for everything but the Hide Park Flasher—"

"We did that!" screamed someone.

"—and that was a woman . . ."

"We did it!" This time the voice was a lot higher. *"Now please can we come out?"*

Carrot stood up and raised the megaphone. "If you gentlemen would care to step out with your hands up?"

"Are you joking?" whimpered someone, against the background of another growl.

"Well, at least with your hands where I can see them."

"You bet, mister!"

Four men stumbled out into the street. Their torn clothing fluttered in the breeze. The apparent leader pointed an angry finger back at the doorway as Carrot walked toward them.

"The owner of that place ought to be prosecuted!" he shouted. "Keeping a wild animal like that in his strongroom, it's disgraceful! We broke in perfectly peacefully and it just attacked us for no reason at all!"

"You shot at Constable Shoe here," said Carrot.

"Only to miss! Only to miss!"

Constable Shoe pointed at the arrow sticking into his breastplate.

"Right where it shows!" he complained. "It's a welding job and we have to pay for our own armor repairs and there'll always be a mark, you know, no matter what I do."

Their horrified gaze took in the stitch marks around his neck and on his hands, and it dawned on them that although the human race came in a variety of colors, very few living people were gray with a hint of green.

"Here, you're a *zombie!*"

"That's right, kick a man when he's dead," said Constable Shoe sharply.

"And you took Corporal Angua hostage. A *lady*," said Carrot, in the same level voice. It was very polite. But it simply suggested that somewhere a fuse was burning, and it would be a good idea not to wait for it to reach the barrel.

"Yes . . . sort of . . . but she must've got away when that *creature* turned up . . ."

"So you left her in there?" said Carrot, still very calm.

The men dropped to their knees. The leader raised his hand imploringly.

"Please! We're just robbers and thieves! We're not bad men!"

Carrot nodded to Constable Shoe. "Take them down to the Yard, constable."

"Right!" said Reg. There was a mean look in his eye as he cocked his crossbow. "I'm down ten dollars thanks to you. So you'd better not try to escape."

"No, sir. Not us."

Carrot wandered into the gloom of the building. Fearful faces peered out of doorways. He gave them a reassuring smile as he walked toward the strongroom.

Corporal Angua was adjusting her uniform.

"I didn't bite anyone, before you start," she said, as he appeared in the doorway. "Not even flesh wounds. I just tore at their trousers. And that was no bed of roses, I might add."

A frightened face appeared round the door.

"Ah, Mr. Vortin," said Carrot. "I think you will find that all is in order. They seem to have dropped everything."

The diamond merchant looked at him in amazement.

"But they had a hostage—"

"They saw the error of their ways," said Carrot.

"And . . . and there were snarling noises . . . sounded like a wolf . . ."

"Ah, yes," said Carrot. "Well, you know, when thieves fall out . . ." Which was no kind of explanation, but because the tone of voice suggested that it *was,* Mr. Vortin accepted it as such for fully five minutes after Carrot and Angua had left.

"Well, that's a nice start to the day," said Carrot.

"Thank you, yes, I wasn't hurt," said Angua.

"It makes it all seem worthwhile, somehow."

"Just my hair messed up and another shirt ruined."

"Well done."

"Sometimes I might suspect that you don't listen to anything I say," said Angua.

"Glad to hear it," said Carrot.

The entire Watch was mustering. Vimes looked down at the sea of faces.

My gods, he thought. How many have we got now? A few years ago you could count the Watch on the fingers of a blind butcher's hand, and now . . .

There's *more* coming in!

He leaned sideways to Captain Carrot. "Who're all these people?"

"Watchmen, sir. You appointed them."

"Did I? I haven't even *met* some of them!"

"You signed the paperwork, sir. And you sign the wage bill every month. Eventually."

There was a hint of criticism in his voice. Vimes's approach to paperwork was not to touch it until someone was shouting, and then at least there would be someone to help him sort through the stacks.

"But how did they join?"

"Usual way, sir. Swore them in, gave them each a helmet—"

"Hey, that's Reg Shoe! He's a zombie! He falls to bits all the time!"

"Very big man in the undead community, sir," said Carrot.

"How come *he* joined?"

"He came round last week to complain about the Watch harassing some bogeymen, sir. He was very, er, vehement, sir. So I persuaded him that what the Watch needed was some expertise, and so he joined up, sir."

"No more complaints?"

"Twice as many, sir. All from undead, sir, and all against Mr. Shoe. Funny, that."

Vimes gave his captain a sideways look.

"He's very hurt about it, sir. He says he's found that the

undead just don't understand the difficulties of policing in a multi-vital society, sir."

Good gods, thought Vimes, that's just what I would have done. But I'd have done it because I'm not a nice person. Carrot *is* a nice person, he's practically got medals for it, surely he wouldn't have . . .

And he knew that he would never know. Somewhere behind Carrot's innocent stare was a steel door.

"*You* enrolled him, did you?"

"Nossir. You did, sir. You signed his joining orders and his kit chitty and his posting orders, sir."

Vimes had another vision of too many documents, hurriedly signed. But he *must* have signed them and they needed the men, true enough. It was just that it ought to be *him* who—

"And anyone of sergeant rank or above can recruit, sir," said Carrot, as if reading his mind. "It's in the General Orders. Page twenty-two, sir. Just below the tea stain."

"And you've recruited . . . how many?"

"Oh, just one or two. We're still very short-handed, sir."

"We are with Reg. His arms keep falling off."

"Aren't you going to talk to the men, sir?"

Vimes looked at the assembled . . . well, multitude. There was no other word. Well, there were plenty, but none that it would be fair to use.

Big ones, short ones, fat ones, troll ones with the lichen still on, bearded dwarf ones, the looming pottery presence of the golem Constable Dorfl, undead ones . . . and even now he wasn't certain if that term should include Corporal Angua, an intelligent girl and a very useful wolf when she had to be. Waifs and strays, Colon had said once. Waifs and bloody strays, because normal people wouldn't be coppers.

Technically they were all in uniform, too, except that mostly they weren't wearing the same uniform as anyone else. Everyone had just been sent down to the armory to collect whatever fitted, and the result was a walking historical exhibit: Funny-Shaped Helmets Through the Ages.

"Er . . . ladies and gentlemen—" he began.

"Be quiet, please, and listen to Commander Vimes!" bellowed Carrot.

Vimes found himself meeting the gaze of Angua, who was leaning against the wall. She rolled her eyes helplessly.

"Yes, *yes,* thank you, captain," said Vimes. He turned back to the massed array of Ankh-Morpork's finest. He opened his mouth. He stared. And then he shut his mouth, all but a corner of it. And said out of that corner: "What's that little lump on Constable Flint's head?"

"That's Probationary Constable Buggy Swires, sir. He likes to get a good view."

"He's a *gnome!*"

"Well done, sir."

"Another one of yours?"

"*Ours,* sir," said Carrot, using his reproachful voice again. "Yes, sir. Attached to the Chitterling Street Station since last week, sir."

"Oh my gods . . ." murmured Vimes.

Buggy Swires saw his stare and saluted. He was five inches tall.

Vimes regathered his mental balance. The long and the short and the tall . . . waifs and strays, all of us.

"I'm not going to keep you long," he said. "You all know me . . . well, *most* of you know me," he added, with a sidelong glance at Carrot, "and I don't make speeches. But I'm sure all of you have noticed the way this Leshp business has got people all stirred up. There's a lot of loose talk about war. Well, war isn't our business. War is soldiers' business. Our business, I think, is to keep the peace. Let me show you this—"

He stood back and pulled something out of his pocket with a flourish. At least, that was the intention. There was a rip as something ceased to be entangled in the lining.

"Damn . . . ah . . ."

He produced a length of shiny black wood from the ragged pocket. There was a large silver knob on the end. The watchmen craned to look.

"This . . . er . . . this . . ." Vimes groped. "This old man turned up from the palace a couple of weeks ago. Gave me this damn thing. Got a label saying *'Regalia of the Watch Commandr., Citie of Ankh-Morporke.'* You know they never throw anything away up at the palace."

He waved it vaguely. The wood was surprisingly heavy.

"It's got the coat of arms on the knob, look." Thirty watchmen tried to see.

"And I thought . . . I thought, good grief, *this* is what I'm supposed to carry? And I thought about it, and then I thought, no, that's right, just once someone got it *right*. It's not even a weapon, it's just a *thing*. It ain't for using, it's just for having. That's what it's all about. Same thing with uniforms. You see, a soldier's uniform, it's to turn him into part of a crowd of other parts all in the same uniform, but a copper's uniform is there to—"

Vimes stopped. Perplexed expressions in front of him told him that he was building a house of cards with too few cards on the bottom.

He coughed.

"*Anyway,*" he went on, with a glare to indicate that everyone should forget the previous twenty seconds, "our job is to *stop* people fighting. There's a lot happening on the street. You've probably heard that they're starting up the regiments again. Well, people can recruit if they like. But we're not going to have any mobs. There's a nasty mood around. I don't know what's going to happen, but we've got to be there when it does." He looked around the room. "Another thing. This new Klatchian envoy or whatever he's called is arriving tomorrow. I don't think the Assassins' Guild has anything planned but *tonight* we're going to check the route the wizards' procession will be taking. A nice little job for the night shift. And tonight we're *all* on the night shift."

There was a groan from the Watch.

"As my old sergeant used to say, if you can't take a joke you shouldn't have joined," said Vimes. "A nice gentle door-to-door inspection, shaking hands with doorknobs, giving the uniform a bit of an airing. Good old-fashioned policing. Any questions? Good. Thank you very much."

There was a general rustling and relaxing among the squad as it dawned on them that they were free to go.

Carrot started to clap.

It wasn't the clap used by middlings to encourage underlings to applaud overlings.* It had genuine enthusiasm behind it which was, somehow, worse. A couple of the more impressionable new constables picked it up and then, in the same way that little pebbles lead the avalanche, the sound of humanoids banging their hands together filled the room.

Vimes glowered.

"Very inspiring, sir!" said Carrot, as the clapping rose to a storm.

Rain poured on Ankh-Morpork. It filled the gutters and overflowed and was then flung away by the wind. It tasted of salt.

The gargoyles had crept out of their daytime shadows and were perched on every cornice and tower, ears and wings outstretched to sieve anything edible out of the water. It was amazing what could fall on Ankh-Morpork. Rains of small fish and frogs were common enough, although bedsteads caused comment.

A broken gutter poured a sheet of water down the window of Ossie Brunt, who was sitting on his bed because there were no chairs or, indeed, any other furniture. He didn't mind at the moment. In a minute or two he might be very angry. And, then again, possibly not.

It was not that Ossie was insane in any way. Friends would have called him a quiet sort who kept himself to himself, but they didn't because he didn't have any friends. There *was* a group of men who went to practice at the archery butts on Tuesday nights, and he sometimes went to a pub with them afterward and sat and listened to them talk, and he'd saved up once and bought a round of drinks, although they probably wouldn't remember or maybe they'd say, "Oh . . . yeah . . . Ossie." People said that. People tended to put him out of their minds, in the same way that you didn't pay much attention to empty space.

He wasn't stupid. He thought a lot about things. Sometimes he'd sit and think for hours, just staring at the opposite wall where the rain came in on damp nights and made a map of Klatch.

---

* The palms are held at right angles to one another and flapped together rather than clapped, while the flapper stares intently at the audience as if to say "We're going to have some applause here or else the whole school is in detention."

Someone hammered on the door. "Mr. Brunt? Are you decent?"

"I'm a bit busy, Mrs. Spent," he said, putting his bow under the bed with his magazines.

"It's about the rent!"

"Yes, Mrs. Spent?"

"You know my rules!"

"I shall pay you tomorrow, Mrs. Spent," said Ossie, looking toward the window.

"Cash in my hand by noon or it's out you go!"

"Yes, Mrs. Spent."

He heard her stamp downstairs again.

He counted to fifty, very carefully, and then reached down and pulled out his bow again.

Angua was on patrol with Nobby Nobbs. This was not an ideal arrangement, but Carrot was on swing patrol and on a night like this Fred Colon, who kept the roster, had an uncanny knack of being on desk duty in the warm. So the spare partners had been thrown together. It was a terrible thought.

"Can I have a word, miss?" said Nobby, as they rattled door-knobs and waved their lanterns into alleyways.

"Yes, Nobby?"

"It's pers'nal."

"Oh."

"Only I'd ask Fred, but he wouldn't understand, and I fink you *would* understand on account of you being a woman. Most of the time, anyway. No offense meant."

"What do you *want,* Nobby?"

"It's about my . . . sexual nature, miss."

Angua said nothing. Rain banged off Nobby's ill-fitting helmet.

"I think it's time I looked it full in the face, miss."

Angua cursed her graphic imagination again.

"And, er . . . how were you thinking of doing that, Nobby?"

"I mean, I sent off for stuff, miss. Creams an' that."

"Creams," said Angua flatly.

"That you rub on," said Nobby helpfully.

"Rub on."

"And a thing you do exercises with—"

"Oh gods . . ."

"Sorry, miss?"

"What? Oh . . . I was just thinking of something else. Do go on. Exercises?"

"Yeah. To build up my biceps and that."

"Oh, *exercises.* Really?" Nobby did not appear to have any biceps to speak of. There wasn't really anything for them to be on. Technically he had arms, because his hands were attached to his shoulders, but that was about all you could say.

Horrified interest got the better of her.

"Why, Nobby?"

He looked down, sheepishly.

"Well . . . I mean . . . you know . . . girls an' that . . ."

To her amazement, Nobby was blushing.

"You mean you . . ." she began. "You want to . . . you're look-ing for . . ."

"Oh, I'm not just after . . . I mean, if you want a thing done properly then . . . I mean, no," said Nobby reproachfully. "What I'm saying is, as you get older, you know, you think about settlin' down, findin' someone who'll go with you hand in hand down life's bumpy highway— Why's your mouth open?"

Angua shut it abruptly.

"But I just don't seem to meet girls," Nobby said. "Well, I mean, I *meet* girls, and then they rush off."

"Despite the cream."

"Right."

"And the exercises."

"Yes."

"Well, you've covered all the angles, I can see that," said Angua. "Beats me where you're going wrong." She sighed. "What about Stamina Thrum, in Elm Street?"

"She's got a wooden leg."

"Well, then . . . Verity Pushpram, nice girl, she runs the clam and cockle barrow in Rime Street?"

"Hammerhead? Stinks of fish all the time. And she's got a squint."

"She's got her own business, though. Does wonderful chowder, too."

"And a squint."

"Not exactly a squint, Nobby."

"Yes, but you know what I mean."

Angua had to admit that she did. Verity had the *opposite* of a squint. Both eyes appeared to be endeavoring to see the adjacent ear. When you talked to her, you had to suppress a feeling that she was about to walk off in two directions. But she could gut fish like a champion.

She sighed again. She was familiar with the syndrome. They *said* they wanted a soulmate and helpmeet but sooner or later the list would include a skin like silk and a chest fit for a herd of cows.

Except for Carrot. That was almost . . . almost one of the *annoying* things about him. She suspected he wouldn't mind if she shaved her head or grew a beard. It wasn't that he wouldn't notice, he just wouldn't *mind,* and for some reason that was very aggravating.

"The only thing I can suggest," she said, "is that women are quite often attracted to men who can make them laugh."

Nobby brightened. "Really?" he said. "I ought to be well in there, then."

"Good."

"People laugh at me all the time."

High above, quite oblivious of the rain that had already soaked him to the skin, Ossie Brunt checked the oilskin cover round his bow and settled down for the long wait.

Rain was a copper's friend. Tonight people were making do with indoor crime.

Vimes stood in the lee of one of the fountains in Sator Square. The fountain hadn't worked for years, but he was getting just as wet as if it were in full flow. He'd never experienced truly horizontal rain before.

There was no one around. The rain marched across the square like . . . like an army . . .

Now *there* was an image from his youth. Funny how they hung around in the dark alleys of your brain and suddenly jumped out on you.

Rain falling on water . . .

Ah, yes . . . When he was a little lad he'd pretended that the raindrops splashing in the running gutters were soldiers. Millions of soldiers. And the bubbles that sometimes went floating by were men on horseback.

Right now he couldn't remember what the occasional dead dog had been. Some kind of siege weapon, possibly.

Water swirled around his boots and dripped off his cape. When he tried to light a cigar the wind blew the match out and the rain poured off his helmet and soaked the cigar in any case.

He grinned in the night.

He was, temporarily, a happy man. He was cold, wet and alone, trying to keep out of the worst of the weather at three o'clock on a ferocious morning. He'd spent some of the best nights of his life like this. At such times you could just . . . sort of hunch your shoulders like *this* and let your head pull in like *this* and you became a little hutch of warmth and peace, the rain banging on your helmet, the mind just ticking over, sorting out the world . . .

It was like this in the old days, when no one cared about the Watch and all you really had to do was keep out of trouble. Those were the days when there wasn't as much to do.

But there *was* as much to do, said an inner voice. You just didn't do it.

He could feel the official truncheon hanging heavily in the special pocket that Sybil herself had sewn in his breeches. Why is it just a bit of wood? he'd asked himself when he'd unwrapped it. Why not a sword? *That's* the symbol of power. And then he'd realized why it couldn't ever be a sword—

"Ho there, good citizen! May I ask your business this brisk morning?"

He sighed. There was a lantern appearing through the murk, surrounded by a halo of water.

Ho there, good citizen . . . There was only one person in the city who would say something like that and mean it.

"It's me, captain."

The halo drew nearer and illuminated the damp face of Captain Carrot. The young man ripped off a salute—at godsdamn three in the morning, Vimes thought—that would have brought a happy tear to the eye of the most psychotic drill sergeant.

"What're you doing out, sir?"

"I just wanted to . . . check up on things," said Vimes.

"You could have left it all to me, sir," said Carrot. "Delegation is the key to successful command."

"Really? Is it?" said Vimes sourly. "My word, we live and learn, don't we." And you certainly learn, he added in the privacy of his head. And he was *almost* sure he was being mean and stupid.

"We've just about finished, sir. We've checked all the empty buildings. And there will be an extra squad of constables on the route. *And* the gargoyles will be up as high as they can. You know how good they are at watching, sir."

"Gargoyles? I thought we just had Constable Downspout . . ."

"And Constable Pediment now, sir."

"One of yours?"

"One of ours, sir. You signed—"

"Yes, yes, I'm sure I did. Damn!"

A gust of wind caught the water pouring from an overloaded gutter and dumped it down Vimes's neck.

"They say this new island's upset the air streams," said Carrot.

"Not just the air," said Vimes. "A lot of damn fuss over a few square miles of silt and some old ruins! Who cares?"

"They say it's strategically very important," said Carrot, falling into step beside him.

"What for? We're not at war with anyone. Hah! But we might go to war to keep some damn island that's only useful in case we have to go to war, right?"

"Oh, his lordship will have it all sorted out today. I'm sure that when moderate-mannered men of goodwill can get round a table there's no problem that can't be resolved," said Carrot cheerfully.

He is, thought Vimes glumly. He really *is* sure. "Know much about Klatch?" he said.

"I've read a little, sir."

"Very sandy place, they say."

"Yes, sir. Apparently."

There was a crash somewhere ahead of them, and a scream. Coppers learned to be good at screams. There was to the connoisseur a world of difference between "I'm drunk and I've just trodden on my fingers and I can't get up!" and "Look out! He's got a knife!"

Both men started to run.

Light blazed out in a narrow street. Heavy footsteps vanished into the darkness.

The light flickered beyond a shop's broken window. Vimes stumbled through the doorway, pulled off his sodden cape and threw it over the fire in the middle of the floor.

There was a hiss, and a smell of hot leather.

Then Vimes stood back and tried to work out where the hell he was.

People were staring at him. Dimly, his mind assembled clues: the turban, the beard, the woman's jewelry . . .

"*Where did he come from? Who is this man?*"

"Er . . . good morning?" he said. "Looks like there's been a bit of an accident?" He raised the cape gingerly.

A broken bottle lay in a pool of sizzling oil.

Vimes looked up at the broken window. "Oh . . ."

The other two people were a boy almost as tall as his father and a small girl trying to hide behind her mother.

Vimes felt his stomach turn to lead.

Carrot arrived in the doorway.

"I lost them," he panted. "There were three of them, I think. Can't see anything in this rain . . . *Oh, it's you, Mr. Goriff. What happened here?*"

"*Captain Carrot! Someone threw a burning bottle through our window and then this beggar man rushed in and put it out!*"

"What'd he say? What did *you* say?" said Vimes. "You *speak* Klatchian?"

"Not very well," said Carrot modestly. "I just can't get the back-of-the-throat sound to—"

"But . . . you can understand what he said?"

"Oh, yes. He just thanked you very much, by the way. *It's all right, Mr. Goriff. He's a watchman.*"

"But *you* speak—"

Carrot knelt down and looked at the broken bottle.

"Oh, you know how it is. You come in here on night shift for a hot caraway bun and you just get chatting. You must have picked up the odd word, sir."

"Well . . . vindaloo, maybe, but . . ."

"This is a firebomb, sir."

"I know, captain."

"This is very bad. Who would do a thing like this?"

"Right now?" said Vimes. "Half the city, I should think."

He looked helplessly at Goriff. He vaguely recognized the face. He vaguely recognized Mrs. Goriff's face. They were . . . faces. They were usually at the other end of some arms holding a portion of curry or a kebab. Sometimes the boy ran the place. The shop opened very early in the morning and very late at night, when the streets were owned by bakers, thieves and watchmen.

Vimes knew the place as Mundane Meals. Nobby Nobbs had said that Goriff had wanted a word that meant ordinary, everyday, straightforward, and had asked around until he found one he liked the sound of.

"Er . . . tell him . . . tell him you're staying here, and I'll go back to the Watch House and send someone out to relieve you," said Vimes.

"Thank you," said Goriff.

"Oh, you underst—" Vimes felt like an idiot. "Of course you do, you must have been here, what, five, six years?"

"Ten years, sir."

"Really?" said Vimes manically. "That long? Really? My word . . . well, I'd better get along . . . Good morning to you—"

He hurried out into the rain.

I must have been going in there for *years*, he thought, as he splashed through the darkness. And I know how to say "vindaloo." And . . . "korma" . . . ? Carrot's hardly been here five minutes and he gargles the language like a native.

Good grief, I can get by in dwarfish and I can at least say, "Put down that rock, you're under arrest," in troll, but . . .

He stamped into the Watch House, water pooling off him. Fred Colon was dozing quietly at the desk. In deference to the fact that he'd known Fred all these years, Vimes was extra noisy about taking off his cape.

When he officially turned round, the sergeant was sitting at attention.

"I didn't know you were on tonight, Mr. Vimes . . ."

"This is unofficial, Fred," said Vimes. He accepted "Mr." from certain people. In an odd way, they'd earned it. "Send someone along to Mundane Meals in Scandal Alley, will you? A bit of trouble there."

He reached the stairs.

"You stopping, sir?" said Fred.

"Oh, yes," said Vimes grimly. "I've got to catch up on the paperwork."

The rain fell on Leshp so hard it probably hadn't been worth the island's bother of rising from the bottom of the sea.

Most of the explorers slept in their boats now. There *were* buildings on the risen island, but . . .

. . . the buildings weren't quite right.

Solid Jackson peered out from the tarpaulin he'd rigged up on deck. Mist was rising off the soaking ground and was made luminous by the occasional flash of lightning.

The city, by storm light, looked far too malevolent. There *were* things he could recognize—columns and steps and archways and so on—but there were others . . . he shuddered. It looked as if people had once tried to add human touches to structures that were already ancient . . .

It was because of his son that everyone was staying in the boats.

A party of Ankh-Morpork fishermen had gone ashore that morning to search for the heaps of treasure that everyone knew littered the ocean bottom and had found a tiled floor, washed clean by the rain. Pretty blue and white squares showed a pattern of waves and shells and, in the middle, a squid.

And Les had said, "That looks pretty big, Dad."

And everyone had looked around at the weed-covered buildings and had shared the Thought, which remained unspoken but was made up of a lot of little thoughts like the occasional ripples in the pools, and the little splashes in the dark water of cellars that made the mind think of claws, winnowing the deeps, and the odd things that sometimes got washed up on beaches or turned up in nets. Sometimes you pulled things over the side that'd put a man off fish for life.

And suddenly no one wanted to explore any more, just in case they found something.

Solid Jackson pulled his head back under the cover.

"Why'n't we going home, Dad?" said his son. "You said this place gives you the willies."

"All right, but they're *Ankh-Morpork* willies, see? And no foreigner's going to get his hands on them."

"Dad?"

"Yes, lad?"

"Who was Mr. Hong?"

"How should I know?"

"Only, when we was all heading back for the boats one of the other men said, 'We all know what happened to Mr. Hong when he opened the Three Jolly Luck Take-Away Fish Bar on the site of the old fish-god temple in Dagon Street on the night of the full moon, don't we . . . ?' Well, *I* don't know."

"Ah . . ." Solid Jackson hesitated. Still, Les was a big lad now . . .

"He . . . closed up and left in a bit of a hurry, lad. So quick he had to leave some things behind."

"Like what?"

"If you must know . . . half an earhole and one kidney."

"Cool!"

The boat rocked, and wood splintered. Jackson jerked the cover up. Spray washed over him. Somewhere close in the wet darkness a voice shouted: "Why you not carrying lights, you second cousin of a jackal?"

Jackson pulled out the lantern and held it up.

"What're you doing in Ankh-Morpork territorial waters, you camel-eating devil?"

"These waters belong to us!"

"We were here first!"

"Yeah? *We* were here first*!*"

"We were here first *first!*"

"You damaged my boat! That's *piracy*, that is!"

There were other shouts around them. In the darkness the two flotillas had collided. Bowsprits tore away rigging. Hulls boomed. The controlled panic that is normal sailing became the frantic panic composed of darkness, spray and too much rigging coming unrigged.

At times like this the ancient traditions of the sea that unite all mariners should come to the fore and see them combine in the face of their common foe, the hungry and relentless ocean.

However, at this point Mr. Arif hit Mr. Jackson over the head with an oar.

"Hnh? Wuh?"

Vimes opened the only eye that appeared to respond. A horrible sight met it.

. . . I read him his rites, whereupon, he said up, yours copper. Sgnt. Detritus then, cautioned him, upon which he said, ouch . . .

There may be a lot of things I'm not good at, thought Vimes, but at least I don't treat the punctuation of a sentence like a game of Pin the Tail on the Donkey . . .

He rolled his head away from Carrot's fractured grammar. The pile of paper shifted under him.

Vimes's desk was becoming famous. Once there were piles, but they had slipped as piles do, forming this dense compacted layer that was now turning into something like peat. It was said there were plates and unfinished meals somewhere down there. No one wanted to check. Some people said they'd heard movement.

There was a genteel cough. Vimes rolled his head again and looked up into the big pink face of Willikins, Lady Sybil's butler. *His* butler too, technically, although Vimes hated to think of him like that.

"I think we had better proceed with alacrity, Sir Samuel. I have brought your dress uniform, and your shaving things are by the basin."

"What? What?"

"You are due at the University in half an hour. Lady Sybil has vouchsafed to me that if you are not there she will utilize your intestines for hosiery accessories, sir."

"Was she smiling?" said Vimes, staggering to his feet and making his way to the steaming basin on the washstand.

"Only slightly, sir."

"Oh gods . . ."

"*Yes,* sir."

Vimes made an attempt at shaving while, behind him, Willikins brushed and polished. Outside, the city's clocks began to strike ten.

It must've been almost four when I sat down, Vimes thought. I know I heard the shift change at eight, and then I had to sort out Nobby's expenses, that's advanced mathematics if ever there was some. . .

He tried to yawn and shave at the same time, which is never a good idea.

"Damn!"

"I shall fetch some tissue paper directly, sir," said Willikins, without looking round. As Vimes dabbed at his chin, the butler went on: "I should like to take this opportunity to raise a matter of some import, sir . . ."

"Yes?" Vimes stared blearily at the red tights that seemed to be a major item of his dress uniform.

"Regretfully, I am afraid I must ask leave to give in my notice, sir. I wish to join the Colors."

"Which colors are these, Willikins?" said Vimes, holding up a shirt with puffed sleeves. Then his brain caught up with his ears. "You want to become a *soldier?*"

"They say Klatch needs to be taught a sharp lesson, sir. A Willikins has never been found wanting when his country calls. I thought that Lord Venturi's Heavy Infantry would do for me. They have a particularly attractive uniform of red and white, sir. With gold frogging."

Vimes pulled his boots on. "You've had military experience, have you?"

"Oh, no, sir. But I am a quick learner, sir, and I believe I have some prowess with the carving knife." The butler's face showed a patriotic alertness.

"On turkeys and so on . . ." said Vimes.

"Yes, sir," said Willikins, buffing up the ceremonial helmet.

"And you're off to fight the screaming hordes in Klatch, are you?"

"If it should come to that, sir," said Willikins. "I think this is adequately polished now, sir."

"A very sandy place, so they say."

"Indeed, sir," said Willikins, adjusting the helmet under Vimes's chin.

"And rocky. Very rocky. Lots of rocks. Dusty, too."

"Very parched in parts, sir, I believe you are correct."

"And so into this land of sand-colored dust and sand-colored rocks and sand-colored sand *you*, Willikins, will march with your expertise in cutlery and your red and white uniform?"

"With the gold frogging, sir." Willikins thrust out his jaw. "Yes, sir. If the need arises."

"You don't see anything wrong with this picture?"

"Sir?"

"Oh, never mind." Vimes yawned. "Well, we shall miss you, Willikins." Others may not, he thought. Especially if they have time for a second shot.

"Oh, Lord Venturi says it'll all be over by Hogswatch, sir."

"Really? I didn't know it had started."

Vimes ran down the stairs and into a smell of curry.

"We saved you some, sir," said Sergeant Colon. "You was asleep when the lad brought it round."

"It was Goriff's kid," said Nobby, chasing a bit of rice around his tin plate. "Enough for half the shift."

"The rewards of duty," said Vimes, hurrying toward the door.

"Bread and mango pickle and everything," said Colon happily. "I've always said old Goriff isn't that bad for a rag'ead."

A pool of sizzling oil . . . Vimes stopped at the door. *The family, huddling together* . . . He took out his watch. It was twenty past ten. If he ran—

"Fred, could you just step up to my office?" he said. "It won't take a moment."

"Right, sir."

Vimes ushered the sergeant up the stairs and closed the door.

Nobby and the other watchmen strained to listen, but there was no sound except for a low murmuring which went on for some time.

The door opened again. Vimes came down the stairs.

"Nobby, come up to the University in five minutes, will you? I want to stay in touch and I'm damned if I'm taking a pigeon with this uniform on."

"Right, sir."

Vimes left.

A few moments later Sergeant Colon walked carefully down to the main office. He had a slightly glassy look and walked back to his desk with the nonchalance that only the extremely worried try to achieve. He toyed with some paper for a while and then said:

"You don't mind what people call *you,* do you, Nobby?"

"I'd be minding the whole time if I minded that, sarge," said Corporal Nobbs cheerfully.

"Right. Right! And *I* don't mind what people call *me,* neither." Colon scratched his head. "Don't make sense, really. I reckon Sir Sam is missing too much sleep."

"He's a very busy man, Fred."

"Trying to do everything, that's his trouble. And . . . Nobby?"

"Yes?"

"It's Sergeant Colon, thanks."

There was sherry. There was always sherry at these occasions. Sam Vimes could regard it dispassionately, since he always drank fruit juice these days. He'd heard they made sherry by letting wine go rotten. He couldn't see the *point* of sherry.

"And you will *try* to look dignified, won't you?" said Lady Sybil, adjusting his cloak.

"Yes, dear."

"What will you try to look?"

"Dignified, dear."

"And *please* try to be diplomatic."

"Yes, dear."

"What will you try to be?"

"Diplomatic, dear."

"You're using your 'henpecked' voice, Sam."

"Yes, dear."

"You know that's not fair."

"No, dear." Vimes raised a hand in a theatrical gesture of submission. "All right, all *right*. It's just these feathers. And these tights." He winced and tried to do some surreptitious rearranging in an effort to prevent himself becoming the city's first hunchgroin. "I mean, supposing people *see* me?"

"Of course they'll see you, Sam. You're leading the procession. And I'm *very* proud of you."

She brushed some lint off his shoulder.*

Feathers in my hat, Vimes thought glumly. And fancy tights. And a shiny breastplate. A breastplate shouldn't be shiny. It should be too dented to take a decent polish. And diplomatic talk? How should I know how to talk diplomatically?

"And now I must go and have a word with Lady Selachii," said Lady Sybil. "You'll be all right, will you? You keep yawning."

"Of course. Didn't get much sleep last night, that's all."

"You promise not to run away?"

"*Me?* I *never* run—"

"You ran away before the big soirée for the Genuan ambassador. Everyone saw you."

"I'd just got news that the De Bris gang were robbing Vortin's strongroom!"

"But *you* don't have to chase everyone, Sam. You employ people for that now."

"We got 'em, though," said Vimes, with satisfaction.

He'd enjoyed it immensely, too. It wasn't just the pursuit that was so invigorating, with his velvet cloak left behind on a tree and his hat in a puddle somewhere, it was the knowledge that while he was doing this he wasn't eating very small sandwiches and making even smaller talk. It wasn't proper police work, Vimes considered, unless you were doing something that someone somewhere would much rather you weren't doing.

---

* Women always do this.

When Sybil had disappeared into the crowd he found a handy shadow and lurked in it. It enabled him to see almost the whole of the University's Great Hall.

He quite liked the wizards. They didn't commit crimes. Not Vimes's type of crimes, anyway. The occult wasn't Vimes's beat. The wizards might well mess up the very fabric of time and space but they didn't lead to paperwork, and that was fine by Vimes.

There were a lot of them in the hall, in all their glory. And there was nothing finer than a wizard dressed up formally, until someone could find a way of inflating a Bird of Paradise, possibly by using an elastic band and some kind of gas. But the wizards were getting a run for their money, because the rest of the guests were either nobles or guild leaders or both, and an occasion like the Convivium brought out the peacock in everyone.

His gaze went from face to chatting face, and he wondered idly what each person was guilty of.†

Quite a few of the ambassadors were there, too. They were easy to pick out. They wore their national costumes, but since by and large their national costumes were what the average peasant wore they looked slightly out of place in them. Their bodies wore feathers and silks, but their minds persistently wore suits.

They chatted in small groups. One or two nodded and smiled to him as they passed.

The world is watching, Vimes thought. If something went wrong and this stupid Leshp business started a war, it's men like these who'd be working out exactly how to deal with the winner, whoever it was. Never mind who started it, never mind how it was fought, they'd want to know how to deal with things *now.* They represented what people called the "international community." And like all uses of the word "community," you were never quite sure what or who it was.

He shrugged. It wasn't his world, thank goodness.

He sidled over to Corporal Nobbs, who was standing by the main doors in the sort of lopsided slouch which was the closest a living Nobbs could come to attention.

"All quiet, Nobby?" he said, out of the corner of his mouth.

---

† The possibility that they were not guilty of anything was one that he didn't even think worthy of consideration.

"Yessir."

"Nothing going on *at all?*"

"Nossir. Not a pigeon anywhere, sir."

"What, nowhere? Nothing?"

"Nossir."

"There was trouble all over the place yesterday!"

"Yessir."

"You did *tell* Fred he was to send a bird if there was anything at all?"

"Yessir."

"The Shades? There's *always* something—"

"Dead quiet, sir."

"Damn!"

Vimes shook his head at the sheer untrustworthiness of Ankh-Morpork's criminal fraternity.

"I suppose you couldn't take a brick and—"

"Lady Sybil was very speffic about how you was to stop here," said Corporal Nobbs, staring straight ahead.

"Speffic?"

"Yeah, sir. She come and have a word with me. Gave me a dollar," said Nobby.

"Ah, Sir Samuel!" said a booming voice behind him, "I don't think you've met Prince Khufurah yet, have you?"

He turned. Archchancellor Ridcully was bearing down on him, towing a couple of swarthy men. Vimes hurriedly put on his official face.

"This is Commander Vimes, gentlemen. Sam . . . no, I'm doing this the wrong way round, aren't I, got the protocol all wrong—so much to sort out, the Bursar's locked himself in the safe again, we don't know how he manages to get the key in there with him, I mean, it's not even as if it's got a keyhole on the inside . . . ."

The first man held out a hand as Ridcully bustled off again. "Prince Khufurah," he said. "My carpet got in only two hours ago."

"Carpet? Oh . . . yes . . . you flew . . ."

"Yes, very chilly and of course you just can't get a good meal. And did you get your man, Sir Samuel?"

"What? Pardon?"

"I believe our ambassador told me you had to leave the reception last week . . . ?" The Prince was a tall man who had probably once been quite athletic until the big dinners had finally weighed him down. And he had a beard. All Klatchians had beards. This Klatchian had intelligent eyes, too. Disconcertingly intelligent. You looked into them and several layers of person looked back at you.

"What? Oh. Yes. Yes, we got 'em all right," said Vimes.

"Well done. He put up a fight, I see."

Vimes looked surprised. The Prince tapped his jaw thoughtfully. Vimes's hand flew up and encountered a little bit of tissue on his own chin.

"Ah . . . er . . . yes . . ."

"Commander Vimes *always* gets his man," said the Prince.

"Well, I wouldn't say I—"

"Vetinari's terrier, I've heard them call you," the Prince went on. "Always hot on the chase, they say, and he won't let go."

Vimes stared into the calm, knowing gaze.

"I suppose, at the end of the day, we're all someone's dog," he said, weakly.

"In fact it is fortuitous I have met you, commander."

"It is?"

"I was just wondering about the meaning of the word shouted at me as we were on our way down here. Would you be so kind?"

"Er . . . if I . . ."

"I believe it was . . . let me see now . . . oh, yes . . . *towelhead.*"

The Prince's eyes stayed locked on Vimes's face.

Vimes was conscious of his own thoughts moving very fast, and they seemed to reach their own decision. We'll explain later, they said. You're too tired for explanations. Right now, with this man, it's oh so much better to be honest . . .

"It . . . refers to your headdress," he said.

"Oh. Is it some kind of obscure joke?"

Of *course* he knows, thought Vimes. And he knows I know . . .

"No. It's an insult," he said eventually.

"Ah? Well, we certainly cannot be held responsible for the ramblings of idiots, commander." The Prince flashed a smile. "I must commend you, incidentally."

"I'm sorry?"

"For your breadth of knowledge. I must have asked a dozen people that question *this morning* and, do you know? Not *one* of them knew what it meant. And they *all* seemed to have caught a cough."

There was a diplomatic pause but, in it, someone sniggered.

Vimes let his glance drift sideways to the other man, who had not been introduced. He was shorter and skinnier than the Prince and, under his black headdress, had the most crowded face Vimes had ever seen. A network of scars surrounded a nose like an eagle's beak. There was a sort of beard and moustache, but the scars had affected the hair growth so much that they stuck out in strange bunches and at odd angles. The man looked as though he had been hit in the mouth by a hedgehog. He could have been any age. Some of the scars looked fresh.

All in all, the man had a face that any policeman would arrest on sight. There was no possible way it could be innocent of *anything.*

He caught Vimes's expression and grinned, and Vimes had never seen so much gold in one mouth. He'd never seen so much gold in one *place.*

Vimes realized he was staring when he ought to have been making polite diplomatic conversation.

"So," he said, "are we going to have a scrap over this Leshp business or what?"

The Prince gave a dismissive shrug.

"Pfui," he said. "A few square miles of uninhabited fertile ground with superb anchorage in an unsurpassed strategic position? What sort of inconsequence is that for civilized people to war over?"

Once again Vimes felt the gaze on him, *reading* him. Well, the hell with it. He said, "Sorry, I'm not good at this diplomacy business. Did you *mean* what you just said then?"

There was another snigger. Vimes turned and looked at the leering bearded face again. And was aware of a smell, no, a *stench* of cloves.

Good grief, he chews *the stinking things . . .*

"Ah," said the Prince, "you haven't met 71-hour Ahmed?"

Ahmed grinned again and bowed. "Offendi," he said, in a voice like a gravel path.

And that seemed to be it. Not "This is 71-hour Ahmed, Cultural Attaché or "71-hour Ahmed, my bodyguard" or even "71-hour Ahmed, walking strongroom and moth killer." It was clear that the next move was up to Vimes.

"That's . . . er . . . that's an unusual name," he said.

"Not at all," said the Prince smoothly. "Ahmed is a very common name in my country."

He leaned forward again. Vimes recognized this as the prelude to a confidential aside. "Incidentally, was that beautiful lady I saw just now your first wife?"

"Er . . . all my wives," said Vimes. "That is—"

"Could I offer you twenty camels for her?"

Vimes looked back into the dark eyes for a moment, glanced at 71-hour Ahmed's 24-carat grin, and said:

"This is another test, isn't it . . . ?"

The Prince straightened up, looking pleased.

"Well done, Sir Samuel. You're *good* at this. Do you know, Mr. Boggis of the Thieves' Guild was prepared to accept fifteen?"

"For Mrs. Boggis?" Vimes waggled a hand dismissively. "Nah . . . four camels, maybe four camels and a goat in a good light. And when she's had a shave."

The milling guests turned at the sound of the Prince's explosion of laughter.

"Very good! Very good! I am afraid, commander, that some of *your* fellow citizens feel that just because *my* people invented advanced mathematics and all-day camping we are complete barbarians who'd try to buy their wives at the drop of, shall we say, a turban. I am surprised they're giving me an honorary degree, considering how incredibly backward I am."

"Oh? What degree is that?" said Vimes. No wonder this man was a diplomat. You couldn't trust him an inch, he thought in loops, and you couldn't help liking him despite it.

The Prince pulled a letter out of his robe.

"Apparently it's a *Doctorum Adamus cum Flabello Dulci*— Is there something wrong, Sir Samuel?"

Vimes managed to turn the treacherous laugh into a coughing fit. "No, no, nothing," he said. "No."

He desperately wanted to change the subject. And fortunately there was something here to provide just the opportunity.

"Why has Mr. Ahmed got such a big curved sword slung on his back?" he said.

"Ah, you are a policeman, you notice such things—"

"It's hardly a concealed weapon, is it? It's nearly bigger than him. He's practically a concealed owner!"

"It's ceremonial," said the Prince. "And he does fret so if he has to leave it behind."

"And what exactly is his—"

"Ah, there you are," said Ridcully. "I think we're just about ready. You know you go right at the front, Sam—"

"Yes, I know," said Vimes. "I was just asking His Highness what—"

"—and if you, Your Highness, and you, Mr. . . . my word, what a big sword, and you come back here and take your place among the honored guests, and we'll be ready in a brace of sheiks . . ."

What a thing it is to have a copper's mind, Vimes thought, as the great file of wizards and guests tried to form a dignified and orderly line behind him. Just because someone makes himself pleasant and likable you start to be suspicious of him, for no other reason than the fact that *anyone* who goes out of their way to be nice to a copper has got something on their mind. Of course, he's a diplomat, but still . . . I just hope he never studied ancient languages, and that's a fact.

Someone tapped Vimes on the shoulder. He turned and looked right into the grin of 71-hour Ahmed.

"If hyou changing your mind, offendi, I give hyou twenty-five camels, no problem," he said, pulling a clove from his teeth. "May your hloins be full of fruit."

He winked. It was the most suggestive gesture Vimes had ever seen. "Is this another—" he began, but the man had vanished into the crowd.

"My loins be full of fruit?" he repeated to himself. "Good grief!"

71-hour Ahmed reappeared at his other elbow in a gust of cloves. "I go, I hcome back," he growled happily. "The Prince hsays the degree is Doctor of Sweet ℱanny Adams. A ʰwizard wheeze, yes? Oh, ʰow we are laughing."

And then he was gone.

The Convivium was Unseen University's Big Day. Originally it had just been the degree ceremony, but over the years it had developed into a kind of celebration of the amicable relationship between the University and the city, in particular celebrating the fact that people were hardly ever turned to clams anymore. In the absence of anything resembling a Lord Mayor's Show or a state opening of Parliament, it was one of the few formal opportunities the citizens had of jeering at their social superiors, or at least at people wearing tights and ridiculous costumes.

It had grown so big that it was now held in the city's Opera House. Distrustful people—that is to say, people like Vimes—considered that this was *so* there could be a procession. There was nothing like the massed ranks of wizardry walking sedately through the city in a spirit of civic amicability to subtly remind the more thoughtful kind of person that it hadn't always been this way. Look at us, the wizards seemed to be saying. We used to rule this city. Look at our big staffs with the knobs on the end. Any one of these could do some very serious damage in the wrong hands so it's a good thing, isn't it, that they're in the right hands at the moment? Isn't it nice that we all get along so well?

And someone, once, had decided that the Commander of the Watch should walk in front, for symbolic reasons. That hadn't mattered for years because there hadn't been a Commander of the Watch, but now there was, and he was Sam Vimes. In a red shirt with silly baggy sleeves, red tights, some kind of puffed shorts in a style that went out of fashion, by the look of it, at the time when flint was at the cutting edge of cutting-edge technology, a tiny shiny breastplate and a helmet with feathers in it.

And he really did need some sleep.

And he had to carry the truncheon.

He kept his eyes fixed on the damn thing as he walked out of the University's main gate. Last night's rain had cleaned the sky. The city steamed.

If he stared at the truncheon he didn't have to see who was giggling at him.

The downside was that he had to keep staring at the thing.

It said, on a little tarnished shield that he'd had to clean before reading it, *Protecter of thee Kinge's Piece.*

That had brightened the occasion slightly.

Feathers and antiques, gold braid and fur . . .

Perhaps it was because he was tired, or just because he was trying to shut out the world, but Vimes found himself slowing down into the traditional watchman's walk and the traditional idling thought process.

It was an almost Pavlovian response.* The legs swung, the feet moved, the mind began to work in a certain way. It wasn't a dream state, exactly. It was just that the ears, nose and eyeballs wired themselves straight into the ancient "suspicious bastard" node of his brain, leaving his higher brain center free to freewheel.

. . . Fur and tights . . . what kind of wear was that for a watchman? Bashed-in armor, greasy leather breeches and a tatty shirt with bloodstains on it, someone else's for preference . . . that was the stuff . . . nice feel of the cobbles through his boots, it was really comforting . . .

Behind him, confusion running up and down the ranks, the procession slowed down to keep in step.

". . . Hah, *Protecter of thee Kinge's Piece* indeed . . . he'd said to the old man who'd delivered it, "Which piece did you have in mind?" but that had fallen on stony ears . . . damn silly thing anyway, he'd thought, a short length of wood with a lump of silver on the end . . . even a constable got a decent sword, what was he supposed to do, *wave* it at people? . . . ye gods, it was months since he'd had a good walk through the streets . . . lot of people about today . . . some parade on, wasn't there . . . ?

"Oh dear," said Captain Carrot, in the crowd. "What's he doing?"

---

* A term invented by the wizard Denephew Boot†, who had found that by a system of rewards and punishments he could train a dog, at the ringing of a bell, to immediately eat a strawberry meringue.

† His parents, who were uncomplicated country people, had wanted a girl. They were expecting to call her Denise.

Next to him an Agatean tourist was industriously pulling the lever of his iconograph.

Commander Vimes stopped and, with a faraway look in his eyes, tucked his truncheon under one arm and reached up to his helmet.

The tourist looked up at Carrot and tugged his shirt politely.

"Please, what is he doing now?" he said.

"Er . . . he's . . . he's taking out . . ."

"Oh, *no* . . ." said Angua.

". . . he's taking the ceremonial packet of cigars out of his helmet," said Carrot. "Oh . . . and he's, he's lighting one . . ."

The tourist pulled the lever a few times.

"Very historic tradition?"

"Memorable," murmured Angua.

The crowd had fallen silent. No one wanted to break Vimes's concentration. There was the big gusty silence of a thousand people holding their breath.

"What's he doing now?" said Carrot.

"Can't you see?" said Angua.

"Not with my hands over my eyes. Oh, the poor man . . ."

"He's . . . he's just blown a smoke ring . . ."

". . . first one of the day, he *always* does that . . ."

". . . and now he's set off again . . . and now he's pulled out the truncheon and he's tossing it up in the air and catching it again, you know the way he does with his sword when he's thinking . . . He looks quite happy . . ."

"I think he's going to really *treasure* this moment of happiness," said Carrot.

Then the murmur started. The procession had halted behind Vimes. Some of the more impressionable people who weren't sure what they should be doing, and those who had partaken too heavily of the University's rather good sherry, started to fumble around on their person for something to throw up in the air and catch. After all, this was a Traditional Ceremony. If you took the view that you were not going to do things because they were apparently ridiculous, you might as well go home right now.

"He's tired, that's what it is," said Carrot. "He's been running around overseeing things for days. Night *and* day watches. You know what a hands-on person he is."

"Let's hope the Patrician will agree to let him stay that way."

"Oh, his lordship wouldn't . . . He wouldn't, would he?"

Laughter was starting. Vimes had started to toss the truncheon from one hand to the other.

"He can make his sword spin three times and still catch it—"

Vimes's head turned. He looked up. His truncheon clattered onto the cobbles and rolled into a puddle, unheeded.

Then he started to run.

Carrot stared at him and then tried to see what the man had been looking at.

"On top of the Barbican . . ." he said. "In that window . . . isn't that someone up there? Excuse me, excuse me, sorry, excuse me—" He began to push his way through the crowd.

Vimes was already a small figure in the distance, his red cloak flying out after him.

"Well? There's lots of people watching the parade from high places," said Angua. "What's so special about—"

"No one should be up there!" said Carrot, starting to run now he was free of the crowd. "It's all sealed up!"

Angua looked around. Every face was turned toward the street theater, and there was a cart nearby. She sighed and strolled behind it wearing an expression of suspicious nonchalance. There was a gasp, a faint but distinctly organic sound, a muffled yelp and then the clank of armor hitting the ground.

Vimes didn't know why he ran. It was a sixth sense. It was when the back of the brain picked up out of the ether that something bad was going to happen, and didn't have time to rationalize, and just took over the spinal cord.

No one could get to the top of the Barbican. The Barbican had been the fortified gateway in the days when Ankh-Morpork didn't regard an attacking army as a marvelous commercial opportunity. Some parts were still in use, but the bulk of it was six or seven stories of ruin, without stairs that any sensible man would trust. For years it had been used as an unofficial source of masonry for the rest of the city. Bits of it fell off on windy nights. Even gargoyles avoided it.

He was aware that far behind him the noise of the crowd became a lot of shouting. One or two people screamed. He didn't turn round. Whatever was going on, Carrot could take care of it.

Something overtook him. It looked like a wolf would look if one of its ancestors had been a long-haired Klatchistan hunting dog, one of those graceful things that were all nose and hair.

It bounded ahead and through the crumbling gateway.

The creature was nowhere to be seen when Vimes arrived. But the absence was not a matter that grabbed at his attention, because of the more pressing presence of the corpse, lying in a mess of fallen masonry.

One of the things Vimes had always said—that is to say, one of the things he said he always said, and no one disagrees with the commanding officer—was that sometimes small details, tiny little details, things that no one would notice in ordinary circumstances, grab your senses by the throat and scream, "See me!"

There was a lingering, spicy scent in the air. And in the gap between a couple of cobblestones was a clove.

It was five o'clock. Vimes and Carrot sat in the Patrician's outer office, in silence except for the irregular ticking of the clock.

After a while Vimes said: "Let me have a look at that again."

Carrot obediently pulled out the small square of paper. Vimes looked at it. There was no mistaking what it showed. He tucked it into his own pocket.

"Er . . . why do you want to keep it, sir?"

"Keep what?" said Vimes.

"The iconograph I borrowed from the tourist."

"I don't know what you're talking about," said Vimes.

"But you—"

"I can't see you going very far in the Watch, captain, if you go around seeing things that aren't there."

"Oh."

The clock seemed to tick louder.

"You're thinking something, sir. Aren't you?"

"It is a use to which I occasionally put my brain, captain. Strange as it may seem."

"*What* are you thinking, sir?"

"What they want me to think," said Vimes.

"Who's *they?*"

"I don't know yet. One step at a time."

A bell tinkled.

Vimes stood up. "You know what I always say," he said.

Carrot removed his helmet and polished it with his sleeve. "Yes, sir. 'Everyone's guilty of something, especially the ones that aren't,' sir."

"No, not that one . . ."

"Er . . . 'Always take into consideration the fact that you might be dead wrong,' sir?"

"No, nor that one either."

"Er . . . 'How come Nobby ever got a job as a watchman?', sir? You say that a lot."

"No! I meant 'Always act stupid,' Carrot."

"Ah, right, sir. From now on I shall remember that you always said that, sir."

They put their helmets under their arms. Vimes knocked at the door.

"Come," said a voice.

The Patrician was standing at the window.

Sitting or standing around the office were Lord Rust and the others. Vimes never quite understood how the civic leaders were chosen. They just seemed to turn up, like a tack on the sole of your shoe.

"Ah, Vimes," said Vetinari.

"Sir."

"Let us not beat about the bush, Vimes. How did the man get up there when your people had so thoroughly checked everything last night? Magic?"

"Couldn't say, sir."

Carrot, still staring straight ahead, blinked.

"Your people *did* check the Barbican, I assume?"

"No, sir."

"They *didn't?*"

"No, sir. I did that myself."

"You physically checked it yourself, Vimes?" said Boggis of the Thieves' Guild.

Captain Carrot could *feel* Vimes's thoughts at this point.

"That is correct . . . Boggis," said Vimes, without turning his head. "But . . . we think someone got in where the windows are boarded up and pulled the boards back after him. Dust has been disturbed and—"

"And you didn't spot this, Vimes?"

Vimes sighed. "It'd be hard enough to spot the nailed-back boards in daylight, Boggis, let alone in the middle of the night." Not that we did, he added to himself. Angua smelled the scent on them.

Lord Vetinari sat down at his desk. "The situation is grave, Vimes."

"Yes, sir?"

"His Highness is very seriously injured. And Prince Cadram, we understand, is beside himself with rage."

"They *insist* on keeping his brother in the embassy," said Lord Rust. "A studied insult. As if we haven't good surgeons in this city."

"That's right, of course," said Vimes. "And many of them could give him a decent shave and a haircut, too."

"Are you making fun of me, Vimes?"

"Certainly not, my lord," said Vimes. "In my opinion, no surgeons anywhere have cleaner sawdust on their floors than the ones in this city."

Rust glared at him.

The Patrician coughed.

"You have identified the assassin?" said the Patrician.

Carrot was expecting Vimes to say, "Alleged assassin, sir," but instead he said:

"Yes. He is— He *was* called Ossie Brunt, sir. No other name that we know. Lived in Market Street. Did odd jobs from time to time. Bit of a loner. No relatives or friends that we can find. We are making enquiries."

"And that's all you fellows know?" said Lord Downey.

"It took some time to identify him, sir," said Vimes stolidly.

"Oh? Why should that be?"

"Couldn't give you the technical answer, sir, but it looked to me like they wouldn't need to make him a coffin, they could just have posted him between two barn doors."

"Was he acting alone?"

"We only found the one body, sir. And a lot of recently fallen masonry, so it looks as—"

"I *meant* does he belong to any organization? Any suggestion that he's anti-Klatchian?"

"Apart from him trying to kill one? Enquiries are continuing."

"Are you taking this *seriously,* Vimes?"

"I have put my best men on the job, sir." *Who's looking worried?* "Sergeant Colon and Corporal Nobbs." *Who's looking relieved?* "Very experienced men. The keystones of the Watch."

"Colon and Nobbs?" said the Patrician. "Really?"

"Yes, sir."

Their gazes met, very briefly.

"We're getting some very threatening noises, Vimes," said Vetinari.

"What can I say, sir? I saw someone up on the tower, I ran, someone shot the Prince with an arrow and then I found the man at the bottom of the tower very obviously dead, with a broken bow and a lot of rock beside him. The storm last night probably loosened things up. I can't make up facts that don't exist, sir."

Carrot watched the faces round the table. The general expression was one of relief.

"A lone bowman," said Vetinari. "An idiot with some kind of mad grudge. Who died in the execution of the, uh, attempted execution. And, of course, valiant action by our watchmen probably at least prevented an immediately fatal shot."

"Valiant action?" said Downey. "I know Captain Carrot here ran toward the VIPs and Vimes headed for the tower, but frankly, Vimes, your strange behavior beforehand—"

"Somewhat immaterial now," said Lord Vetinari. Once again he adopted a slightly faraway voice, as if reporting to somebody else. "If Commander Vimes had not slowed down the procession, the wretch would undoubtedly have got a much better shot. As it was, the man panicked. Yes . . . the Prince, possibly, would accept that."

"Prince?" said Vimes. "But the poor devil—"

"His brother," said the Patrician.

"Ah. The nice one?"

"Thank you, commander," said the Patrician. "Thank you, gentlemen. Do not let me detain you. Oh, Vimes . . . just a brief word, if you would be so good. Not you, Captain Carrot. I'm sure someone is committing some crime somewhere."

Vimes remained staring at the far wall while the room emptied. Vetinari left his chair and went over to the window.

"Strange days indeed, commander," he said.

"Sir."

"For example, I gather that this afternoon Captain Carrot was on the roof of the Opera House firing arrows down toward the archery butts."

"Very keen lad, sir."

"It could well be that the distance between the Opera House and the targets is about the same, you know, as the distance between the top of the Barbican and the spot where the Prince was hit."

"Just fancy that, sir."

Vetinari sighed. "And why was he doing this?"

"It's a funny thing, sir, but he was telling me the other day that in fact it is still law that every citizen should do one hour's archery practice every day. Apparently the law was made in 1356 and it's never been—"

"Do you know why I sent Captain Carrot away just now, Vimes?"

"Couldn't say, sir."

"Captain Carrot is an honest young man, Vimes."

"Yes, sir."

"And did you know that he winces when he hears you tell a direct lie?"

"Really, sir?" *Damn.*

"I can't stand to see his poor face twitch all the time, Vimes."

"Very thoughtful of you, sir."

"Where was the second bowman, Vimes?"

Damn! "Second bowman, sir?"

"Have you ever had a hankering to go on the stage, Vimes?"

Yes, at the moment I'd leap on it wherever it's heading, thought Vimes.

"No, sir."

"Pity. I am certain you're a great loss to the acting profession. I believe you said the man had put the boards back after him."

"Yes, sir."

"*Nailed* them back?"

Blast. "Yes, sir."

"From the outside."

Damn. "Yes, sir."

"A particularly *resourceful* lone bowman, then."

Vimes didn't bother to comment. Vetinari sat down at his desk, raised his steepled fingers to his lips and stared at Vimes over the top of them.

"Colon and Nobbs are investigating this? Really?"

"Yes, sir."

"If I were to ask you why, you'd pretend not to understand?"

Vimes let his forehead wrinkle in honest perplexity. "Sir?"

"If you say 'Sir?' again in that stupid voice, Vimes, I swear there will be trouble."

"They're good men, sir."

"However, some people might consider them to be unimaginative, stolid and . . . how can I put this? . . . possessed of an inbuilt disposition to accept the first explanation that presents itself and then bunk off somewhere for a quiet smoke? A certain lack of imagination? An ability to get out of their depth on a wet pavement? A tendency to rush to judgment?"

"I hope you are not impugning my men, sir."

"Vimes, Sergeant Colon and Corporal Nobbs have never *been* pugn'd in their entire lives."

"Sir?"

"And yet . . . in fact, we do not *need* complications, Vimes. An ingenious lone madman . . . well, there are many madmen. A regrettable incident."

"Yes, sir." The man was looking harassed and Vimes felt there was room for a pinch of sympathy.

"Fred and Nobby don't like complications either, sir."

"We need simple answers, Vimes."

"Sir. Fred and Nobby are *good* at simple."

The Patrician turned away and looked out over the city.

"Ah," he said, in a quieter voice. "Simple men to see the simple truth."

"This is a fact, sir."

"You are learning fast, Vimes."

"Couldn't say about that, sir."

"And when they have found the simple truth, Vimes?"

"Can't argue with the truth, sir."

"In my experience, Vimes, you can argue with anything."

When Vimes had gone Lord Vetinari sat at his desk for a while, staring at nothing. Then he took a key from a drawer and walked across to a wall, where he pressed a particular area.

There was a rattle of a counterweight. The wall swung back.

The Patrician walked softly through the narrow passageway beyond. Here and there it was illuminated by a very faint glow from around the edges of the little panels which, if gently slid back, would allow someone to look out through the eyesockets of a handy portrait.

They were a relic of a previous ruler. Vetinari never bothered with them. Looking out of someone else's eyes wasn't the trick.

There was a certain amount of travel up dark stairways and along musty corridors. Occasionally he'd make movements the meaning of which might not be readily apparent. He'd touch a wall *here* and *here*, apparently without thinking, as he passed. Along one stone-flagged passage, lit only by the gray light from a window forgotten by everyone except the most optimistic flies, he appeared to play a game of hopscotch, robes flying around him and calves twinkling as he skipped from stone to stone.

These various activities did not seem to cause anything to happen. Eventually he reached a door, which he unlocked. He did this with some caution.

The air beyond was full of acrid smoke, and the steady *pop-pop* sound which he had begun to hear farther back along the passage was now quite loud. It faltered for a moment, was followed by a much louder bang, and then a piece of hot metal whirled past the Patrician's ear and buried itself in the wall.

In the smoke a voice said, "Oh dear."

It didn't seem unhappy, but sounded rather like the voice one might use to a sweet and ingratiating little puppy which, despite one's best efforts, is sitting next to a spreading damp patch on the carpet.

As the billows cleared the indistinct shape of the speaker turned to Vetinari with a wan little smile and said, "Fully fifteen seconds this time, my lord! There is no doubt that the *principle* is sound."

That was one of Leonard of Quirm's traits: he picked up conversations out of the air, he assumed everyone was an interested friend, and he took it for granted that you were as intelligent as he was.

Vetinari peered at a small heap of bent and twisted metal.

"What was it, Leonard?" he said.

"An experimental device for turning chemical energy into rotary motion," said Leonard. "The problem, you see, is getting the little pellets of black powder into the combustion chamber at exactly the right speed and one at a time. If two ignite together, well, what we have is the *external* combustion engine."

"And, er, what would be the purpose of it?" said the Patrician.

"I believe it could replace the horse," said Leonard proudly.

They looked at the stricken thing.

"One of the advantages of horses that people often point out," said Vetinari, after some thought, "is that they very seldom explode. Almost never, in my experience, apart from that unfortunate occurrence in the hot summer a few years ago." With fastidious fingers he pulled something out of the mess. It was a pair of cubes, made out of some soft white fur and linked together by a piece of string. There were dots on them.

"Dice?" he said.

Leonard smiled in an embarrassed fashion. "Yes. I can't think why I thought they'd help it go better. It was just, well, an idea. You know how it is."

Lord Vetinari nodded. He knew how it was. He knew how it was far more than Leonard of Quirm did, which was why there was one key to the door and he had it. Not that the man was a prisoner, except by dull, humdrum standards. He appeared rather grateful to be confined in this light, airy attic with as much wood, paper, sticks of charcoal and paint as he desired and no rent or food bills to pay.

In any case, you couldn't really imprison someone like Leonard of Quirm. The most you could do was lock up his body. The gods alone knew where his mind went. And, although he had so much cleverness it leaked continually, he couldn't tell you which way the political wind was blowing even if you fitted him with sails.

Leonard's incredible brain sizzled away alarmingly, an overloaded chip pan on the Stove of Life. It was impossible to know what he would think of next, because he was constantly reprogrammed by the whole universe. The sight of a waterfall or a soaring bird would send him spinning down some new path of practical speculation that invariably ended in a heap of wire and springs and a cry of "I think I know what I did wrong." He'd been a member of most of the craft guilds in the city but had been thrown out for getting impossibly high marks in the exams or, in some cases, correcting the questions. It was said that he'd accidentally blown up the Alchemists' Guild using nothing more than a glass of water, a spoonful of acid, two lengths of wire and a ping-pong ball.

Any sensible ruler would have killed off Leonard, and Lord Vetinari was extremely sensible and often wondered why he had not done so. He'd decided that it was because, imprisoned in the priceless, inquiring amber of Leonard's massive mind, underneath all that bright investigative genius was a kind of willful innocence that might in lesser men be called stupidity. It was the seat and soul of that force which, down the millennia, had caused mankind to stick its fingers in the electric light socket of the Universe and play with the switch to see what happened—and then be very surprised when it did.

It was, in short, something useful. And if the Patrician was anything, he was the political equivalent of the old lady who saves bits of string because you never know when they might come in handy.

After all, you couldn't plan for every eventuality, because that would involve knowing what was going to happen, and if you *knew* what was going to happen, you could probably see to it that it didn't, or at least happened to someone else. So the Patrician never planned. Plans often got in the way.

And, finally, he kept Leonard around because the man was easy to talk to. He never understood what Lord Vetinari was talking about, he had a world view about as complex as that of a concussed duckling and, above all, never really paid attention. This made him an excellent confidant. After all, when you seek advice from someone it's certainly not because you want them to give it. You just want them to be there while you talk to yourself.

"I've just made some tea," said Leonard. "Will you join me?"

He followed the Patrician's gaze to a brown stain all up one wall, which ended in a star of molten metal in the plaster.

"I'm afraid the automatical tea engine went wrong," he said. "I shall have to make it by hand."

"So kind," said Lord Vetinari.

He sat down amidst the easels and, while Leonard busied himself at the fireplace, leafed through the latest sketches. Leonard sketched as automatically as other people scratched; genius—a certain *kind* of genius—fell off him like dandruff.

There was a picture of a man drawing, the lines catching the figure so accurately it appeared to stand out of the paper. And around it, because Leonard never wasted white space, were *other* sketches, scattered aimlessly. A thumb. A bowl of flowers. A device, apparently, for sharpening pencils by water power . . .

Vetinari found what he was looking for in the bottom left-hand corner, sandwiched between a sketch for a new type of screw and a tool for opening oysters. It, or something very much like it, was always there somewhere.

One of the things that made Leonard such a rare prize, and kept him under such secure lock and key, was that he really didn't see any difference between the thumb and the roses and the pencil-sharpener and *this.*

"Ah, the self-portrait," said Leonard, returning with two cups.

"Yes, indeed," said Vetinari. "But my eye was drawn to this little sketch here. The war machine . . . ."

"Oh, that? A mere nothing. Have you ever noticed the way in which the dew on roses—"

"This bit here . . . what is it for?" said Vetinari, pointing persistently.

"Oh, that? That's just the throwing arm for the balls of molten sulfur," said Leonard, picking up a plate of small cakes. "I calculate that one should get a range of almost half a mile, if one detaches the endless belt from the driving wheels and uses the oxen to wind the windlass."

"Really?" said Vetinari, taking in the carefully numbered parts. "And it could be built?"

"What? Oh, yes. Macaroon? In theory."

"In theory?"

"No one would ever actually do it. Raining unquenchable fire down upon fellow humans? Hah!" Leonard sprayed macaroon crumbs. "You'd never find an artisan to build it, or a soldier who would pull the lever . . . That's part 3(b) on the plan, just here, look . . ."

"Ah, yes," said Vetinari. "Anyway," he added, "I imagine these huge power arms here couldn't possibly be operated without them breaking . . ."

"Seasoned ash and yew, laminated and held together by special steel bolts," said Leonard promptly. "I made a few calculations, just there below the sketch of light on a raindrop. As an intellectual exercise, obviously."

Vetinari ran his eye along several lines of Leonard's spidery mirror-writing.

"Oh, yes," he said glumly. He put the paper aside.

"Have I told you that the Klatchian situation is intensely political? Prince Cadram is trying to do a great deal very fast. He needs to consolidate his position. He is depending on support that is somewhat volatile. There are many plotting against him, I understand."

"Really? Well, this is the sort of thing people do," said Leonard. "Incidentally, I've recently been examining cobwebs and, I know this will interest you, their strength in relation to their weight is much greater even than our best steel wire. Isn't that fascinating?"

"What kind of weapon do you intend to make out of them?" said the Patrician.

"Sorry?"

"Oh, nothing. I was just thinking aloud."

"And you haven't touched your tea," said Leonard.

Vetinari looked around the room. It was full of . . . *things.* Tubes and odd paper kites and things that looked like the skeletons of ancient beasts. One of Leonard's saving graces, in a very *real* sense from Vetinari's point of view, was his strange attention span. It wasn't that he soon got bored with things. He didn't seem to get bored with *anything.* But since he was interested in everything in the universe all the time the end result tended to be that an experimental device for disembowelling people at a distance then became a string-weaving machine and ended up as an instrument for ascertaining the specific gravity of cheese.

He was as easily distracted as a kitten. All that business with the flying machine, for example. Giant bat wings hung from the ceiling even now. The Patrician had been more than happy to let him waste his time on that idea, because it was obvious to anyone that no human being would ever be able to flap the wings hard enough.

He needn't have worried. Leonard was his own distraction. He had ended up spending ages designing a special tray so that people could eat their meals in the air.

A truly innocent man. And yet always, always, some little part of him would sketch these wretchedly beguiling engines, with their clouds of smoke and carefully numbered engineering diagrams . . .

"What's this?" Vetinari said, pointing to yet another doodle. It showed a man holding a large metal sphere.

"That? Oh, something of a toy, really. Makes use of the strange properties of some otherwise quite useless metals. They don't like being *squeezed.* So they go bang. With extreme alacrity."

"Another weapon . . ."

"Certainly not, my lord! It would be no possible use as a weapon! I did think it might have a place in the mining industries, though."

"Really . . ."

"For when they need to move mountains out of the way."

"Tell me," Vetinari said, putting this paper aside as well, "you don't have any relatives in Klatch, do you?"

"I don't believe so. My family lived in Quirm for generations."

"Oh. Good. But . . . very clever people in Klatch, are they?"

"Oh, in many disciplines they practically wrote the scroll. Fine metalwork, for example."

"Metalwork . . ." The Patrician sighed.

"And alchemy, of course. Affir Al-chema's *Principia Explosia* has been *the* seminal work for more than a hundred years."

"Alchemy," said the Patrician, glumly. "Sulfur and so forth . . ."

"Yes, indeed."

"But the way you put it, these major achievements were some considerable time ago . . ." Lord Vetinari sounded like a man straining to see a light at the end of the tunnel.

"Certainly! I would be astonished if they haven't made considerable progress!" said Leonard of Quirm happily.

"Ah?" The Patrician sank a little in his chair. It had turned out that the end of the tunnel was on fire.

"A splendid people with much to recommend them," said Leonard. "I always thought it was the presence of the desert. It leads to an urgency of thought. It makes you aware of the briefness of life."

The Patrician glanced at another page. Between a sketch of a bird's wing and a careful drawing of a ball-joint was a little doodle of something with spiked wheels and spinning blades. And then there was the device for moving mountains aside . . .

"The desert is not required," he said. He sighed again and pushed the pages aside. "Have you heard about the lost continent of Leshp?" he said.

"Oh, yes. I did some sketches there a few years ago," said Leonard. "Some interesting aspects, I recall. More tea? I fear you've let that one get cold. Was there anything you particularly wanted?"

The Patrician pinched the bridge of his nose.

"I'm not sure. There is a small problem developing. I thought perhaps you could help. Unfortunately," the Patrician glanced at the sketches again, "I suspect that you can." He stood up, straightened his robe and forced a smile. "You have everything you require?"

"Some more wire would be nice," said Leonard. "And I have run out of Burnt Umber."

"I shall have some sent along directly," said Vetinari. "And now, if you will excuse me—"

He let himself out.

Leonard nodded happily as he cleared away the teacups. The infernal combustion engine was carried to the heap of scrap metal beside the small forge, and he fetched a ladder and removed the piston from the ceiling.

He'd just opened out his easel to start work on a new design when he was aware of a distant pattering. It sounded like someone running but also occasionally pausing to hop sideways on one leg.

Then there was a pause, such as might be made by someone adjusting their clothing and getting their breath back.

The door opened and the Patrician returned. He sat down and looked carefully at Leonard of Quirm.

"You did *what?*" he said.

Vimes turned the clove over and over under the magnifying glass.

"I see tooth marks," he said.

"Yes sir," said Littlebottom, who represented in her entirety the Watch's forensic department. "Looks like someone was chewing it like a toothpick."

Vimes sat back. "I would say," he said, "that this was last touched by a swarthy man of about my height. He had several gold teeth. And a beard. And a slight cast in one eye. Scarred. He was carrying a large weapon. Curved, I'd say. And you'd have to call what he was wearing a turban because it wasn't moving fast enough to be a badger."

Littlebottom looked astonished.

"Detectoring is like gambling," said Vimes, putting down the clove. "The secret is to know the winner in advance. Thank you, corporal. Write down that description and make sure everyone gets a copy, please. He goes by the name of 71-hour Ahmed, heaven knows why. And then go and get some rest."

Vimes turned to face Carrot and Angua, who had crammed into the tiny little room, and nodded at the girl.

"I followed the clove smell all the way down to the docks," she said.

"And then?"

"Then I lost it, sir." Angua looked embarrassed. "I didn't have any trouble through the fish market, sir. Or in the slaughterhouse district. And then it went into the spice market—"

"Ah. I see. And didn't come out again?"

"In a way, sir. Or came out going fifty different ways. Sorry."

"Can't be helped. Carrot?"

"I did what you said, sir. The top of the Opera House is about the right distance from our archery butts. I used a bow just like the one he used, sir—"

Vimes raised a finger. Carrot stared, and then said slowly: ". . . like . . . the one you found next to him . . ."

"Right. And?"

"It's a Burleigh and Stronginthearm 'Shureshotte Five,' sir. A bow for the expert. I'm not a great bowman but I could at least hit the target at that elevation. But . . ."

"I'm ahead of you," said Vimes. "You're a big lad, Carrot. Our late Ossie had arms like Nobby. I could put my hand round them."

"Yes, sir. It's a hundred-pound draw. I doubt if he could even pull the string back."

"I'd hate to watch him try. Good grief . . . the only thing he could be sure of hitting with a bow like that would be his foot. By the way, do you think anyone saw you up there?"

"I doubt it, sir. I was right in among the chimneys and the air vents."

Vimes sighed. "Captain, I expect if you'd done it in a cellar at midnight his lordship would have said 'Wasn't it rather dark down there?' next morning."

He took out the by now rather creased picture. There was Carrot—or at least Carrot's arm and ear—as he ran toward the procession. And there, among the people in the procession turning to look at him, was the face of the Prince. There was no sign of 71-hour Ahmed. He'd been at the soirée, hadn't he? But then there'd been all that milling around at the door, people changing places, treading on one another's robes, nipping back to the privy, walking into one another . . . He could have gone *anywhere*.

"And the Prince fell as you got to him? With the arrow in his back? He was still facing you?"

"Yes, sir. I'm sure of that. Everyone else was milling around, of course . . ."

"So he was shot in the back by a man in front of him who could not possibly have used the bow that he didn't shoot him with from the wrong direction . . ."

There was a tapping at the window.

"That'll be Downspout," said Vimes, without looking around. "I sent him on an errand . . ."

Downspout never quite fitted in. It wasn't that he didn't get on with people, because he hardly ever *met* people, except those whose activities took them above, say, second-floor level. Constable Downspout's beat was the rooftops. Very slowly. He'd come down for the Watch's Hogswatch party and had poured gravy in his ears to show willing, but gargoyles got very nervy indoors at ground level and he had soon exited via the chimney and his paper squeaker had echoed out forlornly amongst the snowy rooftops all night.

But gargoyles were good at watching, and good at remembering, and very, very good at being patient.

Vimes opened the window. Moving jerkily, Downspout unfolded himself into the room and then quickly scrambled up onto a corner of Vimes's desk, for the comfort that it brought.

Angua and Carrot stared at the arrow the gargoyle held in his hand.

"Ah, well done," said Vimes, in the same even voice. "Where did you find it, Downspout?"

Downspout spluttered a series of guttural syllables only pronounceable by someone with a mouth shaped like a pipe.

"In the wall on the second floor of the dress shop in the Plaza of Broken Moons," Carrot translated.

"eshk," said Downspout.

"That's barely halfway to Sator Square, sir."

"Yes," said Vimes. "A small weak man trying to pull a heavy bow, the arrow wobbling all over the place . . . Thank you very much, Downspout. There will be an extra pigeon for you this week."

"nkorr," said Downspout, and clambered back out of the window.

"Excuse me, sir?" said Angua. She took the arrow from Vimes and, closing her eyes, sniffed at it gingerly.

"Oh, yes . . . Ossie," she said. "All over it . . ."

"Thank you, corporal. It's as well to be sure."

Carrot took the arrow from the werewolf and looked at it critically. "Huh. Peacock feathers and a plated point. It's the sort of thing an amateur buys because he thinks it'll magically improve his shot. Showy."

"Right," said Vimes. "You, Carrot, and you, Angua . . . you're on the case."

"Sir, I don't understand," said Carrot. "I am perplexed. I thought you said Fred and Nobby were investigating this?"

"Yes," said Vimes.

"But—"

"Sergeant Colon and Corporal Nobbs are investigating why the late Ossie tried to kill the Prince. And do you know what? They're going to find lots of clues. I just *know* it. I can feel it in my water."

"But we know he *couldn't*—" said Carrot.

"Isn't this fun?" said Vimes. "I don't want you to get in Fred's way. Just . . . ask around. Try Done It Duncan, or Sidney Lopsides, hah, there's a man with his ear to the ground all right. Or the Agony Aunts, or Lily Goodtime. Or Mr. Slider, haven't seen him around for a while, but—"

"He's dead, sir," said Carrot.

"What, Smelly Slider? When?"

"Last month, sir. He got hit by a falling bedstead. Freak accident, sir."

"No one told *me*."

"You were busy, sir. But you put some money in the envelope when Fred brought it round, sir. Ten dollars, which Fred remarked was very generous."

Vimes sighed. Oh, yes, the envelopes. Fred was always wandering around with an envelope these days. Someone was always leaving, or some friend of the Watch was in trouble, or there was a raffle, or the tea money was low again, or some complicated explanation . . . so Vimes just put some money in. Simplest way.

Old Smelly Slider . . .

"You should've mentioned it," he said reproachfully.

"You've been working hard, sir."

"Any other street news you haven't mentioned, captain?"

"Not that I can think of, sir."

"All right. Well . . . see which way the wind is blowing. Very carefully. And—trust no one."

Carrot looked worried.

"Er . . . I can trust Angua, can't I?" he said.

"Well, of *course* you—"

"And you, presumably."

"Me, well, obviously. That goes without say—"

"Corporal Littlebottom? She can be very helpful—"

"Cheery, yes, certainly you can trust—"

"Sergeant Detritus? I always thought he was very trust—"

"Detritus, oh yes, he—"

"Nobby? Should I—"

"Carrot, I understand what he *means,*" said Angua, tugging his arm.

Carrot looked a little crestfallen. "I've never liked . . . you know, underhand things," he mumbled.

"I don't want any written reports," said Vimes, grateful for that small mercy. "This is . . . unofficial. But *officially* unofficial, if you see what I mean."

Angua nodded. Carrot just stayed looking dismal.

She's a werewolf, thought Vimes, *of course* she understands. And you'd think a man who is technically a dwarf'd be able to fold his head around the idea of subterfuge.

"Look, just . . . listen to the streets," said Vimes. "The streets know everything. Talk to . . . Blind Hugh—"

"I'm afraid he passed away last month," said Carrot.

"Did he? No one told me!"

"I thought I sent you a memo, sir."

Vimes glanced guiltily at his overloaded desk, and then shrugged.

"Have a quiet look at things. Get to the bottom of things. And trust no— Trust practically no one. All right? Except trustworthy people."

*　　*　　*

"Come on, open up! Watch business!"

Corporal Nobbs pulled at Sergeant Colon's sleeve and whispered in his ear.

"*Not* Watch business!" said Colon, pounding the door again. "Nothing to do with the Watch at all! We are just civilians, all right?"

The door opened a crack.

"Yes?" said a voice that counted its small change.

"We have to ask you some questions, missus."

"*Are* you the Watch?" said the voice.

"No! I think I just made that clear—"

"Piss off, copper!"

The door slammed.

"You sure this is the right place, sarge?"

"Harry Chestnuts said he saw Ossie going in here. Come on, open up!"

"Everyone's looking at us, sarge," said Nobby. Doors and windows had opened all along the street.

"And don't call me sarge when we're in plain clothes!"

"Right you are, Fred."

"That's—" Colon hesitated in an agony of status. "Well, that's *Frederick* to you, Nobby."

"And they're giggling, Fred . . . er . . . erick."

"We don't want to make a cock-up of this, Nobby."

"Right, Frederick. And that's Cecil, thank you."

"Cecil?"

"That is my name," said Nobby coldly.

"Have it your way," said Colon. "Just remember who's the superior civilian around here, all right?"

He hammered on the door again.

"We hear you've got a room to let, missus!" he yelled.

"Brilliant, Frederick," said Nobby. "That was bloody *brilliant!*"

"Well, I *am* the sergeant, right?" Colon whispered.

"No."

"Er . . . yeah . . . right . . . well, just you remember that, right?"

The door snapped open.

The woman within had one of those faces that had settled over the years, as though it had been made of butter and then left in the sun. But age hadn't been able to do much with her hair. It was a violent ginger and piled up like a threatening thunderhead.

"Room? You shoulda said," she said. "Two dollars a week, no pets, no cookin', no wimmin after six a.m., if you don't want it thousands do, are you with the circus? You look like you're with the circus."*

"We're—" Colon began, and then stopped. There were undoubtedly a large number of things to be apart from policemen, but there and then he couldn't think of any of them.

"—actors," said Nobby.

"Then it's payment a week in advance," said the woman. "And no filthy foreign habits. This is a respectable house," she added, in defiance of evidence so far.

"We ought to see the room first," said Colon.

"Oh, the choosy sort, eh?"

She led them upstairs.

The room vacated so terminally by Ossie was small and bare. A few items of clothing hung on nails in the wall, and a heap of wrappers and greasy bags indicated that Ossie had been a man who ate, as it were, off the street.

"Whose is this stuff?" said Sergeant Colon.

"Oh, he's gone now. I *told* him he'd be out if he didn't pay up. I'll throw it out afore you settle in."

"We'll get rid of it for you," said Sergeant Colon. He fumbled in his pouch and produced a couple of dollars. "Here you are, Miss—?"

"*Mrs.* Spent," said Mrs. Spent. She gave them a lopsided look. "Are you both stopping here or what?"

"Nah, I've just come along as his chaperon," said Colon, giving her a friendly grin. "He has to fight women off when they find out about his sexual magnetism."

Mrs. Spent gave the shocked Nobby a sharp look and bustled out of the room.

---

* Plain clothes was the problem. Both the men had been used to uniforms all their lives. Sergeant Colon's only suit had been bought by a man two stone lighter and ten years younger, so the buttons creaked under tension, and Nobby's idea of plain clothes was the ribbon-and-bell-bedecked costume he wore as a leading member of the Ankh-Morpork Folk Dance and Song Society. Small children had followed them in the street to see where the show was going to be.

"What'd you go and say that for?" said Nobby.

"It's got rid of her, hasn't it?"

"You were having a go at me, don't deny it! Just because I'm going through a bit of an emotional wossname, eh?"

"It was just a joke, Nobby. Just a joke."

Nobby peered under the narrow bed.

"Wow!" he said, all emotional wossnames forgotten.

"What is it? What is it?" said Colon.

"It looks like a complete run of *Bows and Ammo!* And . . ." Nobby pulled another stack of badly engraved magazines out into the light, "here's *Warrior of Fortune*, look! And *Practical Siege Weapons* . . ."

Colon leafed through page after page of very similar-looking people holding very similar weapons of personal destruction.

"You got to be a bit odd to sit around all day reading this kind of thing," he said.

"Yeah," said Nobby. "Here, don't put that one back, that's last August's issue, I ain't got that one. Hang on, there's a box right at the back . . ."

He wriggled out, towing a small box with him. It was locked, but the cheap metal gave way when he accidentally levered at the lid.

Silver coins gleamed. Lots and lots of them.

"Whoops . . ." he muttered. "We're in trouble now . . ."

"That's *Klatchian* money, that is!" said Colon. "Sometimes people slip you one instead of a half-dollar in your change. Look, there's all curly writing on them!"

"We're in *big* trouble," said Nobby.

"No, no, no, this is a Clue what we have found by patient detectoring," said Sergeant Colon. "And it's going to be a feather in our caps and no mistake when Mister Vimes hears about it!"

"How much do you reckon there is?"

"Got to be hundreds and hundreds of dollars' worth," said Colon. "And that's a lot of money to a Klatchian. You can probably live like a king for a year on a dollar, in Klatch."

"It wasn't *very* patient detectoring," said Nobby doubtfully. "All I did was look under the bed."

"Ah, but that's because you is trained," said Colon. "Your

basic *civilian* wouldn't think of that, right? Ah, it all begins to make sense!"

"Does it? Why would the Klatchians give him money to shoot a Klatchian?" said Nobby.

Colon tapped the side of his nose. *"Politics,"* he said.

"Ah, *politics,"* said Nobby. "Ah, well, *politics.* I see. *Politics.* Right. So why?"

"Aha," said Colon again, tapping the other side of his nose.

"Why're you picking your nose, sarge?"

"I'm *tapping* it," said Colon severely. "That's to show I'm in the know."

"In the nose," said Nobby cheerfully.

"It's just the sort of underhand cunning thing they'd do," said Colon.

"Payin' us to kill them?" said Nobby.

"Ah, you see, some Klatchian nob gets topped *here,* and then *they* can send a snotty note saying, 'You killed our big nob, you foreign nephews of dogs, this means war!' see? A perfect excuse."

"Do you *need* an excuse to have a war?" said Nobby. "I mean, who for? Can't you just say, 'You got lots of cash and land but I've got a big sword so divvy up right now, chop chop?' That's what *I'd* do," said Corporal Nobbs, military strategist. "And I wouldn't even say *that* until after I'd attacked."

"Ah, but that's 'cos you don't know about politics," said Colon. "You can't do that stuff anymore. Mark my words, this case has got politics written all over it. That's why old Vimes put me on it, depend upon it. Politics. Young Carrot's all very well, but you need an experienced man of the world in these delicate political situations."

"You've certainly got the nose-tapping just right," said Nobby. "I generally miss."

But he felt troubled, if not in his nose then in whatever small organ propelled his blood around his body. This didn't feel right. Nothing much in Nobby's life had ever felt right, so he knew very well how the feeling felt.

He looked up at the bare walls and down at the rough floorboards.

"There's a bit of sand on the floor," he said.

"Another clue, then," said Colon happily. "A Klatchian has

been here. Bugger all else but sand in Klatch. Still got some in his sandals."

Nobby opened the window. It gave on to a gently sloping roof. Someone could get through it easily and be away over the tiles and into the maze of chimneys.

"He could've gone in and out this way, sarge," he volunteered.

"Good point, Nobby. Write that down. Evidence of conniving and sneaking around."

Nobby peered down. "Here, there's glass outside, Fred . . ."

Sergeant Colon joined him at the stricken window. One of the panes had been smashed. Outside, glass glittered on the tiles.

"That could be a clue, eh?" said Nobby, hopefully.

"It certainly is," said Sergeant Colon. "See the glass fell *outside* the window? Everyone knows you look at which way the glass falls. I reckon he was just testing his bow and it went off while it was loaded."

"That's clever, sarge," said Nobby.

"That's *detectoring*," said Colon. "It's no good just *looking* at things, Nobby. You got to *think* straight, too."

"*Cecil*, sarge."

"That's Frederick, Cecil. Come on, I think we've wrapped this up nicely. Old Vimes says he wants a report toot sweet."

Nobby looked out of the broken window. The roof abutted the end wall of a much larger warehouse. For a moment he found himself thinking bendy rather than straight, but he reasoned that his thinking was only a corporal's thinking, and worth far less per thought than a sergeant's thinking, so he kept his private thoughts to himself.

As they went downstairs Mrs. Spent watched them suspiciously through a barely opened doorway at the far end of the hall, clearly ready to slam it shut at the first suggestion of any sexual magnetism.

"It's not as if I even know where to *get* a sexual magnet," Nobby muttered. "And she didn't even laugh."

. . . *Also, we went to the bow shops in the Street of Cunning Artificers and showed the iconograph to the man in Burleigh and*

Stronginthearm, who vouchsafed, that is him, e.g, he was refer-ring to the Diseased . . .

"Oh, my . . ." Vimes's lips moved slightly as his gaze went back up the page.

. . . also in addition to the Klatchian money you could tell one of them had been there because of, e.g, the sand on the floor . . .

"He'd still got sand in his sandals?" murmured Vimes. "Good grief."

"*Sam?*"

Vimes looked up from his reading.

"Your soup will be cold," said Lady Sybil from the far end of the table. "You've been holding that spoonful in the air for the last five minutes by the clock."

"Sorry, dear."

"What are you reading?"

"Oh, just a little masterpiece," said Vimes, pushing Fred Colon's report aside.

"Interesting, is it?" said Lady Sybil a little sourly.

"Practically unparalleled," said Vimes. "The only things they haven't found are the bunch of dates and the camel hidden under the pillow . . ."

Belatedly, his nuptial radar detected a certain chilliness from the far side of the cruet.

"Is, er, there something wrong, dear?" he said.

"Can you remember when we last had dinner together, Sam?"

"Tuesday, wasn't it?"

"That was the Guild of Merchants' annual dinner, Sam."

Vimes's brow wrinkled. "But you were there too, weren't you?"

A further subtle change in the dragonhouse quotient told him that this was not a well chosen answer.

"And then you rushed off afterward because of that business with the barber in Gleam Street."

"Sweeney Jones," said Vimes. "Well, he *was* killing people, Sybil. The best you could say is that he didn't mean to. He was just very bad at shaving—"

"But *you* didn't have to go, I'm sure."

"Policing's a twenty-four-hour job, dear."

"Only for you! Your constables do their ten hours and that's *it*. But you're *always* working. It's not good for you. You're always running around during the day, and when I wake up in the middle of the night there's always a cold space beside me . . ."

The dots hung in the air, the ghosts of words unsaid. Little things, thought Vimes. That's how a war starts.

"There's so much to do, Sybil," he said, as patiently as he could.

"There's always been a lot to do. And the bigger the Watch gets the *more* there is to do, have you noticed that?"

Vimes nodded. That was true. Rotas, receipts, notebooks, reports . . . the Watch might or might not be making a difference in the city, but it was certainly frightening a lot of trees.

"You ought to delegate," said Lady Sybil.

"So he tells me," muttered Vimes.

"Pardon?"

"Just thinking aloud, dear." Vimes pushed the paperwork away. "I'll tell you what . . . let's have an evening in," he said. "There's a nice fire in the drawing room—"

"Er . . . no, Sam, there isn't."

"Hasn't young Forthright lit it?" Forthright was the Boy; it came as news to Vimes that this was an official servant position, but the Boy's job was to light the fires, clean the privies, help the gardener and take the blame.

"He's gone off to be a drummer boy in the Duke of Eorle's regiment," said Lady Sybil.

"Him too? He seemed a bright lad! Isn't he too young?"

"He said he was going to lie about his age."

"I hope he lies about his musical ability. I've heard him whistling." Vimes shook his head. "Whatever possessed him to do such a daft thing?"

"He thinks the uniform will impress the girls."

Sybil gave him a gentle smile. An evening at home suddenly began to seem very inviting.

"Well, it won't take a genius to find the woodshed," said Vimes. "And then we can bolt the doors and—"

One of the aforesaid doors shook to the sound of frantic knocking.

Vimes caught Sybil's gaze.

"Go on, then. Answer it," she sighed, and sat down.

The door admitted Corporal Littlebottom, seriously out of breath.

"You . . . got to come quick, sir . . . it's . . . murder this . . . time!"

Vimes looked helplessly at his wife.

"Of course you must go," she said.

Angua brushed out her hair in front of the mirror.

"I don't like this," said Carrot. "It's not a proper way to behave."

She patted him on the shoulder. "Don't *worry*," she said. "Vimes explained it all. You're acting as though we're doing something *wrong*."

"I like being a watchman," said Carrot, still in the mournful depths. "And you've got to wear a uniform. If you *don't* wear a uniform it's like spying on people. He *knows* I think that."

Angua looked at his short red hair and honest ears.

"I've taken a lot of the work off his shoulders," Carrot went on. "He doesn't have to go on patrol at *all,* but he still tries to do everything."

"Perhaps he doesn't want you to be quite so helpful?" said Angua, as tactfully as possible.

"It's not as if he's getting any younger, either. I've tried to point that out."

"That was kind of you."

"And I've never *worn* plainclothes."

"On you they'll never be very plain," said Angua, pulling on her coat. It was a relief to be out of that armor. As for Carrot, there was no disguising him. The size, the ears, the red hair, the expression of muscular good-naturedness . . .

"I suppose a werewolf is in plainclothes all the time, when you think about it," said Carrot.

"Thank you, Carrot. And you are absolutely right."

"I just don't feel comfortable, living a lie."

"Walk a mile on these paws."

"Pardon?"

"Oh . . . nothing."

Goriff's son Janil had been angry. He didn't know why. The anger was built up of a lot of things. The fire bomb last night was a big part. So were some of the words he'd been hearing in the street. He'd had an argument with his father about sending that food round to the Watch House this morning. They were an official part of the city. They had those stupid badges. They had uniforms. He was angry about a lot of things, including the fact that he was thirteen.

So when, at nine in the evening while his father was baking bread, the door had slammed back and a man had rushed in, Janil had pulled his father's elderly crossbow from under the counter and aimed it where he thought the heart was and pulled the trigger.

Carrot stamped his feet once or twice and looked around.

"Here," he said. "I was standing *here*. And the Prince was . . . in that direction."

Angua obediently walked across the square. Several people turned to look curiously at Carrot.

"All right . . . stop . . . no, on a bit . . . stop . . . turn a little bit to the left . . . I mean my left . . . back a bit . . . now throw your arms up . . ."

He walked over to her and followed her gaze.

"He was shot from the University?"

"Looks like the library building," said Angua. "But a wizard wouldn't do it, surely? They keep out of that sort of thing."

"Oh, it's not too hard to get in there, even when the gates are shut," said Carrot. "Let's try the unofficial way, shall we?"

"Okay. Carrot?"

"Yes?"

"The false moustache . . . it's not you, you know. And the nose is far too pink."

"Doesn't it make me look inconspicuous?"

"No. And the hat . . . I should lose the hat, too. It is a *good* hat," she added quickly. "But a brown bowler . . . it's not your style. It doesn't suit you."

"Exactly!" said Carrot. "If it *was* my style, people would know it's me, right?"

"I mean it makes you look like a twerp, Carrot."

"Do I normally look like a twerp?"

"No, not—"

"Aha!" Carrot fumbled in the pocket of his large brown overcoat. "I got this book of disguises from the joke shop in Phedre Road, look. Funny thing, Nobby was in there buying stuff too. I asked him why and he said it was desperate measures. What d'you think he meant by that?"

"I can't imagine," said Angua.

"It's just amazing the stuff they've got. False hair, false noses, false beards, even false . . ." He hesitated, and began to blush. "Even false . . . you know, chests. For ladies. But I can't imagine for the life of me why they'd want to disguise those."

He probably couldn't, Angua thought. She took the very small book from Carrot and glanced through it. She sighed.

"Carrot, these disguises are meant for a potato."

"Are they?"

"Look, they're all on potatoes, see?"

"I thought that was just for display."

"Carrot, it's got 'Mr. Spuddy Face' on it."

Behind his thick black moustache Carrot looked hurt and perplexed. "What does a potato want a disguise for?" he said.

They'd reached the alley alongside the University that had been known informally as Scholars' Entry for so many centuries that this was now on a nameplate at one end. A couple of student wizards went past.

The unofficial entrance to the University has always been known only to students. What most students failed to remember was that the senior members of the faculty had also been students once, and also liked to get out and about after the official shutting of the gates. This naturally led to a certain amount of embarrassment and diplomacy on dark evenings.

Carrot and Angua waited patiently as a few more students climbed over, followed by the Dean.

"Good evening, sir," said Carrot, politely.

"Good evening to you, Spuddy," said the Dean, and ambled off into the night.

"You see?"

"Ah, but he didn't call me Carrot," said Carrot. "The *principle* is sound."

They dropped down onto lawns of academia and headed for the library.

"It'll be shut," said Angua.

"Remember, we have a man on the inside," said Carrot, and knocked.

The door opened a little way. "Ook?"

Carrot raised his horrible little round hat.

"Good evening, sir, I wonder if we could come in? It's Watch business."

"Ook eek ook?"

"Er . . ."

"What did he say?" said Angua.

"If you must know, he said, 'My goodness me, a walking potato,'" said Carrot.

The Librarian wrinkled his nose at Angua. He did not like the smell of werewolves. But he beckoned them inside and then left them waiting while he knuckled back to his desk and rummaged in a drawer. He produced a Watch Special Constable's badge on a string, which he hung around the general area where his neck should have been, and then stood as much to attention as an orangutan can, which is not a great deal. The central ape gets the idea but outlying areas are slow to catch on.

"Ook ook!"

"Was that 'How may I be of assistance, Captain Tuber?'" said Angua.

"We need to have a look on the fifth floor, overlooking the square," said Carrot, a shade coldly.

"Ook oook—ook."

"He says that's just old storerooms," said Carrot.

"And that last 'ook'?" said Angua.

"'Mr. Horrible Hat,'" said Carrot.

"Still, he hasn't worked out who you are, eh?" said Angua.

The fifth floor was a corridor of airless rooms, smelling sadly of old, unwanted books. They were stacked not on shelves but on wide racks, bundled up with string. A lot of them were battered and missing their covers. Judging by what remained, though, they were old textbooks that not even the most ardent bibliophile could treasure.

Carrot picked up a torn copy of Woddeley's *Occult Primer*. Several loose pages fell out. Angua picked one up.

"'Chapter Fifteen, Elementary Necromancy,'" she read aloud. "'Lesson One: Correct Use of Shovel . . .'"

She put it down again and sniffed the air. The presence of the Librarian filled the nasal room like an elephant in a matchbox, but—

"Someone else has been in here," she said. "In the last couple of days. Could you leave us, sir? When it comes to odors, you're a bit . . . forthright . . ."

"Ook?"

The Librarian nodded at Carrot, shrugged at Angua and ambled out.

"Don't move," said Angua. "Stay right where you are, Carrot. Don't disturb the air . . ."

She inched forward carefully.

Her ears told her the Librarian was down the corridor, because she could hear the floorboards creaking. But her nose told her that he was still here. He was a little fuzzy, but—

"I'm going to have to change," she said. "I can't get a proper picture this way. It's too strange."

Carrot obediently shut his eyes. She'd forbidden him to watch her en route from a human to a wolf, because of the unpleasant nature of the shapes in between. Back in Überwald people went from one shape to the other as naturally as ordinary humans would put on a different coat, but even there it was considered polite to do it behind a bush.

When he reopened them Angua was slinking forward, her whole being concentrated in her nose.

The olfactory presence of the Librarian was a complex shape, a mere purple blur where he had been moving but almost a solid figure where he'd been standing still. Hands, face, lips . . . they'd be just the center of an expanding cloud in a few hours' time, but now she could still smell them out.

There must be only the tiniest air currents in here. There weren't even any flies buzzing in the dead air to cause a ripple of disturbance.

She edged nearer to the window. Vision was a mere shadowy presence, providing a charcoal sketch of a room over which the scents painted their glorious colors.

By the window . . . by the window . . .

Yes! A man had stood there, and by the scent of it he hadn't moved for some time. The smell wavered in the air, on the edge of her nasal skill. The curling, billowing traces said that the window had been opened and closed again, and was there just the merest, tiniest suggestion that he'd held an arm out in front of him?

Her nose raced, trying to form original shapes from the patterns hanging in the room like dead smoke . . .

When she'd finished, Angua went back to her pile of clothes and coughed politely while she was pulling on her boots.

"There *was* a man standing by the window," she said. "Long hair, a bit dry, stinks of expensive shampoo. He was the man who nailed the boards back after Ossie got into the Barbican."

"Are you sure?"

"Is this nose ever wrong?"

"Sorry. Go on."

"I'd say he was heavyset, a bit bulky for his height. He doesn't wash a lot, but when he does he uses Windpike's Soap, the cheap brand. But expensive shampoo, which is odd. Quite new boots. And a green coat."

"You can smell the color?"

"No. The dye. It comes from Sto Lat, I think. And . . . I *think* he shot a bow. An *expensive* bow. There's a hint of silk in the air, and that's what the strongest bowstrings are made of, isn't it? And you wouldn't put one of those on a cheap bow."

Carrot stood by the window. "He got a good view," he said, and looked down at the floor. And then at the sill. And on the shelves nearby.

"How long was he here?"

"Two or three hours, I'd say."

"He didn't move around much."

"No."

"Or smoke, or spit. He just stood and waited. A professional. Mr. Vimes was *right*."

"A lot more professional than Ossie," said Angua.

"Green coat," said Carrot, as if thinking aloud. "Green coat, green coat . . ."

"Oh . . . and bad dandruff," said Angua, standing up.

"Snowy Slopes?!" shouted Carrot.

"What?"

"Really bad dandruff?"

"Oh, yes, it—"

"That's why they call him Snowy," said Carrot. "Daceyville Slopes, the man with the reinforced comb. But I'd heard he'd moved to Sto Lat—"

In unison they said: "—where the dye comes from—"

"Is he good with a bow?" said Angua.

"Very good. He's good at killing people he never met, too."

"He's an Assassin, is he?"

"Oh, no. He just kills people for money. No style. Snowy can barely read and write."

Carrot scratched his head in sympathetic recollection. "He doesn't even look at complicated pictures. We'd have got him last year, but he shook his head fast and got away while we were trying to dig out Nobby. Well, well. I wonder where he's staying?"

"Don't ask me to follow him in these streets. Thousands of people will have walked over the trail."

"Oh, there's people who will know. Someone sees everything in this town."

Mr. Slopes?

Snowy Slopes gingerly felt his neck, or at least the neck of his soul. The human soul tends to keep to the shape of the original body for some time after death. Habit is a wonderful thing.

"Who the *hell* was he?" he said.

Not someone you know? said Death.

"Well, no! I don't know many people who cut my head off!"

Snowy Slopes's body had knocked against the table as it fell.

Several bottles of medicated shampoo now dripped and mixed their contents into the other more intimate fluids from the Slopes corpse.

"That stuff with the special oil in it cost me nearly four dollars," said Snowy. Yet, somehow, it all seemed slightly . . . irrelevant now. Death happens to other people. The other person in this case had been him. That is, the one down there. Not the one standing here looking at it. In life, Snowy hadn't even been able to *spell* "metaphysical," but he was already beginning to view life in a different way. From the outside, for a start.

"Four dollars," he repeated. "I never even had time to try it!"

IT WOULDN'T HAVE WORKED, said Death, patting the man on a fading shoulder. BUT, IF I MIGHT SUGGEST THAT YOU LOOK ON THE BRIGHT SIDE, IT WILL NO LONGER BE NECESSARY.

"No more dandruff?" said Snowy, now quite transparent and fading fast.

EVER, said Death. TRUST ME ON THIS.

Commander Vimes ran down darkened streets, trying to buckle on his breastplate as he ran.

"All right, Cheery, what's happening?"

"They say a Klatchian killed someone, sir. There's a mob up in Scandal Alley and it's looking bad. I was on the desk and I thought you ought to be told, sir."

"Right!"

"And anyway I couldn't find Captain Carrot, sir."

A little bit of acid ink scribbled its subtle entry on the ledger of Vimes's soul.

"Oh, gods . . . so who's the officer in charge?"

"Sergeant Detritus, sir."

It seemed to the dwarf that she was suddenly standing still. Commander Vimes had become a rapidly disappearing blur.

With the calm expression of someone who was methodically doing his duty, Detritus picked up a man and used him to hit some other men. When he had a clear area around him and a groaning heap of former rioters, he climbed the heap and cupped his hands round his mouth.

"Listen to me, youse people!"

A troll shouting at the top of his voice could easily be heard above a riot. When he seemed to have their attention he pulled a scroll out of his breastplate and waved it over his head.

"Dis is der Riot Act," he said. "You know what dat means? It means if'n I reads it out and youse don't disb . . . disp . . . go away, der Watch can use deadly force, you unnerstand?"

"What did you just use, then?" moaned someone from underneath his feet.

"Dat was you helpin' der Watch," said Detritus, shifting his weight.

He unrolled the scroll.

Although there was some scuffling in alleyways and shouts from the next street, a ring of silence expanded outward from the troll. An almost genetic component of the citizens of Ankh-Morpork was their ability to spot an opportunity for amusement.

Detritus held the document at arm's length. And then a few inches from his face. He tried turning it round a few times.

His lips moved uneasily.

Finally, he leaned down and showed it to Constable Visit.

"What dis word?"

"That's 'Whereby,' sergeant."

"I knew dat."

He straightened up again.

"'Whereby . . . it is . . .'" Beads of the troll equivalent of sweat began to form on Detritus's forehead. "'Whereby it is . . . ack-no-legg-ed . . .'"

"Acknowledged," whispered Constable Visit.

"I knew dat." Detritus stared at the paper again, and then gave up. "Youse don't want to stand here listenin' to me all day!" he bellowed. "Dis is der Riot Act and you've all got to read it, right? Pass it round."

"What if we don't read it?" said a voice in the crowd.

"You got to read it. It *legal*."

"And then what happens?"

"Den I shoot you," said Detritus.

"That's not allowed!" said another voice. "You've got to shout 'Stop! Armed Watchman!' first."

"Sure, dat suits me," said Detritus. He shrugged one huge shoulder to bring his crossbow under his arm. It was a siege bow, intended to be mounted on the cart. The bolt was six feet long. "It harder to hit runnin' targets."

He released the safety catch.

"Anyone finishing readin' dat thing yet?"

"Sergeant!"

Vimes pushed his way through the crowd. And it *was* a crowd now. Ankh-Morpork was always a good audience.

There was a clang as Detritus saluted.

"Were you proposing to shoot these people in cold blood, sergeant?"

"Nossir. Just a warning shot inna head, sir."

"Really? Just give me a moment to talk to them, then."

Vimes looked at the man next to him. He was holding a flaming torch in one hand and a long length of wood in the other. He gave Vimes the nervously defiant stare of someone who has just felt the ground shift under his feet.

Vimes pulled the torch toward him and lit a cigar. "What's happening here, friend?"

"The Klatchians have been shooting people, Mr. Vimes! Unprovoked attack!"

"Really?"

"People have been killed!"

"Who?"

"I . . . there were . . . everyone *knows* they've been killing people!" The man's mental footsteps found safer ground. "Who do they think they are, coming over—"

"That's enough," said Vimes. He stood back and raised his voice.

"I recognize a lot of you," he said. "And I know you've got homes to go to. See this?" He pulled his baton of office out of his pocket. "This says I've got to keep the peace. So in ten seconds I'm going somewhere else to find some peace to keep, but Detritus is going to stay here. And I just hope he doesn't do anything to disgrace the uniform. Or get it very dirty, at least."

Irony was not a degree-level subject among the listeners, but the brighter ones recognized Vimes's expression. It said that here was a man hanging on to his patience by his teeth.

The mob dispersed, going ragged at the edges as people legged it down side alleys, threw away their makeshift weapons and emerged at the other end walking the grave, thoughtful walk of honest citizens.

"All right, what *happened?*" said Vimes, turning to the troll.

"We're hearing where dis boy shot dis man," said Detritus. "We got here, next minute it rainin' people from everywhere, shoutin'.'"

"He smote him as Hudrun smote the fleshpots of Ur," said Constable Visit.*

"Smote?" said Vimes, bewildered. "He killed someone?"

"Not by der way der man was cussing, sir," said Detritus. "Hit him in der arm. His friends brought him round der Watch House to complain. He a baker on der night shift. He said he was late for work, he come runnin' in to pick up his dinner, next minute he flat on der floor."

Vimes walked across the street and tried the door of the shop. It opened a little way, and then fetched up against what seemed to be a barricade. Furniture had been piled up against the window as well.

"How many people were there, constable?"

"A multitude thereof, sir."

And four people in here, thought Vimes. A family. The door moved a fraction and Vimes realized he was ducking even before the crossbow protruded.

There was the *thung* of the string. The bolt tumbled rather than sped. It corkscrewed wildly across the alley and was almost moving sideways when it hit the opposite wall.

---

* Constable Visit-The-Ungodly-With-Explanatory-Pamphlets was a good copper, Vimes always said, and that was his highest term of praise. He was an Omnian with his countrymen's almost pathological interest in evangelical religion and spent all his wages on pamphlets; he even had his own printing press. The results were handed out to anyone interested and everyone who wasn't interested as well. Even Detritus couldn't clear a crowd faster than Visit, Vimes said. And on his days off he could be seen tramping the streets with his colleague, Smite-The-Unbeliever-With-Cunning-Arguments. So far they hadn't made a single convert. Vimes thought that Visit was probably a really nice man underneath it all, but somehow he could never face the task of finding out.

"Look," said Vimes, keeping his body down but raising his voice. "Anyone who got hit with *that,* it must have been an accident. This is the Watch. Open the door. Otherwise Detritus will open it. And when he opens a door, it stays open. You know what I mean?"

There was no reply.

"All right. Detritus, just step over here—"

There was a hissed argument inside, and then the sound of scraping as furniture was moved.

He tried the door. It swung inward.

The family were at the far end of the room. Vimes felt eight eyes on him. The atmosphere had a hot, worrying feel, spiced with the smell of burnt food.

Mr. Goriff was holding the crossbow gingerly, and the expression on his son's face told Vimes a lot of what he needed to know.

"All *right,*" he said. "Now you all listen to me. I'm not arresting anyone right now, you hear? This sounds like one of those things that make his lordship yawn. But you'd do better spending the rest of the night in the Watch House. I can't spare the men to stand guard here. Do you understand? I *could* arrest you. But this is just a request."

Mr. Goriff cleared his throat.

"The man I shot—" he began, and left the question and the lie hanging in the air.

Vimes forced himself not to glance at the boy. "Not badly hurt," he said.

"He . . . ran in," said Mr. Goriff. "And after last night—"

"You thought you were being attacked again and grabbed the crossbow?"

"Yes," said the boy, defiantly, before his father could speak.

There was a brief argument in Klatchian. Then Mr. Goriff said:

"We must leave the house?"

"For your own good. We'll try to have someone watch it. Now, get something together and go off with the sergeant. And give me that crossbow."

Goriff handed it over with a look of relief. It was a typical Saturday Night Special, so badly made and erratic that the only safe place to be when it was fired would be directly behind it, and even then you would be running a risk. And then no one had told its owner that under the counter in a steamy shop and a perpetual rain of grease wasn't the best place to keep it strung. The string sagged. Probably the only way you could reliably hurt someone with it was to beat them over the head.

Vimes waited until they'd been ushered out and took a last look around the room. It wasn't large. In the kitchen behind the shop something spicy in a pot was boiling dry. After burning his fingers a couple of times he managed to tip the pot onto the fire to put it out and then, vaguely remembering his mother doing something like this, put the pot under the pump to soak.

Then he barricaded the windows as best he could and went out, locking the door behind him. A discreetly obvious brass Thieves' Guild plaque over the door told the world that Mr. Goriff had conscientiously paid his annual fee,* but the world had plenty of less formal dangers and so Vimes took a piece of chalk out of his pocket and wrote on the door:

UnDer THE ProTeCtIOn Of THE WAtcH

As an afterthought he signed it:

SgT. DetrITus

In the imaginations of the less civically minded the majesty of the rule of law didn't carry anything like as much weight as the dread of Detritus.

The Riot Act! Where the *hell* had he dredged that from? Carrot, probably. It hadn't been used for as long as Vimes could remember, and that was no wonder when you knew what it really did. Even Vetinari would hesitate to use it. Now it was nothing more than a phrase. Thank goodness for trollish illiteracy . . .

It was when Vimes stood back to admire his handiwork that

---

* And would not, therefore, be officially burgled. Ankh-Morpork had a very direct approach to the idea of insurance. When the middle-man was cut out, that wasn't a figure of speech.

he saw the glow in the sky over Park Lane, almost at the same time as he heard the clatter of iron boots on the street.

"Oh, hello, Littlebottom," he said. "What now? Don't tell me—someone's set fire to the Klatchian embassy."

"All right, sir," said the dwarf. She stood uncertainly in the middle of the alley, looking worried.

"Well?" said Vimes.

"Er . . . you said—"

With a sinking feeling Vimes remembered that the generic dwarfish skill with iron was matched only by the fumble-fingered grasp of irony.

"The Klatchian embassy is *really* on fire?"

"Yes, sir!"

Mrs. Spent opened the door a crack.

"Yes?"

"I'm a friend of . . ." Carrot hesitated, wondering if Fred would have given his real name. "Er . . . big fat man, suit doesn't fit—"

"The one who goes around with the sex maniac?"

"Pardon?"

"Skinny little twerp, dresses like a clown?"

"They said you'd have a room," said Carrot desperately.

"They've got it," said Mrs. Spent, trying to shut the door.

"They said I could use it—"

"No sublettin'!"

"They said I should pay you two dollars!"

The pressure of the door was released a little.

"On top of what they paid?" said Mrs. Spent.

"Of course."

"Well . . ." She looked Carrot up and down and sniffed. "All right. What shift are you on?"

"Sorry?"

"You're a watchman, right?"

"Er . . ." Carrot hesitated, and then raised his voice. "No, I am not a watchman. Haha, you think I'm a watchman? Do I look like a watchman?"

"Yes, you do," said Mrs. Spent. "You're Captain Carrot. I *seen* you walking about the town. Still, I suppose even coppers have to sleep somewhere."

On the roof, Angua rolled her eyes.

"No wimmin, no cookin', no music, no pets," said Mrs. Spent, as she led the way up the creaking stairs.

Angua waited in the dark until she heard the window open.

"She's gone," Carrot hissed.

"There's glass on the tiles out here, just like Fred reported," said Angua, as she swung herself over the sill. Inside the room she took a deep breath and shut her eyes.

First she had to forget the smell of Carrot—anxious sweat, soap, the lingering hints of armor polish . . .

. . . and Fred Colon, all perspiration with a hint of beer, and then the odd ointment Nobby used for his skin condition, and the smells of feet, bodies, clothes, polish, fingernails . . .

After an hour it was possible for the eye of the nose to see someone walk across the room, frozen in time by their smell. But after a day smells criss-crossed and entangled. You had to take them apart, remove the familiar pieces, and what you had left—

"They're so mixed up!"

"All right, all right," said Carrot soothingly.

"At least three people! But I think one of them is Ossie . . . It's stronger round the bed . . . and . . ."

She opened her eyes wide and looked down at the floor. "Somewhere here!"

"What? What is?"

Angua crouched down with her nose just above the floorboards.

"I can smell it but I can't see it!"

A knife appeared in front of her. Carrot got down on his knees and ran the blade along the dust-filled crack between the floorboards.

Something splintery and brown popped up. It had been trodden on and rolled underfoot, but at this distance even Carrot could pick up traces of the clove smell. "Do you think Ossie made a lot of apple pies?" he whispered.

"No cookin', remember?" said Angua, and grinned.

"There's something else . . ."

Carrot levered out more dirt and dust. In it, something glittered. "Fred said all the glass was outside, didn't he?"

"Yes."

"Well, supposing we assume that someone didn't pick up *all* the bits when they broke in?"

"For someone that doesn't like lying, Carrot, you can be quite devious, you know?"

"Just logical. There's glass outside the window, but all that means is that there is glass outside the window. Commander Vimes always says there're no such things as clues. It's how you look at them."

"You think someone broke in and then carefully put the glass outside?"

"Could be."

"Carrot? Why are we whispering?"

"No wimmin, remember?"

"And no pets," said Angua. "So she's got me coming *and* going. Don't look like that," she added, when she saw his face. "It's only bad taste if someone else says it. *I'm* allowed."

Carrot scratched up some more glass fragments. Angua looked under the bed and pulled out the battered magazines.

"Ye gods, do people really read this stuff?" she said, flicking through *Bows and Ammo.* "'Testing the Locksley Reflex 7: A Whole Lotta Bow' . . . 'Footsore! We test the Ten Best Caltrops!' . . . and what's this magazine . . . ? *Warrior of Fortune?*"

"There's always little wars somewhere," said Carrot, pulling out the box of money.

"But will you look at the size of this ax here? 'Get A Head, Get A Burleigh and Stronginthearm "Streetsweeper" And Win By A Neck!' Well, it must be true what they say about men who like big weapons . . ."

"And that is?" said Carrot, lifting the lid of the box.

She looked at the top of his head. As always, Carrot radiated innocence like a small sun. But he'd . . . They'd . . . *Surely* he . . .

"They, er . . . they're rather small," she said.

"Oh, that's true," said Carrot, picking up some of the Klatchian coins. "Look at dwarfs. Never happier than with a chopper the same size as them. And Nobby's fascinated by weapons and he's practically dwarf-sized."

"Er . . ."

Technically, Angua was sure she knew Carrot better than anyone else. She was pretty sure he cared a lot for her. He seldom said so, he just assumed that she knew. She'd known other men, although turning into a wolf for part of the month was one of those little flaws that could put any *normal* man off and, up until Carrot, always had. And she knew the sort of things men said in what might be called the heat of the moment and then forgot. But when Carrot said things, you knew that *he* felt that everything was now settled until further notice, so if she made any comment he'd be genuinely surprised that she'd forgotten what it was he had said and would probably quote date and time.

And yet all the time there was this feeling that the greater part of him was always deep, deep inside, looking out. No one could be so simple, no one could be so creatively *dumb,* without being very intelligent. It was like being an actor. Only a very good actor was any good at being a bad actor.

"Rather a lonely person, our Nobby," said Carrot.

"Well, yes . . ."

"But I'm sure he'll find the right person for him," Carrot added, cheerfully.

Probably in a bottle, said Angua to herself. She remembered the conversation with him. It was a terrible thing to think, but there was something itchy about the thought of Nobby being allowed in the gene pool, even at the shallow end.

"You know, these coins are odd," said Carrot.

"How do you mean?" said Angua, grateful for the distraction.

"Why would he be paid in Klatchian *wols?* He wouldn't be able to spend them here, and the money changers don't give very good rates." Carrot tossed a coin in the air and caught it. "When we were leaving, Mr. Vimes said to me, 'Make sure you find the bunch of dates and the camel hidden under the pillow.' I think I know what he meant."

"Sand on the floor," said Angua. "Now, isn't that's an *obvious* clue? You can tell they were Klatchian because of the sand in their sandals!"

"But these cloves . . ." Carrot prodded the little bud. "It's not as if it's a common habit, even among Klatchians. *That's* not a very obvious clue, is it?"

"It smells newer," said Angua. "I'd say he was here last night."

"*After* Ossie was dead?"

"Yes."

"Why?"

"How should I know? What kind of name is 71-hour Ahmed?" said Angua.

Carrot shrugged. "I don't know. I *think* Mr. Vimes thinks that someone in Ankh-Morpork wants us to believe that Klatchians paid to have the Prince killed. That sounds . . . nasty but logical. But I don't understand why a *real* Klatchian would get involved . . ."

Their eyes met.

"Politics?" they said together.

"For enough money, a lot of people would do *anything*," said Angua.

There was a sudden and ferocious knocking at the door.

"Have you got someone in there?" said Mrs. Spent.

"Out of the window!" said Carrot.

"Why don't I just stay and rip her throat out?" said Angua. "All right, all right, it was a *joke*, all right?" she said, swinging her legs over the sill.

Ankh-Morpork no longer had a fire brigade. The citizens had a rather disturbingly direct way of thinking at times, and it did not take long for people to see the rather obvious flaw in paying a group of people by the number of fires they put out. The penny really dropped shortly after Charcoal Tuesday.

Since then they had relied on the good old principle of enlightened self-interest. People living close to a burning building did their best to douse the fire, because the thatch they saved might be their own.

But the crowd watching the burning embassy were doing so in a hollow-eyed, distant way, as if it was all taking place on some distant planet.

They moved aside automatically as Vimes elbowed his way

through to the space in front of the gates. Flames were already licking from every ground-floor window, and they could make out scurrying silhouettes in the flickering light.

He turned to the crowd. "Come on! What's up with you? Get a bucket chain going!"

"It's *their* bloody embassy," said a voice.

"Yeah. 's Klatchian soil, right?"

"Can't go on Klatchian soil."

"That'd be an *invasion,* that would."

"They wouldn't let us," said a small boy holding a bucket.

Vimes looked at the embassy gateway. There were a couple of guards. Their worried glances kept going back from the fire behind them to the crowd in front. They were nervous men, but it was much worse than that, because they were nervous men holding big swords.

He advanced on them, trying to smile and holding his badge out in front of him. It had a shield on it. It was not a very big shield.

"Commander Vimes, Ankh-Morpork City Watch," he said, in what he hoped was a helpful and friendly voice.

A guard waved him away. "Ḥyou be off!"

"Ah . . ." said Vimes. He looked down at the cobbles of the gateway and then back up at the guard. Somewhere in the flames someone was screaming.

"You! Come here! You see this?" he shouted at the guard, pointing down. The man took a hesitant step forward.

"That's Ankh-Morpork soil down there, my friend," said Vimes. "And you're standing on it and you're obstructing me in my—" he rammed his fist as hard as he could into the guard's stomach "—duty!"

He was already kicking out as the other guard rushed him. He caught him on the knee. Something went click. It felt like Vimes's own ankle.

Cursing and limping slightly, he ran on into the embassy and caught a scurrying man by his robe.

"Are there people still in there? Are there *people* in there?"

The man gave Vimes a panicky look. The armfuls of paper he'd been carrying spilled onto the ground.

Someone else grabbed his shoulder. "Can you climb, Mr. Vimes?"

"Who're—"

The newcomer turned to the cowering paper-carrier and struck him heavily across the face. "Rescuer of paper!"

As the man fell back his turban was snatched from his head.

"This way!" The figure plunged off through the smoke. Vimes hurried after him until they reached a wall, with a drainpipe attached.

"How did you—?"

"Up! Up!"

Vimes put one foot in the man's cupped hands, managed to get the other one on a bracket, and forced himself upward.

"Hurry!"

He managed to half climb, half pull himself up the pipe, little fireworks of pain exploding up and down his legs as he reached a parapet and hauled himself over. The other man rose behind him as if he'd run up the wall.

There was a strip of cloth hiding the lower half of his face. He thrust another strip toward Vimes.

"Across your nose and mouth!" he commanded. "For the smoke!"

It was boiling across the roof. Beside Vimes a chimneypot gushed a roaring tongue of flame.

The rest of the unwound turban was thrust into his hands.

"You take this side, I'll take the other," said the apparition, and darted away again into the smoke.

"But wh—"

Vimes could feel the heat through his boots. He edged away across the roof, and heard the shouting coming from below.

When he leaned over the edge here he could see the window some way below him. Someone had smashed a pane, because a hand was waving.

There was more commotion down in the courtyard. Amid a press of figures he could make out the huge shape of Constable Dorfl, a golem and quite definitely fireproof. But Dorfl was bad enough at stairs as it was. There weren't many that could take the weight.

The hand in the smoke stopped waving.

Vimes looked down again.

Can you fly, Mr. Vimes?

He looked at the chimney, belching flame.

He looked at the unwound turban.

A lot of Sam Vimes's brain had shut down, although the bits relaying the twinges of pain from his legs were operating with distressing efficiency. But there were still some thoughts operating down around the core, and they delivered for his consideration the insight:

. . . tough-looking cloth . . .

He looked back at the chimney. It looked stout enough.

The window was about six feet below.

Vimes began to move automatically.

So, purely theoretically, if a man were to wrap one end of the cloth round the belching stack like *this* and pay it out like *this* and lower himself over the parapet like *this* and kick himself away from the wall like *this,* then when he swung back again his feet ought to be able to smash his way through the other panes of the window, like *this*—

A cart squeaked along the wet street. Its progress was erratic because no two of its wheels were the same size, so it rocked and wobbled and skidded and probably involved more effort to pull than it saved overall, especially since its contents appeared to be rubbish. But then, so did its owner.

Who was about the size of a man, but bent almost double, and was covered with hair or rags or quite possibly a matted mixture of both that was so felted and unwashed that small plants had taken root on it. If the thing had stopped walking and crouched down, it would have given an astonishingly good impression of a long-neglected compost heap. As it walked along, it snuffled.

A foot was stuck out to impede its progress.

"Good evening, Stoolie," said Carrot as the cart halted.

The heap stopped. Part of it tilted upward.

"Geroff," it muttered, from somewhere in the thatch.

"Now, now, Stoolie, let's help one another, shall we? You help me, and I'll help you."

"B'g'r 'ff, c'p'r."

"Well, you tell *me* things I want to know," said Carrot, "and I won't search your cart."

"I hate gnolls," said Angua. "They smell *awful*."

"Oh, that's hardly fair. The streets'd be a lot dirtier without you and yours, eh, Stoolie?" said Carrot, still speaking quite pleasantly. "You pick up this, you pick up that, maybe bash it against a wall until it stops struggling—"

"'s a vile accur'cy," said the gnoll. There was a bubbling noise that might have been a chuckle.

"So I'm hearing you might know where Snowy Slopes is these days," said Carrot.

"D'nno n'thin'."

"Fine." Carrot produced a three-tined garden fork and walked round to the cart, which dripped.

"D'nno n'thin' *ab't*—" said the gnoll quickly.

"Yes?" said Carrot, fork poised.

"D'nno n'thin' ab't t' sweetsh'p 'n M'ney Tr'p L'ne."

"The one with the Rooms To Let sign?"

"R't."

"Well done. Thank you for being a good citizen," said Carrot. "Incidentally, we passed a dead seagull on the way here. It's in Brewer Street. I bet if you hurried you could beat the rush."

"H't d'gg'ty," snuffled the gnoll. The cart started to judder forward. The watchmen watched it lurch and scrape around the corner.

"They're good fellows at heart," said Carrot. "I think it says a lot for the spirit of tolerance in this city that even gnolls can call it home."

"They turn my stomach," said Angua, as they set off again. "That one had plants growing on him!"

"Mr. Vimes says we ought to do something for them," said Carrot.

"All heart, that man."

"With a flamethrower, he says."

"Wouldn't work. Too soggy. Has anyone ever *really* found out what they eat?"

"It's better to think of them as . . . cleaners. You certainly don't see as much rubbish and dead animals on the streets as you used to."

"Yes, but have you ever seen a gnoll with a brush and shovel?"

"Well, that's society for you, I'm afraid," said Carrot. "Everything is dumped on the people below until you find someone who's prepared to eat it. That's what Mr. Vimes says."

"Yes," said Angua. They walked in silence for a while, and then she said, "You care a lot about what Mr. Vimes says, don't you . . . ?"

"He is a fine officer and an example to us all."

"And . . . you've never thought of getting a job in Quirm or somewhere, have you? The other cities are headhunting Ankh-Morpork watchmen now."

"What, leave Ankh-Morpork?" The tone of voice included the answer.

"No . . . I suppose not," said Angua sadly.

"Anyway, I don't know what Mr. Vimes would do without me running around all the time."

"It's a point of view, certainly," said Angua.

It wasn't far to Money Trap Lane. It was in a ghetto of what Lord Rust would probably call "skilled artisans," the people too low down the social scale to be movers and shakers but slightly too high to be easily moved or shook. The sanders and polishers, generally. The people who hadn't got very much but were proud even of that. There were little clues. Shiny house numbers, for a start. And, on the walls of houses that were effectively just one long continuous row, after centuries of building and inbuilding, very careful boundaries in the paint where people had brushed up to the very border of their property and not a gnat's blink to each side. Carrot always said it showed the people were the kind who instinctively realized that civilization was based on a shared respect for ownership; Angua thought they were just tight little bastards who'd sell you the time of day.

Carrot walked noiselessly down the alley beside the sweetshop. There was a rough wooden staircase going up to the first floor. He pointed silently to the midden below it.

It seemed to consist almost entirely of bottles.

"Big drinker?" Angua mouthed. Carrot shook his head.

She crouched down and looked at the labels, but her nose was already giving her a hint. *Dibbler's Homoeopathic Shampoo. Mere and Stingbat's Herbal Wash—with Herbs! Rinse 'n' Run Scalp Tonic—with Extra Herbs! . . .*

There were others. Herbs, she thought. Chuck a handful of weeds in the pot and you've got herbs . . .

Carrot was starting up the stairs when she put her hand on his shoulder. There was another smell. It was one that drove through all the other scents of the streets like a spear. It was one that a werewolf's nose is particularly attuned to.

He nodded and went carefully to the door. Then he pointed down. There was a stain under the gap.

Carrot drew his sword and kicked the door open.

Daceyville Slopes hadn't taken his condition lightly. Bottles of all shapes and colors occupied most flat surfaces, giving testimony to the alchemist's art and humanity's optimism.

The suds of his latest experiment were still in a bowl on the table, and his body on the floor had a towel around his neck. The watchmen looked down at it. Snowy had cleaned, washed and gone.

"I think we can say life is extinct," said Carrot.

"Yuk," said Angua. She grabbed the open shampoo bottle and sniffed deeply. The sickly scent of marinated herbs assailed her sinuses, but anything was better than the sharp, beguiling smell of blood.

"I wonder where his head is at?" said Carrot, in a determinedly matter-of-fact voice. "Oh, it's rolled over there . . . What's the horrible smell?"

"This!" Angua flourished the shampoo. "Four dollars a bottle, it says. Sheesh!"

Angua took another deep sniff at the herbal goo, to drown out the call of the wolf.

"Doesn't look as if they stole anything," said Carrot. "Unless they were *very* neat— What's the matter?"

"Don't ask!"

She managed to get a window open and sucked down great draughts of comparatively fresh air, while Carrot went through the corpse's pockets.

"Er . . . you can't tell if there's a clove around, can you?" he said.

"Carrot! Please! This is a room with blood all over the floor! Have you *any idea?* Excuse me . . ."

She rushed out and down the steps. The alley had the generic smell of all alleys everywhere, overlaid on the basic all-embracing smell of the city. But at least it didn't make your hair grow and your teeth try to lengthen. She leaned against the wall and fought for control. Shampoo? She could have saved Snowy a hell of a lot of money with just one careful bite. Then he'd know *all* about a really bad hair day . . .

Carrot came down a couple of minutes later, locking the door behind him.

"Are you feeling better?"

"A bit . . ."

"There was something else," said Carrot, looking thoughtful. "I think he wrote a note before he died. But it's all rather odd." He waved in the air what looked like a cheap notepad. "This needs careful looking at." He shook his head. "Poor old Snowy."

"He was a killer!"

"Yes, but that's a nasty way to die."

"Decapitation? With a very sharp sword, by the look of it. I can think of worse."

"Yes, but I can't help thinking that if only the chap had better hair or had found the right shampoo at an early age he'd have led a different life . . ."

"Well, at least he won't have to worry about dandruff anymore."

"That was a little tasteless."

"Sorry, but you know how blood makes me tense."

"*Your* hair always looks amazing," said Carrot, changing the subject with, Angua thought, unusual tact. "I don't know what you use, but it's a shame he never tried it."

"I doubt if he went to the right shop," said Angua. "It says 'For a Glossy Coat' on the bottles I usually buy— What's the matter?"

"Can you smell smoke?" said Carrot.

"Carrot, it's going to be five minutes before I can smell *anything* except—"

But he was staring past her, at the big red glow in the sky.

* * *

Vimes coughed. And then coughed some more. And eventually opened his streaming eyes in the confident expectation of seeing his own lungs in front of him.

"Glass of water, Mr. Vimes?"

Vimes peered through the tears at the shifting shape of Fred Colon.

"Thanks, Fred. What's the horrible burning smell?"

"It's you, sir."

Vimes was sitting on a low wall outside the wreck of the embassy. Cool air washed around him. He felt like underdone beef. The heat was *radiating* off him.

"You was passed on for a while there, sir," said Sergeant Colon helpfully. "But everyone saw you swing in that window, sir! *And* you threw that woman out for Detritus to catch! That'll be a feather in your cap and no mistake, sir! I bet the ragh— I bet the Klatchians'll be giving you the Order of the Camel or something for *this* night's work, sir!" Colon beamed, bursting with pride by association.

"A feather in my cap . . ." murmured Vimes. He undid his helmet and with a certain amount of exhausted delight saw that every single plume had been burned to a stub.

He blinked slowly.

"What about the man, Fred? Did he get out?"

"What man?"

"There was . . ." Vimes blinked again. Various parts of his body, aware that he hadn't been taking calls, were ringing in to complain.

There had been . . . *some man? Vimes had landed on a bed or something, and there was a woman clutching at him, and he had smashed out what was left of the window, seen the big, broad and above all strong arms of Detritus down below, and had thrown her out as politely as the circumstances allowed. Then the man from the roof had come out of the smoke again, carrying another figure over his shoulder, screamed something at him and beckoned him to follow and . . .*

. . . then the floor had given way . . .

"There were . . . two other people in there," he said, coughing again.

"They didn't get out the front way, then," said Colon.

"How did *I* get out?" said Vimes.

"Oh, Dorfl was stamping on the fire down below, sir. Very handy, a ceramic constable. You landed right on him, so of course he stopped what he was doing and brought you out. 's gonna be handshakes and buns all round in the morning, sir!"

There weren't any right now, Vimes noted. There were still plenty of people around, carrying bundles, putting out small fires, arguing with one another . . . but there was a big hole where congratulating-the-hero-of-the-hour should have been.

"Oh, everyone's always a bit preoccupied after something like this, sir," said Colon, as if reading his thoughts.

"I think I'll have a nice cold bath," said Vimes, to the world in general. "And then some sleep. Sybil's got some wonderful ointment for burns . . . Ah, hello, you two."

"We saw the fire—" Carrot began, running up. "Is it all over?"

"Mr. Vimes saved the day!" said Sergeant Colon excitedly. "Just went straight in and saved everyone, in the finest tradition of the Watch!"

"Fred?" said Vimes, wearily.

"Yessir?"

"Fred, the finest tradition of the Watch is having a quiet smoke somewhere out of the wind at three a.m. Let's not get carried away, eh?"

Colon looked crestfallen. "Well—" he began.

Vimes staggered to his feet and patted his sergeant on the back.

"Oh, all right, it's a tradition," he conceded. "You can do the next one, Fred. And now," he steadied himself as he stood up, "I'm going down to the Yard to write my report."

"You're covered in ash and you're swaying," said Carrot. "I should just get on home, sir."

"Oh no," said Vimes. "Got to do the paperwork. Anyone know the time?"

"Bingeley-bingeley beep!" said a cheerful voice from his pocket.

"Damn!" said Vimes, but it was too late.

"It is," said the voice, which had the squeaky friendly quality that begs to be strangled, "about . . . nineish."

"Nineish?"

"Yep. Nineish. Precisely about nineish."

Vimes rolled his eyes. "*Precisely* about nineish?" he said, pulling a small box out of his pocket and opening the lid. The demon inside gave him an angry look.

"Yesterday you *said*," it said, "that if I, and I quote, Didn't Stop all that Eight Fifty-Six and Six Seconds Precisely business I Would Be Looking at a Hammer From Below. And when I said, Mr. Insert Name Here, that this would invalidate my warranty, you said that I could take my warranty and—"

"I thought you'd lost that thing," said Carrot.

"Hah," said the Dis-organizer, "really? You thought he did? I don't call putting something in your trouser pockets just before they go into the wash *losing* it."

"That was an accident," muttered Vimes.

"Oh? Oh? And dropping me in the dragon's feeding bowl, that was accidental too, was it?" The demon mumbled to itself for a moment and then said, "Anyway, do you want to know your appointments for this evening?"

Vimes looked at the smoldering wreckage of the embassy.

"Do tell," he said.

"You don't have any," said the demon sulkily. "You haven't told me any."

"You see?" said Vimes. "*That's* what drives me livid! Why should I have to tell *you*? Why didn't you tell *me*, 'Eightish: break up riot at Mundane Meals and stop Detritus shooting people,' eh?"

"You didn't tell me to tell you!"

"I didn't *know!* And that's how real life works! How can I tell you to warn me about things that no one knows are going to happen? If you were any good, that'd be *your* job!"

"He writes in the manual," said the demon nastily. "Did you know that, everybody? *He writes in the manual.*"

"Well, of course I make notes—"

"He's actually sneakily trying to keep his diary in the manual so his wife won't find out he's never bothered to learn how to use me," said the demon.

"What about the *Vimes* manual, then?" snapped Vimes. "I notice you've never bothered to learn how to use *me!*"

The demon hesitated. "Humans come with a manual?" it said.

"It'd be a damn good idea!" said Vimes.

"True," murmured Angua.

"It could say things like 'Chapter One: Bingeley-bingeley beep and other damn fool things to spring on people at six in the morning,'" said Vimes, his eyes wild. "And 'Troubleshooting: my owner keeps trying to drop me in the privy, what am I doing wrong?' And—"

Carrot patted him gently on the back. "I should sign off now, sir," he said gently. "It's been a busy few days."

Vimes rubbed his forehead. "I daresay I *could* do with a rest," he said. "Come on, there's nothing more to see here. Let's go home."

"I thought you said you weren't going—" Carrot began, but Vimes's mind was already scolding him.

"I meant the Yard, of course," he said. "I'll go *home* afterward."

A ball of lamplight floated through the Ramkin library, drifting across the shelves of huge, leather-bound books.

Many of them had never been read, Sybil knew. Various ancestors had simply ordered them from the engravers and put them on the shelves, because a library was something you had to have, don'tcherknow, like a stableyard and a servants' wing and some ghastly landscaping mistake created by "Bloody Stupid" Johnson, although in the latter case her grandfather had shot the man before he could do any real damage.

She held the lamp higher.

Ramkins looked down their noses at her from their frames, through the brown varnish of the centuries. Portraits were another thing that had been collected out of unregarded habit.

Most of them were of men. They were invariably in armor and always on horseback. And every single one of them had fought the sworn enemies of Ankh-Morpork.

In recent times this had been quite difficult and her grandfather, for example, had to lead an expedition all the way to Howondaland in order to find some sworn enemies, although there was an adequate supply and a lot of swearing by the time he left. Earlier, of course, it had been a lot easier. Ramkin regiments had fought the city's enemies all over the Sto Plains and had inflicted heroic casualties, quite often on people in the opposing armies.*

There were a *few* women among the sitters, none of them holding anything heavier than a glove or a small pet dragon. Their job had largely been to roll bandages and await the return of their husbands with, she liked to think, resolution and fortitude and a general hope that said husbands would return with as many of their bits as possible.

The point was, though, that they never *thought* about it. There was a war, and off they went. If there wasn't a war, they looked for one. They didn't even use words like "duty." It was all built in at bone level.

She sighed. It was all so *difficult* these days, and Lady Sybil came from a class that was not used to difficulty, or at least the kind that couldn't be sorted out by shouting at a servant. Five hundred years ago one of her ancestors had cut off a Klatchian's head in battle and had brought it home on a pole, and no one thought any the worse of him, given what the Klatchians would have cut off if they'd caught him. That seemed straightforward. You fought them, they fought you, everyone knew the rules, and if you got your head cut off you jolly well didn't blub about it afterward.

Certainly, things were *better* now. But they were just . . . more difficult.

And of course some of those antique husbands were away for months or years at a time, and for them wives and families were pretty much like the library and stableyard and the Johnson Exploding Pagoda. You got them sorted out and then didn't think much about it. At least Sam was home every day.

Well, most days. Every night, anyway.

Well . . . part of most nights, certainly.

At least they ate meals together.

Well, most meals.

---

* It is a long-cherished tradition among a certain type of military thinker that huge casualties are the main thing. If they are on the other side then this is a valuable bonus.

Well, at least they made a *start* on most meals.

Well, at least she knew he was never very far away, just somewhere where he was trying to do too much and run too fast and people were trying to kill him.

All in all, she considered, she was jolly lucky.

Vimes stared at Carrot, who was standing in front of his desk.

"So what does all that add up to?" he said. "The man we know *didn't* get the Prince is dead. The man who probably *did* . . . is dead. Someone tried very clumsily to make it look as if Ossie was paid by the Klatchians. Okay, I can see why someone might want to do that. That's what Fred calls *politics*. They get Snowy to do the real business, and he helps poor dumb Ossie who's there to take the fall, and then the Watch *proves* that Ossie was in the pay of the Klatchians and that's *another* reason for fighting. And Snowy just slopes off. Only someone cured his dandruff for him."

"*After* he'd written something, sir," said Carrot.

"Ah . . . yes."

Vimes looked at the notepad retrieved from Snowy's room. It was a crude affair, the wads of mismatched bits of scrap that the engravers sold off cheaply. He sniffed at it.

"Soap on the edges," he said.

"His new shampoo," said Carrot. "First time he'd used it."

"How do you know?"

"We looked at all the bottles on the heap, sir."

"Hmm. Looks like fresh blood here, at the spine, where they're stitched together . . ."

"His, sir," said Angua.

Vimes nodded. You never argued with Angua about blood.

"But none of the actual pages have blood on them . . ." said Vimes. "Which is a bit odd. Messy business, decapitation. People tend to . . . spray. So the top page—"

"—has been taken away, sir," said Carrot, grinning and nodding. "But that's not the funny part, sir. See if you can guess, sir!"

Vimes glared at him and then moved the lamp closer. "Very faint impression of writing on the top page . . ." he muttered. "Can't make it out . . ."

"We can't either, sir. We know he wrote in pencil, sir. There was one on the table."

"*Very* faint traces," said Vimes. "Blokes like Snowy write as though they're chipping stone." He flicked the notebook. "Someone tore out . . . not just the page he'd written on but several below it as well."

"Clever, eh, sir? Everyone knows—"

"—you can read the suspicious note by looking at the marks on the page below," said Vimes. He tossed the book onto the table again. "Hmm. There's a message there, yes . . ."

"Perhaps he was blackmailing whoever's behind all this?" said Angua.

"That's not his style," said Vimes. "No, what I meant was—"

There was a knock on the door, and Fred Colon entered.

"Brung you a mug of coffee," he said, "and there's a bunch of wo— Klatchians to see you downstairs, Mr. Vimes. Probably come to give you a medal and gabble at you in their lingo. And if you're on for late supper, Mrs. Goriff's doing goat and rice and foreign gravy."

"I suppose I'd better go down and see them," said Vimes. "But I haven't even had time for a wash—"

"That's evidence of your heroic endeavors," said Colon stoutly.

"Oh, all right."

Unease began about halfway down the stairs. Vimes had never run into a group of citizens wishing to give him a medal and so he did not have a lot of experience on this score, but the group waiting for him in a tight cluster near the sergeant's desk did not look like a committee of welcome.

They *were* Klatchian. At least, they were wearing foreign-looking clothes and one or two of them had caught more sun than you generally got in Ankh-Morpork. The feeling crept over Vimes that Klatch was a very big place in which his city and the whole of the Sto Plains would be lost, and so there must be room in it for all kinds of peoples, including this short chap in the red fez who was practically vibrating with indignation.

"Are you the man Vimes?" the enfezzed one demanded.

"Well, I'm Commander Vimes—"

"We demand the release of the Goriff family! And we won't take any excuses!"

Vimes blinked. "Release?"

"You have locked them up! And confiscated their shop!"

Vimes stared at the man, and then he looked across the room at Sergeant Detritus.

"Where did you put the family, sergeant?"

Detritus saluted. "In der cells, sir."

"Aha!" said the man in the fez. "You admit it!"

"Excuse me, who *are* you?" said Vimes, blinking with tiredness.

"I don't have to tell you and you can't beat it out of me!" said the man, sticking out his chest.

"Oh, thank you for telling me," said Vimes. "I do hate wasted effort."

"Oh, hello, Mr. Wazir," said Carrot, appearing behind Vimes. "Did you get the note about that book?"

There was one of those silences that happen when everyone has to reprogram their faces.

Then Vimes said, "What?"

"Mr. Wazir sells books in Widdy Street," said Carrot. "Only I asked him for some books on Klatch, you see, and one of the ones he gave me was *The Perfumed Allotment, or, The Garden of Delights*. And I didn't mind because the Klatchians invented gardens, sir, so I thought it might be a very useful cultural insight. Get inside the Klatchian mind, as it were. Only it, er, it . . . er . . . well, it wasn't about gardening . . . er . . . ." He started to blush.

"Yes, yes, all right, bring it back if you like," said Mr. Wazir, looking a little derailed.

"I just thought you ought to know in case you hadn't . . . in case you sold . . . well . . . it could shock the impressionable, you know, a book like that . . ."

"Yes, fine—"

"Corporal Angua was so shocked she couldn't stop laughing," Carrot went on.

"I will have your money sent round directly," said Wazir. His expression turned vengeful again. He glared at Vimes.

"Books are unimportant at this time! We demand you release my countrymen now!"

"Detritus, why the hell did you put them in the cells?" said Vimes wearily.

"What else we got, sir? Dey're not locked in and dey got clean blankets."

"There's your explanation," said Vimes. "They're our guests."

"In the cells!" said Wazir, relishing the word.

"They're free to go whenever they like," said Vimes.

"I'm sure they are *now*," said Wazir, contriving to indicate that only his arrival had prevented officially sanctioned bloodshed. "You can be sure the Patrician will hear about this!"

"He hears about everything else," said Vimes. "But if they leave here, who is going to protect them?"

"We are! Their fellow countrymen!"

"How?"

Wazir almost stood to attention. "By force of arms, if necessary."

"Oh, *good*," said Vimes. "Then there'll be *two* mobs—"

"Bingeley-bingeley beep!"

"Damn!" Vimes slapped at his pocket. "I don't *want* to know I haven't got any appointments!"

"You have one at eleven pee em. The Rats Chamber, at the palace," said the Dis-organizer.

"Don't be stupid!"

"Please yourself."

"And shut up."

"I was just trying to help."

"Shut up." Vimes turned back to the Klatchian bookseller.

"Mr. Wazir, if Goriff wants to leave with you, we won't stop him—"

"Aha! You may well try!"

Vimes told himself that there was no reason at all why a Klatchian couldn't be a pompous little troublemaker. But he felt uneasy about it, like a man edging along the side of a very deep crevasse.

"Sergeant Colon?"

"Yessir!"

"See to this, will you?"

"Yessir!"

"Diplomatically."

"Right, sir!" Colon tapped the side of his nose. "Is this politics, sir?"

"Just . . . just go and fetch the Goriff family and they can . . ." Vimes waved a hand vaguely. "They can do whatever they like."

He turned and walked up the stairs.

"Someone has to protect my people's rights!" shouted Wazir.

They heard Vimes stop halfway up the stairs. The board creaked under his weight for a second. Then he continued upward, and several of the watchmen started breathing again.

Vimes shut his office door behind him.

Politics! He sat down and scrabbled through the papers. It was much easier to think about crime. Give him good honest crime any time.

He tried to shut out the outside world.

Someone had beheaded Snowy Slopes. That was a *fact.* You couldn't put it down to a shaving accident, or unreasonably strong shampoo.

And Snowy had attempted to shoot the Prince.

And so had Ossie, but Ossie only *thought* he was an assassin. Everyone else thought he was a weird little twerp who was as impressionable as wet clay.

A lovely idea, though. You used a *real* murderer, a nice quiet professional, and then you had—Vimes smiled grimly—someone else to take the fall. And if he hadn't taken a less metaphorical fall the poor twisted little sod would have *believed* he was the murderer.

And the Watch was supposed to believe it was a Klatchian plot.

Sand in their sandals . . . The *nerve* of it! Did they think he was stupid? He wished Fred had carefully swept up the sand, because he was damn well going to find out who'd put it there and they were going to *eat* it. Someone wanted Vimes to chase Klatchians.

The man on the burning roof. Did he fit in? Did he *have* to fit in? What could Vimes recall? A man in a robe, his face hidden. And a voice of a man not just used to giving commands—*Vimes* was used to giving commands—but also used to having commands obeyed, whereas a member of the Watch treated orders as suggestions.

But some things didn't have to fit. That was where "clues" let you down. And the damn notebook. That was the oddest thing yet. So *someone* had carefully ripped out several pages after Snowy had written whatever he'd written. Someone bright enough to know the trick of looking at the pages underneath for faint impressions.

So why not pinch the whole pad?

It was all too complicated. But somewhere was the one thing that'd make it simple, that would turn it all into sense—

He flung down his pencil and wrenched open the door to the stairs.

"What the hell's all this noise?" he yelled.

Sergeant Colon was halfway up the stairs.

"It was Mr. Goriff and Mr. Wazir having a bit of what you might call an argy-bargy, sir. Someone set fire to someone else's country two hundred years ago, Carrot says."

"What, just *now?*"

"'s all Klatchian to me, sir. Anyway, Wazir's gone off with his nose in a sling."

"Wazir comes from Smale, you see," said Carrot. "And Mr. Gorriff comes from Elharib, and the two countries only stopped fighting ten years ago. Religious differences."

"Run out of weapons?" said Vimes.

"Ran out of rocks, sir. They ran out of weapons last century."

Vimes shook his head. "That always chews me up," he said. "People killing one another just because their gods have squabbled—"

"Oh, they've got the same god, sir. Apparently it's over a word in their holy book, sir. The Elharibians say it translates as 'god' and the Smalies say it's 'man.'"

"How can you mix them up?"

"Well, there's only one tiny dot difference in the script, you see. And some people reckon it's only a bit of fly dirt in any case."

"Centuries of war because a fly crapped in the wrong place?"

"It could have been worse," said Carrot. "If it had been slightly to the left the word would have been 'liquorice.'"

Vimes shook his head. Carrot was good at picking up this sort of thing. And I know how to ask for vindaloo, he thought. And it turns out that's just a Klatchian word meaning "mouth-scalding gristle for macho foreign idiots."

"I wish we understood more about Klatch," he said.

Sergeant Colon tapped the side of his nose conspiratorially.

"Know the enemy, eh, sir?" he said.

"Oh, I know the *enemy*," said Vimes. "It's Klatchians I want to find out about."

"Commander Vimes?"

The watchmen looked round. Vimes narrowed his eyes.

"You're one of Rust's men, aren't you?"

The young man saluted.

"Lieutenant Hornett, sir." He hesitated. "Er . . . his lordship has sent me to ask you if you and your senior officers would be so good as to come to the palace at your convenience, sir."

"Really? Those were his words?"

The lieutenant decided that honesty was the only policy.

"In fact he said, 'Get Vimes and his mob up here right now,' sir."

"Oh, did he?" said Vimes.

"Bingeley-bingeley beep!" said a small triumphant voice from his pocket. "The time is eleven pee em precisely!"

The door opened before Nobby knocked, and a small stout woman glared out at him.

"Yes, I am!" she snapped.

Nobby stood with his hand still raised. "Er . . . are you Mrs. Cake?" he said.

"Yes, but I don't hold with doing it except for money."

Nobby's hand did not move.

"Er . . . you can tell the future, right?" said Nobby.

They stared at one another. Then Mrs. Cake thumped her own ear a couple of times, and blinked.

"Drat! Left my precognition on again." Her gaze unfocused for a moment as she replayed the recent conversation in the privacy of her head.

"I think we're sorted out," she said. She looked at Nobby and sniffed. "You'd better come in. Mind the carpet, it's just been

122

washed. And I can only give you ten minutes 'cos I've got cabbage boilin'."

She led Corporal Nobbs into her tiny front room. A lot of it was occupied by a round table covered with a green cloth. There was a crystal ball on the table, not very well covered by a pink knitted lady in a crinoline dress.

Mrs. Cake motioned Nobby to sit down. He obediently did so. The smell of cabbage drifted through the room.

"A bloke in the pub told me about you," Nobby mumbled. "Said you do mediuming."

"Would you care to tell me your problem?" said Mrs. Cake. She looked at Nobby again and, in a state of certainty that had nothing to do with precognition and everything to do with observation, added: "That is, which of your problems do you want to know about?"

Nobby coughed. "Er . . . it's a bit . . . you know . . . intimate. Affairs of the heart, sort of thing."

"Are *women* involved?" said Mrs. Cake cautiously.

"Er . . . I hope so. What else is there?"

Mrs. Cake visibly relaxed.

"I just want to know if I'm going to meet any," Nobby went on.

"I see." Mrs. Cake gave a kind of facial shrug. It wasn't up to her to tell people how to waste their money. "Well, there's the tenpenny future. That's what you see. And there's the ten-dollar future. That's what you get."

"Ten dollars? That's more'n a week's pay! I'd better take the tenpenny one."

"A very wise choice," said Mrs. Cake. "Give me your paw."

"Hand," said Nobby.

"That's what I said."

Mrs. Cake examined Nobby's outstretched palm while taking care not to touch it.

"Are you going to moan and roll your eyes and stuff?" said Nobby, a man out to get his tenpenn'orth.

"I don't have to take cheek," said Mrs. Cake, without looking up. "That sort of—"

She peered closer, and then gave Nobby a sharp look.

"Have you been playing with this hand?"

"Pardon?"

Mrs. Cake whipped the crinoline lady off the crystal and glared into the depths. After a while she shook her head.

"I don't know, I'm sure . . . oh, well." She cleared her throat and spoke in a more sibylic voice. "Mr. Nobbs, I see you surrounded by dusky ladies in a hot place. Looks a bit foreign to me. They're laughing and chatting with you . . . in fact, one of them's just handed you a drink . . ."

"None of 'em are shouting or anything?" said Nobby, mystified.

"Doesn't look like it," said Mrs. Cake, equally fascinated. "They seem quite happy."

"You can't see any . . . magnets?"

"What're they?"

"Dunno," Nobby admitted. "I 'spect you'd know 'em if you saw 'em."

Mrs. Cake, despite a certain rigidity of character, couldn't help but be aware of a drift in Nobby's speculation.

"Some of the ladies look . . . nubile," she hinted.

"Ah, right," said Nobby, his expression not changing in any way.

"If you understand what I mean . . ."

"Right. Yes. Nubile. Right."

Mrs. Cake gave up. Nobby counted out ten pennies.

"And that'll be soon, will it?" said Nobby.

"Oh yes. I can't see very far for tenpence."

"Happy young ladies . . ." mused Nobby. "Nubile, too. Definitely something to think about."

After he'd gone, Mrs. Cake went back to her crystal and sneaked a whole ten dollars' worth of precognition for her own curiosity and satisfaction, and laughed about it all afternoon.

Vimes was only half surprised when the doors to the Rats Chamber opened and there, sitting at the head of the table, was Lord Rust. The Patrician wasn't there.

He was *half* surprised. That is, at a certain shallow level he thought, that's odd, I thought you couldn't budge the man with a siege weapon. But at a dark level, where the daylight seldom penetrated, he thought: *of course.* At a time like this men like Rust rise to the top. It's like stirring a swamp with a stick. Really big bubbles are suddenly on the surface and there's a bad smell about everything. Nevertheless, he saluted and said:

"Lord Vetinari on his holidays, then?"

"Lord Vetinari stepped down this evening, Vimes," said Lord Rust. "Pro tem, of course. Just for the duration of the emergency."

"Really?" said Vimes.

"Yes. And I have to say that he anticipated a certain . . . cynicism on your part, commander, and therefore asked me to give you this letter. You will see that it is sealed with his seal."

Vimes looked at the envelope. There was certainly the official seal in the wax, but—

He met Lord Rust's gaze and at least that suspicion faded. Rust wouldn't try a trick like that. Men like Rust had a moral code of sorts, and some things weren't *honorable.* You could own a street of crowded houses where people lived like cockroaches and the cockroaches lived like kings and that was perfectly okay, but Rust would probably die before he'd descend to forgery.

"I see, sir," said Vimes. "You wanted me?"

"Commander Vimes, I must ask you to take the Klatchians resident in the city into custody."

"On what charge, sir?"

"Commander, we are on the verge of *war* with Klatch. Surely you understand?"

"No, sir."

"We are talking about spying, commander. Sabotage, even," said Lord Rust. "To be frank . . . the city is to be placed under martial law."

"Yessir? What kind of law's that, sir?" said Vimes, staring straight ahead.

"You know very well, Vimes."

"Is it the kind where you shout 'Stop!' *before* you fire, sir, or the other kind?"

"Ah. I *see.*" Rust stood up and leaned forward.

"It pleased you to be . . . *smart* with Lord Vetinari, and for some reason he indulged you," he said. "I, on the other hand, know your type."

"My type?"

"It seems to me that the streets are full of crimes, commander. Unlicensed begging, public nuisances . . . but you seem to turn a blind eye, you seem to think you should have bigger ideas. But you are not required to have big ideas, commander. You are a thief-taker, nothing more. Are you eyeballing me, Vimes?"

"I was trying not to turn a blind eye, sir."

"You seem to feel, Vimes, that the law is some kind of big glowing light in the sky which is not subject to control. And you are wrong. The law is what we tell it to be. I'm not going to add 'Do you understand?' because I *know* you understand and I am not going to try to reason with you. I know a rank bad hat when I see one."

"Bad hat?" said Vimes weakly.

"Commander Vimes," he said, "I had hoped to avoid this, but the last few days point to a succession of astonishing judgemental errors on your part. The Prince Khufurah was shot, and you seemed helpless to prevent this or find the criminal responsible. Mobs appear to run around the city unimpeded, I gather that one of your sergeants proposed to shoot innocent people in the head, and we have just heard that you took it upon yourself to arrest an innocent businessman and lock him in the cells for no reason at all."

Vimes heard Colon gasp. But it sounded a long way off. He could feel everything crumbling under him, but his mind seemed to be flying now, flapping through a pink sky where nothing mattered very much.

"Oh, I don't know about that, sir," he said. "He was guilty of repeatedly being Klatchian, wasn't he? Don't you want me to do that to all of 'em?"

"And if this was not enough," Rust went on, "we are told, and in other circumstances I would find this *very* hard to believe, even of a counter-jumper like you, that earlier tonight you, being quite unprovoked, assaulted two Klatchian guards, trespassed on Klatchian soil, entered the women's quarters, abducted two Klatchians from their beds, ordered the destruction of Klatchian property and . . . well, frankly, acted quite disgracefully."

What is the point of arguing? Vimes thought. Why play cards with a shaved deck? And yet—

"Two Klatchians, sir?"

"It seems Prince Khufurah has been kidnapped, Vimes. I find it hard to believe that even *you* would attempt that, but the Klatchians seem to be suggesting this. You were seen entering their property illegally. And you appear to have dragged a helpless lady from her bed. What have you got to say about that?"

"It was on fire at the time, sir."

Lieutenant Hornett stepped forward and whispered something. Lord Rust subsided a bit.

"All right. Very well. There were perhaps mitigating circumstances, but politically it was a most ill-advised action, Vimes. I cannot pretend to know what has happened to the Prince, but frankly you seem to have taken a positive delight in making matters worse."

Can you climb, Mr. Vimes? Vimes said nothing. The other man had been carrying something bulky over his shoulder . . .

"You are removed from authority, commander. And the Watch will come under the direct command of this council. Is that understood?"

Rust turned to Carrot. "Captain Carrot, many of us here have heard . . . good reports about you, and by due authority I hereby appoint you acting Commander of the Watch—"

Vimes shut his eyes.

Carrot saluted smartly. "No! Sir!"

Vimes opened his eyes wide.

"Really?" Rust stared at Carrot for a few moments, and then gave a little shrug.

"Ah, well . . . loyalty is a fine thing. Sergeant Colon?"

"Sir!"

"In the circumstances, and since you are the most experienced noncommissioned officer and have an exemp— and have a military record, you will take command of the Watch for the duration of the . . . emergency."

"Nossir!"

"That was an instruction, sergeant."

Beads of sweat began to form on Colon's brow. "Nossir!"

"Sergeant!"

"You can put it where the sun does not shine, sir!" said Colon desperately.

Once again, Vimes saw Rust's milky-blue stare. Rust never looked surprised. And since he knew that a mere sergeant would never dare offer cheeky defiance, he erased Sergeant Colon from the immediate universe.

The gaze turned briefly to Detritus.

And he doesn't know how to speak to a troll, Vimes thought. And he was once again impressed, in the same dark way, by the manner in which Rust dealt with the problem. He dealt with it by making it not be there.

"Who is the senior corporal in the Watch, Sir Samuel?"

"That would be Corporal Nobbs."

The committee went into a huddle. There was a rush of whispering, in which the words "—an absolute little *tit*—" could be heard several times. Finally Rust looked up again.

"And the next in seniority?"

"Let me see . . . that would be Corporal Stronginthearm," said Vimes. He felt oddly light-headed.

"Perhaps *he* is a man who can take orders."

"He's a dwarf, you idiot!"

Not a muscle moved on Rust's face. There was a *clink* as Vimes's badge was set neatly on the table.

"I don't have to take this," Vimes said calmly.

"Oh, so you'd rather be a civilian, would you?"

"*A watchman is a civilian, you inbred streak of piss!*"

Rust's brain erased the sounds that his ears could not possibly have heard.

"And the keys to the armory, Sir Samuel," he said.

They jangled as they landed on the table.

"And do the rest of you have any empty gestures to make?" said Lord Rust.

Sergeant Colon took his grimy badge out of his pocket and was a little disappointed that it didn't make a defiant tinkle when he threw it on the table but instead bounced and smashed the water jug.

"I got my badge carved on my arm," Detritus rumbled. "Someone c'n try an' take it off if dey likes."

Carrot laid his badge down very carefully.

Rust raised his eyebrows. "You too, captain?"

"Yes, sir."

"I would have thought that *you* at least—"

He stopped and looked up in annoyance as the doors opened. A couple of the palace guards ran in, with a group of Klatchians behind them.

The council got to their feet in a hurry.

Vimes recognized the Klatchian in the center of the group. He'd seen him around at official functions and, if it hadn't been for the fact that the man was a Klatchian, would have marked him down as a shifty piece of work.

"Who's he?" he whispered to Carrot.

"Prince Kalif. He's the deputy ambassador."

"Another prince?"

The man came to a halt in front of the table, glanced at Vimes with no show of recognition and bowed to Lord Rust.

"Prince Kalif," said Lord Rust. "Your arrival is unannounced but nevertheless—"

"I have grave news, my lord." Even in his stunned state, a part of Vimes registered that the voice was different. Khufurah had learned his second language on the street, but this one had had tutors.

"At a time like this, what news isn't?" said Rust.

"There have been developments on the new land. Regrettable incidents. And indeed in Ankh-Morpork, too." He glanced at Vimes again. "Although here, I must say, reports are confused. Lord Rust, I have to tell you we are, technically, at war."

"*Technically* at war?" said Vimes.

"I am afraid events are carrying us forward," said Kalif. "The situation is delicate."

They know they're going to fight, Vimes thought. This is just like the start of a dance, where you hang around looking at your partner . . .

"I must tell you that you are being given twelve hours to remove all your citizens from Leshp," said Kalif. "If that is done, matters will be happily resolved. For the present."

"Our response is that *you* have twelve hours to quit Leshp," said Rust. "If that is not done, then we will take . . . steps . . ."

Kalif bowed slightly. "We understand one another. A formal

document will be with you shortly and, no doubt, we will be receiving one from you."

"Indeed."

"Here, hang on, you can't just—" Vimes began.

"Sir Samuel, you are no longer Commander of the Watch and you have no place at these proceedings," said Rust sharply. He turned back to the Prince.

"It is unfortunate that things have come to this," he said stiffly.

"Indeed. But there comes a time when words are no longer sufficient."

"I must agree with you. And then it is time to test one's strength."

Vimes stared in fascinated horror from one face to the other.

"We will, of course, allow you time to quit your embassy. Such of it as remains."

"So kind. And of course we will extend to you the same courtesy." Kalif bowed slightly.

So did Rust.

"After all, just because our countries are at war is no reason why we should not respect one another as friends," said Lord Rust.

"What? Yes, it bloody well is!" said Vimes. "I can't *believe* this! You can't just stand there and . . . good grief, whatever happened to diplomacy?"

"War, Vimes, is a continuation of diplomacy by other means," said Lord Rust. "As you would know, if you were really a gentleman."

"And you Klatchians are as bad," Vimes went on. "It's that green mouldy mutton Jenkins sells. You've all got Foaming Sheep Disease. You can't just stand there and—"

"Sir Samuel, you are, as you are at pains to point out, a civilian," said Rust. "As such, you have no place here!"

Vimes didn't bother with a salute but just turned away and walked out of the room. The rest of the squad followed him in silence back to Pseudopolis Yard.

"I told him he could put it where the sun didn't shine," said Sergeant Colon, as they crossed the Brass Bridge.

"That's right," said Vimes woodenly. "Well done."

"Right to his face. 'Where the sun don't shine.' Just like that," said Colon. It was a little difficult to tell from his tone whether this was a matter of pride or dread.

"I'm afraid Lord Rust is technically correct, sir," said Carrot.

"Really."

"Yes, Mr. Vimes. The safety of the city is of paramount importance, so in times of war the civil power is subject to military authority."

"Hah."

"I *told* him," said Fred Colon. "Right where the sun does not shine, I said."

"The deputy ambassador didn't mention Prince Khufurah," said Carrot. "That was odd."

"I'm going home," said Vimes.

"We're nearly there, sir," said Carrot.

"I mean *home* home. I need some sleep."

"Yes, sir. What shall I tell the lads, sir?"

"Tell them anything you like."

"I looked him right in the eye and I told him, I said, you can put it right where the—" mused Sergeant Colon.

"You want me an' some of der boys go and sort out dat Rust later on?" said Detritus. "It no problem. He bound to be guilty o' somethin'."

"No!"

Vimes's head felt so light now that he couldn't touch the ground with a rope. He left them outside the Yard and let his head drag him on and up the hill and round the corner and into the house and past his astonished wife and up the stairs and into the bedroom, where he fell full length on the bed and was asleep before he hit it.

At nine next morning the first recruits for Lord Venturi's Heavy Infantry paraded down Broadway.

The watchmen went out to watch. That was all that was left for them to do.

"Isn't that Mr. Vimes's butler?" said Angua, pointing to the stiff figure of Willikins in the front rank.

"Yeah, and that's his kitchen boy banging the drum in front," said Nobby.

"You were a . . . military man, weren't you, Fred?" said Carrot, as the parade passed by.

"Yes, sir. Duke of Eorle's First Heavy Infantry, sir. The Pheasant Pluckers."

"Pardon?" said Angua.

"Nickname for the regiment, miss. Oh, from ages ago. They were bivvywhacking on some estate and came across a lot of pheasant pens and, well, you know, having to live off the land and everything . . . anyway, that's why we always wore a pheasant feather on our helmets. Traditional, see?"

Already old Fred's face was creasing up in the soft expression of someone who has been mugged in Memory Lane.

"We even had a marching song," he said. "Mind you, it was quite hard to sing right. Er . . . sorry, miss?"

"Oh, it's all right, sergeant," said Angua. "I often start to laugh like that for no reason at all."

Fred Colon once again stared dreamily at nothing. "And o'course before that I was in the Duke of Quirm's Middleweight Infantry. Saw a lot of action with them."

"I'm sure you did," said Carrot, while Angua entertained cynical thoughts about the actual distance of Fred's vantage point. "Your distinguished military career has obviously given you many pleasant memories."

"The ladies liked the uniform," said Fred Colon, with the unspoken rider that sometimes a growing lad needed all the help he could get. "An' it . . . weelll . . ."

"Yes, sarge?"

Colon looked awkward, as if the bunched underwear of the past was tangling itself in the crotch of recollection.

"It was . . . more easier, sir. Than being a copper, I mean. I mean, you're a soldier, right, and the other buggers is the enemy. You march into some big field somewhere and all form up into them oblongs, and then a bloke with the feathery helmet gives the order, and you all forms up into big arrows—"

"Good gods, do people really do that? I thought it was just how they drew the battle plans!"

"Well, the old duke, sir, he did it by the book . . . anyway, it's just a case of watching your back and walloping any bloke in the wrong uniform. But . . ." Fred Colon's face screwed up in agonized thought, "well, when you're a copper, well, you dunno the good guys from the bad guys without a map, miss, and that's a fact."

"But . . . there's *military* law, isn't there?"

"Well, yes . . . but when it's pissing with rain and you're up to your tonk— your waist in dead horses and someone gives you an order, that ain't the time to look up the book of rules, miss. Anyway, most of it's about when you're allowed to get shot, sir."

"Oh, I'm sure there's more to it than that, sergeant."

"Oh, prob'ly, sir," Colon conceded diplomatically.

"I'm sure there's lots of stuff about not killing enemy soldiers who've surrendered, for instance."

"Oh, yerss, there's *that,* captain. Doesn't say you can't duff 'em up a bit, of course. Give 'em a little something to remember you by."

"Not *torture?*" said Angua.

"Oh, *no,* miss. But . . ." Memory Lane for Colon had turned into a bad road through a dark valley ". . . well, when your best mate's got an arrow in his eye an' there's blokes and horses screamin' all round you and you're scared shi— you're *really* scared, an' you come across one of the enemy . . . well, for some reason or other you've got this kinda urge to give him a bit of a . . . nudge, sort of thing. Just . . . you know . . . like, maybe in twenty years' time his leg'll twinge a bit on frosty days and he'll remember what he done, that's all."

He rummaged in a pocket and produced a very small book, which he held up for inspection.

"This belonged to my great-grandad," he said. "He was in the scrap we had against Pseudopolis and my great-gran gave him this book of prayers for soldiers, 'cos you need all the prayers you can get, believe you me, and he stuck it in the top pocket of his jerkin, 'cos he couldn't afford armor, and next day in battle—whoosh, this arrow came out of nowhere, wham, straight into this book and it went all the way through to the last page before stopping, look. You can see the hole."

"Pretty miraculous," Carrot agreed.

"Yeah, it was, I s'pose," said the sergeant. He looked ruefully at the battered volume. "Shame about the other seventeen arrows, really."

The drumming died away. The remnant of the Watch tried to avoid one another's gaze.

Then an imperious voice said, "Why aren't you in uniform, young man?"

Nobby turned. He was being addressed by an elderly lady with a certain turkey-like cast of feature and a capital punishment expression.

"Me? Got one, missus," said Nobby, pointing to his battered helmet.

"A *proper* uniform," snapped the woman, handing him a white feather. "What will *you* be doing when the Klatchians are ravishing us in our beds?"

She glared at the rest of the guards and swept on. Angua saw several others like her passing along the crowds of spectators. Here and there was a flash of white.

"I'll be thinking: those Klatchians are jolly brave," said Carrot. "I'm afraid, Nobby, that the white feather is to shame you into joining up."

"Oh, that's all right, then," said Nobby, a man for whom shame held no shame. "What am I supposed to do with it?"

"That reminds me . . . did I tell you what I said to Lord Rust?" said Sergeant Colon, nervously.

"Seventeen times so far," said Angua, watching the women with the feathers. She added, apparently to herself, "'Come back with your shield or on it.'"

"I wonder if I can get the lady to give me any more?" said Nobby.

"What was that?" said Carrot.

"These feathers," said Nobby. "They look like real goose. I've got a use for a lot more of these—"

"I *meant* what was it that Angua said?" said Carrot.

"What? Oh . . . it's just something women used to say when they sent their men off to war. Come back with your shield, or on it."

"*On* your shield?" said Nobby. "You mean like . . . sledging, sort of thing?"

"Like dead," said Angua. "It meant come back a winner or not at all."

"Well, I *always* came back with my shield," said Nobby. "No problem there."

"Nobby," sighed Colon, "you used to come back with your shield, everyone *else's* shield, a sack of teeth and fifteen pairs of still-warm boots. On a cart."

"We-ell, no point in going to war unless you're on the winning side," said Nobby, sticking the white feather in his helmet.

"Nobby, you was *always* on the winning side, the reason bein', you used to lurk aroun' the edges to see who was winning and then pull the right uniform off'f some poor dead sod. I used to hear where the generals kept an eye on what you were wearin' so they'd know how the battle was going."

"Lots of soldiers have served in lots of regiments," said Nobby.

"Right, what you say is true. Only not usually during the same battle," said Sergeant Colon.

They trooped back into the Watch House. Most of the shift had taken the day off. After all, who was in charge? What were they supposed to be doing today? The only ones left were those who never thought of themselves as off duty, and the new recruits who hadn't had their keen edge blunted.

"I'm sure Mr. Vimes'll think of something," said Carrot. "Look, I'd better take the Goriffs back to their shop. Mr. Goriff says he's going to pack up and leave. A lot of Klatchians are leaving. You can't blame them, either."

Dreams rising with him like bubbles, Vimes surfaced from the black fathoms of sleep.

Normally, these days, he treasured the moment of waking. It was when solutions presented themselves. He assumed bits of his brain came out at night and worked on the problems of the previous day, handing him the result just as he opened his eyes.

All that arrived now were memories. He winced. Another memory turned up. He groaned. The sound of his badge bouncing on the table replayed itself. He swore.

He swung his legs off the covers and groped for the bedside table.

"Bingeley-bingeley beep!"

"Oh, *no* . . . All right, what's the time?"

"One o'clock pee em! Hello, Insert Name Here!"

Vimes looked blearily at the Dis-organizer. One day, he knew, he really *would* have to try to understand the manual for the damn thing. Either that or drop it off a cliff.*

"What—" he began, and then groaned again. The twanging sound made by the unwound turban as it took his weight had just come back to haunt him.

"Sam?" The bedroom door was pushed open and Sybil came in carrying a cup.

"Yes, dear?"

"How do you feel?"

"I've got bruises on my brui—" Another memory crawled up from the pit of guilt. "Oh, good grief, did I really call him a long streak of—?"

"*Yes,*" said his wife. "Fred Colon came round this morning and told me all about it. And a very good description, I'd say. I went out with Ronnie Rust once. Bit of a cold fish."

Another recollection burst like a ball of marsh gas in Vimes's head.

"Did Fred tell you where he said Rust could put his badge?"

"Yes. Three times. It seems to be weighing on his mind. Anyway, knowing Ronnie, he'd have to use a hammer."

Vimes had long ago got used to the fact that the aristocracy all seemed to know one another by their first name.

"And did Fred tell you anything else?" he said timidly.

"Yes. About the shop and the fire and everything. I'm proud of you." She gave him a kiss.

"What do I do now?" he said.

"Drink your tea and have a wash and a shave."

"I ought to go down to the Watch House and—"

"A shave! There's hot water in the jug."

When she had left he hauled himself upright and tottered into

---

* One of the universal rules of happiness is: always be wary of any helpful item that weighs less than its operating manual.

his bathroom. There was, indeed, a jug of hot water on the marble washstand.

He looked at the face in the mirror. Unfortunately, it was his. Perhaps if he shaved it first . . . ? And then he could wash the bits that were left.

Fragments of the night before kept on respectfully drawing themselves to his attention. It was a shame about that guard, but sometimes you just couldn't stand and argue—

He shouldn't have done that with his badge. It wasn't like the old days. He had *responsibilities.* He should've stayed on and made things just a little less—

No. That never worked.

He managed to get the lather on his face. The Riot Act! Good grief . . . He stropped his razor thoughtfully. Rust's milky eyes stared out of his memory. Bastard! Men like that thought, they really thought, that the Watch was a kind of sheepdog, to nip at the heels of the flock, bark when spoken to and never, ever, bite the shepherd . . .

Oh yes. Vimes knew in his bones who the enemy was.

Except—

No badge, no Watch, no job . . .

Another memory arrived, late.

Lather still dripping down his shirt, he pulled Vetinari's sealed letter out of his pocket and slit it open with the razor.

There was a blank sheet of paper inside. He turned it over, and there was nothing on the other side either. Mystified, he glanced at the envelope.

Sir Samuel Vimes, Knight.

Nice of him to be so precise about it, Vimes thought. What was the point of a message with no message? Some people might absentmindedly have slipped the wrong piece of paper in an envelope, but Vetinari wouldn't. What was the point of sending him a note telling him he was a knight, for gods' sake, he knew *that* embarrassing fact well enough—

Another little memory burst open as silently as a mouse passing wind in a hurricane.

Who'd said it? Any gentleman—

Vimes stared. Well, he *was* a gentleman, wasn't he? It was official. And then he *didn't* shout, and he *didn't* run out of the room.

He finished shaving, had a wash and put on a change of under-wear, very calmly.

Downstairs, Sybil had cooked him a meal. She wasn't a very good cook. This was fine by Vimes, because he wasn't a very good eater. After a lifetime of street meals his stomach wasn't set up right. What it craved was little crunchy brown bits, the food group of the gods, and Sybil reliably always left the pan too long on the dragon.

She eyed him carefully as he chewed his fried egg and stared into the middle distance. Her manner was that of someone with a portable safety net watching a man on the high wire.

After a while, as she watched him crack open a sausage, he said, "Do we have any books on chivalry, dear?"

"Hundreds, Sam."

"Is there any one which tells you what . . . you know, what it's all about? I mean, what you have to do if you're a knight, say? Responsibilities and so on?"

"Most of them, I should think."

"Good. I think I shall do a little reading." Vimes hit the bacon with his fork. It shattered very satisfactorily.

Afterward, he went into the library. Twenty minutes later, he came back out for a pencil and some paper.

Ten minutes after that, Lady Sybil took him a cup of coffee. He was hidden behind a pile of books, and apparently deep in *Life of Chivalrie*. She crept out and went into her own study, where she settled down to update her dragon-breeding records.

It was an hour later when she heard him step out into the hall.

He was humming under his breath, tunelessly, with the far-away look of preoccupation that means that some Big Thought has required the shutting down of all non-essential processes. He was also re-radiating the field of angered innocence that was, to her, part of his essential Vimesness.

"Are you going out, Sam?"

"Yes. I'm just going to kick some arse, dear."

"Oh, *good*. Just be sure you wrap up well, then."

The Goriff family trudged along silently beside Carrot.

"I'm sorry about your shop, Mr. Goriff," he said.

Goriff shifted the load he was carrying. "We can start other shops," he said.

"We'll certainly keep an eye on it," said Carrot. "And . . . when all this is over, you can come back."

"Thank you."

His son said something in Klatchian. There was a brief family argument.

"I appreciate your strength of feeling," said Carrot, going red, "although I must say I think your language was a little strong."

"My son is sorry," said Goriff automatically. "He did not remember that you speak Kl—"

"No, I'm not! Why should we run away?" said the boy. "We *live* here! I've never *seen* Klatch!"

"Oh, well, that will be something to look forward to," said Carrot. "I hear it has many fine—"

"Are you *stupid?*" said Janil. He shook himself free of his father's grasp and confronted Carrot. "I don't care! I don't want all this stuff about the moon rising over the Mountains of the Sun! I get that at home all the time! I live *here!*"

"Now, you really ought to listen to your parents—"

"Why? My dad works all the time and now he's being pushed out! What good's that? We ought to stay here and defend what's ours!"

"Ah, well, you shouldn't take the law into your own hands—"

"Why not?"

"It's our job—"

"But you're not doing it!"

There was a rattle of Klatchian from Mr. Goriff.

"He says I've got to apologize," said Janil sullenly. "I'm sorry."

"So am I," said Carrot.

The boy's father gave him that complicated shrug used by adults in a situation involving adolescents.

"You'll be back, I know it," said Carrot.

"We shall see."

They went down the quay toward a waiting boat. It was a Klatchian ship. People lined the rails, people who were getting out with what they could carry before they could only get out with what they wore. The watchmen found themselves under hostile scrutiny.

"Surely Rust isn't already forcing Klatchians out of their homes?" said Angua.

"We can tell which way the wind is blowing," said Goriff calmly.

Carrot sniffed the salt air. "It's blowing from Klatch," he said.

"For you, perhaps," said Goriff.

A whip cracked behind them and they stood aside as several coaches rumbled by. A blind at the window was pulled aside momentarily. Carrot caught a brief glimpse of a face, all gold teeth and black beard, before the cloth twitched back.

"That's *him,* isn't it?"

There was a faint grunt from Angua. She had her eyes closed, as she always did when she was letting her nose do the seeing . . .

"Cloves," she murmured, and then grabbed Carrot's arm.

"*Don't* run after it! There's armed men on that ship! What will they think when they see a soldier running toward them?"

"I'm not a soldier!"

"How long do you think they'll spend working out the difference?"

The coach pushed through the press of people on the dock. The crowd surged back around it.

"There's boxes being unloaded— I can't quite see . . ." said Carrot, shading his eyes. "Look, I'm sure they'll understand if—"

71-hour Ahmed stepped out onto the dock and looked back toward the watchmen. There was a momentary sparkle as he grinned. They saw his hand reach over his shoulder and come back holding the curved sword.

"I can't just let him get away," said Carrot. "He's a suspect! Look, he's laughing at us!"

"With diplomatic impunity," said Angua. "But there's a lot of armed men down there."

"My strength is as the strength of ten because my heart is pure," said Carrot.

"Really? Well, there's eleven of them."

71-hour Ahmed threw his sword in the air. It spun a couple of times, making a *whum-whum* noise, and then his hand shot out and caught it by the handle as it fell.

"That's what Mr. Vimes was doing," said Carrot, through gritted teeth. "Now he's taunting us—"

"You will be killed if you go on the ship," said Goriff behind him. "I know that man."

"You do? How?"

"He is feared in the whole of Klatch. That is 71-hour Ahmed!"

"Yes, *why* is—"

"You haven't heard of him? And he is a D'reg!" Mrs. Goriff pulled at her husband's arm.

"Dreg?" said Angua.

"A warlike desert tribe," said Carrot. "Very fierce. Honorable, though. They say that if a D'reg is your friend he's your friend for the rest of your life."

"And if he's *not* your friend?"

"That's about five seconds."

He drew his sword. "Nevertheless," he added, "we can't let—"

"I have said too much. We must go," said Goriff. The family picked up their bundles.

"Look, there might be another way to find out about him," said Angua. She pointed at the carriage.

A couple of lean, long-haired and extremely graceful dogs had been let out and were straining at their leashes as they led the way up the gangplank.

"Klatchistan hunting dogs," she said. "The Klatchian nobility are very keen on them, I understand."

"They look a bit like—" Carrot began, and then the penny dropped. "No, I can't let you go on there by yourself," he said. "Something would go wrong."

"I stand a much better chance than you would, believe me," said Angua quickly. "They won't be leaving until the tide changes, in any case."

"It's too dangerous."

"Well, they *are* supposed to be our enemies."

"I meant for *you!*"

"Why?" said Angua. "I've never heard of werewolves in Klatch, so they probably don't know how to deal with us."

She undid the little leather collar that held her badge and handed it to Carrot.

"Don't *worry*," she said. "If the worst comes to the worst, I'll dive overboard."

"Into the *river?*"

"Even the river Ankh can't kill a werewolf." Angua glanced at the turgid water. "Probably, anyway."

Sergeant Colon and Corporal Nobbs had gone on patrol. They weren't sure why they were patrolling, and what they were supposed to do if they saw a crime, although many years of training had enabled them not to see some quite large crimes. But they were creatures of habit. They were watchmen, so they patrolled. They didn't patrol with a purpose. They patrolled, as it were, in pure essence. Nobby's progress wasn't helped by the large, leather-bound book in his arms.

"A war'd do this place good," said Sergeant Colon, after a while. "Put some backbone in people. Everything's gone all to pot these days."

"Not like when we were kids, sarge."

"Not like when we were kids indeed, Nobby."

"People trusted one another in them days, didn't they, sarge?"

"People trusted one another, Nobby."

"Yes, sarge. I know. And people didn't have to lock their doors, did they?"

"That's right, Nobby. And people were always ready to help. They were always in and out of one another's houses."

"'sright, sarge," said Nobby vehemently. "I know no one ever locked their houses down *our* street."

"That's what I'm talking about. That's my point."

"It was 'cos the bastards even used to steal the locks."

Colon considered the truth of this.

"Yes, but at least it was each other's stuff they were nicking, Nobby. It's not like they was *foreigners.*"

"Right."

They strolled on for a while, each entangled in his own thoughts.

"Sarge?"

"Yes, Nobby?"

"Where's Nubilia?"

"Nubilia?"

"It's got to be a place, I reckon. Pretty warm there, I think."

"Ah, *Nubilia*," said Colon. He invented desperately. "Right. Yes. It's one of them Klatchian places. Yeah. Got lots of sand. And mountains. Exports dates. Why'd you want to know?"

"Oh . . . no reason."

"Nobby?"

"Yes, sarge?"

"Why are you carrying that huge book?"

"Hah, clever idea, sarge. I saw what you said about that book of your great-grandad, so if there's any fighting I got this one off'f Washpot. It's *The Book of Om*. Five inches thick."

"It's a bit big for a pocket, Nobby. It's a bit big for a *cart*, to be honest."

"I thought I could make sort of braces to carry it. I reckon even a longbow could only get an arrow as far as the Apocrypha."

A familiar creak made them look up.

A Klatchian's head was swinging in the breeze.

"Fancy a pint?" said Sergeant Colon. "Big Anjie brews up some that's a treat."

"Better not, sarge. Mr. Vimes is in a bit of a mood."

Colon sighed. "You're right."

Nobby looked up at the head again. It was wooden. It had been repainted many times over the centuries. The Klatchian was smiling very happily for someone who'd never have to buy a shirt ever again.

"The Klatchian's Head. My grandad said *his* grandad remembered when it was still the real one," Colon said. "Of course, it was about the size of a walnut by then."

"Bit . . . nasty, sticking up a bloke's head for a pub sign," said Nobby.

"*No*, Nobby. Spoils of war, right? Some bloke came back from one of the wars with a souvenir, stuck it on a pole and opened a pub. The Klatchian's Head. Teach 'em not to do it again."

"I used to get into enough trouble just for nicking boots," said Nobby.

"More robust times, Nobby."

"You ever *met* a Klatchian, sarge?" said Nobby, as they began to pace the length of the quiet street. "I mean one of the wild ones."

"Well, no . . . but you know what? They're allowed three wives! That's criminal, that is."

"Yeah, 'cos here's me and I ain't got one," said Nobby.

"And they eat funny grub. Curry and that."

Nobby gave this some thought. "Like . . . we do, when we're on late duty."

"Weelll, yerss—but they don't do it properly—"

"You mean runny ear-wax yellow with peas and currants in, like your mum used to do?"

"Right! You poke around as much as you like in a Klatchian curry and you won't find a single *piece* of swede."

"And I heard where they eat sheep's eyeballs, too," said Nobby, international gastra-gnome.

"Right again."

"Not decent ordinary stuff like lambs' fry or sweetbreads, then?"

"That's . . . right."

Colon felt that he was being got at in some way.

"Look, Nobby, when all's said and done they ain't the right color, and there's an end to it."

"Good job you found out, Fred!" said Nobby, so cheerfully that Sergeant Colon was almost sure that he meant it.

"Well, it's obvious," he conceded.

"Er . . . what *is* the right color?" said Nobby.

"White, of course!"

"Not brick-red, then? 'Cos *you*—"

"Are you winding me up, Corporal Nobbs?"

"'Course not, sarge. So . . . what color am I?"

That caused Sergeant Colon to think. You could have found, somewhere on Corporal Nobbs, a shade appropriate to every climate on the disc and a few found only in specialist medical books.

"White's . . . white's a state of, you know . . . *mind*," he said. "It's like . . . doing an honest day's work for an honest day's pay, that sort of thing. And washing regular."

"Not lazing around, sort of thing."

"Right."

"Or . . . like . . . working all hours like Goriff does."

"Nobby—"

"And you never see those kids of his with dirty clo—"

"Nobby, you're just trying to get me going, right? You *know* we're better'n Klatchians. Otherwise, what's the point? Anyway, if we're going to fight 'em, you could get locked up for going around talking treachery."

"Are you going to fight them, Fred?"

Fred Colon scratched his chin. "Well, as a hexperienced milit'ry man, I suppose I'll have to . . ."

"What're you going to do? Join a regiment and go to the front?"

"We-ell . . . my fore-tay lies in training, so I reckon I'd better stay here and train up the new recruits."

"Here at the back, you might say."

"We all have to do our bit, Nobby. If it was down to me I'd be out there like a shot to give Johnny Klatchian a taste of cold steel."

"Their razor-sharp swords wouldn't worry you, then?"

"I should laugh at them with scorn, Nobby."

"But s'posing the Klatchians attack here? Then *you'll* be at the front, and the front will be at the back."

"I'll sort of try for a posting in the middle . . ."

"The middle of the front or—"

"Gentlemen?"

They looked round to find that they had been followed by a man of medium height but with an extraordinary head. It wasn't that he had gone bald. He had quite a lot of hair, which was long and curly and reached almost to his shoulders, and his beard was large enough to conceal a small chicken. But his head had simply risen through his hair, like a kind of intrusive dome.

He gave them a friendly smile.

"Am I by any chance addressing the heroic Sergeant Colon and the—" The man looked at Nobby. Expressions of amazement, dread, interest and charity passed across his otherwise sunny countenance like storm-driven clouds. "And *the* Corporal Nobbs?" he finished.

"That is us, citizen," said Colon.

"Ah, good. I was very specifically told to find you. It's quite amazing, you know. No one had even broken into the boathouse, although I must say I did design the locks rather well. And all I've had to do is replace the leatherwork around the joints and grease it up . . . oh, do excuse me, I've got rather ahead of myself. Now . . . there was a message I had to give you . . . What was it now?. . . Something about your hands . . ." He reached down into the large canvas bag by his feet and pulled out a long tube, which he handed to Nobby.

"I do apologize about this," he said, producing a smaller tube and handing it to Colon. "I had to do things in such a hurry, there really was no time to finish it off properly, and frankly the materials are not very good—"

Colon looked at his tube. It was pointed at one end.

"This is a firework rocket," he said. "Look, it's got 'A riot of colored balls and stars' on it . . ."

"Yes, I do *so* apologize," said the man, lifting a complex little arrangement of wood and metal out of the bag. "May I have the tube back, corporal?" He took it and screwed the arrangement on to one end. "Thank you . . . yes, I'm afraid that without my lathe and, indeed, my forge, I really have had to make do with what I could find lying around . . . Could I have the rocket back, please? Thank you."

"They don't go properly without a stick," said Nobby.

"Oh, in fact they do," said the man. "Just not very accurately."

He raised the tube to shoulder height and peered into a small wire grid.

"That seems about right," he said.

"And they don't go along," said Nobby. "They just go up."

"A common misconception," said Leonard of Quirm, turning to face them.

Colon could see the tip of the rocket in the depths of the tube, and had a sudden image of stars and balls.

"Now, apparently you two have to step into this alley here and come with me," said Leonard. "I'm very sorry about this, but his lordship has explained to me at great length how the needs of society as a whole may have to overrule the rights of a particular individual. Oh, and I've just remembered. You have to put your hands up."

Sand had been spilled across the big table in the Rats Chamber.

Lord Rust felt a sensation akin to pleasure as he surveyed it.

There were the little square boxes for the towns and cities, and cut-out palm trees to indicate the known oasisies. And, although he was uneasy about the word "oasisies," Lord Rust looked at it and saw that it was good. Especially since it was a map of Klatch and everyone knew that Klatch was sand anyway, which made it rather satisfying in an existential sort of way, although this sand here had been commandeered from the heap behind Chalky the troll's wholesale pottery and bore the occasional cigarette end and trace of feline incontinence that would probably not be found in the real desert, or certainly not to scale.

"*Here* would be a good landing area," he said, pointing with his stick.

His equerry tried to look helpful. "The El Kinte peninsula," he said. "That's the closest point to us, sir."

"Exactly! We can be across the straits in jig time."

"Very good, sir," said Lieutenant Hornett, "but . . . you don't think the enemy might be expecting us there? It being such an obvious landing site?"

"Not obvious at all to the trained military thinker, sir! They won't be expecting us there precisely *because* it is so obvious, d'y'see?"

"You mean . . . they'll think only a complete idiot would land there, sir?"

"Correct! And they know we're *not* complete idiots, sir, and therefore that will be the last place they will be expecting us, d'y'see? They'll be expecting us somewhere like"—his stick stabbed into the sand— "here."

Hornett looked closely. In the street outside, someone started to bang a drum.

"Oh, you mean Eritor," he said. "Where I believe there is a concealed landing area, and two days forced march through good cover would have us at the heart of the empire, sir."

"Exactly!"

"Whereas landing at El Kinte means three days over sand dunes and past the fortified city of Gebra . . ."

"Precisely. Wide-open spaces! And that is where we can practice the *art* of warfare." Lord Rust raised his voice above the drumming. "That's how you settle these things. One decisive battle. Us

147

on one side, the Klatchians on the other. THAT IS HOW THESE THINGS ARE D—"

He threw down his pointer. "Who the devil is making that infernal noise?"

The equerry walked across to the window. "It's someone else recruiting, sir," he said.

"But we're all here!"

The equerry hesitated, as the bearers of bad tidings to short-tempered men often do.

"It's Vimes, sir . . ."

"Recruiting for the *Watch?*"

"Er . . . no, my lord. For a regiment. Er . . . the banner says 'Sir Samuel Vimes's First of Foot,' my lord—"

"The arrogance of the man. Go and— No, I'll go myself!"

There was a crowd in the street. In the center there rose the bulk of Constable Dorfl, and a key thing about the golem was that if he was banging a drum then no one was going to ask him to stop. No one except possibly Lord Rust, who strode up and snatched the drumsticks out of his hands.

"Yerss, it are species of your choice's life in der First of Foot!" shouted Sergeant Detritus, unaware of the events going on behind him. "You learnin' a trade! You learnin' self-respek! Also you get spiffy uniform plus all der boots you can eat—here, dat's my banner!"

"What's the meaning of this?" said Rust, flinging the home-made banner onto the ground. "Vimes can't do this!"

A figure detached itself from the wall, where it had been watching the show.

"You know, I rather think I can," said Vimes. He handed Rust a piece of paper. "It's all here, my lord. With references citing the highest authorities, in case you are in any doubt."

"Citing the—?"

"On the role of a knight, my lord. In fact the *duties* of a knight, funnily enough. A lot of it is pretty damn stupid stuff, riding around the place on one of those bloody great horses with curtains round it and so on, but *one* of them says in time of need a knight *has* to raise and maintain—you'll laugh when I tell you this—a body of armed soldiers! No one could have been more surprised than me, I don't mind telling you! Seems there's nothing for it but I have to go out and get some chaps together. Of course, most of the Watch have joined, well, you know how it is, disciplined lads, anxious to do their bit, so that saved *me* a bit of effort. Except for Nobby Nobbs, 'cos he says if he leaves it till Thursday he's going to have enough white feathers for a mattress."

Rust's expression would have preserved meat for a year.

"This is a nonsense," he said. "And you, Vimes, certainly are no knight. Only a king can make—"

"There's a good few lordships in this city created by the Patricians," said Vimes. "Your friend Lord Downey, for one. You were saying?"

"Then if you persist in playing games I will say that before a knight is created he must spend a night's vigil watching his armor—"

"Practically every night of my life," said Vimes. "A man doesn't keep an eye on his armor round here, that man's got no armor in the morning."

"In *prayer,*" said Rust sharply.

"That's me," said Vimes. "Not a night has gone by without me thinking, 'Ye gods, I hope I get through this alive.'"

"—and he must have proved himself on the field of combat. Against other trained men, Vimes. Not vermin and thugs."

Vimes started to undo the strap of his helmet.

"Well, this isn't the best of moments, my lord, but if someone'll hold your coat I can spare you five minutes . . ."

In Vimes's eyes Rust recognized the fiery gleam of burning boats.

"I know what you're doing, Vimes, and I am not going to rise to it," he said, taking a step back. "In any case, you have had no formal training in arms."

"That's true," said Vimes. "You've got me there, right enough. No one ever trained me in arms. I was lucky there." He leaned closer and lowered his voice so that the watching crowd wouldn't hear. "Y'see, I *know* what 'training in arms' means, Ronald. There hasn't been a real war in ages. So it's all prancing around wearing padded waistcoats and waving swords with knobs on the end so no one'll really get hurt, isn't it? But down in the Shades no one's had any training in arms either. Wouldn't know an épée from a saber. No, what they're *good* at is a broken bottle in one hand and a length of four-by-two in the other and when you face 'em, Ronnie, you know you aren't going off for a laugh and a jolly drink afterward, 'cos they want you *dead.* They want to *kill* you, you see, Ron? And by the time you've swung your nice shiny broadsword they've carved their name and address on your stomach. And *that's* where I got *my* training in arms. Well . . . fists and knees and teeth and elbows, mostly."

"You, sir, are *no gentleman,*" said Rust.

"I *knew* there was something about me that I liked."

"Can you not even see that you can't enroll . . . dwarfs and trolls in an Ankh-Morpork regiment?"

"It just says 'armed soldiers,' and dwarfs come with their own axes. A great saving. Besides, if you've ever seen them really fight, then you must've been on the same side."

"Vimes—"

"It's Sir Samuel, my lord."

Rust seemed to think for a moment.

"Very well, then," he said. "Then you and your . . . regiment come under my command—"

"Strangely, no," said Vimes swiftly. "Under the command of the King or his duly appointed representative, it says in Scavone's *Chivalric Law and Usage.* And, of course, there has been no duly appointed representative ever since some complete bastard cut off the last king's head. Oh, assorted bods appeared to have been ruling the city, but according to the *chivalric tradition—*"

Rust stopped to think again. He had the look of a lawnmower just after the grass has organized a workers' collective. There was a definite suggestion that, deep inside, he knew this was not really happening. It could not be happening because this sort of thing did not happen. Any contradictory evidence could be safely ignored. However, it might be necessary to find some motions to go through.

"I think you'll find that, legally, your position—" he began, and his eyes bulged for a moment as Vimes interrupted him cheerfully.

"Oh, there might be a few problems, I grant you. But if you ask

Mr. Slant he'll say 'This is a very interesting case,' which as you know is lawyer-talk for 'One thousand dollars a day plus expenses and it'll take months.' So I'll leave you to get on with it, shall I? Got such a lot of things to do, you know. I think the swatches for the new uniforms should be in my office about now, it's so important to look right on the battlefield, isn't it?"

Rust gave Vimes another look, and then strode away.

Detritus stamped to attention beside Vimes and his salute clanged smartly off his helmet.

"What we doin' now, sir?"

"We can pack up now, I think. All the lads have joined up?"

"Yessir!"

"You told them it wasn't compulsory?"

"Yessir! I said, 'It ain't compuls'ry, you just gotta,' sir."

"Detritus, I wanted *volunteers.*"

"'sright, sir. They volunteered all right, I saw to that."

Vimes sighed as he walked back to his office. But they were probably safe. He was pretty sure he was legally sound and if he knew anything about Rust, the man would respect the letter of the law. Such men did, in a chilly way. Besides, thirty men in the Watch simply didn't figure in the great scheme of things. Rust could ignore them.

Suddenly there's a war brewing, Vimes thought, and they all come back. Civil order is turned upside down, because that's the *rules.* And people like Rust are at the top of the heap again. You have these aristocrats lazing around for years, and suddenly the old armor's out and the sword is being taken down from over the fireplace. They think there's going to be a war and all they can think about is that wars can be won or lost . . .

Someone's behind this. Someone wants to see a war. Someone paid to have Ossie and Snowy killed. Someone wanted the Prince dead. I've got to remember that. This isn't a war. This is a crime.

And then he realized he was wondering if the attack on Goriff's shop had been organized by the same people, and whether those same people had set fire to the embassy.

And *then* he realized why he was thinking like this.

It was because he wanted there to be conspirators. It was much better to imagine men in some smoky room somewhere, made mad and cynical by privilege and power, plotting over the brandy. You had to cling to this sort of image, because if you didn't then you might have to face the fact that bad things happened because ordinary people, the kind who brushed the dog and told their children bedtime stories, were capable of then going out and doing horrible things to other ordinary people. It was so much easier to blame it on Them. It was bleakly depressing to think that They were Us. If it was Them, then nothing was anyone's fault. If it was Us, what did that make Me? After all, I'm one of Us. I must be. I've certainly never thought of myself as one of Them. *No one* ever thinks of themselves as one of Them. We're always one of Us. It's Them that do the bad things.

Around about this time, in his former life, Vimes would be taking the cap off a bottle, and wouldn't be too bothered about the bottle's contents so long as they crinkled paint—

"Ook?"

"Oh, hello. What can I do for— oh, yes, I asked about books on Klatch . . . Is that all?"

The Librarian shyly held out a small, battered green book. Vimes had been expecting something bigger, but he took it anyway. It paid to look at any book the orangutan gave you. He matched you up to books. Vimes supposed it was a knack, in the same way that an undertaker was very good at judging heights.

On the spine, in very faded gold lettering, were the words *"VENI VIDI VICI: A Soldier's Life* by Gen. A. Tacticus."

Nobby and Sergeant Colon edged along the alley.

"I know who he is!" Fred hissed. "That's Leonard of Quirm, that is! He went missing five years ago!"

"So he's called Leonard and he's from Quirm, so what?" said Nobby.

"He's a raving genius!"

"He's a loony."

"Yeah, well, they say there's a thin line between genius and madness . . ."

"He's fallen off it, then."

The voice behind them said, "Oh, dear, this won't do at all, will it . . . ? I can't deny it, you were quite right, the accuracy would be quite unacceptable at any reasonable range. Could you bear to stop a moment, please?"

They turned. Leonard was already dismantling the tube.

"If you could just hang on to this bit, corporal . . . and, sergeant, if you would be so good as to hold this piece steady . . . some sort of fins should do it, I'm sure I had a suitable piece of wood somewhere . . ." Leonard began to pat his pockets.

The watchmen realized that the man holding them up had paused to redesign his weapon and had given it to them to hold while he looked for a screwdriver. This was a thing that did not often happen.

Nobby silently took the rocket from Colon and pushed it into the tube.

"What's this bit here, mister?" he said.

Leonard glanced up briefly in between patting his pockets.

"Oh, that is the trigger," he said. "Which, as you can see, rubs against the flint and—"

"*Good.*"

There was a short burst of flame and rather more black smoke.

"Oh, dear," said Leonard.

The watchmen turned, like men dreading what they were about to see. The rocket had shot the length of the alley and through the window of a house.

"Ah . . . putting 'This Way Up' on the projectile would be an important safety point to bear in mind for the new design," said Leonard. "Now, where's that notebook . . . ?"

"I think we'd better leave," said Colon, moving backward. "Very fast."

Inside the house there was an explosion of stars and balls to delight young and old but not the troll who had just opened the door.

"Ah, really?" said Leonard. "Well, if speed is required, I have this very interesting design for a two-wheeled—"

Acting on an unspoken agreement, the watchmen each put a hand under a shoulder, lifted him off the ground, and ran for it.

"Oh, dear," said Leonard, as he was dragged backward.

The watchmen dived into a side alley, and then jinked and

dodged along several others with quiet professionalism. Finally they leaned Leonard against a wall and peered round the end of the alley.

"All clear," said Nobby. "They went the other way."

"Right," said Colon. "Now, what was you doing? I mean, you might be a genius like I heard, Mister da Quirm, but when it comes to threatening people you're as clever as an inflatable dartboard."

"I appear to have been a bit of a juggins, don't I?" Leonard agreed. "But I do implore you to come with me. I'm afraid I thought that as warriors you would be more inclined to understand force—"

"Well, yes, we're *warriors*," said Sergeant Colon. "But—"

"'ere, have you got another one of these rockets?" said Nobby, hefting the tube onto his shoulder again. He had the special gleam in his eye that a small man gets when he's laid his hands on a big, big weapon.

"I *may* have," said Leonard, and the gleam in *his* eye was the mad twinkle of the naturally innocent when they think they're being cunning. "Why don't we go and see? You see, I was told to fetch you by any means necessary."

"Bribery sounds good," said Nobby. He put his eye to the tube's sights and started making "whoosh" noises.

"Who told you to fetch us?" said Colon.

"Lord Vetinari."

"The Patrician wants *us?*"

"Yes. He said you have special qualities and must come at once."

"To the *palace?* I heard he'd done a runner."

"Oh, no. To the, er . . . to the, er . . . docks . . ."

"Special qualities, eh?" said Colon.

"Er, sarge . . ." Nobby began.

"Now then, Nobby," said Colon importantly. "It's about time we were given some recognition, you know that. Hexperienced officers are the backbone of the force. Seems to me," he went on, "seems to *me* that this is a case of cometh the time, cometh the man."

"When's he cometh?"

"I'm talking about us. Men with special qualities."

Nobby nodded, but with a certain amount of reluctance. In many ways he was a much clearer thinker than his superior officer, and he was worrying about "special qualities." Being picked for something because of your "special qualities" was tantamount to being volunteered. Anyway, what was so special about "special qualities"? *Limpets* had special qualities.

"Will we go undercover again?" said Colon.

Leonard blinked. "There . . . yes, I think I can say there is a strong *under* element involved. Yes, indeed."

"Sarge—"

"You just be quiet, corporal." Colon pulled Nobby closer. "Undercover means not getting stabbed and shot at, right?" he whispered. "And what's the most important thing a professional soldier wants not to happen to him?"

"Not getting stabbed and shot," said Nobby automatically.

"Right! So let's be going, Mr. Quirm! The call has come!"

"Well done!" said Leonard. "Tell me, sergeant, are you of a nautical persuasion?"

Colon saluted again. "Nossir! Happily married man, sir!"

"I meant, have you ploughed the ocean waves at all?"

Colon gave him a cunning look.

"Ah, you can't catch me with that one, sir," he said. "Everyone knows the horses would sink."

Leonard paused for a moment and retuned his brain to Radio Colon.

"Have you, in the past, floated around, on the sea, in a boat, at all?"

"Me, sir? Not me, sir. It's the sight of the waves going up and down, sir."

"Really?" said Leonard. "Well, happily, that will not be a problem."

All right, start again . . .

Assembling facts, that's what it was about . . .

The world watched. Someone *wanted* the Watch to say that the assassination had been inspired by Klatch. Who?

Someone had also beheaded Snowy Slopes where he stood and left him deader than six buckets of fish bait.

A vision of 71-hour Ahmed's big curved sword presented itself for his attention. So . . .

. . . let's assume that Ahmed was Khufurah's servant or body-guard, and he'd found out . . .

No, how could that work? Who'd tell him?

Well, maybe he'd found out *somehow,* and that meant that he might also know who'd paid the man . . .

Vimes sat back. It was still a mystery but he'd solve it, he knew he would. He'd assemble the facts, analyze them, look at them from every angle with an open mind, and *find out exactly how Lord Rust had organized it.*

Rank bad hat! He didn't have to sit still for something like that, especially from a man who rhymed "house" with "mice."

His eye was caught by the ancient book. General Tacticus. Every kid knew about him. Ankh-Morpork had ruled a huge empire and a lot of it had been in Klatch, thanks to him. Except there wasn't any thanks *for* him, strangely enough. Vimes had never quite known why, but the city seemed to be rather ashamed of the general.

One reason, of course, was that he'd ended up fighting Ankh-Morpork. The city of Genua had run out of royalty, inbreeding having progressed to the point where the sole remaining example consisted mostly of teeth, and senior courtiers had written to Ankh-Morpork asking for help.

There'd been a lot of that sort of thing, Vimes had been surprised to learn. The little kingdoms of the Sto Plains were forever scrounging spare royalty off one another. The King had sent Tacticus out of sheer exasperation. It's hard to run a proper empire when you're constantly getting bloodstained letters on the lines of: *Dear sire, I beg to inform you that we have conquered Betrek, Smale and Ushistan. Please send AM$20,000 back pay.* The man never knew when to stop. So he was hastily made a duke and packed off to Genua, whereupon his first action was to consider what was that city's greatest military threat and then, having identified it, to declare war on Ankh-Morpork.

But what else had anyone expected? He'd done his duty. He'd

brought back heaps of spoils, lots of captives and, almost uniquely among Ankh-Morpork's military leaders, most of his men. Vimes suspected that this last fact was one reason why history didn't approve. There was a suggestion that this was, in some way, not playing fair.

"Veni, vidi, vici." That was what the man was supposed to have said when he'd conquered . . . where? Pseudopolis, wasn't it? Or Al-Khali? Or Quirm? Maybe Sto Lat? That was in the old days when you attacked anyone else's city on principle, and went back and did them over again if they looked like getting up. And in those days, you didn't care if the world watched. You *wanted* them to watch, and learn. *"Veni, vidi, vici."* I came, I saw, I conquered.

As a comment it always struck Vimes as a bit too pat. It wasn't the sort of thing you came up with on the spur of the moment, was it? It sounded as if he had worked it out. He'd probably spent long evenings in his tent, looking up in the dictionary short words beginning with V and trying them out . . . *Veni, vermini, vomui,* I came, I got ratted, I threw up? *Visi, veneri, vamoosi,* I visited, I caught an embarrassing disease, I ran away? It must have been a big relief to come up with three short acceptable words. He probably made them up *first,* and then went off to see somewhere and conquer it.

He opened the book at random.

"It is always useful to face an enemy who is prepared to die for his country," he read. *"This means that both you and he have exactly the same aim in mind."*

"Hah!"

"Bingeley-bingeley b—"

Vimes's hand slammed down on the box.

"Yes? What is it?"

"Three oh five pee em, Interview with Cpl Littlebottom re Missing Sgt Colon," said the demon sulkily.

"I never arranged anything like— Who told you—? Are you telling me that I've got an appointment and I don't know about it?"

"That's right."

"So how do *you* know about it?"

"You *told* me to know about it. Last night," said the demon.

"You *can* tell me about appointments I don't know about?" said Vimes.

"They're still appointments *sine qua* appointments," said the demon. "They exist, as it were, in appointment phase space."

"What the hell does that mean?"

"Look," said the demon patiently, "you can have an appointment at any time, right? So therefore *any* appointment exists *in potentia*—"

"Where's that?"

"Any *particular* appointment simply collapses the waveform," said the demon. "I merely select the most likely one from the projected matrix."

"You're just making this up," said Vimes. "If you were right, then any second now—"

Someone knocked at the door. It was a polite, tentative tap.

Vimes didn't take his eyes off the smirking demon.

"Is that you, Corporal Littlebottom?" he said.

"Yes, sir. Sergeant Colon has sent a pigeon. I thought you ought to see it, sir."

"Come in!"

A small roll of thin paper was placed on his desk. He read:

Have volunteered for a mission of Vital Importance. Nobby is here also. There will be statchoos of us when this day's work is over. PS Someone I can't tell you who says this note will self-destruct in five seconds, he is sorry he hasn't got good chemicles to do it better—

The paper began to crinkle around the edges and then vanished in a small puff of acrid smoke.

Vimes stared at the little pile of ash that remained.

"I suppose it's a mercy they didn't blow up the pigeon, sir," said Cheery.

"What the hell are they up to? Well, I can't chase around after them. Thanks, Cheery."

The dwarf saluted and departed.

"Coincidence," said Vimes.

"All right, then," said the demon. "Bingeley-bingeley beep! Three fifteen pee em, Emergency Meeting with Captain Carrot."

It was a cylinder, tapering to a point at both ends. At one end the taper was quite complex, the cylinder narrowing in a succession of smaller and smaller rings, overlapping one another until they ended in a large fishtail. Oiled leather could be seen gleaming in the gaps between the metal.

At the other end, extending from the cylinder for all the world like the horn of a unicorn, was a very long and pointed screw thread.

The whole thing was mounted on a crude trolley, which was in turn riding on a pair of iron rails that disappeared into the black water at the far end of the boathouse.

"Looks like a giant fish to me," said Colon. "Made of tin."

"With an 'orn," said Nobby.

"It'll never float," said Colon. "I can see where you've gone wrong there. Everyone knows metal sinks."

"Not *entirely* true," said Leonard, diplomatically. "In any case, this boat is *designed* to sink."

"What?"

"Propulsion was a major headache, I'm afraid," said Leonard, climbing up a stepladder. "I thought of paddles and oars, and even some kind of screw, and then I thought: dolphins, that's the ticket! They move extremely fast with barely an effort. That's out at sea, of course, we only get the shovel-nosed dolphin in our estuary here. The linkage rods are a bit complicated but I used to be able to get quite a turn of speed. The pedalling can be somewhat tiresome, but with three of us we should be able to get up to some quite satisfactory accelerations. It's amazing what you can do when you imitate nature, I just wish my flying exp— Oh . . . where did you go . . . ?"

It would be difficult to establish what part of satisfactorily accelerating nature the watchmen were trying to imitate, but it was a part which tended to get stuck in doors a lot.

They stopped struggling and began to back into the room.

"Ah, sergeant," said Lord Vetinari, entering in front of them. "And Corporal Nobbs, too. Leonard has explained everything to you?"

"You can't ask us to go in that thing, sir! It'll be suicide!" said Colon.

The Patrician brought his hands together in front of his lips in the manner of someone praying, and sucked air thoughtfully.

"No. No, I think you are wrong," he said at last, as if reaching a conclusion on some complex metaphysical conundrum. "I think that, in all probability, going into that thing would be a valiant and possibly rewarding deed. I would venture to suggest that, in fact, it is *not* going that would be suicidal. But I would appreciate your views."

Lord Vetinari was not a heavily built man and, these days, he walked with the aid of an ebony cane. No one could remember seeing him handle a weapon, and a flash of unaccustomed insight told Sergeant Colon that this was not in fact a comforting thought at all. They said he'd been educated at the Assassins' School, but no one remembered what weapons he'd learned. He'd studied languages. And suddenly, with him in front of you, this didn't seem like the soft option.

Sergeant Colon saluted, always a useful thing to do in an emergency such as this, and shouted: "Corporal Nobbs, why aren't you in the . . . the metal sinking fish thing?"

"Sarge?"

"Let's see you get up them steps, lad . . . hup hup hup . . ."

Nobby scrambled up the ladder and disappeared. Colon saluted again. You could usually tell his nervousness by the smartness of his salute. You could have cut bread with this one.

"Ready to go, *sah!*" he shouted.

"Well done, sergeant," said Vetinari. "You're displaying exactly those special qualities I'm looking for—"

"—'ere, sarge," came a metallic voice from the belly of the fish, "*there's all chains and cogwheels in here. What's this do?*" The big auger in front of the thing started to squeak round.

Leonard appeared from behind the fish.

"I think we should all get in," he said. "I've lit the candle that'll burn down and sever the string that'll release the weight that'll pull the blocks out."

"Er . . . what is this thing called?" said Colon, as he followed the Patrician up the ladder.

"Well, because it is *submersed* in a *marine* environment I've always called it the Going-Under-The-Water-Safely Device," said Leonard, behind him.* "But usually I just think of it as the Boat."

He reached behind him and shut the lid.

After a moment any listener in the boathouse would have heard a complicated clonk as bolts slid into place.

The candle burned down and severed the string that released the weight that pulled the blocks out and, slowly at first, the Boat slid down the rails and into the dark water which, after a second or two, closed over it with a gloop.

No one took any notice of Angua as she trotted up the gangplank. The important thing, she knew, was to look at home. No one bothered a large dog that looked as though it knew where it was going.

People were milling about on deck in the manner peculiar to nonsailors on board ship, not sure of what they should be doing or where they should refrain from doing it. Some of the more stoic ones had made little camps, defining with bundles and pieces of cloth tiny areas of private property. They reminded Angua of the bicolored drainpipes and microscopically delineated household boundaries in Money Trap Lane, showing yet another way of drawing a line in the sand. This is Mine, and that is Yours. Trespass on Mine, and you'll get Yours.

There were a couple of guards standing on either side of the door to the cabins. They hadn't been told to stop dogs.

Scents led down below. She could smell the other dogs and a strong odor of cloves.

At the end of the narrow passage a door was ajar. She forced it open with her nose and looked around.

The dogs were lying on a rug on one side of a large cabin. Other dogs might have barked, but these just turned their beautiful heads toward her, sighted down the length of their noses and examined her carefully.

A narrow bed beyond them was half concealed by silk hang-

---

* Thinking up good names was, oddly enough, one area where Leonard of Quirm's genius tended to give up.

ings. 71-hour Ahmed was bending over it, but he turned when she entered.

He glanced toward the dogs and gave her a puzzled look. Then, to her amazement, he sat down on the deck in front of her.

"And who do you belong to?" he said in perfect Morporkian.

Angua wagged her tail. There was someone in the bed, she could smell them, but they wouldn't be a problem. Jaw muscles strong enough to sever someone's neck help you to feel relaxed in most situations.

Ahmed patted her on the head. Very few people have ever done that to a werewolf without having to get people to cut up their meals for them in future, but Angua had learned self-control.

Then he stood up and went to the door. She heard him say something to someone outside, and then he came back into the room and smiled at her.

"I go, I come back . . ."

He opened a small cupboard and took out a jewelled dog collar. "You shall have a collar. Oh, and here is some food," he added, as a servant brought in some bowls. "'Knick-knack, paddywack, give a dog a bone' is a rhyme I hear your Ankh-Morpork children sing, but a paddywack is a ball of gristle suitable only for animal food and who knows what part of the animal is its knick-knack . . ."

The plate was put in front of Angua. The other dogs stirred, but Ahmed snapped a word at them and they settled back again.

The food was . . . dog food. In Ankh-Morpork terms, it meant something that you wouldn't even put in a sausage, and there are very few things that a man with a big enough mincer cannot put in a sausage.

The little central human part of her was revolted, but the werewolf drooled at the sight of every glistening tube and wobbly fat bit—

It was on a silver plate.

She looked up. Ahmed was watching her carefully.

Of course, the royal dogs were treated like kings, all those diamond collars . . . It didn't have to mean he *knew*—

"Not hungry?" he said. "Your mouth says you are."

Something snapped around her neck as she spun around to

bite. Her teeth closed on a mouthful of greasy cloth but that wasn't as important as the pain.

"His Highness has always liked fine collars on his dogs," said 71-hour Ahmed, through the red mist. "Rubies, emeralds . . . and diamonds, Miss Angua." His face came down level with hers. "Set in silver."

". . . A crucial factor, I have always found, is NOT the size of the forces. It is the positioning and commitment of reserves, the bringing of power to a point . . ."

Vimes tried to concentrate on Tacticus. But there were two distractions. One was that the grinning face of 71-hour Ahmed looked out at him from every line. The other was his watch, which he had propped up against the Dis-organizer. It was powered by actual clockwork and was much more reliable. And it never needed feeding. It ticked quietly. As far as it was concerned, he could forget his appointments. He liked it.

The second hand was just curving toward the top of the minute when he heard someone coming up the stairs.

"Come in, captain," said Vimes. There was a snigger from the box.

Carrot's face was pinker than normal.

"Something's happened to Angua," said Vimes.

The high color drained from Carrot's face. "How did you know that?"

Vimes firmly closed the lid on the sniggering demon. "Let's call it intuition, shall we? I'm right, am I?"

"Yes, sir! She went aboard a Klatchian boat and now it's sailing! She hasn't come off!"

"What the hell did she go on board for?"

"We were after Ahmed! And he looked as if he was taking someone with him, sir. Someone *ill*, sir!"

"He's left? But the diplomats are still—"

Vimes stopped. There was, if you didn't know Carrot, something wrong with the situation. There were people who, when their girlfriend was spirited away on a foreign ship, would have dived into the Ankh, or at least run briskly along the crust, leapt aboard and dealt out merry hell on a democratic basis. Of course, at a time like this that would be a dumb thing to do. The sensible approach *would* be to let people know, but even so—

But Carrot really did believe that personal wasn't the same as important. Of course, Vimes believed the same thing. You had to hope that when push came to shove you'd act the right way. But there was something slightly creepy about someone who didn't just believe it, but lived their life by it. It was as unnerving as meeting a really poor priest.

Obviously, it was a consideration that if someone had captured Angua you knew that the rescue you were going to probably wouldn't be hers.

But . . .

The gods alone knew what would happen if he left now. The city had gone war mad. Big things were happening. At a time like this, every cell in his body was telling him that the Commander of the Watch had Responsibilities . . .

He drummed his fingers on the desk. In times like this, it was vital to make the right decision. That was what he was paid for. *Responsibility* . . .

He ought to stay here, and do the best he could.

But . . . history was full of the bones of good men who'd followed bad orders in the hope that they could soften the blow. Oh, yes, there were worse things they could do, but most of them began right where they started following bad orders.

His eyes went from Carrot to the Dis-organizer and then to the tottering mounds of paperwork on his desk.

Blow that! He was a thief-taker! He'd *always* be a thief-taker! Why lie?

"Damned if I'll let Ahmed get back to Klatch!" he said, standing up. "Fast boat, was it?"

"Yes, but it looked pretty heavy in the water."

"Then maybe we can catch it up before it goes very far—"

As he hurried forward he had, just for a second, the strange sensation that he was two people. And this was because, for the merest fraction of a second, he *was* two people. They were both called Samuel Vimes.

To history, choices are merely directions. The Trousers of Time opened up and Vimes began to hurtle down one leg of them.

And, somewhere else, the Vimes who made a different choice began to drop into a different future.

They both darted back to grab their Dis-organizers. By the most outrageous of freak chances, quite uniquely, in this split second of decision, they each got the wrong one.

And sometimes the avalanche depends on one snowflake. Sometimes a pebble is allowed to find out what might have happened—if only it had bounced the other way.

The wizards of Ankh-Morpork had been very firm on the subject of printing. It's not happening here, they said. Supposing, they said, someone printed a book on magic and then broke up the type again and used it for a book on, say, cookery? The metal would remember. Spells aren't just words. They have extra dimensions of existence. We'd be up to here in talking soufflés. Besides, someone might print *thousands* of the damn things, many of which could well be read by unsuitable people.

The Engravers' Guild was also against printing. There was something pure, they said, about an engraved page of text. It was there, whole, unsullied. Their members could do very fine work at very reasonable rates. Allowing unskilled people to bash lumps of type together showed a disrespect for words and no good would come of it.

The only attempt ever to set up a printing press in Ankh-Morpork had ended in a mysterious fire and the death by suicide of the luckless printer. Everyone knew it was suicide because he'd left a note. The fact that this had been engraved on the head of a pin was considered an irrelevant detail.

And the Patrician was against printing because if people knew too much it would only bother them.

So people relied on word of mouth, which worked very well because the mouths were so close together. A lot of them were just below the noses of the members of the Beggars' Guild,* citizens

---

* Except in the particular case of Sidney Lopsides, who was paid two dollars a day from City funds to wear a sack over his head. It wasn't that he was spectacularly deformed, as such, it was merely that anyone who saw him spent the rest of the day with an unnerving feeling that they were upside down.

generally regarded as reasonably reliable and well informed. Some of them were highly thought of for their sports coverage.

Lord Rust looked thoughtfully at Cumbling Michael, a Grade II Mutterer.

"And what happened next?"

Cumbling Michael scratched his wrist. He'd recently got his extra grade because he'd finally managed to catch a disfiguring but harmless skin disease.

"Mr. Carrot was in there about two minutes, m'lord. Then they all come runnin' out, right, an' they—"

"Who were *they?*" said Rust. He fought off an urge to scratch his own arm.

"There was Carrot an' Vimes anna dwarf an' a zombie an' all of them, m'lord. They ran all the way to the docks, m'lord, and Vimes saw Captain Jenkins and he said—"

"Ah, Captain Jenkins! This is your lucky day!"

The captain looked up from the rope he was coiling. No one likes being told it's their lucky day. That sort of thing does not bode well. When someone tells you it's your lucky day, something bad is about to happen.

"It is?" he said.

"Yes, because you have an unrivaled opportunity to aid the war effort!"

"I have?"

"And also to demonstrate your patriotism," Carrot added.

"I do?"

"We need to borrow your boat," said Vimes.

"Bugger off!"

"I'm choosing to believe that was a salty nautical expression meaning 'Why, certainly,'" said Vimes. "Captain Carrot?"

"Sir."

"You and Detritus go and look behind that false partition in the hold," said Vimes.

"Right, sir," said Carrot, walking toward the ladder.

"There's no false partition in the hold!" snapped Jenkins. "And I know the law, and you can't—"

There was a crash of timber from below.

"If that *wasn't* a false partition, our Carrot's gone and knocked a hole in the side," said Vimes calmly, watching the captain.

"Er . . ."

"I know the law too," said Vimes. He drew his sword. "See this?" he said, holding it up. "This is *military* law. And military law is a sword. Not a two-edged sword. There's only one edge, and it's pointing at you. Found anything, Carrot?"

Carrot appeared over the edge of the hold. There was a crossbow in his hand.

"I do declare," said Vimes, "but that looks to me like a Burleigh and Stronginthearm 'Viper' Mk 3, which kills people but leaves buildings standing."

"There's crates and crates of stuff," said Carrot.

"'s no law—" Jenkins began, but he sounded as if the bottom was dropping out of his world.

"You know, I think there probably *is* some law against selling weapons to the enemy in times of war," said Vimes. "Of course, there might not be. Tell you what," he added brightly, "why don't we all go along to Sator Square? It's full of people around this time, all very keen on the war and cheering our brave lads . . . Why don't we go along and put it to them? You told me I ought to listen to the voice of the people. Odd thing, ain't it . . . you meet people one at a time, they seem decent, they got brains that work, and then they get together and you hear the *voice* of the people. And it snarls."

"That's mob rule!"

"Oh, no, surely not," said Vimes. "Call it democratic justice."

"One man, one rock," Detritus volunteered.

Jenkins looked like a man afraid the world was about to drop out of his bottom. He glared at Vimes and then at Carrot, and saw no help there.

"Of course, you'd have nothing to fear from *us*," said Vimes. "Although you might trip on your way down the stairs to the cells."

"There's no stairs down to your cells!"

"Stairs can be arranged."

"Please, Mr. Jenkins," said Carrot, the good cop.

"I wasn't . . . taking . . . the weapons to . . . Klatch," Jenkins said slowly, as if he was reading the words very painfully off some interior script. "I had . . . in fact . . . bought them to . . . donate them . . . to . . ."

"Yes? Yes?" said Vimes.

". . . our . . . brave lads," said Jenkins.

"Well done!" said Carrot.

"And you'd be happy to . . . ?" Vimes prompted.

"And . . . I'd be happy to . . . lend my boat to the war effort," said Jenkins, sweating.

"A true patriot," said Vimes.

Jenkins writhed.

"Who told you there was a false panel in the hold?" he demanded. "It was a guess, right?"

"Right," said Vimes.

"Aha! I *knew* you were only guessing!"

"Patriotic *and* clever," said Vimes. "Now . . . how do you make this thing go fast?"

Lord Rust tapped his fingers on the table.

"What did he take the boat *for*?"

"Dunno, m'lord," said Cumbling Michael, scratching his head.

"Damn! Did anyone else see them?"

"Oh, there weren't many people around, m'lord."

"That's a small mercy, at least."

"Just me and Foul Ole Ron and the Duck Man and Ringo Eyebrows and No Way José and Sidney Lopsides and that bastard Stoolie and Whistling Dick and a few others, m'lord."

Rust sank back in his chair and put a pale hand over his face. In Ankh-Morpork the night had a thousand eyes and so did the day, and it also had five hundred mouths and nine hundred and ninety-nine ears.*

"The Klatchians *must* know, then," he said. "A detachment of Ankh-Morpork soldiery has taken ship for Klatch. An invasion force."

---

* Sidney Lopsides again.

"Oh, you could hardly call it—" Lieutenant Hornett began.

"The Klatchians will call it that. Besides, the troll Detritus is with them," said Rust.

Hornett looked glum. Detritus was an invasion force all by himself.

"What ships have we commandeered?" said Rust.

"There's more than twenty now, if you include the *Indestructible*, the *Indolence* and the . . ." Lieutenant Hornett looked at his list again, ". . . and the *Prid of Ankh-Morpork*, sir."

"The *Prid?*"

"I'm afraid so, sir."

"We should be able to take more than a thousand men and two hundred horses, then."

"Why not let Vimes go?" said Lord Selachii. "Let the Klatchians deal with him, and good riddance."

"And give them a victory over Ankh-Morpork forces? That's how they will see it. Damn the man. He forces our hand. But still, perhaps it is for the best. We should embark."

"Are we entirely ready, sir?" said Lieutenant Hornett, with the special inflection that means "We are not entirely ready, sir."

"We had better be. Glory awaits, gentlemen. In the words of General Tacticus, let us take history by the scrotum. Of course, he was not a very honorable fighter."

White sunlight etched dark shadows in Prince Cadram's palace. He too had a map of Klatch, made of tiny colored tiles set into the floor. He sat looking at it pensively.

"Just one boat?" he said.

General Ashal, his chief adviser, nodded. And added: "Our scryers can't get a very clear picture over that distance, but we do believe one of the men to be Vimes. You recall the name, sire."

"Ah, the *useful* Commander Vimes." The Prince smiled.

"Indeed. And since then there has been a lot of activity all along the docks. We have to take the view that the expeditionary force is setting out."

"I thought we had at least a week, Ashal."

"It is certainly puzzling. They cannot possibly be prepared, sire. Something must have happened."

Cadram sighed. "Oh, well, let us follow where fate points the way. Where will they attack?"

"Gebra, sire. I'm sure of it."

"Our most heavily fortified city? Surely not. Only an idiot would do that."

"I have studied Lord Rust in some depth, sire. Remember that he doesn't expect us to fight, so the size of our forces really doesn't worry him." The general smiled. It was a neat, thin little smile. "And of course in attacking *us* he is piling infamy upon infamy. The other coastal states will take note."

"A change of plan, then," said Cadram. "Ankh-Morpork can wait."

"A wise move, sire. As always."

"Any news of my poor brother?"

"Alas no, sire."

"Our agents must search harder. The world is watching, Ashal."

"Correct, sire."

"Sarge?"

"Yes, Nobby?"

"Tell me again about our special qualities."

"Shut up and keep pedalling, Nobby."

"Right, sarge."

It was quite dark in the Boat. A candle swung from a bracket over Leonard of Quirm's bowed head as he sat steering with two levers. Around Nobby, pulleys rattled and little chains clicked. It was like being inside a sewing machine. A damp one, too. Condensation dropped off the ceiling in a steady stream.

They had been pedaling for ten minutes. Leonard had spent most of the time talking excitedly. Nobby got the impression he didn't get out much. He talked about *everything*.

There were the tanks of air, for example. Nobby was happy to accept that you could squeeze air up really small, and that was what was in the groaning, creaking steel-bound casks strapped to the walls. It was what happened to the air afterward that came as a surprise.

"Bubbles!" said Leonard. "Dolphins again, you see? They don't swim through the water, they fly through a cloud of bubbles. Which is much easier, of course. I add a little soap, which seems to improve matters."

"He thinks dolphins fly, sarge," whispered Nobby.

"Just keep pedaling."

Sergeant Colon risked a glance behind him.

Lord Vetinari was sitting on an upturned box amidst the clicking chains, with several of Leonard's sketches open on his knees.

"Carry on, sergeant," said the Patrician.

"Right, sir."

The Boat was moving faster now they were away from the city. There was even a brackish light filtering through the little glass windows.

"Mr. Leonard," said Nobby.

"Yes?"

"Where're we going?"

"His lordship wishes to go to Leshp."

"Yes, I thought it'd be something like that," said Nobby. "I thought: 'Where don't I want to go?' And the answer just popped into my head, just like that. Only I don't think we'll get there, the reason bein', in about another five minutes my knees are going to fall off . . ."

"Oh, my word, you won't have to *pedal* all the way," said Leonard. "What did you think the big auger on the nose is for?"

"That?" said Nobby. "I thought that was for drillin' into the bottom of enemy ships—"

"*What?*" Leonard spun around in his seat, a look of horror on his face.

"Sink ships? Sink *ships?* With *people* on them?"

"Well . . . yes . . ."

"Corporal Nobbs, I think you are a very misguided young . . . man," said Leonard stiffly. "Use the Boat to sink ships? That would be terrible! In any case, no sailor would dream of doing such a dishonorable thing!"

"Sorry . . ."

"The auger, I would have you know, is for *attaching* us to passing ships in the manner of the remora, the sucker-fish which attaches itself to sharks. A few turns is all that is necessary for a firm attachment."

"So . . . you couldn't bore all the way through the hull, then?"

"Only if you were a very careless and extremely thoughtless young man!"

The ocean waves may not be ploughable, but the crust of the river Ankh downstream from the city was known to sprout small bushes in the summertime. The *Milka* moved slowly, leaving a furrow behind it.

"Can't you go faster?" said Vimes.

"Why, certainly," said Jenkins nastily. "Where would you like us to put the extra mast?"

"The ship's just a dot," said Carrot. "Why aren't we gaining on them?"

"It's a bigger ship so it has got what we technically call *more sails,*" said Jenkins. "And they're fast hulls on those Klatchian boats. And we've got a full hold—"

He stopped, but it was too late.

"Captain Carrot?" said Vimes.

"Sir?"

"Throw everything overboard," said Vimes.

"Not the crossbows! They cost more than a hundred dollars ea—"

Jenkins stopped. Vimes's expression said, very clearly, that there were a whole lot of things that could be thrown off the boat, and it would be a good idea not to be among them.

"Go and pull some ropes, Mr. Jenkins," he said.

He watched the captain stamp off. A few moments later there was a splash. Vimes looked over the side and saw a crate bob for a moment and then sink. And he felt happy. Thief-taker, Rust had called him. The man had meant it as an insult, but it'd do. Theft was the only crime, whether the loot was gold, innocence, land or life. And for the thief-taker, there was the chase . . . There were several more splashes. Vimes fancied the ship surged forward.

. . . the chase. Because the chase was simpler than the capture.

Once you'd caught someone it got complicated, but the chase was pure and free. Much better than prodding at clues and peering at notebooks. He flees, I chase. Simple.

Vetinari's terrier, eh?

"Bingeley-bingeley beep!" said his pocket.

"Don't tell me," said Vimes. "It's something like 'Five pee em, At Sea,' yes?"

"Er . . . no," said the Dis-organizer. "Says here 'Violent Row With Lord Rust,' Insert Name Here."

"Aren't you supposed to tell me what I'm going to do?" said Vimes, opening the box.

"Er . . . what you *should* be doing," said the demon, looking very worried. "What you *should* be doing. I don't understand it . . . er . . . something seems to be wrong . . .*"*

Angua stopped trying to rub the collar off against a bulkhead. It wasn't working, and the silver pressing against her skin seemed to freeze her and burn her at the same time.

Apart from that—and a silver collar on a werewolf was a fairly major *that*—she'd been treated well. They'd left a plate of food, a *wooden* plate, and she'd let her wolf side eat it while the human side shut its eyes and held its nose. There was a bowl of water, quite fresh by Ankh-Morpork standards. She could see the bottom of the bowl, at least.

It was so hard to *think* in wolf shape. It was like trying to unlock a door while drunk. It was possible, but you had to concentrate every step of the way.

There was a sound.

Her ears pricked up.

Something tapped once or twice under the hull. She hoped it was a reef. That meant . . . land, possibly . . . with any luck she could swim ashore . . .

Something clinked. She'd forgotten about the chain. It was hardly necessary. She felt as weak as a kitten.

There was a rhythmic noise, like something chewing at the wood.

A tiny metal point splintered through the wall just in front of her nose, and rose an inch.

And someone spoke. It sounded far off and distorted, and perhaps only a werewolf would have heard it, but words were happening, somewhere under her paws.

"—can stop pedaling now, Corporal Nobbs."

"I am knackered, sarge. Is there anything to eat?"

"There's some more of that garlic sausage. Or there's the cheese. Or cold beans."

"We're in a tin with no air and we're supposed to eat cheese? I ain't even going to comment on the beans."

"I'm very sorry, gentlemen. Things were rather rushed and I had to take food which would keep."

"It's just that it's getting a bit . . . crowded, if you get my meaning."

"I will pay out the rope as soon as it's dark and we can surface and take on air."

"Just so long as we get rid of the air we've got, that's all I'm saying . . ."

Angua's brows wrinkled as she tried to make sense of this. The voices were familiar. Even muffled as they were, she recognized the tones. The vague feeling that fought its way through the mists of animal intellect was: friends.

The tiny little unchangeable center of her thought: good grief, next thing I'll be licking hands.

She laid her head down near the point again.

"—way to do it, young man. There you go again! Sink ships? I can't imagine how anyone could think of such a thing!"

Names. Some of those voices had . . . names.

Thinking was getting harder. That was the silver at work. But if she stopped, she might forget how to start again.

She stared at the point of metal. The point of *metal* with *sharp* edges.

The tiny human part of her mind raged at the wolf brain, trying to get it to understand what it needed to do.

It was after midnight.

The lookout man knelt on the deck in front of 71-hour Ahmed and trembled.

"I know what I saw, *wali*," he moaned. "And the others saw it too! Something rose up behind the ship and began chasing us! A monster!"

Ahmed looked at the captain, who shrugged. "Who knows what lies on the floor of the sea, *wali?*"

"Its breath!" moaned the seaman. "There was a great roar of breath like the stink of a thousand privies! And then it spoke!"

"Really?" said Ahmed. "This is not usual. What did it say?"

"I did not understand!" The man's face screwed up as he tried to assemble the unfamiliar syllables. "It sounded like . . ." he swallowed, and went on, "*'Ye gods, that was better out than in, sarge!'*"

Ahmed stared at him. "And what did that mean to you?" he said.

"I do not know, *wali!*"

"You have not spent much time in Ankh-Morpork?"

"No, *wali!*"

"Then return to your post."

The man stumbled out.

"We have lost speed, *wali,*" said the captain.

"Perhaps the sea monster is clutching at our keel?"

"It pleases you to joke, lord. But who knows what has been disturbed by the rising of the new land?"

"I shall have to see for myself," said 71-hour Ahmed.

He walked alone to the stern of the ship. Dark waters sucked and splashed and left a phosphorescent glow edging the wake.

He watched for a long time. People bad at watching didn't last long in the desert, where a shadow in the moonlight could be just a shadow or it could be someone anxious to help you on your way to Paradise. The D'regs came across many shadows of the latter persuasion.

D'reg wasn't their name for themselves, although they tended to adopt it now out of pride. The word meant *enemy.* Everyone's. And if anyone else wasn't around, then one another's.

If he concentrated, he might believe that there was a darker shape about a hundred yards behind the ship, very low in the water. Waves were breaking where waves shouldn't be. It looked as though the ship was being followed by a reef.

Well, well . . .

71-hour Ahmed was not *super*stitious. He *was* substitious, which put him in a minority among humans. He didn't believe in the things everyone believed in but which nevertheless weren't true. He believed instead in the things that were true in which no one else believed. There are many such substitions, ranging from "It'll get better if you don't pick at it" all the way up to "Sometimes things just happen."

Currently he was disinclined to believe in sea monsters, especially ones that spoke in the language of Ankh-Morpork, but he did believe that there were a lot of things in the world that he didn't know about.

In the far distance he could see the lights of a ship. It didn't seem to be gaining on them.

This was much more worrying.

In the darkness 71-hour Ahmed reached over his shoulder and grasped the handle of his sword.

Above him, the mainsail creaked in the wind.

Sergeant Colon knew he was facing one of the most dangerous moments in his career.

There was nothing for it. He was out of options.

"Er . . . if I add this A and this O and this I and this D," he said, the sweat pouring down his pink cheeks, "then I can use that V to make 'avoid.' Er . . . and that gets me, er, a . . . what d'you call these blue squares, Len?"

"A 'Three Times Ye Value of Thee Letter' score," said Leonard of Quirm.

"Well done, sergeant," said Lord Vetinari. "I do believe that puts you in the lead."

"Er . . . I do believe it does, sir," squeaked Sergeant Colon.

"*However*, I find that you have left me the use of my U, N and A, B, L, E," the Patrician went on, "which incidentally lands me on this Three Times the Whole Worde square and, I rather suspect, wins me the game."

Sergeant Colon sagged with relief.

"A capital game, Leonard," said Vetinari. "What did you say it was called?"

"I call it the 'Make Words With Letters That Have All Been Mixed Up Game,' my lord."

"Ah. Yes. Obviously. Well done."

"Huh, an' I got three points," mumbled Nobby. "They was perfectly good words that you wouldn't let me have, too."

"I'm sure the gentlemen don't want to know those words," said Colon severely.

"I'd have got ten points for that X."

Leonard looked up. "Strange. We seem to have stopped moving . . ."

He reached up and opened the hatch. Damp night air poured in, and there was the sound of voices, quite close, echoing loudly as voices do when heard across water.

"Heathen Klatchian talk," said Colon. "What are they gabblin' about?"

"'What nephew of a camel cut the rigging?'" said Lord Vetinari, without looking up. "'Not just the ropes, look at this sail— Here, give me a hand . . .'"

"I didn't know you spoke Klatchian, my lord."

"Not a word," said Lord Vetinari.

"But you—"

"I did not," said Vetinari calmly.

"Ah . . . right . . ."

"Where are we, Leonard?"

"Well, er, my star charts are all out of date, of course, but if you would care to wait until the sun rises, and I've invented a device for ascertaining position by reference to the sun, and devised a satisfactorily accurate watch—"

"Where are we *now*, Leonard?"

"Er . . . in the middle of the Circle Sea, I suspect."

"The middle?"

"Pretty close, I should say. Look, if I can measure the wind speed—"

"Then Leshp should be in this vicinity?"

"Oh, yes, I should—"

"Good. Unhitch us from this apparently stricken ship while we still have the cover of darkness and in the morning I wish to see this troublesome land. In the meantime, I suggest that everyone gets some sleep."

Sergeant Colon did not get a lot of sleep. This was partly

because he was woken up several times by sawing and banging coming from the front of the Boat, and partly because water kept dripping on his head, but mainly because the lull in activity was causing him to consider his position.

Sometimes when he woke up he saw the Patrician hunched over Leonard's drawings, a gaunt silhouette in the light of the candle—reading, making notes . . .

He was in the immediate company of a man even the Assassins' Guild was frightened of, another man who would stay up all night in order to invent an alarm clock to wake him up in the morning, and a man who had never knowingly changed his underwear.

And he was at sea.

He tried to look on the bright side. What was the main reason why he hated boats? The fact that they sank, right? But this one had the sinking *built in* right from the start. And you didn't have to watch the waves going *up* and *down,* because they were already above you.

All this was logical. It just wasn't very comforting.

When he awoke at one point there were faint voices coming from the other end of the vessel.

"—don't quite understand, my lord. Why them?"

"They do what they're told, they tend to believe the last thing they heard, they're not bright enough to ask questions, and they have that certain unshakeable loyalty available to those unencumbered by too much intelligence."

"I suppose so, my lord."

"Such men are valuable, believe me."

Sergeant Colon turned over and tried to make himself comfortable. Glad I'm not like *those* poor bastards, he thought as he drifted off to sleep on the bosom of the deep. I'm a man with special qualities.

Vimes shook his head. The stern light of the Klatchian ship was barely visible in the gloom.

"Are we gaining on them?" he said.

Captain Jenkins nodded. "We might be. There's a lot of sea between us."

"And has *all* excess weight been thrown overboard?"

"Yes! What do you want me to do, shave my beard off?"

Carrot's face appeared over the edge of the hold. "All the lads are bedded down, sir."

"Right."

"I'll turn in for a few hours too, sir, if it's all right with you."

"Sorry, captain?"

"I'll get my head down, sir."

"But . . . but—" Vimes waved vaguely at the darkening horizon, "we're in hot pursuit of your girlfriend! Among other things," he added.

"Yes, sir."

"So aren't you . . . you mean you can . . . you want to . . . captain, you intend to go and have *a bit of a nap?*"

"To be fresh for when we catch up with them. Yes, sir. If I spend the whole night staring out there worrying then I'll probably be a bit useless when we catch up with them, sir."

It made sense. It really *did* make sense. Of *course* it made sense. Vimes could see the sense all over it. Carrot had actually sat down and thought *sensibly* about things.

"You'll be able to *get* to sleep, will you?" he said weakly.

"Oh, yes. I owe it to Angua."

"Oh. Well . . . goodnight, then."

Carrot disappeared into the hold again.

"Good heavens," said Jenkins. "Is he real?"

"Yes," said Vimes.

"I mean . . . would you go and bang your ear if we was chasing *your* lady in that ship?"

Vimes said nothing.

Jenkins sniggered. "Mind you, if it was Lady Sybil, she'd be a bit lower on the waterline—"

"You just watch the . . . the sea. Don't run into any damn whales or anything," said Vimes, and strode up to the sharp end.

Carrot, he thought. If you didn't know him, you wouldn't believe it . . .

"They're slowing, Mr. Vimes!" Jenkins called out.

"What?"

"I reckon they're slowing down, I said!"

"Good."

"So what're you going to do when we catch them?"

"Er . . ." Vimes hadn't given this a lot of thought. But he recalled a very bad woodcut he'd once seen in a book about pirates.

"We'll swing across on to them with our cutlasses in our teeth?" he said.

"Really?" said Jenkins. "That's good. I haven't seen that done in years. Only ever seen it done once, in fact."

"Oh, yes?"

"Yes, this lad'd seen the idea in a book and he swung across into the other ship's rigging with his cutlass clenched, as you say, between his teeth."

"Yes?"

"Topless Harry, we wrote on his coffin."

"Oh."

"I don't know if you've ever seen a soft-boiled egg after you've picked up your knife and sli—"

"All right, I see the point. What do you suggest?"

"Grapnels. You can't beat grapnels. Catch 'em on the other ship and just pull 'em toward you."

"And you've got grapnels?"

"Oh, yes. Saw some only today, in fact."

"Good. Then—"

"As I recall," Jenkins went on relentlessly, "it was when your Sergeant Detritus was chucking stuff over the side and he said, 'What shall we do with dese bendy, hooky things, sir?' and someone, can't recall his name just at this minute, said, 'They're dead weight, throw them over.'"

"Why didn't you say something?"

"Oh, well, I didn't like to," said Jenkins. "You were doing so well."

"Don't mess me about, captain. Otherwise I'll clap you in irons."

"No, you ain't going to do that, and I'll tell you why. First, 'cos when Captain Carrot said, 'These chains, sir, what shall I do with them?' you said—"

"Now, you listen to—"

"—and, second, I don't reckon you know anything about

ships, oh deary me. We don't clap people in irons, we put them in chains. Do you know how to splice the mainbrace? 'Cos I don't. All that yohoho stuff's for landlubbers, or it would be if we ever used words like landlubber. Do you know the difference between port and starboard? I don't. I've never even drunk starboard. Shiver my timber!"

"Isn't it 'shiver my timbers'?"

"I've been ill." Captain Jenkins spun the wheel. "Also, this is a frisky wind and me and my crew know how to pull the strings that make the big square canvas things work properly. If your men tried it you'd soon find out how far it is to land."

"How far is it to land?"

"About thirty fathoms, hereabouts."

The light was noticeably nearer.

"Bingeley-bingeley beep!"

"Good grief, what *now?*" said Vimes.

"Eight pee em. Er . . . Narrowly Escape Assassination by Klatchian Spy?"

Vimes went cold. "Where?" he said, looking around wildly.

"Corner of Brewer Street and Broadway," said the little sing-song voice.

"But I'm not there!"

"What's the point of having appointments, then? What's the point of my making an effort? You *told* me you wanted to know what you *ought* to—"

"Listen, you don't have an appointment for being assassinated!"

The demon went silent for a moment, and then said:

"You mean it should be on your To Do list?" Its voice was trembling.

"You mean like: 'To Do: Die'?"

"Look, it's no good taking it out on me just because you're not on the right time line!"

"What the hell does that mean?"

"Aha, I *knew* you didn't read the manual! Chapter xvii-2(c) makes it very clear that sticking to one reality is vitally important, otherwise the Uncertainty Principle says—"

"Forget I asked, all right?"

Vimes glared at Jenkins and at the distant ship.

"We'll do this my way, wherever the hell we are," he said. He strode to the hold and pulled aside a hatchway. "Detritus?"

The Klatchian sailors struggled with the canvas while their captain screamed at them.

71-hour Ahmed didn't scream. He just stood with his sword in his hand, watching.

The captain hurried over to him, trembling with fear and holding a length of rope.

"See, *wali?*" he said. "Someone cut it!"

"Who would do that?" said 71-hour Ahmed quietly.

"I do not know, but when I find him—"

"The dogs are almost on us," said Ahmed. "You and your men will work faster."

"Who could have done such a thing?" said the captain. "You were here, how could they—?"

His gaze flickered from the cut rope to the sword.

"Was there something you wished to say?" said Ahmed.

The captain hadn't got where he was by being stupid. He spun round.

"Get that sail up right now, you festering sons of bitches!" he screamed.

"Good," said 71-hour Ahmed.

Detritus's crossbow was originally a three-man siege weapon, but he had removed the windlass as an unnecessary encumbrance. He cocked it by hand. Usually the mere sight of the troll pulling the string back with one finger was enough to make the strong-willed surrender.

He looked doubtfully at the distant light.

"It a million-to-one chance," he said. "Got to be closer'n this."

"Just hit it below the waterline so they can't cut the rope," said Vimes.

"Right. Right."

"What's the problem, sergeant?"

"We headin' for Klatch, right?"

"Well, in that direction, yes."

"Only . . . I'm gonna be really stoopid in Klatch, 'cos a der heat, right?"

"I hope we're going to stop them before we get there, Detritus."

"I ain't keen on bein' stoopid. I know people say, that troll Detritus, he ficker than a, than a—"

"—brick sandwich—" said Vimes, staring at the light.

"Right. Only I hearin' it get really, really *hot* in der desert . . ."

The troll looked so mournful that Vimes felt moved to give him a cheerful slap on the back.

"Then let's stop them now, eh?" he said, shaking his hand hurriedly to stop the stinging.

The other ship was so close they could see the sailors working feverishly on the deck. The mainsail billowed in the lamplight.

Detritus raised the bow.

A ball of blue-green light glowed on the tip of the arrow. The troll stared at it.

Then green fire ran down the masts and, when it hit the deck, burst into dozens of green balls that rolled, cracking and spitting, over the planks.

"Dey're usin' magic?" said Detritus. A green flame spluttered over his helmet.

"What is this, Jenkins?" said Vimes.

"It ain't magic, it's *worse'n* magic," said the captain, hurrying forward. "All right, lads, get those sails down right now!"

"You leave them where they are!" shouted Vimes.

"You know what this *is?*"

"It dun't even feel warm," said Detritus, poking the flame on the crossbow.

"Don't touch it! Don't *touch* it! That's St. Ungulant's Fire, that is! It means we're going to die in a dreadful storm!"

Vimes looked up. Clouds were racing across— No, they were *pouring into* the sky in great twisting billows, like ink streaming into water. Blue light flashed somewhere inside them. The ship lurched.

"Look, we got to lose some sail!" shouted Jenkins. "That's the only way—"

"No one touches anything!" shouted Vimes. Green fire skimmed along the tops of the waves now. "Detritus, arrest any man who touches anything!"

"Right."

"We want to go fast, after all," Vimes said, above the hissing and the distant crackle of thunder.

Jenkins gawped at him as the ship lunged beneath them.

"You're mad! Have you any idea what happens to a ship that tries to— You haven't got *any* idea, have you? This ain't normal weather! You have to ride it out careful! You can't try to run ahead of it!"

Something slippery landed on Detritus's head and bounced on to the deck, where it tried to slither away.

"And now it's raining fish!" Jenkins moaned.

The clouds formed a yellow haze, lit almost constantly by the lightning. And it was warm. That was the strangest thing. The wind howled like a sack full of cats and the waves were turning into walls on either side of the ship, but the air felt like an oven.

"Look, even the Klatchians are reducing sail!" shouted Jenkins, in a shower of shrimp.

"Good. We'll catch them up."

"Mad! *Ouch!*"

Something hard rebounded from his hat, hit the rail and rolled to a stop by Vimes's feet.

It was a brass knob.

"Oh, *no,*" moaned Jenkins, putting his arms over his head. "Now it's bloody bedsteads again!"

The captain of the Klatchian ship was not an argumentative man when he was anywhere near 71-hour Ahmed. He just looked at the straining sails and calculated his chances of Paradise.

"Perhaps the dog who cut the sail loose did us a favor!" he shouted, above the roar of the wind.

Ahmed said nothing. He kept looking back. The occasional burst of electric storm light showed the ship behind, aflame with green light.

Then he looked at the cold fire streaming behind their own masts.

"Can you see that light on the edge of the flames?" he said.

"My lord?"

"Can you, man?"

"Er . . . no . . ."

"Of course you can't! But can you see where the light isn't?"

The captain stared at him and then looked up again in terrified obedience. And there *was* somewhere where the light wasn't. As the fizzing green tongues waved in the wind they seemed to be edged with . . . blackness, perhaps, or a moving hole in space.

"That's octarine!" shouted Ahmed, as another wave sloshed over the deck. "Only wizards can see it! There's magic in these storms! That's why the weather is so bad!"

The ship screamed in every joint as it hit the waves again.

"We're coming right out of the water!" wept Jenkins. "We're just going from crest to crest!"

"Good! It won't be so bumpy!" shouted Vimes. "We should pick up speed again now we've got those bedsteads over the side! Does it often rain bedsteads out here?"

"What do *you* think?"

"I'm not a nautical man!"

"No, rains of bedsteads are *not* an everyday occurrence! Nor are coal scuttles!" Jenkins added, as something black crashed off a rail and over the side. "We just get the normal stuff, you know! Rain! Snow! Sleet! Fish!"

Another squall blew across the bounding boat and the deck was suddenly covered with flashing silver.

"Back to fish!" shouted Vimes. "That's better, surely?"

"No! It's worse!"

"Why!"

Jenkins held up a tin.

"These are sardines!"

The ship thumped into another wave, groaned, and took flight again.

The cold green fire was everywhere. Every nail of the deck sprouted its flame, every rope and ladder had its green outline.

And the feeling crept over Vimes that it was holding the ship

185

together. He wasn't at all sure that it was just light. It moved too purposefully. It crackled, but it didn't sting. It looked as though it was having fun—

The ship landed. Water washed over Vimes.

"Captain Jenkins!"

"Yes?"

"Why're we playing with this wheel? It's not as if the rudder's in the water!"

They let go. The spokes blurred for a moment, and then stopped as the fire wrapped itself around them.

Then it rained cake.

The Watch had tried to make themselves comfortable in the hold, but there were difficulties. There wasn't any area of floor which at some point in every ten seconds wasn't an area of wall.

Nevertheless, someone was snoring.

"How can anyone sleep in *this?*" said Reg Shoe.

"Captain Carrot can," said Cheery. She was hacking at something with her ax.

Carrot had wedged himself into a corner. Occasionally he mumbled something, and shifted position.

"Like a baby. Beats me how he's managing it," said Reg Shoe. "Of course, any minute this thing is going to fall apart."

"Yes, but dat shouldn't worry you, should it?" said Detritus. "On account of you bein' dead already?"

"So? I end up at the bottom of the sea knee-deep in whale droppings? And it'll be a long walk home in the dark. Not to mention the problems if a shark tries to eat me."

"I shall fear not. According to the Testament of Mezerek, the fisherman Nonpo spent four days in the belly of a giant fish," said Constable Visit.

The thunder seemed particularly loud in the silence.

"Washpot, are we talking miracles here?" said Reg eventually. "Or just a very slow digestive process?"

"You would be better employed considering the state of your immortal soul than making jokes," said Constable Visit severely.

"It's the state of my immortal body that's worrying me," said Reg.

"I have a leaflet here which will bring you considerable—" Visit began.

"Washpot, is it big enough to be folded into a boat that'll save us all?"

Constable Visit pounced on the opening. "Aha, yes, metaphorically it *is*—"

"Hasn't this ship *got* a lifeboat?" said Cheery hurriedly. "I'm sure I saw one when we came on."

"Yeah . . . lifeboat," said Detritus.

"Anyone want a sardine?" said Cheery. "I've managed to get a tin open."

"Lifeboat," Detritus repeated. He sounded like someone exploring an unpleasant truth. "Like . . . a big, heavy thing which would've slowed us down . . . ?"

"Yes, I saw it, I know I did," said Reg.

"Yeah . . . dere was one," said Detritus. "Dat was a lifeboat, was it?"

"At the very least we ought to get somewhere sheltered and drop the anchor."

"Yeah . . . anchor . . ." mused Detritus. "Dat's a big thing kinda hooks on, right?"

"Of course."

"Kinda heavy thing?"

"Obviously!"

"Right. An' . . . er . . . if it was dropped a long time ago, on accounta bein' heavy, dat wouldn't do us much good now?"

"Hardly." Reg Shoe glared through the hatchway. The sky was a dirty yellow blanket, criss-crossed with fire. Thunder boomed continuously.

"I wonder how far the barometer's sunk?" he said.

"All der way," said Detritus gloomily. "Trust me on dis."

It was in the nature of a D'reg to open doors carefully. There was generally an enemy on the other side. Sooner or later.

He saw the collar lying on the floor, right by a little fountain of water trickling from the hull, and swore under his breath.

Ahmed waited just a moment, and then pushed the door back quickly. It rattled against the wall.

"I don't intend to harm you," he said to the gloom of the bilges. "If that was my intention, by now you'd—"

She wished she'd used the wolf. There would have been no problem with the wolf. That *was* the problem. She'd easily win, but then she'd be nervy and frightened. A human could stay on top of that. A wolf might not. She'd do the wrong things, panicky things, *animal* things.

She pushed him hard as she dropped down from above the door, somersaulted backward, slammed the door and turned the key.

The sword came through the planking like a hot knife through runny lard.

There was a gasp beside her. She spun round and saw two men holding a net. They would have thrown it over the wolf. What they hadn't been expecting was a naked woman. The sudden appearance of a naked woman always causes a rethink of anyone's immediate plans.

She kicked them both hard and ran in the opposite direction, opened the first door at random and slammed it behind her.

It was the cabin with the dogs in it. They sprang to their feet, opened their mouths—and slunk down again. A werewolf can have considerable power over other animals, whatever shape she's in, although it is largely the power to make them cringe and try to look inedible.

She hurried past them and pulled at one of the hangings over the bunk.

The man in the bunk opened his eyes. He was a Klatchian, but pale with weakness and pain. There were dark rings under his eyes.

"Ah," he said, "it would appear that I have died and gone to Paradise. Are you a *houri?*"

"I don't have to take that kind of language, thank you," said Angua, ripping the silk in two with a practiced hand.

She was aware that she had a slight advantage over male werewolves in that naked women caused fewer complaints, although the downside was that they got some pressing invitations. Some kind of covering was essential, for modesty and the prevention of inconvenient bouncing, which was why fashioning impromptu clothes out of anything to hand was a lesser-known werewolf skill.

Angua stopped. Of course, to the unpracticed eye all Klatchians looked alike, but then to a werewolf all humans looked alike: they looked appetizing. She'd learned to discern.

"Are you Prince Khufurah?"

"I am. And you are . . . ?"

The door was kicked open. Angua leapt toward the window and flung aside the bar restraining the shutters. Water funneled into the cabin, drenching her, but she managed to scramble up and out.

"Just passing through?" the Prince murmured.

71-hour Ahmed strode to the window and looked out. Green-blue waves edged with fire fought outside as the ship heaved. No one could stay afloat in a sea like that.

He turned and looked along the hull to where Angua was clinging to a trailing line.

She saw him wink at her. Then he turned away and she heard him say, "She must have drowned. Back to your posts!"

Presently, up on the deck, a hatch closed.

The sun rose in a cloudless sky.

A watcher, if such had been out here, would have noticed a slight difference in the way the swells were moving on this tiny patch of sea.

They might even have wondered about the piece of bent piping which turned with a faint squeaking noise.

Had they been able to place an ear to it, they would have heard the following:

"—idea while I was dozing off. Piece of pipe, two angled mirrors—the solution to all our steering and air problems!"

"Fascinating. A Seeing-Things-Pipe-You-Can-Breathe-Down."

"My goodness, how did you know it was called that, my lord?"

"A lucky guess."

"'ere, someone's re-designed my pedaling seat, it's *comfortable—*"

"Ah, yes, corporal, I took some measurements while you were asleep and rebuilt it for a better anatomical configu—"

"You took measurements?"

"Oh, yes, I—"

"What, of my . . . saddlery regions?"

"Oh, please don't be concerned, anatomy is something of a passion with me—"

"Is it? Is it? Well, you can stop being passionate about mine for a start—"

"Here, I can see an island of some sort!"

The pipe squeaked around.

"Ah, Leshp. And I see people. To your pedals, gentlemen. Let us explore the ocean's bottom . . ."

"I expect we shall, with *him* steering—"

"Shut up, Nobby."

The pipe slid down into the waves. There was a little flurry of bubbles and a damp argument about whose job it should have been to put the cork in, and then the patch of sea that had been empty was, somehow, a little bit emptier still.

There weren't any fish.

At a time like this Solid Jackson would have even been prepared to eat Curious Squid.

But the sea was empty. And it smelled wrong. It fizzed gently. Solid could see little bubbles breaking on the surface, which burst with a smell of sulfur and rotting eggs. He guessed that the rise of the land must have stirred up a lot of mud. It was bad enough at the bottom of a pond, all those frogs and bugs and things, and this was the sea—

He tried hard to reverse that train of thought, but it kept on rising from the depths like a . . . like a . . .

Why were there no fish? Oh, there'd been the storm last night, but generally you got better fishing in these parts after a storm because it . . . stirred . . . up . . .

The raft rocked.

He was beginning to think it might be a good idea to go home, but that'd mean leaving the land to the Klatchians, and that'd happen over his dead body.

The treacherous internal voice said: Funnily enough, they never found Mr. Hong's body. Not most of the important bits, anyway.

"I think, think, I think we'll be getting back now," he said to his son.

"Oh, Dad," said Les. "Another dinner of limpets and seaweed?"

"Nothing wrong with seaweed," said Jackson. "It's full of nourishing . . . seaweed. 's got iron in it. Good for you, iron."

"Why don't we boil an anchor, then?"

"None of your lip, son."

"The Klatchians have got bread," said Les. "They brought flour with them. And they've got firewood." This was a sore point with Jackson. Efforts to make seaweed combust had not been successful.

"Yeah, but you wouldn't like their bread," said Jackson. "It's all flat and got no proper crust—"

A breeze blew the scent of baking over the water. It carried a hint of spices.

"They're baking bread! On *our* property!"

"Well, they say it's *their*—"

Jackson grabbed the piece of broken plank he used as an oar and began to scull furiously toward the shore. The fact that this only made the raft go round in circles added to his fury.

"They bloody move in right next to us and all we get is the stink of foreign food—"

"Why's your mouth watering, Dad?"

"And how come they've got wood, may I ask?"

"I think the current takes the driftwood to their side of the island, Dad—"

"See? They're stealing our driftwood! Our damn driftwood! Hah! Well, we'll—"

"But I thought we agreed that the bit over *there* was theirs, and—"

Jackson had finally remembered how to propel a raft with one oar.

"That wasn't an agreement," he said, creating foam as the oar thrashed back and forth, "that was just an . . . an arrangement.

It's not as if they *created* the driftwood. It just turned up. Accident of geography. It is a natural resource, right? It don't *belong* to anyone—"

The raft hit something which made a metallic sound. But they were still a hundred yards from the rocks.

Something else, long and bent at the end, rose up with a creaking noise. It twisted around until it pointed at Jackson.

"Excuse me," it said, in a tinny yet polite voice, "but this is Leshp, isn't it?"

Jackson made a sound in his throat.

"Only," the thing went on, "the water's a little cloudy and I thought we might have been going the wrong way for the last twenty minutes."

"Leshp!" squeaked Jackson, in an unnaturally high-pitched voice.

"Ah, good. Thank you so much. Good day to you."

The appendage sank slowly into the sea again. The last sounds from it, erupting on the surface in a cloud of bubbles, were, ". . . don't forget to put the cork in— *You've forgot to put the cor—*"

The bubbles stopped.

After a while Les said, "Dad, what was—?"

"It wasn't anything!" snapped his father. "That sort of thing doesn't happen!"

The raft shot forward. You could have waterski'd behind it.

Another important thing about the Boat, thought Sergeant Colon gloomily as they slipped back into a blue twilight, was that you couldn't bale out the bilges. It *was* the bilges.

He was pedaling with his feet in water and he was suffering simultaneously from claustrophobia and agoraphobia. He was afraid of everything in *here* and everything out *there* at the same time. Plus, there were unpleasantnesses out there, moving past as the Boat drifted down the wall of rock. Feelers waved. There were claws. *Things* scuttled into the waving weeds. Giant clams watched Sergeant Colon with their lips.

The Boat creaked.

"Sarge," said Nobby, as they looked out at the wonders of the deep.

"Yes, Nobby?"

"You know they say every tiny part of your body is replaced every seven years?"

"A well-known fact," said Sergeant Colon.

"Right. So . . . I've got a tattoo on my arm, right? Had it done eight years ago. So . . . how come it's still there?"

Giant seaweeds winnowed the gloom.

"Interesting point," quavered Colon. "Er . . ."

"I mean, okay, new tiny bits of skin float in, but that means it ought to be all new and pink by now."

A fish with a nose like a saw swam past.

In the middle of all his other fears, Sergeant Colon tried to think fast.

"What happens," he said, "is that all the blue skin bits are replaced by other blue skin bits. Off'f other people's tattoos."

"So . . . I've got other people's tattoos now?"

"Er . . . yes."

"Amazing. 'cos it still looks like mine. 's got the crossed daggers and 'WUM.'"

"Wum?"

"It was gonna be 'Mum' but I passed out and Needle Ned didn't notice I was upside down."

"I should've thought he'd notice that . . ."

"He was pissed, too. C'mon, sarge, you know it's not a proper tattoo unless no one can remember how it got there."

Leonard and the Patrician were staring out at the submarine landscape.

"What're they looking for?" said Colon.

"Leonard keeps talking about hieroglyphs," said Nobby. "What're they, sarge?"

Colon hesitated, but not for long. "A type of mollusc, corporal."

"Cor, you know everything, sarge," said Nobby admiringly. "That's what hieroglyphs are, is it? So, if we go any deeper, they'll be loweroglyphs?"

There was something slightly off-putting about Nobby's grin. Sergeant Colon decided to go for broke.

"Don't be daft, Nobby. 'Loweroglyphs if you go lower . . .' Oh, deary me."

"Sorry, sarge."

"Everyone knows you don't get loweroglyphs in these waters."

A couple of Curious Squid peered at them, curiously.

Jenkins's ship was a floating wreck.

Several sails were in tatters. Rigging and other string that Vimes refused to learn the nautical names for covered the deck and trailed in the water.

Such sail as remained was moving them along in the brisk breeze.

Atop the mast the lookout cupped his hands around his mouth and leaned down.

"Land ahoy!"

"Even I can see that," said Vimes. "Why does he have to shout?"

"It's lucky," said Jenkins. He squinted into the haze. "But your friend ain't heading for Gebra. Wonder where he's going?"

Vimes stared at the pale yellow mass on the horizon, and then up at Carrot.

"We'll get her back, don't worry," he said.

"I wasn't actually worrying, sir. Although I am very concerned," said Carrot.

"Er . . . right . . ." Vimes waved his arms helplessly. "Er . . . everyone fit and well? The men in good heart, are they?"

"It would help morale no end if you were to say a few words, sir."

The monstrous regiment of watchmen had lined up on the deck, blinking in the sunshine. Oh, dear. Round up the unusual suspects. One dwarf, one human who was brought up as a dwarf and thinks like a manual of etiquette, one zombie, one troll, me and, oh, no, one religious fanatic—

Constable Visit saluted. "Permission to speak, sir."

"Go ahead," mumbled Vimes.

"I'm pleased to tell you, sir, that our mission is clearly divinely approved of, sir. I refer to the rain of sardines which sustained us in our extremity, sir."

"We were a little hungry, I wouldn't say we were in extremi—"

"With respect, sir," said Constable Visit firmly, "the pattern is firmly established, sir. Yes, indeed. The Sykoolites when being pursued in the wilderness by the forces of Offlerian Mitolites, sir, were sustained by a rain of celestial biscuits, sir. Chocolate ones, sir."

"Perfectly normal phenomenon," muttered Constable Shoe. "Probably swept up by the wind passing a baker's shop—"

Visit glared at him, and went on: "And the Murmurians, when driven into the mountains by the tribes of Miskmik, would not have survived but for a magical rain of elephants, sir—"

"Elephants?"

"Well, one elephant, sir," Visit conceded. "But it splashed."

"Perfectly normal phenomenon," said Constable Shoe. "Probably an elephant was picked up by a freak—"

"*And when they were thirsty* in the desert, sir, the Four Tribes of Khanli were succored by a sudden and supernatural rain of rain, sir."

"A rain of rain?" said Vimes, almost mesmerized by Visit's absolute conviction.

"Perfectly normal phenomenon," sneered Reg Shoe. "Probably water was evaporated from the ocean, was blown through the sky, condensed around nuclei when it ran into cold air, and precipitated . . ." He stopped, and continued irritably, "Anyway, I don't believe it."

"So . . . which particular deity is on our case?" said Vimes, hopefully.

"I shall definitely inform you as soon as I have ascertained this, sir."

"Er . . . very good, constable."

Vimes took a step back. "I don't pretend this is going to be easy, men," he said. "But our mission is to catch up with Angua and this bastard Ahmed and shake the truth out of him. Unfortunately, this means we will be following him through his own country, with which we are at war. This is bound to put a few barriers in our way. But we should not let the prospect of being tortured to death dismay us, eh?"

"Fortune favors the brave, sir," said Carrot cheerfully.

"Good. Good. Pleased to hear it, captain. What is her position

195

vis à vis heavily armed, well prepared and excessively manned armies?"

"Oh, no one's ever heard of Fortune favoring them, sir."

"According to General Tacticus, it's because they favor themselves," said Vimes. He opened the battered book. Bits of paper and string indicated his many bookmarks. "In fact, men, the general has this to say about ensuring against defeat when outnumbered, out-weaponed and out-positioned. It is . . ." he turned the page, "*'Don't Have a Battle.'*"

"Sounds like a clever man," said Jenkins. He pointed to the yellow horizon.

"See all that stuff in the air?" he said. "What do you think *that* is?"

"Mist?" said Vimes.

"Hah, yes. *Klatchian* mist! It's a sandstorm! The sand blows about all the time. Vicious stuff. If you want to sharpen your sword, just hold it up in the air."

"Oh."

"And it's just as well because otherwise you'd see Mount Gebra. And below it is what they call the Fist of Gebra. It's a town but there's a bloody great fort, walls thirty feet thick. 's like a big city all by itself. 's got room inside for thousands of armed men, war elephants, battle camels, everything. And if you saw *that*, you'd want me to turn around right now. What's your famous general got to say about it, eh?"

"I think I saw *something* . . ." said Vimes. He flicked to another page. "Ah, yes, he says, *'After the first battle of Sto Lat, I formulated a policy which has stood me in good stead in other battles. It is this: if the enemy has an impregnable stronghold, see he stays there.'*"

"That's a *lot* of help," said Jenkins.

Vimes slipped the book into a pocket.

"So, Constable Visit, there's a god on our side, is there?"

"Certainly, sir."

"But probably also a god on *their* side as well?"

"Very likely, sir. There's a god on every side."

"Let's hope they balance out, then."

*   *   *

The Klatchian ship's boat hit the water with the gentlest of splashes. This was because 71-hour Ahmed was standing by the winches with his sword at the ready, which had the effect of making the men lowering the boat take some trouble over their task.

"When we are away you may take the ship into Gebra," he said to the captain.

The captain trembled. "What shall I tell them, *wali?*"

"Tell them the truth . . . eventually. The commander of the garrison is a man of no breeding and will torture you a little bit. Save up the truth until you need it. That will make him happy. It will help you to say that I forced you."

"Oh, I will. I *will* . . . tell that lie," the captain added quickly.

Ahmed nodded, slid down the rope into the boat and set it adrift.

The crew watched him row through the surf.

This wasn't a nice beach. It was a wrecking coast. Ribcages of broken ships crumbled into the sand. Bones and driftwood and bleached white seaweed mounded along the high tide line. And beyond, the dunes of the real desert rose. Even down here sand stung the eyes and gritted the teeth.

"There's sudden death on that beach," said the first mate, looking over the rail and trying to blink his eyes clear.

"Yes," said the captain. "He's just got out of the boat."

The figure on the beach pulled the other, recumbent figure out of the boat and dragged him out of reach of the waves. The mate raised his bow.

"I could kill him from here, master. Just say the word."

"How sure are you? Because you'd better be *really* sure. First, if you miss him you're dead and, second, if you hit him, you're *still* dead. Look up there."

On the high distant dunes, dark against the sand-filled sky, there were mounted figures. The mate dropped his bow.

"How did they know we were here?"

"Oh, they watch the sea," said the captain. "D'regs like a good shipwreck as much as anyone else. More, in fact. A lot more."

As they turned away from the rail, something leapt from the hull and entered the water with barely a splash.

* * *

Detritus tried to lurk in the shade, but there was not a lot of it about. The heat came off the high desert ahead of them like a blowtorch.

"I'm gonna get fick," he muttered.

There was a shout from the lookout.

"He says someone's climbing the dunes," said Carrot. "Carrying someone else, he says."

"Er . . . female?"

"Look, sir, I know Angua. She's not the useless type. She doesn't stand there and scream helplessly. She makes other people do that."

"Well . . . if you're sure . . ." Vimes turned to Jenkins. "Don't bother to chase the ship, captain. Just keep heading for the shore."

"I don't work like that, mister. For one thing, that's a damn difficult shore, the wind's always against you, and there's some very nasty currents. Many an incautious sailorman has left his bones to bleach on those sands. No, we'll stand out a little way and you can lower the— well, if we had a boat anymore, you could lower it . . . and we'll drop the anchor, oh, no, tell a lie, it turned out to be too heavy, didn't it—"

"You just keep straight on," said Vimes.

"We'll all be killed."

"Think of it as the lesser of two evils."

"What's the other one?"

Vimes drew his sword.

"Me."

The Boat squeaked through the mysterious depths of the ocean. Leonard spent a lot of time looking out of the tiny windows, particularly interested in pieces of seaweed which, to Sergeant Colon, looked like pieces of seaweed.

"Do you note the fine strands of Dropley's Etoliated Bladderwrack?" said Leonard. "That's the brown stuff. A marvelous growth which, of course, you will see as significant."

"Could we just assume for the moment that I have neglected my seaweed studies in recent years?" said the Patrician.

"Really? Oh, the loss is entirely yours, I assure you. The point *is,* of course, that the Etoliated Bladderwrack is never usually found growing above thirty fathoms, and it's only ten here."

"Ah." The Patrician flicked through a stack of Leonard's drawings. "And the hieroglyphs—an alphabet of signs and colors. Colors as a language . . . what a fascinating idea . . ."

"An *emotional* intensifier," said Leonard. "But of course we ourselves use something like it. Red for danger and so on. I never did succeed in translating it, though."

"Colors as a language . . ." murmured Lord Vetinari.

Sergeant Colon cleared his throat. "I know something about seaweed, sir."

"Yes, sergeant?"

"Yessir! If it's wet, sir, it means it's going to rain."

"Well done, sergeant," said Lord Vetinari, without turning his head. "I think it is quite possible that I will never forget you said that."

Sergeant Colon beamed. He had Made A Contribution.

Nobby nudged him. "What're we doing down here, sarge? I mean, what's it all about? Poking around, looking at weird marks on the rocks, going in and out of caves . . . and the smell . . . well . . ."

"It's not me," said Sergeant Colon.

"Smells like . . . sulfur . . ."

Little bubbles streamed past the window.

"It stunk up on the surface, too," Nobby went on.

"Nearly finished, gentlemen," said Lord Vetinari, putting the papers aside. "One last little venture and then we can surface. Very well, Leonard . . . take us *underneath.*"

"Er . . . aren't we underneath already, sir?" said Colon.

"Only underneath the sea, sergeant."

"Ah. Right." Colon gave this due consideration. "Is there anything else to be under, then, sir?"

"Yes, sergeant. Now we're going under the land."

* * *

The beach was a lot closer now. The watchmen couldn't help noticing that the sailors were all hurrying to the blunt end of the ship and hanging on to any small, lightweight and above all, buoyant objects they could find.

"This seems close enough," said Vimes. "Right. Stop here."

"Stop here? How?"

"Don't ask me, I'm no sailor. Aren't there some sort of brakes?"

Jenkins stared at him. "You— you landlubber!"

"I thought you never used the word!"

"I never met one like you before! You even think we call the bows the sharp en—"

It was, the crew agreed later, one of the strangest landings in the history of bad seamanship. The shelving of the beach must have been right and the tide as well, because the ship did not so much hit the beach as sail up it, rising out of the water as the keel de-barnacled itself on the sand. Finally the forces of wind, water, impetus and friction all met at the point marked "fall over slowly."

It did so, earning the title of "world's most laughable ship-wreck."

"Well, that might have been worse," said Vimes, when the splintering noises had died away.

He eased himself out of a tangle of canvas and adjusted his helmet with as much aplomb as he could muster.

He heard a groan from the lopsided hold.

"Is dat you, Cheery?"

"Yes, Detritus."

"Is dis me?"

"No!"

"Sorry."

Carrot eased his way down the sloping deck and jumped onto the damp sand. He saluted.

"All present and lightly bruised, sir. Shall we establish a beachhead?"

"A what?"

"We have to dig in, sir."

Vimes looked both ways along the beach, if such a sunny-sounding word could be applied to the forsaken strand. It was really just a hem to the land. Nothing stirred except the heat haze and, in the distance, one or two carrion birds.

"What for?" he said.

"Establish a defensible position. It's just one of those things soldiers do, sir."

Vimes glanced at the birds. They were approaching with a kind of sidling sideways hop, ready to move in just as soon as anyone had been dead for a few days. Then he flicked through *Tacticus* until the word "beachhead" caught his eye.

"It says here 'If you want your men to spend much time wielding a shovel, encourage them to become farmers,'" he said. "So I think we'll press on. He can't have got very far. We'll be back soon."

Jenkins waded out of the surf. He didn't look angry. He was a man who had passed through the fires of anger and was now in some strange peaceful bay beyond them. He pointed a quivering finger at his stricken ship and said "Muh . . . ?"

"Pretty good shape, all things considered," said Vimes.

"Muh?"

"I'm sure you and your salty sailors will be able to float it again."

"Muh . . ."

Jenkins and his wading crew watched the regiment as it slithered and complained its way up the side of the dune. Eventually the crew went into a huddle and drew lots and the cook, who was always unlucky in games of chance, approached the captain.

"Never mind, captain," he said, "we can probably find some decent balks of timber in all this driftwood, and a few days' work with block and tackle should—"

"Muh."

"Only . . . we'd better get started 'cos he said they won't be long . . ."

"They won't be back!" said the captain. "The water they've got won't last a day up there! They haven't got the right gear! And once they're out of sight of the sea they'll get lost!"

"Good!"

*   *   *

It took half an hour to get to the top of the dune. The sand had been stamped down but, even as Vimes watched, the wind caught the particles and nibbled away at the prints.

"Camel tracks," said Vimes. "Well, camels don't go all that fast. Let's—"

"I think Detritus is having real trouble, sir," said Carrot.

The troll was standing with his knuckles on the ground. The motor of his cooling helmet sounded harsh for a moment in the dry air, and then stopped as the sand got into the mechanism.

"Feelin' fick," he muttered. "My brain hurts."

"Quick, hold your shield over his head," said Vimes. "Give him some shade!"

"He's never going to make it, sir," said Carrot. "Let's send him back down to the boat."

"We need him! Quick, Cheery, fan him with your ax!"

At which point, the sand stood up and drew a hundred swords.

"Bingeley-bingeley beep!" said a cheerful if somewhat muffled voice. "Eleven eh em, Get Haircut . . . er . . . that's right . . . isn't it?"

It wasn't large, but slabs of collapsing building had smashed together in such a way that they made a cistern that the rain had filled half full.

Solid Jackson slapped his son on the back.

"Fresh water! At last!" he said. "Well done, lad."

"You see, I was looking at these sort of painting things, Dad, and then—"

"Yeah, yeah, pictures of octopuses, very nice," said Jackson. "Hah! The ball is on the other foot now and no mistake! It's *our* water on *our* side of the island, and I'd just like to see them greasy buggers claim otherwise. Let 'em keep their damn driftwood and suck water out of fishes!"

"Yeah, Dad," said Les. "And we can trade them some of the water for wood and flour, right?"

His father waved a hand cautiously. *"Maybe,"* he said. "No need to rush into that, though. We're pretty close to finding a seaweed that'll burn. I mean, what're our long-term objectives here?"

"Cooking meals and keeping warm?" said Les hopefully.

"Well, *initially*," said Jackson. "That's obvious. But you know what they say, lad. 'Give a man a fire and he's warm for a day, but set fire to him and he's warm for the rest of his life.' See my point?"

"I don't think that's actually what the saying is—"

"I mean, we can stop here living on water and raw fish for . . . well, practically forever. But that lot can't go without proper fresh water for much longer. See? So they'll have to come begging to us, right? And then we deal on our terms, eh?"

He put his arm around his son's reluctant shoulders and waved a hand at the landscape.

"I mean, I started out with nothing, son, except that old boat that your grandad left me, but—"

"—you worked and scraped—" said Les wearily.

"—I worked and scraped—"

"—and you've always kept your head above water—"

"—right, I've always kept my head above water—"

"And you've always wanted to leave me something that—Ow!"

"Stop making fun of your dad!" said Jackson. "Otherwise I'll wallop the other ear. Look, you see this land? You see it?"

"I see it, Dad."

"It's a *land of opportunity*."

"But there's no fresh water and all the ground's full of salt, Dad, and it smells *bad!*"

"That's the smell of freedom, that is."

"Smells like someone did a really big fart, Dad— Ow!"

"Sometimes the two are very similar! And it's *your* future I'm thinking of, lad!"

Les looked at the acres of decomposing seaweed in front of him.

He was learning to be a fisherman like his father before him because that's how the family had always done it and he was too good-natured to argue, although he actually wanted to be a painter like no one in the family had ever been before. He was noticing things, and they worried him even though he couldn't quite say why.

But the buildings didn't look right. Here and there were definite bits of, well, architecture, like Morporkian pillars and the remains of Klatchian arches, but they'd been added to buildings that looked as though some ham-fisted people had just piled rocks on top of one another. And then in other places the slabs had been stacked *on top* of ancient brick walls and tiled floors. He couldn't imagine who'd done the tiling, but they did like pictures of octopussies.

The feeling was stealing over him that Morporkians and Klatchians arguing over who owned this piece of old sea bottom was *extremely* pointless.

"Er . . . I'm thinking about my future too, Dad," he said. "I really am."

Far below Solid Jackson's feet, the Boat surfaced. Sergeant Colon reached automatically for the screws that held the lid shut.

"Don't open it, sergeant!" shouted Leonard, rising from his seat.

"The air's getting pretty lived-in, sir—"

"It's worse outside."

"Worse than in here?"

"I'm almost certain."

"But we're on the surface!"

"*A* surface, sergeant," said Lord Vetinari. Beside him, Nobby uncorked the seeing device and peered through it.

"We're in a cave?" said Colon.

"Er . . . sarge . . ." said Nobby.

"Capital! Well worked out," said Lord Vetinari. "Yes. A cave. You could say that."

"Er . . . sarge?" said Nobby again, nudging Colon. "This isn't a cave, sarge! It's bigger than a cave, sarge!"

"What, you mean . . . like a cavern?"

"Bigger!"

"Bigger'n a cavern? More like a . . . *big* cavern?"

"Yeah, that'd be about right," said Nobby, taking his eye away from the device. "Have a look yourself, sarge."

Sergeant Colon peered into the tube.

Instead of the darkness he was half expecting, he saw the sea's surface, bubbling like a boiling saucepan. Green and yellow flashes of lightning danced across the water, illuminating a distant wall that seemed practically a horizon . . .

The tube squeaked around. If this was a cave, it was at least a couple of miles across.

"How long, do you think?" said Lord Vetinari, behind him.

"Well, the rock has a large proportion of tufa and pumice, very light, and once floated up the build-up of gas starts to escape very rapidly because of the swell," said Leonard. "I don't know . . . perhaps another week . . . and then I think it takes a very long time for a sufficient bubble to build up again . . ."

"What're they saying, sarge?" said Nobby. "This place *floats?*"

"A most unusual natural phenomenon," Leonard went on. "I'd have thought it was just a legend had I not seen it for myself . . ."

"Of course it's not floating," said Sergeant Colon. "Honestly, Nobby, how're you ever going to find out anything when you ask daft questions like that? Land's heavier than water, right? That's why you find it at the bottom of the sea."

"Yes, but he said pumice, and my gran had a pumice stone that worked a treat for getting tough skin off'f your feet in the tub and that'd float—"

"That sort of thing happens in bath tubs *maybe*," said Colon. "Not in real life. This is just a phenomena. It's not *real*. Next thing you'll be saying there's rocks up in the sky."

"Yeah, but—"

"I am a sergeant, Nobby."

"Yes, sarge."

"It puts me in mind," said Leonard, "of those nautical stories about giant turtles that sleep on the surface, thus causing sailors to think they are an island. Of course, you don't get giant turtles that small."

"Hey, Mr. Quirm, this is an amazing boat," said Nobby.

"Thank you."

"I bet you could even smash up ships with it if you wanted."

There was an embarrassed silence.

"Altogether an interesting experience," said Lord Vetinari, making some notes. "And now, gentlemen—downward and onward, please . . ."

* * *

The watchmen drew their weapons.

"They're D'regs, sir," said Carrot. "But—this is all wrong . . ."

"What do you mean?"

"We're not dead yet."

They're watching us like cats watch mice, thought Vimes. We can't run away and we can't win a fight, and they want to see what we'll do next.

"What does General Tacticus have to say about this, sir?" said Carrot.

There's a hundred of them, thought Vimes. And six of us. Except that Detritus is drifting off and there's no knowing what particular commandment Visit is obeying right now and Reg's arms tend to drop off when he gets excited—

"I don't know," he said. "Probably something on the lines of Don't Allow This to Happen."

"Why don't you check, sir?" said Carrot, not taking his eyes off the watching D'regs.

"What?"

"I said, why don't you check, sir?"

"Right now?"

"It might be worth a try, sir."

"That's crazy, captain."

"Yes, sir. The D'regs have some very strange notions about crazy people, sir."

Vimes pulled out the battered book. The D'reg nearest to him, with a grin almost as wide and as curved as his sword, had a certain additional swagger that suggested chieftainship. A huge ancient crossbow was slung on his back.

"I say!" said Vimes. "Could we just delay things a little?" He strode toward the man, who looked very surprised, and waved the book in the air. "This is a book by General Tacticus, don't know if you've ever heard of him, quite a big name in these parts once, probably slaughtered your great-great-great-great-grandfather in fact, and I just want to take a moment to see what he has to say about this situation. You don't mind, do you?"

The man gave Vimes a puzzled look.

"This may take a second, there's no index, but I think I saw something—"

The chieftain took a step backward and looked at the men next to him, who shrugged.

"I wonder if you could help me with this word here?" Vimes went on, reaching the man's side and holding the book under his nose. He got another puzzled grin.

What Vimes did next was known in Ankh-Morpork's alleyways as the Friendly Handshake, and consisted largely of driving his elbow into the man's stomach, then bringing his knee up to meet the man's chin on its way down, gritting his own teeth because of the pain in both knee and ankle, and then drawing his sword and holding it to the D'reg's throat before he could scramble up.

"Now, captain," said Vimes, "I'd like you to say in a loud clear voice that unless they back off a really long way, this gentleman here is going to be in some very serious legal trouble."

"Mr. Vimes, I don't think—"

"Do it!"

The D'reg looked into his eyes while Carrot hawked his way through the demand. The man was *still* grinning.

Vimes couldn't risk shifting his gaze, but he sensed some puzzlement and confusion among the tribesmen.

Then, as one man, they charged.

A Klatchian fishing boat, whose captain knew which way the wind was blowing, made its way back to the harbor of Al-Khali. It seemed to the captain that, despite the favorable wind, he wasn't making quite the speed he should. He put it down to barnacles.

Vimes awoke with a noseful of camel. There are far worse awakenings, but not as many as you might think.

By turning his head, which took some effort, he ascertained that the camel was sitting down. By the sound of things, it was digesting something explosive.

Now, how had he got here . . . Oh, gods . . .

But it *should* have worked . . . It was *classic.* You threatened to cut off the head and the body just folded up. That was how everyone reacted, wasn't it? That was practically how civilization worked . . .

Put it down to cultural differences, then.

On the other hand, he wasn't dead. According to Carrot, knowing the D'regs for five minutes and still being alive at the end of it meant that they really, really liked you.

On the *other* other hand, he'd just given their head man a Handshake, which influenced people without making friends.

Well, no sense lying over this saddle bound hand and foot and dying of sunstroke all day. He ought to start being a leader of men again, and would do so just as soon as he could get this camel out of his mouth.

"Bingeley-bingeley beep?"

"Yes?" said Vimes, struggling with his bonds.

"Would you like to know about the appointments you missed?"

"No! I'm trying to get these damn ropes untied!"

"Do you want me to put that on your To Do list?"

"Oh, you've woken up, sir."

It sounded like Carrot's voice and it was the sort of thing he'd say. Vimes tried to turn his head.

What he saw was mainly a white sheet, but it then became Carrot's face, upside down.

"They asked if they should untie you but I said you hadn't been getting enough rest lately," Carrot went on.

"Captain, my arms and legs have gone to sleep . . ." Vimes began.

"Oh, well done, sir! That's a start, at least."

"Carrot?"

"Yes, sir?"

"I want you to listen very carefully to the order I am about to give you."

"Certainly, sir."

"The point I'm making is that it won't be a request or a suggestion or some sort of hint."

"Understood, sir."

"I have, as you know, always encouraged my officers to think for themselves and not blindly obey me, but sometimes in any organization it is necessary for instructions to be followed to the letter and with alacrity."

"Right, sir."

"Untie me right now or you'll bloody well live to regret untying me!"

"Er, sir, I believe there is an inadvertent inconsistency in—"

"Carrot!"

"Of course, sir."

His ropes were cut. He slid down onto the sand. The camel turned its head, looked at him with its nostrils for a moment, and then looked away.

Vimes managed to sit upright while Carrot busied himself cutting the rest of his bonds.

"Captain, why are you wearing a white sheet?"

"It's a *burnous,* sir. Very practical for desert wear. The D'regs gave them to us."

"Us?"

"The rest of us, sir."

"Everyone's okay?"

"Oh, yes."

"But they attacked—"

"Yes, sir. But they only wanted to take us prisoner, sir. One of them did accidentally cut Reg's head off, but he did help him sew it on again, so no real harm done there."

"I thought D'regs didn't take prisoners . . . ?"

"Beats me too, sir. But they say if we try to escape they'll cut our feet off, and Reg says he hasn't got enough thread for everyone, sir."

Vimes rubbed his head. Someone had hit him so hard his helmet was dented.

"What went wrong?" he said. "I had their boss down!"

"As I understand it, sir, the D'regs think that any leader who is stupid enough to be defeated so easily isn't worth following. It's a Klatchian thing."

Vimes tried to persuade himself that there wasn't a hint of sarcasm in Carrot's voice as he went on: "They're not really very interested in leaders, sir, to tell you the truth. They look on them as a sort of ornament. You know . . . just someone to shout 'Charge!' sir."

"A leader has to do other things, Carrot."

"The D'regs think 'Charge!' pretty well covers all of them, sir."

Vimes managed to stand up. Strange muscles twanged in his legs. He tottered forward.

"Here, let me give you a hand . . ." said Carrot, catching him.

The sun was setting. Ragged tents clustered below one of the dunes, and there was the glow of firelight. Someone was laughing. It didn't *sound* like a prison. But then, thought Vimes, the desert was probably better than bars. He wouldn't even know which way to run, feet or no feet.

"The D'regs, like all Klatchians, are a very hospitable people," said Carrot, as if he'd memorized this. "They take hospitality very, very seriously."

Their captors were sitting round the fire. So were the watchmen. They'd also been persuaded to dress more suitably, which meant that Cheery looked like a girl in her mum's dress, apart from the iron helmet, and Reg Shoe looked *like* a mummy, and Detritus was a small snow-covered mountain.

"He's gone very . . . insensible in all this heat," whispered Carrot. "And that's Constable Visit over there, arguing religion. There are six hundred and fifty-three religions on the Klatchian continent."

"He must be having fun."

"And this is Jabbar," said Carrot. Exhibit A, who looked like a slightly older version of 71-hour Ahmed, stood up and salaamed to Vimes.

"Offendi," he said.

"He's their . . . well, he's like an official wise man," said Carrot.

"Oh, so he's not the one who tells them to charge?" said Vimes. His head buzzed with the heat.

"No, that's the leader," said Carrot. "Whenever they have one."

"So perhaps Jabbar tells them when it's *wise* to charge?" said Vimes brightly.

"It's always wise to charge, offendi," said Jabbar. He bowed again. "My tent is your tent," he said.

"It is?" said Vimes.

"My wives are your wives . . ."

Vimes looked panicky. "They are? Really?"

"My food is your food . . ." Jabbar went on.

Vimes stared down at the dish by the fire. It looked like a sheep or a goat had been the main course. And the man bent down, picked up a morsel and handed it to him.

Sam Vimes looked at the mouthful. And it looked back.

"The best part," said Jabbar, and made appreciative sucking noises. He added something in Klatchian. There was some muffled laughter from the other men around the fire.

"This looks like a sheep's eyeball," said Vimes, doubtfully.

"Yes, sir," said Carrot. "But it is unwise to—"

"You know what?" Vimes went on. "I think this is a little game called 'Let's see what offendi will swallow.' And I'm not swallowing this, my friend."

Jabbar gave him an appraising look.

The sniggering stopped.

"Then it is true that you can see further than most," he said.

"So can this food," said Vimes. "My father told me never to eat anything that can wink back."

There was one of those little *hanging-by-a-thread* moments, which might suddenly rock one way or the other into a gale of laughter or sudden death.

Then Jabbar slapped Vimes on the back. The eyeball shot off his palm and into the shadows.

"Well done! Extremely good! First time it have not worked in twenty year! Now sit down and have proper rice and sheep just like mother!"

There was a certain feeling of relaxation. Vimes found himself pulled down. Bottoms shuffled aside to make room for him and a big slab of bread dripping with meat was put in front of him. Vimes prodded at it as politely as he dared, and then took the usual view that, if you can recognize at least half of it, it's probably okay to eat the rest.

"So we're your prisoners, Mr. Jabbar?"

"Honored guests! My tent is—"

"But . . . how can I put this? . . . you want us to enjoy your hospitality for some time?"

"We have tradition," said Jabbar. "A man who is a guest in your tent, even if he is your worst enemy, you owe him hospitality for tree dace."

"Tree dace, eh?" said Vimes.

"I learn language on . . ." Jabbar waved a hand vaguely, "you know, wooden ting, a camel of the sea—"

"Boat?"

"Right! But too many water!" He slapped Vimes on the back again, so that hot fat spilled into his lap. "Any road up, lots speaking Morporkian these dace, offendi. It is language of . . . merchant." He put an inflection on the word that suggested it was the same as "earthworm."

"So you have to know how to say things like 'Give us all your money'?" said Vimes.

"Why ask?" said Jabbar. "We take it anyway. But now . . ." he spat at the fire with amazing accuracy ". . . they say, we got to stop, this is wrong. What harm do we do?"

"Apart from killing people and taking all their merchandise?" said Vimes.

Jabbar laughed again. "*Wali* said you were a big diplomatic! But we don't kill merchants, why should we kill merchants? What is the sense? How foolish to be killing gift horse that lays the golden egg!"

"You could make money exhibiting it, certainly," said Vimes.

"We kill merchants, we rob too much, they never come back. Dumb. We let them go, they get rich again, our *sons* rob them. Such is wisdom."

"Ah . . . it's a sort of agriculture," said Vimes.

"Right! But if you plant merchants, they don't grow so good."

Vimes realized that it was getting colder as the sun went down. In fact, a lot colder. He inched closer to the fire.

"Why is he called 71-hour Ahmed?" he said.

The murmur of conversation stopped. Suddenly all eyes were on Jabbar, except the one that had ended up in the shadows.

"*Not* so diplomatic," said Jabbar.

"We chase him up here, then suddenly we're ambushed by you. That seems—"

"I know nothing," said Jabbar.

"Why won't you—?" Vimes began.

"Er, sir," said Carrot urgently. "That would be very unwise, sir. Look, I had a bit of a talk with Jabbar while you were . . . resting. It's a bit political, I'm afraid."

"What isn't?"

"Prince Cadram is trying to unite the whole of Klatch, you see."

"Dragging it kicking and screaming into the Century of the Fruitbat?"

"Why, yes, sir, how did—?"

"Just a lucky guess. Go on."

"But he has been having trouble," said Carrot.

"What kind?" said Vimes.

"Us," said Jabbar proudly.

"None of the tribes like the idea, sir," Carrot went on. "They've always fought among themselves, and now most of them are fighting him. Historically, sir, Klatch isn't so much an empire as an argument."

"He say, you must be educated. You must be learning to pay taxes. We do not wish to be educated about taxes," said Jabbar.

"So you think you're fighting for your freedom?" said Vimes.

Jabbar hesitated, and looked at Carrot. There was a brief exchange in Klatchian. Then Carrot said: "That's a rather difficult question for a D'reg, sir. You see, their word for 'freedom' is the same as their word for 'fighting.'"

"They certainly make their language do a lot of work, don't they . . . ?"

Vimes was feeling better in the colder air. He took out a crushed and damp packet of cigars, pulled a coal out of the fire, and took a deep drag.

"So . . . Prince Charming's got a lot of troubles at home, has he? Does Vetinari know this?"

"Does a camel shit in the desert, sir?"

"You're really getting the hang of Klatch, aren't you?" said Vimes.

Jabbar rumbled something. There was more laughter.

"Er . . . Jabbar says a camel certainly *does* shit in the desert, sir, otherwise you wouldn't have anything to light your cigar with, sir."

Once again, there was one of those moments when Vimes felt that he was under close scrutiny. Be diplomatic, Vetinari had told him.

He took another deep draw. "Improves the flavor," he said. "Remind me to take some home."

In Jabbar's eyes, the judges held up at least a couple of grudging eights.

"A man on a horse came and said we must fight the foreign dogs—"

"That's us, sir," said Carrot helpfully.

"—because you have stolen an island that is under the sea. But what is that to us? We know no harm of you foreign devils, but the men who oil their beards in Al-Khali we do not like. So we send him back."

"All of him?" said Vimes.

"We are not barbaric. He was clearly a madman. But we kept his horse."

"And 71-hour Ahmed told you to keep us, didn't he?" said Vimes.

"No one orders the D'regs! It is our pleasure to keep you here!"

"And when will it be your pleasure to let us go? When Ahmed tells you?"

Jabbar stared at the fire. "I will not speak of him. He is devious and cunning and not to be trusted."

"But *you* are D'regs, too."

"Yes!" Jabbar slapped Vimes on the back again. "We know what we are talking about!"

The Klatchian fishing boat was a mile or two out of harbor when it seemed to its captain that it was suddenly riding better in the water. Perhaps the barnacles have dropped off, he thought.

When his boat was lost in the evening mists a length of bent pipe rose slowly out of the swell and squeaked around until it faced the coast.

A distant tinny voice said: "Oh, no . . ."

And another tinny voice said: "What's up, sarge?"

"Take a look through this!"

"Okay." There was a pause.

Then the second tinny voice said: "Oh, bugger . . ."

What was riding at anchor before the city of Al-Khali wasn't a fleet. It was a fleet of fleets. The masts looked like a floating forest.

Down below, Lord Vetinari took his turn to peer through the pipe.

"So many ships," he said. "In such a short time, too. How very well organized. Very well organized. One might almost say . . . *astonishingly* well organized. As they say, 'If you would seek war, prepare for war.'"

"I believe, my lord, the saying is 'If you would seek peace, prepare for war,'" Leonard ventured.

Vetinari put his head on one side and his lips moved as he repeated the phrase to himself. Finally he said, "No, no. I just don't see that one at all."

He ducked back into his seat.

"Let us proceed with care," he said. "We can go ashore under cover of darkness."

"Er . . . can we maybe go ashore under cover of cover?" said Sergeant Colon.

"In fact these extra ships will make our plan that much easier," said the Patrician, ignoring him.

"Our plan?" said Colon.

"People within the Klatchian hegemony come in every shape and color." Vetinari glanced at Nobby. "Practically every shape and color," he added. "So our appearance on the streets should not cause undue comment." He glanced at Nobby again. "To any great extent."

"But we're wearing our uniforms, sir," said Sergeant Colon. "It's not like we can say we're on our way to a fancy-dress party."

"Well, I'm not taking mine off," said Nobby firmly. "I'm not running around in my drawers. Not in a port. Sailors are at sea a long time. You hear stories."

"That'd be *worse*," said the sergeant, without wasting time calculating how long any sailor would need to be at sea before the vision of Nobby Nobbs would present itself as anything other than a target, "'cos if we're not in uniform, we'll be spies—and you know what happens to spies."

"Are you going to tell me, sarge?"

"Excuse me, your lordship?" Sergeant Colon raised his voice. The Patrician looked up from a conversation with Leonard.

"Yes, sergeant?"

"What do they do to spies in Klatch, sir?"

"Er . . . let me see . . ." said Leonard. "Oh, yes . . . I believe they give you to the women."

Nobby brightened up. "Oh, well, that doesn't sound too bad—"

"Er, no, Nobby—" Colon began.

"—'cos I've seen the pictures in that book *The Perfumed Allotment* that Corporal Angua was reading, and—"

"—no, *listen*, Nobby, you've got the wrong—"

"—I mean, blimey, I didn't know you could *do* that with a—"

"—Nobby, *listen*—"

"—and then there's this bit where she—"

"Corporal Nobbs!" Colon yelled.

"Yes, sarge?"

Colon leaned forward and whispered in Nobby's ear. The corporal's expression changed, slowly.

"They really—"

"*Yes,* Nobby."

"They *really*—"

"Yes, Nobby."

"They don't do that at home."

"We ain't at home, Nobby. I wish we was."

"Although you hear stories about the Agony Aunts, sarge."

"Gentlemen," said Lord Vetinari. "I am afraid Leonard is being rather fanciful. That may apply to some of the mountain tribes, but Klatch *is* an ancient civilization and that sort of thing is not done officially. I should imagine they'd give you a cigarette."

"A cigarette?" said Fred.

"Yes, sergeant. And a nice sunny wall to stand in front of."

Sergeant Colon examined this for any downside. "A nice roll-up and a wall to lean against?" he said.

"I think they prefer you to stand up straight, sergeant."

"Fair enough. No need to be sloppy just because you're a prisoner. Oh, *well*. I don't mind risking it, then."

"Well done," said the Patrician calmly. "Tell me, sergeant . . . in your long military career, did anyone ever consider promoting you to an officer?"

"Nossir!"

"I cannot think why."

Night poured over the desert. It came suddenly, in purple. In the clear air, the stars drilled down out of the sky, reminding any thoughtful watcher that it is in the deserts and high places that religions are generated. When men see nothing but bottomless infinity over their heads they have always had a driving and desperate urge to find someone to put in the way.

Life emerged from the burrows and fissures. Soon, the desert was filled with the buzz and click and screech of creatures which, lacking mankind's superior brainpower, did not concern themselves with finding someone to blame and instead tried to find someone to eat.

At around three in the morning Sam Vimes walked out of the tent for a smoke. The cold air hit him like a door. It was *freezing*. That wasn't what was supposed to happen in deserts, was it? Deserts were all hot sand and camels and . . . and . . . he struggled for a while, as a man whose geographical knowledge got severely cramped once you got off paved road . . . camels, yes, and dates. And possibly bananas and coconuts. But the temperature here made your breath tinkle in the air.

He waved his cigar packet theatrically at a D'reg who was lounging near the tent. The man shrugged.

The fire was just a heap of gray, but Vimes poked around in the vain hope of finding a glowing ember.

He was amazed at how angry he was. Ahmed was the key, he *knew* it. And now they were stuck out here in the desert, the man had gone, and they were in the hands of . . . quiet, likeable people, fair enough. Brigands, maybe, the dry land equivalent of pirates, but Carrot would have said they were jolly good chaps for all that. If you were content to be their guest then they were as nice as pie, or sheep's eyeball and treacle or whatever you got out here—

Something moved in the moonlight. A shadow slipped down the side of a dune.

Something howled, out in the desert night.

Tiny hairs rose, all down Vimes's back, just like they had for his distant ancestors.

The night is always old. He'd walked too often down dark streets in the secret hours and felt the night stretching away, and known in his blood that while days and kings and empires come and go, the night is always the same age, always aeons deep. Terrors unfolded in the velvet shadows and while the nature of the talons may change, the nature of the beast does not.

He stood up quietly, and reached for his sword.

It wasn't there.

They'd taken it away. They'd not even—

"A fine night," said a voice beside him.

Jabbar was standing by his shoulder.

"Who is out there?" Vimes hissed.

"An enemy."

"Which one?"

Teeth gleamed in the shadows.

"We will find out, offendi."

"Why would they attack you now?"

"Maybe they think we have something they want, offendi."

More shadows slid across the desert.

And one rose up right behind Jabbar, reached down and picked him up. A huge gray hand dragged his sword out of his belt.

"What do you want me to do with him, Mr. Vimes?"

"Detritus?"

The troll saluted with the hand that still held the D'reg.

"All present and correct, sir!"

"But—" And then Vimes realized. "It's freezing cold! Your brain's working again?"

"With rather more efficiency, sir."

"Is this a djinn?" said Jabbar.

"I don't know, but I could certainly do with one," said Vimes. He finally managed to locate some matches in his pocket, and lit one. "Put him down, sergeant," he said, puffing his cigar into life. "Jabbar, this is Sergeant Detritus. He could break every bone in your body, including some of the small ones in the fingers which are quite hard to do—"

The darkness went *shwup* and something whispered past the back of his neck, just a slice of a second before Jabbar cannoned into him and bore him to the ground.

"They shoot at the light!"

"Mwwf?"

Vimes raised his head cautiously and spat out sand and fragments of tobacco.

"Mr. Vimes?"

Only Carrot could whisper like that. He associated whispering with concealment and untruth and compromised by whispering very loudly. To Vimes's horror the man came round the edge of a tent holding a tiny lamp.

"Put that damn—"

But he didn't have time to finish the sentence because, somewhere out in the night, a man screamed. It was a high-pitched scream and was suddenly cut off.

"Ah," said Carrot, crouching down by Vimes and blowing out the lamp. "That was Angua."

"That was nothing like— Oh. Yeah, I think I see what you mean," Vimes said, uneasily. "She's out there, is she?"

"I heard her earlier. She's probably enjoying herself. She doesn't really get much of a chance to let herself go in Ankh-Morpork."

"Er . . . no . . ." Vimes had a mental picture of a werewolf letting go. But surely, Angua wouldn't—

"You two, uh . . . you're getting along okay, are you?" he said, trying to make out shapes in the darkness.

"Oh, fine, sir. Fine."

So her turning into a wolf occasionally doesn't worry you? Vimes couldn't bring himself to say it.

"No . . . problems, then?"

"Oh, not really, sir. She buys her own dog biscuits and she's got her own flap in the door. When it's full moon I don't really get involved."

There were shouts in the night and then a shape erupted from the darkness, streaked past Vimes, and disappeared into a tent. It didn't wait for a door. It simply hit the cloth at full speed and continued until the tent collapsed around it.

"And what is *that?*" said Jabbar.

"This may take some explaining," said Vimes, picking himself up.

Carrot and Detritus were already hauling at the collapsed tent.

"We are D'regs," said Jabbar reproachfully. "We are supposed to fold tents silently in the night, not—"

There was *enough* moonlight. Angua sat up and snatched a piece of tent out of Carrot's hands.

"Thank *you,*" she said, wrapping it around her. "And before anyone says anything, I just bit him on the bum. Hard. And that was not the soft option, let me tell you."

Jabbar looked back into the desert, and then down at the sand, and then at Angua. Vimes could *see* him thinking, and put a fraternal arm around his shoulders.

"I'd better explain—" he began.

"There's a couple of hundred soldiers out there!" Angua snapped.

"—later."

"They're taking up positions all round you! And they don't look nice! Has anyone got any clothes that might fit? And some decent food? And a drink! There's no *water* in this place!"

"They will not dare attack before dawn," said Jabbar.

"And what will you do, sir?" said Carrot.

"At dawn we will charge!"

"Ah. Uh. I wonder if I could suggest an alternative approach?"

"Alternative? It is *right* to charge! Charging is what dawn is *for.*"

Carrot saluted Vimes. "I've been reading your book, sir. While you were . . . asleep. Tacticus's got quite a lot to say about how to deal with overwhelming odds, sir."

"Yes?"

"He says take every opportunity to turn them into underwhelming odds, sir. We could attack now."

"But it's dark, man!"

"It's just as dark for the enemy, sir."

"I mean it's pitch-black! You wouldn't know who the hell you were fighting! Half the time you'd be shooting your own side!"

"*We* wouldn't, sir, because there'd only be a few of us. Sir? All we need to do is crawl out there, make a bit of noise, and then let them get on with it. Tacticus says all armies are the same size in the night, sir."

"There might be something in that," said Angua. "They're crawling around in ones and twos, and they're dressed pretty much like—" She waved a hand at Jabbar.

"This is Jabbar," said Carrot. "He's sort of not the leader."

Jabbar grinned nervously. "It happens often in your country, where dogs turn into naked women?"

"Sometimes days can go past and it doesn't happen at all," Angua snapped. "I'd like some clothes, please. And a sword, if there's going to be fighting."

"Um, I think Klatchians have a very particular view about women fighting—" Carrot began.

"Yes!" said Jabbar. "We expect them to be good at it, Blue Eyes. We are D'regs!"

The Boat surfaced in the scummy dead water under a jetty. The lid opened slowly.

"Smells like home," said Nobby.

"You can't trust the water," said Sergeant Colon.

"But I don't trust the water at home, sarge."

Fred Colon managed to get a foothold on the greasy wood. It was, in theory, quite a heroic enterprise. He and Nobby Nobbs, the bold warriors, were venturing forth in hostile territory. Unfortunately, he knew they were doing it because Lord Vetinari was sitting in the Boat and would raise his eyebrows in no uncertain manner if they refused.

Colon had always thought that heroes had some special kind of clockwork that made them go out and die famously for god, country and apple pie, or whatever particular delicacy their mother made. It had never occurred to him that they might do it because they'd get yelled at if they didn't.

He reached down.

"Come on up, Nobby," he said. "And remember we're doing this for the gods, Ankh-Morpork and—" It seemed to Colon that a foodstuff would indeed be somehow appropriate. "And my mum's famous knuckle sandwich!"

"Our mum never made us knuckle sandwiches," said Nobby, as he hauled himself onto the planks. "But you'd be amazed at what she could do with a bit of cheese . . ."

"Yeah, all right, but that ain't much of a battle cry, is it? 'For the gods, Ankh-Morpork and amazing things Nobby's mum can do with cheese'? That'll strike fear in the hearts of the enemy!" said Sergeant Colon, as they crept forward.

"Oh, well, if *that's* what you're after, you want my mum's Distressed Pudding and custard," said Nobby.

"Frightening, is it?"

"They wouldn't want to know about it, sarge."

The docks of Al-Khali were like docks everywhere, because all docks everywhere are connected. Men have to put things on and off boats. There are only a limited number of ways to do this. So all docks look the same. Some are hotter, some are damper, there are always piles of vaguely forgotten-looking things.

In the distance there was the glow of the city, which seemed quite unaware of the enemy incursion.

"'Get us some clothes so that we'll blend in,'" muttered Colon. "That's all very well to say."

"Nah, nah, that's *easy*," said Nobby. "*Everyone* knows how to do *that* one. You lurk in an alley somewhere, right, and you wait until a couple of blokes come by and you lure them into the alley, see, and there's a couple of thumps, and then you come out wearing their clothes."

"That works, does it?"

"Never fails, sarge," said Nobby confidently.

The desert looked like snow in the moonlight.

Vimes found himself quite at ease with the Tacticus method of fighting. It was how coppers had always fought. A proper copper didn't line up with a lot of other coppers and rush at people. A copper lurked in the shadows, walked quietly and bided his time. In all honesty, of course, the time he bided until was the point when the criminal had already *committed* the crime and was carrying the loot. Otherwise, what was the point? You had to be realistic. "We got the man what done it" carries a lot more gravitas than "We got the man what looked as if he was going to do it," especially when people say, "Prove it."

Somewhere off to the left, in the distance, someone screamed.

Vimes was a bit uneasy in this robe, though. It was like going into battle in a nightshirt.

Because he wasn't at all certain he could kill a man who wasn't actively trying to kill *him*. Of course, *technically* any armed Klatchian these days was actively trying to kill him. That was what war was about. But—

He raised his head over the top of the dune. A Klatchian warrior was looking the other way. Vimes crept—

"Bingeley-bingeley beep! This is your seven eh em alarm call, Insert Name Here! At least I hope—"

"Huh?"

"Damn!"

Vimes reacted first and punched the man on the nose. Since there was no point in waiting to see what effect this would have, he threw himself forward and the two of them rolled down the other side of the freezing dune, struggling and punching.

"—but my real-time function seems erratic at the moment—"

The Klatchian was smaller than Vimes. He was younger, too. But it was unfortunate for him that he appeared to be too young to have learned the repertoire of dirty fighting that spelled survival in Ankh-Morpork's back streets. Vimes, on the other hand, was prepared to hit anything *with* anything. The point was that the opponent shouldn't get up again. Everything else was decoration.

They slid to a halt at the bottom of the dune, with Vimes on top and the Klatchian groaning.

"Things To Do," the Dis-organizer shrilled: "Ache."

And then . . . It was probably throat-cutting time. Back home Vimes could have dragged him off to the cells, in the knowledge that everything would look better in the morning, but the desert had no such options.

No, he couldn't do that. Thump the bloke senseless. That was the merciful way.

"Vindaloo! Vindaloo!"

Vimes's fist stayed raised.

"What?"

"That's you, isn't it? Mr. Vimes? Vindaloo!"

Vimes pulled a fold of cloth away from the figure's face.

"Are you *Goriff's* boy?"

"I didn't want to be here, Mr. Vimes!" The words came fast, desperate.

"All right, all right, I'm not going to hurt you . . ."

Vimes lowered his fist and stood up, pulling the boy up after him.

"Talk later," he muttered. "Come on!"

"No! Everyone knows what the D'regs do to their captives!"

"Well *I'm* their captive and they'll have to do it to both of us, okay? Keep away from the more amusing food and you'll probably be okay."

Someone whistled in the darkness.

"Come *on*, lad!" hissed Vimes. "No harm's going to come to you! Well . . . less than'd come if you stayed here. All right?"

This time he didn't give the boy time to argue, but dragged him along. As he headed toward the D'regs' camp, other figures slid down the dunes.

One of them had an arm missing and had a sword sticking in him.

"How did you get on, Reg?" said Vimes.

"A bit odd, sir. After the first one chopped my arm off and stabbed me, the rest of them seemed to keep out of my way. Honestly, you'd think they'd never seen a man stabbed before."

"Did you *find* your arm?"

Reg waved something in the air.

"That's another thing," he said. "I hit a few of them with it and they ran off screaming."

"It's your type of unarmed combat," said Vimes. "It probably takes some getting used to."

"Is that a prisoner you've got there?"

"In a way." Vimes glanced around. "He seems to have fainted. I can't think why."

Reg leaned closer. "These foreigners are a bit weird," he said.
"Reg?"
"Yes?"
"Your ear's hanging off."
"Is it? Wretched thing. You'd think a nail would work, wouldn't you?"

Sergeant Colon looked up at the stars. They looked down at him. At least Fred Colon had a choice.

Beside him, Corporal Nobbs gave a groan. But the attackers had left him his pants. There are some places where the boldest dare not go, and those areas of Nobby upward of the knees and downward of the stomach were among them.

Well, Colon thought of them as attackers. Technically, he supposed they were defenders. Aggressive defenders.

"Just run all that past me again, will you?" he said.

"We find a couple of blokes about our height and weight—"

"We did that."

"We lure them into this alley—"

"We did that."

"I take a swing at them with a length of wood and hit you by accident in the dark and they get angry and turn out to be thieves and nick all our clothes."

"We weren't supposed to do that."

"Well it worked *basically*," said Nobby, managing to get to his knees. "We could give it another go."

"Nobby, you're in a port in a foreign city clad only in your, and I use this word with feeling, Nobby, your unmentionables. This is not the point to start talking about luring people into alleys. There could be talk."

"Angua always says that nakedness is the national costume everywhere, sarge."

"She was talking about herself, Nobby," said Colon, sidling along in the shadows. "It's different for you."

He peered around the other end of the alley. There was noise and chatter from the building that formed one of the walls. A couple of laden donkeys waited patiently outside.

"Nip out and grab one of those packs, right?"

"Why me, sarge?"

"'cos you're the corporal and I'm the sergeant. And you've got more on than me."

Grumbling under his breath, Nobby edged into the narrow street and unfastened a tether as fast as he could. The animal followed him obediently.

Sergeant Colon pulled at the pack.

"If push comes to shove we can wear the sacks," he said. "That'll— What's this?"

He held up something red.

"Flowerpot?" said Nobby helpfully.

"It's a fez! Some Klatchians wear 'em. Looks like we've struck lucky. Whoops, here's another one. Try it on, Nobby. And . . . looks like one of them nightshirts they wear . . . and here's another one of those, too. We're home and dry, Nobby."

"They're a bit short, sarge."

"Beggars can't be choosers," said Colon, struggling into the costume. "Go on, put your fez on."

"It makes me look like a twit, sarge."

"Look, I'll put mine on, all right?"

"Then we'll be fez to fez, sarge."

Sergeant Colon gave him a severe look. "Did you have that one prepared, Nobby?"

"No, sarge, I just made it up in my head right then."

"Well, look, no calling me sarge. That doesn't sound Klatchian."

"Nor does Nobby, sa— Sorry . . ."

"Oh, I dunno . . . you could be . . . Knobi . . . or Nhobi . . . or Gnobbee . . . Sounds pretty Klatchian to me."

"What's a good Klatchian name for you, then? I don't know hardly any," said Nhobi.

Sergeant Colon didn't answer. He was peering round the corner again.

"His lordship did say we was not to hang about," Nobby murmured.

"Yeah, but inside that tin can, well, it smells pretty *lived-in,* if you know what I mean. What I wouldn't give for—"

There was a bellow behind them. They turned.

There were three Klatchian soldiers. Or possibly watchmen. Nobby and Sergeant Colon didn't look much further than the swords.

The leader growled a question at them.

"What did he say?" Nobby quavered.

"Dunno!"

"Where you from?" said the leader, in Morporkian.

"What? Oh . . . er . . ." Colon hesitated, waiting for shiny death.

"Hah, yes." The guard lowered his sword and jerked a thumb toward the docks. "You get back to your detachment now!"

"Right!" said Nobby.

"What your name?" one of the guards demanded.

"Nhobi," said Nobby. This seemed to pass.

"And you, fat one?"

Colon was panicking on the spot. He sought desperately for any name that sounded Klatchian, and there was only one that presented itself and which was absolutely and authentically Klatchian.

"Al," he said, his knees trembling.

"You get back right now or there will be trouble!"

The watchmen ran for it, dragging the donkey behind them, and didn't stop until they were on the greasy jetty, which somehow felt like home.

"What was that all about, s— Al?" said Nobby. "All they wanted to do was push us around a bit! Typical Watch behavior," he added. "Not ours, of course."

"I suppose we had the right clothes on . . ."

"You didn't even tell them where we came from! *And* they spoke our language!"

"Well, they . . . I mean . . . *anyone* ought to be able to speak Morporkian," said Colon, gradually regaining his mental balance. "Even babies learn it. I bet it comes easy after learning somethin' as complicated as Klatchian."

"What're we going to do with the donkey, Al?"

"Do you think it can pedal?"

"I doubt it."

"Then leave it up here."

"But it'll get pinched, Al."

"Oh, these Klatchians'll pinch anything."

"Not like us, eh, Al?"

Nobby looked at the forest of masts filling the bay.

"Looks like even more of 'em from here," he said. "You could walk from boat to boat for a mile. What're they all here for?"

"Don't be daft, Nobby. It's obvious. They're to take everyone to Ankh-Morpork!"

"What for? We don't eat that much cur—"

"*Invasion,* Nobby! There's a war on, remember?"

They looked back at the ships. Riding lights gleamed on the water.

The bit of it that was immediately below them bubbled for a moment, and then the hull of the Boat rose a few inches above the surface. The lid unscrewed and Leonard's worried face appeared.

"Ah, there you are," he said. "We were getting concerned . . ."

They lowered themselves down into the fetid interior of the vessel.

Lord Vetinari was sitting with a pad of paper across his knees, writing carefully. He glanced up briefly.

"Report."

Nobby fidgeted while Sergeant Colon delivered a more or less accurate account, although there was some witty repartee with the Klatchian guards that the corporal had not hitherto recalled.

Vetinari did not look up. Still writing, he said, "Sergeant, Ur is an old country Rimward of the kingdom of Djelibeybi, whose occupants are a byword for bucolic stupidity. For some reason, I cannot think why, the guard must have assumed you were from there. And Morporkian is something of a lingua franca even in the Klatchian empire. When someone from Hersheba needs to trade with someone from Istanzia, they will undoubtedly haggle in Morporkian. This will serve us well, of course. The force that is being assembled here must mean that practically every man is a distant stranger with outlandish ways. Provided we do not act *too* foreign, we should pass muster. This means not asking for curry with swede and currants in it and refraining from ordering pints of Winkle's Old Peculiar, do I make myself clear?"

"Er . . . what is it we're going to *do,* sir?"

"We will reconnoiter initially."

"Ah, right. Yes. Very important."

"And then seek out the Klatchian high command. Thanks to Leonard I have a little . . . package to deliver. I hope it will end the war very quickly."

Sergeant Colon looked blank. At some point in the last few seconds the conversation had run away with him.

"Sorry, sir . . . you said high command, sir."

"Yes, sergeant."

"Like . . . the top brass, or turbans or whatever . . . all surrounded by crack troops, sir. That's where you always put the best troops, around the top brass."

"I expect this will be the case, yes. In fact, I rather hope it is."

Sergeant Colon, once again, tried to keep up.

"Ah. Right. And we'll go and look for them, will we, sir?"

"I can hardly ask them to come to us, sergeant."

"Right, sir. I can see that. It could get a bit crowded."

At last, Lord Vetinari looked up.

"Is there some problem, sergeant?"

And Sergeant Colon once again knew a secret about bravery. It was arguably a kind of enhanced cowardice—the knowledge that while death *may* await you if you advance it will be a picnic compared to the *certain* living hell that awaits should you retreat.

"Er . . . not as such, sir," he said.

"Very well." Vetinari pushed his paperwork aside. "If there is more suitable clothing in your bag, I will get changed and we can take a look at Al-Khali."

"Oh, gods . . ."

"Sorry, sergeant?"

"Oh, good, sir."

"Good." Vetinari began to pull other items out of the liberated sack. There was a set of juggler's clubs, a bag of colored balls and finally a placard, such as might be placed to one side of the stage during an artiste's performance.

"'Gulli, Gulli and Beti,'" he read. "'Exotic tricks and dances.' Hmm," he added. "It would seem there was a lady among the owners of this sack."

The watchmen looked at the gauzy material that came out of the sack next. Nobby's eyes bulged.

"What are *them?*"

"I believe they are called harem pants, corporal."

"They're very—"

"Curiously, the purpose of the clothing of the nautch girl or exotic dancer has always been less to reveal and more to suggest the *imminence* of revelation," said the Patrician.

Nobby looked down at his costume, and then at Sergeant Al-Colon in *his* costume, and said cheerfully, "Well, I ain't sure it's going to suit you, sir."

He regretted the words immediately.

"I hadn't intended that they should suit *me*," said the Patrician calmly. "Please pass me your fez, Corporal Beti."

The subtle, deceiving dawn-before-dawn slid over the desert, and the commander of the Klatchian detachment wasn't happy about it.

The D'regs always attacked at dawn. All of them. It didn't matter how many of them there were, or how many of you there were. Anyway, the whole tribe attacked. It wasn't just the women and children, but the camels, goats, sheep and chickens, too. Of course you were expecting them and bows could cut them down, but . . . they always appeared suddenly, as if even the desert had spat them out. Get it wrong, be too slow, and you'd be hacked, kicked, butted, pecked and viciously spat at.

His troops lay in wait. Well, if you could call them troops. He'd *said* they were overstretched . . . well, he hadn't actually *said,* because that sort of thing could get you into trouble in this man's army, but he'd thought it very hard. Half of them were keen kids who thought that if you went into battle shouting and waving your sword in the air the enemy just ran away. They'd never faced a D'reg chicken coming in at eye height.

As for the rest of it . . . in the night people had run into one another, ambushed one another by mistake and were now as jittery as peas on a drum. A man had lost his sword and swore that someone had walked away with it stuck right through him. And some kind of rock had got up and walked around hitting people. With other people.

The sun was well up now.

"It's the waiting that's the worst part," said his sergeant, next to him.

"It *might* be the worst part," said the commander. "Or, there again, the bit where they suddenly rise out of the desert and cut you in half might be the worst part." He stared mournfully at the treacherously empty sand. "Or the bit where a maddened sheep tries to gnaw your nose off might be the worst part. In fact, when you think of all the things that can happen when you're sur-rounded by a horde of screaming D'regs, the bit where they aren't there at all is, I think you'll find, the *best* part."

The sergeant wasn't trained for this sort of thing. So he said, "They're late."

"Good. Rather them than us."

"Sun's right up now, sir."

The commander looked at his shadow. It was full day, and the sand was mercifully free of his blood. The commander had been pacifying various recalcitrant parts of Klatch for long enough to wonder why, if he was pacifying people, he always seemed to be fighting them. Experience had taught him never to say things like "I don't like it, it's too quiet." There was no such thing as too quiet.

"They might have decamped in the night, sir," said the sergeant.

"That doesn't sound like the D'regs. They never run away. Anyway, I can see their tents."

"Why don't we rush 'em, sir?"

"You haven't fought D'regs before, sergeant?"

"No, sir. I've been pacifying the Mad Savatars in Uhistan, though, and they're—"

"The D'regs are worse, sergeant. They pacify right back at you."

"I didn't say how mad the Savatars were, sir."

"Compared to the D'regs, they were merely slightly vexed."

The sergeant felt that his reputation was being impugned.

"How about I take a few men and investigate, sir?"

The commander glanced at the sun again. Already the air was too hot to breathe.

"Oh, very *well.* Let's go."

The Klatchians advanced on the camp. There were the tents, and the ash of fires. But there were no camels and horses, merely a long scuffed trail leading off among the dunes.

Morale began to rise a little. Attacking a dangerous enemy who isn't there is one of the more attractive forms of warfare, and there was a certain amount of assertion about how lucky the D'regs were to have run away in time, and some extemporizing on the subject of what the soldiers would have done to the D'regs if they'd caught them . . .

"Who's that?" said the sergeant.

A figure appeared between the dunes, riding on a camel. His white robes fluttered in the breeze.

He slid down when he reached the Klatchians, and waved at them.

"Good morning, gentlemen! May I persuade you to surrender?"

"Who are you?"

"Captain Carrot, sir. If you would be kind enough to lay down your weapons no one will get hurt."

The commander looked up. Blobs were appearing along the tops of the dunes. They rose, and turned out to be heads.

"They're . . . D'regs, sir!" said the sergeant.

"No. D'regs would be charging, sergeant."

"Oh, sorry. Shall I tell them to charge?" said Carrot. "Is that what you'd prefer?"

The D'regs were all along the dunes now. The climbing sun glittered off metal.

"Are you telling me," the commander began slowly, "that you can persuade D'regs *not* to charge?"

"It was tricky, but I think they've got the idea," said Carrot.

The commander considered his position. There were D'regs on either side. His troop were practically huddling together. And this red-headed, blue-eyed man was smiling at him.

"How do they feel about the merciful treatment of prisoners?" he ventured.

"I think they could get the hang of it. If I insist."

The commander glanced at the silent D'regs again.

"Why?" he said. "*Why* aren't they fighting us?" he said.

"My commander says he doesn't want unnecessary loss of life, sir," said Carrot. "That's Commander Vimes, sir. He's sitting on that dune up there."

"*You* can persuade armed D'regs not to charge and *you* have a commander?"

"Yes, sir. He says this is a police action."

The commander swallowed. "We give in," he said.

"What, just like that, sir?" said his sergeant. "Without a fight?"

"*Yes*, sergeant. Without a fight. This man can make water run uphill and *he* has a commander. I love the idea of giving in without a fight. I've fought for ten years and giving in without a fight is what I've always wanted to do."

Water dripped off the Boat's metal ceiling and blobbed onto the paper in front of Leonard of Quirm. He wiped it away. It might have been boring, waiting in a small metal can under a nondescript jetty, but Leonard had no concept of the term.

Absentmindedly, he jotted a brief sketch of an improved ventilation system.

He started to watch his own hand. Almost without his guidance, taking its instructions from somewhere else in his head, it drew a cutaway of a much larger version of the Boat. Here, here and here . . . there could be a bank of a hundred oars rather than pedals, each one manned—his pencil caressed the paper—by a well-muscled and not overdressed young warrior. A boat that would pass unseen under other boats, take men wherever they needed to go. *Here* a giant saw, affixed to the roof, so that when rowed at speed it could cut the hulls of enemy ships. And *here* and *here* a tube . . .

He stopped and stared at his drawing for a while. Then he sighed and started to tear it up.

Vimes watched from the dune. He couldn't hear much from up here, but he didn't need to.

Angua sat down beside him. "It's working, isn't it?" she said.

"Yes."

"What's he going to do?"

"Oh, he'll take their weapons and let 'em go, I suppose."

"Why do people follow him?" said Angua.

"Well, you're his girlfriend, you ought—"

"That's different. I love him because he's kind without thinking about it. He doesn't watch his own thoughts like other people do. When he does good things it's because he's decided to do them, not because he's trying to measure up to something. He's so simple. Anyway, I'm a wolf living with people, and there's a name for wolves that live with people. If he whistled, I'd come running."

Vimes tried not to show his embarrassment.

Angua smiled. "Don't worry, Mr. Vimes. You've said it yourself. Sooner or later, we're *all* someone's dog."

"It's like hypnotism," said Vimes hurriedly. "People follow him to see what's going to happen next. They tell themselves that they're just going along with it for a while and can stop any time they want to, but they never want to. It's damn magic."

"No. Have you ever really watched him? I bet he'd found out everything about Jabbar by the time he'd talked to him for ten minutes. I bet he knows the name of every camel. And he'll remember it all. People don't take that much interest in other people, usually." Her fingers idly traced a pattern in the sand. "So he makes you feel important."

"Politicians do that—" Vimes began.

"Not the way he does, believe me. I expect Lord Vetinari remembers facts about people—"

"Oh, you'd better believe *that!*"

"—but Carrot takes an *interest*. He doesn't even think about it. He makes space in his head for people. He takes an interest, and so people think they're interesting. They feel . . . better when he's around."

Vimes glanced down. Her fingers were drawing aimlessly in the sand again. We're all changing in the desert, he thought. It's not like the city, hemming your thoughts in. You can feel your mind expand to the horizons. No wonder this is where religions start. And suddenly here I am, probably not legally, just trying to do my job. Why? Because I'm too damn stupid to stop and think before I give chase, that's why. Even Carrot knew better than to do that. *I'd* have just chased after Ahmed's ship without a thought, but he was bright enough to report back to me first. He did what a responsible officer ought to do, but me . . .

"Vetinari's terrier," he said aloud. "Chase first, and think about it afterward—"

His eye caught the distant bulk of Gebra. Out there was a Klatchian army, and somewhere over *there* was the Ankh-Morpork army, and he was with a handful of people and no plan because he'd chased first and—

"But I had to," he said. "Any copper wouldn't have let a suspect like Ahmed get—"

Once again he had the feeling that the problem he was facing wasn't really a problem at all. It was something very obvious. *He* was the problem. He wasn't thinking right.

Come to think of it, he hadn't really *thought* at all.

He glanced down again at the trapped company. They had stripped down to their loincloths and were looking very sheepish, as men generally do in their underwear.

Carrot's white robe still flapped in the breeze. He hasn't been here a day, thought Vimes, and already he's wearing the desert like a pair of sandals.

". . . er . . . bingeley-bingeley beep?"

"Is that your demon diary?" said Angua.

Vimes rolled his eyes. "Yes. Although it seems to be talking about someone else."

". . . er . . . three pee em," the demon muttered slowly, ". . . day not filled in . . . Check Wall Defenses . . ."

"See? It thinks I'm in Ankh-Morpork! It cost Sybil three hundred dollars and it can't even keep track of where I am."

He flicked his cigar butt away and stood up.

"I'd better get down there," he said. "After all, I *am* the boss."

He slithered his way down the dune and strolled toward Carrot, who salaamed to him.

"A salute would do, captain, thanks all the same."

"Sorry, sir. I think I got a bit carried away."

"Why've you made them strip off?"

"Makes them a bit of a laughingstock when they return, sir. A blow to their pride." He leaned closer and whispered, "I've let their commander keep his clothes on, though. It doesn't do to show up the officers."

"Really?" said Vimes.

"And some want to join us, sir. There's Goriff's lad and a few others. They were just dragooned into the army yesterday. They don't even know why they're fighting. So I said they could."

Vimes took the captain aside. "Er . . . I don't remember suggesting that any of the prisoners joined us," he said quietly.

"Well, sir . . . I thought, what with our army approaching, and since quite a lot of these lads are from various corners of the empire and don't like the Klatchians any more than we do, I thought that a flying column of guerrilla fighters—"

"We aren't soldiers!"

"Er, I thought we *were* soldiers—"

"Yes, yes, all right. In a *way* . . . but really we're coppers, like we've always been. We don't kill people unless—"

Ahmed? Everyone's slightly on edge when he's around, he worries people, he gets information from all over the place, he seems to go where he pleases, and he's always around when there's trouble— Damn damn *damn* . . .

He ran through the crowd until he reached Jabbar, who was watching Carrot with the usual puzzled smile that Carrot caused in innocent bystanders.

"Tree dace," said Vimes. "Three days. That's seventy-two hours!"

"Yes, offendi?" said Jabbar. It was the voice of someone who recognized dawn, noon and sunset, and just let everything in between happen whenever it liked.

"So why's he called 71-hour Ahmed? What's so special about the extra hour?"

Jabbar grinned nervously.

"Did he *do* something after seventy-one hours?" said Vimes.

Jabbar folded his arms. "I will not say."

"He told you to keep us here?"

"Yes."

"But not to kill us."

"Oh, I would not kill my friend Sir Sam Mule—"

"And don't give me all that eyeball rubbish," said Vimes. "He wanted time to get somewhere and do something, right?"

"I will not say."

"You don't need to," said Vimes. "Because we are *leaving.* And if you kill us . . . well, probably you can. But 71-hour Ahmed would not like that, I expect."

Jabbar looked like a man making a difficult decision.

"He will be coming back!" he said. "Tomorrow! No problem!"

"I'm not waiting! And I don't think he wants me killed, Jabbar. He wants me alive. Carrot?"

Carrot hurried over. "Yes, sir?"

Vimes was aware that Jabbar was staring at him in horror.

"We've lost Ahmed," he said. "Even Angua can't pick up his trail with the sand blowing all over the place. We've got no place here. We're not *needed* here."

"But we *are,* sir!" Carrot burst out. "We could help the desert tribes—"

"Oh, you want to stay and fight?" said Vimes. "Against the Klatchians?"

"Against the *bad* Klatchians, sir."

"Ah, well, that's the trick, isn't it? When one of them comes screaming at you waving a sword, how do you spot his moral character? Well, you can stay if you like and fight for the good name of Ankh-Morpork. It should be a pretty short fight. But I'm off. Jenkins probably hasn't got afloat again. Okay, Jabbar?"

The D'reg was staring at the desert sand between his feet.

"You know where he is now, don't you?" Vimes prompted.

"Yes."

"Tell me."

"No. I swore to him."

"But D'regs are oath-breakers. Everyone knows that."

Jabbar gave Vimes a grin. "Oh, *oaths.* Stupid things. I gave him my *word.*"

"He won't break it, sir," said Carrot. "D'regs are very particular about things like that. It's only when they swear on gods and things that they'll ever break an oath."

"I will not tell you where he is," said Jabbar. "But . . ." he grinned again, but there was no humor in it, "how brave are you, Mr. Vimes?"

"Stop *complaining*, Nobby."

"I'm not complaining. I'm just sayin' these trousers are a bit draughty, that's all I'm saying."

"They look good on you, though."

"And what're these tin bowls supposed to be doing?"

"They're supposed to be protecting the bits you haven't got, Nobby."

"The way this breeze is blowing, I could do with some to protect the bits I *have*."

"Just try and act ladylike, will you, Nobby?"

Which would be hard, Sergeant Colon had to admit. The lady for whom the clothes had been made had been quite tall and somewhat full-figured, whereas Nobby without his armor could have hidden behind a short stick if you attached a toast rack to it about two-thirds of the way up. He looked like a gauzy accordion with a lot of jewelry. In theory, the costume would have been quite revealing, if Corporal Nobbs was something you wished to see revealed, but there were so many billows and folds now that all one could reliably say was that he was in there somewhere. He was leading the donkey, which seemed to like him. Animals tended to like Nobby. He didn't smell wrong.

"And them boots don't work," Sergeant Colon went on.

"Why not? You kept *yours* on."

"Yeah, but I'm not supposed to be a flower of the desert, right? A moon of someone's delight shouldn't kick up sparks when she walks, am I right?"

"They belonged to my gran, I ain't leaving 'em around for anyone to nick, and I ain't mooning for anyone's delight," said Nobby sulkily.

Lord Vetinari strode on ahead. The streets were already filling up. Al-Khali liked to get the business of the day started in the cool of dawn, before full day flamethrowered the landscape. No one paid the newcomers any attention, although a few people did turn round to watch Corporal Nobbs. Goats and chickens ambled out of the way as they passed.

"Watch out for people trying to sell you dirty postcards, Nobby," said Colon. "My uncle was here once and he said some bloke tried to sell him a pack of dirty postcards for five dollars. Disgusted, he was."

"Yeah, 'cos you can get 'em in the Shades for two dollars," said Nobby.

"That's what he said. *And* they were Ankh-Morpork ones. Trying to flog us our own dirty postcards? I call that disgusting, frankly."

"Good morning, sultan!" said a cheerful and somehow familiar voice. "New in town, are we?"

All three of them turned to a figure that had magically appeared from the mouth of an alleyway.

"Indeed, yes," said the Patrician.

"I could see you were! Everyone is, these days. And it is *your* lucky day, shah! I am here to help, right? You want something, I got it!"

Sergeant Colon had been staring at the newcomer. He said, in a faraway voice, "Your name's going to be something like . . . Al-jibla or something, right?"

"Heard about me, have you?" said the trader jovially.

"Sort of, yeah," said Colon slowly. "You're amazingly . . . familiar."

Lord Vetinari pushed him aside. "We are strolling entertainers," he said. "We were hoping to get an engagement at the Prince's palace . . . Perhaps you could help?"

The man rubbed his beard thoughtfully, causing various particles to cascade into the little bowls in his tray.

"Dunno about the palace," he said. "What's it you do?"

"We practice juggling, fire-eating, that sort of thing," said Vetinari.

"Do we?" said Colon.

Al-jibla nodded at Nobby. "What does . . ."

". . . she . . ." said Lord Vetinari helpfully.

". . . she do?"

"Exotic dancing," said Vetinari, while Nobby scowled.

"Pretty exotic, I should think," said Al-jibla.

"You'd be amazed."

A couple of armed men had drifted over to them. Sergeant Colon's heart sank. In those bearded faces he saw himself and Nobby, who at home would always saunter over to anything on the street that looked interesting.

"You are jugglers, are you?" said one of them. "Let's see you juggle, then."

Lord Vetinari gave them a blank look and then glanced down at the tray around Al-jibla's neck. Among the more identifiable foodstuffs were a number of green melons.

"Very well," he said, and picked up three of them.

Sergeant Colon shut his eyes.

After a few seconds he opened them again because a guard had said, "All right, but anyone can do it with three."

"In that case perhaps Mr. Al-jibla will throw me a few more?" said the Patrician, as the balls spun through his hands.

Sergeant Colon shut his eyes again.

After a short while a guard said, "Seven is pretty good. But it's just melons."

Colon opened his eyes.

The Klatchian guard twitched his robe aside. Half a dozen throwing knives glinted. And so did his teeth.

Lord Vetinari nodded. To Colon's growing surprise he did not seem to be watching the tumbling melons at all.

"Four melons and three knives," he said. "If you would care to give the knives to my charming assistant, Beti . . ."

"*Who?*" said Nobby.

"Oh? Why not seven knives, then?"

"Kind sirs, that would be too simple," said Lord Vetinari.* "I am but a humble tumbler. Please let me practice my art."

"*Beti?*" said Nobby, glowering under his veils.

Three fruits arced gently out of the green whirl and thumped on to Al-jibla's tray.

The guards looked carefully, and to Colon's mind nervously, at the cross-dressed figure of the cross corporal.

---

* Jugglers will tell you that juggling with items that are identical is always easier than a mixture of all shapes and sizes. This is even the case with chainsaws, although of course when the juggler misses the first chainsaw it is only the *start* of his problems. Some more will be along very shortly.

"She's not going to do any kind of dance, is she?" one of them ventured.

"No!" snapped Beti.

"Promise?"†

Nobby grabbed three of the knives and tugged them out of the man's belt.

"I'll give them to his lor— to him, shall I, Beti?" said Colon, suddenly quite sure that keeping the Patrician alive was almost certainly the only way to avoid a brief cigarette in the sunshine. He was also aware that other people were drifting over to watch the show.

"To me, please . . . Al," said the Patrician, nodding.

Colon tossed him the knives, slowly and gingerly. He's going to try to stab the guards, he thought. It's a *ruse*. And then everyone's going to tear us apart.

Now the circling blur glinted in the sunlight. There was a murmur of approval from the crowd.

"Yet somehow dull," said the Patrician.

And his hands moved in a complex pattern that suggested that his wrists must have moved through one another at least twice.

The tangled ball of hurtling fruit and cutlery leapt into the air.

Three melons dropped to the ground, cut cleanly in two.

Three knives thudded into the dust a few inches from their owner's sandals.

And Sergeant Colon looked up and into a growing, greenish, expanding—

The melon exploded, and so did the audience, but both their laughter and the humor was slightly lost on Colon as he scraped over-ripe pith out of his ears.

The survival instinct cut in again. Stagger around backward, it said. So he staggered around backward, waving his legs in the air. Fall down heavily, it said. So he sat down, and almost squashed a

---

† Corporal Nobbs's appearance could best be summarized this way.

One of the minor laws of the narrative universe is that any homely featured man who has, for some reason, to disguise himself as a woman will apparently become attractive to some otherwise perfectly sane men with, as the ancient scrolls say, hilarious results.

In this case the laws were fighting against the fact of Corporal Nobby Nobbs, and gave up.

chicken. Lose your dignity, it said; of all the things you've got, it's the one you can most afford to lose.

Lord Vetinari helped him up. "Our very lives depend on your appearing to be a stupid fat idiot," he hissed, putting Colon's fez back on his head.

"I ain't very good at acting, sir—"

"Good!"

"Yessir."

The Patrician scooped up three melon halves and positively *skipped* over to a stall that a woman had just set up, snatching an egg from a basket as he went past. Sergeant Colon blinked again. This was not . . . *real.* The Patrician didn't do this sort of thing . . .

"Ladies and gentlemen! You see—an egg! And here we have a—melon rind! Egg, melon! Melon, egg! We put the melon over the egg!" His hands darted across the three halves, switching them at bewildering speed. "Round and round they go, just like that! Now . . . where's the egg? What about you, shah?"

Al-jibla smirked.

"'s the one on the left," he said. "It always is."

Lord Vetinari lifted the melon. The board below was eggless.

"And you, noble guardsman?"

"'s got to be the one in the middle," said the guard.

"Yes, of course . . . oh, dear, it isn't . . ."

The crowd looked at the last melon. They were street people. They knew the score. When the object can be under one of three things, and it's already turned out not to be under two of them, then the one place it was certainly not going to be was under the third. Only some kind of gullible fool would believe something like that. Of *course* there was going to be a trick. There always *was* a trick. But you watched it, in order to see a trick done well.

Lord Vetinari raised the melon nevertheless, and the crowd nodded in satisfaction. Of *course* it wasn't there. It'd be a pretty poor day for street entertainment if things were where they were supposed to be.

Sergeant Colon knew what was going to happen next, and he knew this because for the last minute or so something had been pecking at his head.

Aware that this was probably his moment, he raised his fez and revealed a very small fluffy chick.

"Have you got a towel? I am afraid it has just gone to the toilet on my head, sir."

There was laughter, some applause and, to his amazement, a tinkling of coins around his feet.

"And finally," said the Patrician, "the beautiful Beti will do an exotic dance."

The crowd fell silent.

Then someone at the back said, "How much do we have to pay for her not to?"

"Right! I've just about had enough of this!" Veils flying out behind her, bangles jingling, elbows waving viciously and boots kicking up sparks, the lovely Beti strode into the crowd. "Which of you said that?"

People shrank away from her. *Armies* would have retreated. And there, revealed like a jellyfish deserted by a suddenly ebbing tide, was a small man about to fry in the wrath of the ascendant Nobbs.

"I meant no offense, oh, doe-eyed one—"

"Oh? Pastry-faced, am I?" Nobby flung out an arm in a crash of bracelets and knocked the man over. "You've got a lot to learn about women, young man!" And then, because a Nobbs could never resist a prone target, the petite Beti drew back a steel-capped boot—

"Beti!" snapped the Patrician.

"Oh, right, yeah, *right,*" said Nobby, with veiled contempt. "Everyone can tell me what to do, right? Just because I happen to be the woman around here I'm just supposed to accept it all, eh?"

"No, you just ain't supposed to kick him inna fork," hissed Colon, pulling him away. "It don't look good." Although, he noted, the women in the crowd seemed to be disappointed by the sudden curtailment of the performance.

"And there are many strange stories we can tell you!" shouted the Patrician.

"Beti certainly could," murmured Colon, and was kicked sharply on his ankle.

"And many strange sights we can show you!"

"Beti cert— Aargh!"

"But for now we will seek the shade of yonder caravanserai . . ."

"What're we doing?"

"We're going to the pub."

The crowd began to disperse, but with occasional amused glances back at the trio.

One of the guards nodded at Colon. "Nice show," he said. "Especially the bit where your lady didn't remove any veils—" He darted behind his colleague as Nobby spun round like an avenging angel.

"Sergeant," the Patrician whispered. "It is very important that we learn the current whereabouts of Prince Cadram, do you understand? In taverns, people talk. Let us keep our ears open."

The tavern wasn't Colon's idea of a pub. For one thing, most of it had no roof. Arched walls surrounded a courtyard. A grapevine grew out of a huge cracked urn and had been teased overhead on trellises. There was the gentle sound of tinkling water, and unlike the Mended Drum this was not because the bar backed onto the privies but because of a small fountain in the middle of the cobbles. And it was cool, much cooler than in the street, even though the vine leaves scarcely hid the sky.

"Didn't know you could juggle, sir," Colon whispered to Lord Vetinari.

"You mean you can't, sergeant?"

"Nossir!"

"How strange. It's hardly a skill, is it? One knows what the objects are and where they want to go. After that it's just a case of letting them occupy the correct positions in time and space."

"You're dead good at it, sir. Practice often, do you?"

"Until today, I've never tried." Lord Vetinari looked at Colon's astonished expression. "After Ankh-Morpork, sergeant, a handful of flying melons present a very minor problem indeed."

"I'm amazed, sir."

"And in politics, sergeant, it is always important to know where the chicken is."

Colon raised his fez. "Is this one still on my head?"

"It seems to have gone to sleep. I wouldn't disturb it, if I were you."

"'ere, you, juggler . . . she can't come in here!"

They looked up. Someone with a face and apron that said

"barman" in seven hundred languages was standing over them, a wine jug in each hand.

"No women in here," he went on.

"Why not?" said Nobby.

"No women asking questions, neither."

"Why not?"

"'cos it is written, that's why."

"Where'm I supposed to go, then?"

The barman shrugged. "Who knows where women go?"

"Off you go, Beti," said the Patrician. "And . . . listen for information!"

Nobby grabbed the cup of wine from Colon and gulped it down.

"I dunno," he moaned, "I've only been a woman ten minutes and already I hate you male bastards."

"I dunno what's got into him, sir," whispered Colon as Nobby stamped out. "He ain't like this normally. I thought Klatchian women did what they were told!"

"Does *your* wife do what she's told, sergeant?"

"Well, yeah, obviously, a man's got to be the master in his own house, that's what I always say—"

"So why are you, I hear, always putting up kitchen furniture?"

"Well, obviously, you've got to listen to—"

"In fact Klatchian history is full of famous examples of women who even went to war with their men," said the Patrician.

"What? On the same side?"

"Prince Arkven's wife Tistam used to ride into the battle with her husband and, according to legend, killed ten thousand thousand men."

"That's a lot of men."

"Legends are prone to inflation. However, I believe there is good historical evidence that Queen Sowawondra of Sumtri had more than thirty thousand people put to death during her reign. She could be quite touchy, they say."

"You should hear my wife if I don't put the plates away," said Sergeant Colon gloomily.

"Now we are integrated with the local population, sergeant," said the Patrician, "we must find out what is happening. Although an invasion is clearly planned, I feel sure Prince Cadram will have reserved some forces in case of land attack. It would be nice to know where they are, because that's where he will be."

"Right."

"You think you can handle this?"

"Yessir. I know Klatchians, sir. Don't you worry about that."

"Here's some money. Buy drinks for people. Mingle."

"Right."

"Not too many drinks, but as much mingling as you are capable of."

"I'm a good mingler, sir."

"Off you go, then."

"Sir?"

"Yes?"

"I'm a bit worried about . . . Beti, sir. Going off like that. Anything might happen to hi . . . her." But he spoke with some hesitation. There wasn't much you could imagine happening to Corporal Nobbs.

"I'm sure we shall hear about it if there are any problems," said the Patrician.

"You're right there, sir."

Colon sidled over to a group of men who were sitting in a rough circle on the floor, talking quietly amongst themselves and eating from a large dish.

He sat down. The men on either side of him obediently shuffled along.

Now then, how did you . . . ah, right . . . *anyone* knew how Klatchians talked . . .

"Greetings, fellow brothers of the dessert," he said. "I don't know about you, but I could just do with a plate of sheep's eyeballs, eh? I bet you boys can't wait to be back on your camels, I know I can't. I spit upon the defiling dogs of Ankh-Morpork. Anyone had any baksheesh lately? You can call me Al."

"Excuse me, are you the lady who is with the clowns?"

Corporal Nobbs, who had been trudging along gloomily, looked up. He was being addressed by a pleasant-faced young woman. A woman actually talking to him by choice was a novelty. Smiling while doing so was unheard of.

"Er . . . yeah. Right. That's me." He swallowed. "Beti."

"My name is Bana. Would you like to come and talk with us?"

Nobby looked past her. There were a number of women of varying ages sitting around a large well. One of them waved at him shyly.

He blinked. This was uncharted territory. He looked down at his clothes, which were already the worse for wear. His clothes always looked the worse for wear five minutes after he'd put them on.

"Oh, don't worry," said the girl. "We know how it is. But you looked so alone. And perhaps you can help us . . ."

They were among the group now. There were women of every legitimate shape and size, and so far none of them had said "Yuk," an experience hitherto unchronicled in Nobby's personal history. In a detached, light-headed way, Corporal Nobbs felt that he was entering Paradise, and it was only an unfortunate detail that he'd come in via the wrong door.

"We are trying to comfort Netal," said the girl. "Her betrothed won't marry her tomorrow."

"The swine," said Nobby.

One of the girls, eyes red with crying, looked up sharply.

"He *wanted* to," she sobbed. "But he's been taken off to fight in Gebra! All over some island no one's heard of! And all my family are here!"

"Who took him off?" said Nobby.

"He took himself off," snapped an older woman. Clothing differences aside, there was something hauntingly familiar about her, and Nobby realized that if you cut her in half the words "mother-in-law" would be all the way through.

"Oh, Mrs. Atbar," said Netal, "he said it was his *duty*. Anyway, all the boys have had to go."

"Men!" said Nobby, rolling his eyes.

"I expect you'd know a lot about the pleasures of men, then," said Mother-in-Law sourly.

"Mother!"

"Who, me?" said Nobby, forgetting himself for a moment. "Oh, yeah. Lots."

"You *do?*"

"Why not? Beer's favorite," said Nobby. "But you can't beat a good cigar, as long as it's free."

"Hah!" Mother-in-Law picked up a basket of washing and stamped away, followed by most of the older women. The others laughed. Even the disappointed Netal smiled.

"I *think* that's not what she meant," said Bana. To a chorus of giggles, she leaned down and whispered in Nobby's ear.

His expression did not change but it did seem to solidify.

"Oh, *that,*" he said.

There were some worlds of experience which Nobby had only contemplated on a map, but he knew what she was talking about. Of course he'd patrolled certain parts of the Shades in his time—the ones where young ladies tended to hang around without very much to do, and probably catching cold too—but those areas of police work that in other places might be of interest to a Vice Squad now tended to be looked after by the Guild of Seamstresses themselves. People who neglected to obey the . . . no, not the law as such, call them the *unwritten rules* . . . as laid down by Mrs. Palm and her committee of very experienced ladies* attracted the attention of the Agony Aunts, Dotsie and Sadie, and might or might not be seen again. Even Mr. Vimes approved of the arrangement. It didn't cause paperwork.

"Oh, yeah," said Nobby, still staring at some inner screen.

Of course, he *knew* what . . .

"Oh, *that,*" he mumbled. "Well, I've seen a thing or two," he added. Largely on postcards, he had to admit.

"It must be wonderful to have so much freedom," said Bana.

"Er . . ."

Netal burst out crying again. Her friends fluttered around her.

"I don't see why the men have to go off like this," said Bana. "My betrothed has gone too."

There was a cackle from a very old woman sitting by the well. "I can tell you why, dears. Because it's better than growing melons all day. It's better than women."

---

* And Mr Harris of the Blue Cat Club. His admission caused a lot of argument in the Guild, who knew competition when they saw it, but Mrs. Palm overruled opposition on the basis, she said, that unnatural acts were only natural.

"Men think war is better than women?"

"It's always fresh, it's always young, and you can make a good fight last all day."

"But they get killed!"

"Better to die in battle than in bed, they say." She cracked a toothless grin. "But there are good ways for a man to die in bed, eh, Beti?"

Nobby hoped the glow of his ears wasn't singeing his veil. Suddenly, he felt he'd caught up with his future. Ten damn pence' worth of it hit him in the face.

"'scuse me," he said. "Are any of you Nubilians?"

"What are Nubilians?" said Bana.

"It's a country round here," said Nobby. He added hopefully, "Isn't it?"

Not a single face suggested that this was so.

Nobby sighed. His hand reached up to his ear for a cigarette end, but it came down again empty.

"I'll tell you this, girls," he said. "I wish I'd settled for the ten-dollar version. Don't you just sometimes want to sit down and cry?"

"You look even sadder than Netal," said Bana. "Isn't there some way we can cheer you up?"

Nobby stared at her for a moment, and then started to sob.

Everyone was staring at Colon, their food halfway to their lips.

"Did I just hear him say that. Faifal? What do I want to be on a camel for? I'm a plumber!"

"He is the clown with the juggler. I think. The poor man is several palms short of an oasis."

"I mean the bloody things spit and they're a bugger to get up the stairs with your toolbox—"

"Now, come on, it's not his fault, let's show a little charity." The speaker cleared his throat. "Good morning, friend," he said. "May we invite you to share our couscous?"

Sergeant Colon peered at the bowl, and then dipped in a finger and tasted it.

"Hey, this is semolina! You've got *semolina!* It's just ordinary semol—" He stopped, and coughed. "Yeah, right. Thanks. Got any strawberry jam?"

The host looked at his friends. They shrugged.

"We know not of this 'strawberry hjam' of which you speak," he said carefully. "We prefer it with lamb." He offered Colon a long wooden skewer.

"Oh, you gotta have strawberry jam," said Colon, carried away. "When we were kids we'd stir it in and . . . and . . ." He looked at their faces. "O'course, that was back in Ur," he said.

The men nodded at one another. Suddenly it was all clear.

Colon belched loudly.

From the looks he got from everyone else, he was the only one who'd heard of this common Klatchian custom.

"So," he said, "where's the army these days? Approximately?"

"Why do you ask, o full-of-gas one?"

"Oh, we thought we could make a bit of cash entertaining the troops," said Colon. He was immensely proud of this idea. "You know . . . a smile, a song, a lack of exotic dancing. But that means we got to know where they are, see?"

"Excuse me, fat one, but can you understand what I am saying?"

"Yes, it's very tasty," Colon hazarded.

"Ah, I thought so. So he's a spy. But whose?"

"Really? Who would be so stupid as to use a joke like this as a spy?"

"Ankh-Morpork?"

"Oh, come on! He's pretending to be an Ankh-Morpork spy, perhaps. But they're cunning over there—"

"You think? A people who make curry out of something called powder and you think they're clever?"

"I reckon he's from Muntab. They're always watching us."

"And pretending to be from Ankh-Morpork?"

"Well, if you were trying to look like a joke Morporkian pretending to be Klatchian, wouldn't you look like that?"

"But why'd he pretend to be from there?"

"Ah . . . politics."

"Let's call the Watch, then."

"Are you mad? We've been talking to him! They will be . . . inquisitive."

"Good point. I know . . ."

Faifal gave Colon a big grin.

"I did hear the entire army has marched away to 𝔈n al Ꙅams la Ꙇaisa," he said. "But don't tell anyone."

"Have they?" Colon glanced at the other men. They were watching him with curiously deadpan expressions.

"Sounds like a massive place, with a name like that," he said.

"Oh, huge," said his neighbor. One of the other men made a noise that you might think was a suppressed chuckle.

"It's a long way, is it?"

"No, very close. You're practically on top of it," said Faifal. He nudged a colleague, whose shoulders were shaking.

"Oh, *right*. Big army, is it?"

"Could easily be very big, yes."

"Fine. Fine," said Colon. "Er . . . anyone got a pencil? I could've sworn I had one when—"

There was a noise outside the tavern. It was the sound of many women laughing, which is always a disquieting noise to men.* Customers peered suspiciously through the vines.

Colon and the rest of the crowd looked around an urn at the group by the well. An old lady was rolling on the ground, laughing, and various younger ones were leaning against one another for support.

He heard one of them say, "What did he say again?"

"He said, 'That's funny, it's never done that when *I've* tried it!'"

"Yeah, *that's* true!" cackled the old woman. "It never does!"

"'That's funny, it's never done that when I've tried it,'" Nobby repeated.

Colon groaned. That was the voice and tone of Corporal Nobbs in storytelling mode, when wood could scorch at ten yards.

"'scuse me," he muttered, and forced his way through the press to the gateway.

"Have you heard the one about the ki . . . the sultan who was afraid his wife . . . one of his wives . . . would be unfaithful to him while he was away?"

"We haven't heard *any* stories like *these*, Beti!" Bana gasped.

---

* Usually because they suspect the joke's on them.

"Really? Oh, I've got a thousand and one of 'em. Well, anyway, he went and saw the wise old blacksmith, right, and *he* said—"

"You can't go round telling stories like that, cor— Beti," Colon panted as he lumbered to a halt.

Nobby realized that a change had come over the group. Now he was surrounded by women who were in the presence of a man. A known man, he corrected himself.

Several of them were blushing. They hadn't blushed before.

"Why not?" said Beti nastily.

"You'll offend people," said Colon uncertainly.

"Er, we are not offended, sir," said Bana, in a small humble voice. "We think Beti's stories are very . . . instructive. Especially the one about the man who went into the tavern with the very small musician."

"And that was pretty hard to translate," said Nobby, "because they don't really know what a piano *is* in Klatch. But it turns out there's this kind of stringed—"

"And it was very interesting about the man with his arms and legs in plaster," said Netal.

"Yeah, and they laughed even though they don't have the same kind of doorbells here," said Nobby. "Here, you don't have to go—"

But the group around the well was dispersing. Water jugs were being picked up and carried away. A kind of preoccupied busyness came over the women.

Bana nodded at Beti. "Er . . . thank you. It's been very . . . interesting. But we must go. It was so kind of you to talk to us."

"Er, no, don't go . . ."

A faint suggestion of perfume hung in the air.

Beti glared at Colon. "Sometimes I really want to give you a right ding alongside the lughole," she growled. "My first bloody chance in *years* and you—"

She stopped. There was a crowd of puzzled yet disapproving faces behind Colon.

And things might have ended otherwise had it not been for the braying of the donkey, from above.

The stolen donkey, easily pulling away from Nobby's inexpert tether, had wandered off in search of food. She vaguely associated this with the doorway to her stable and therefore with doorways in general, and so had wandered through the nearest open one.

There had been some narrow spiral stairs inside, but her stall was pretty narrow and steps didn't worry a donkey that was used to the streets of Al-Khali.

It was only a disappointment when the steps came to an end and there was *still* no hay.

"Oh no," said someone behind Colon. "There's a donkey up the minaret *again*."

There were groans all round.

"What's wrong with that? What goes up must come down," said Colon.

"You don't know?" said one of his dining companions. "You don't have *minarets* in Ur?"

"Er—" said Colon.

"We have plenty of donkeys," said Lord Vetinari. There was general laughter, most of it directed at Colon.

One of the men pointed to the dim interior of the minaret.

"Look . . . see?"

"A very narrow, winding staircase," said the Patrician. "So . . . ?"

"There's nowhere to turn at the top, right? Oh, any fool can get a donkey *up* a minaret. But have you ever tried getting an animal to go backward down a narrow staircase in the dark? Can't be done."

"There's something about a rising staircase," said someone else. "It attracts donkeys. They think there's something at the top."

"We had to push the last one off, didn't we?" said one of the guards.

"Right. It splashed," said his comrade in arms.

"No one is pushing Valerie off'f *anything*," snarled Beti. "Any one of you tries anything like that and, s'welp me, you'll feel the wrong end of—" He stopped, and a wide horrible grin appeared behind the veil. "I mean, I'll give you a great big soppy *kiss*."

Several men at the back of the crowd took to their heels.

"There's no need to get nasty," said the guard.

"I *mean* it!" said Beti, advancing.

The cowering guard cringed. "Can't you do anything with her, sirs?"

"Us?" said Lord Vetinari. "'fraid not. Oh, dear . . . it's going to be like that business in Djelibeybi all over again, Al."

"Oh, dear," said Colon, mugging loyally. The crowd, or at least that part that thought itself sufficiently far away from Beti, started to grin. This was street theater.

"I don't know if they ever got that man down off the flagpole," Vetinari went on.

"Oh, *most* of 'im, they did," said Colon.

"Tell you what, tell you what," said the guard hurriedly, "suppose we get a rope round it—"

"—her—" Beti growled.

"Her, right, and then—"

"You'd need at least three men up there and there ain't no room!"

"Sir, I've got an idea," whispered one of the guards.

"I should make it quick," said Colon. "'cos there's no stopping Beti once she gets going."

The guards held a whispered argument.

"We'd get into trouble if we do that! You know all that stuff we were told about the war effort! That's why they were all confiscated!"

"No one will miss it for five minutes!"

"Yeah, but you want to tell the Prince we lost one?"

"All right, but do you want to explain to her?"

They both looked at Beti.

"And they're easy to steer, after all," one whispered.

"Valerie?" said Sergeant Colon.

"There is a problem?" Beti demanded.

"No! No. It's a fine name for a donkey, N— Beti."

"No one is to do anything," said one of the guards. "We will return."

"What was all that about?" said Colon, watching them go.

"Oh, they've probably gone to get a carpet," said someone.

"Very nice, but I don't see how that'd help," said Beti.

"A flying one."

"Oh, *right,*" said Colon. "They've got one of those up at the University—"

"Ur has a university?"

"Oh, indeed," said the Patrician. "How do you think Al learned what a donkey looks like?"

Once again, laughter dispelled doubt. Colon grinned uncertainly.

"I'm really getting good at this stupid idiot stuff, aren't I?" he said. "It just sort of happens!"

"Marvelous," said Lord Vetinari.

There was another angry braying from far above.

"Trouble is, they're all locked up because of the war effort," said someone behind them.

A piece of mud brick shattered on the ground nearby.

"The way it's thrashing around up there, it's going to fall off anyway."

"Perhaps I should *persuade* her to come down," said the Patrician.

"Can't be done, offendi. You can't get past on the stairs, you can't turn it round, and it won't come down backward."

"I shall consider the situation," said the Patrician.

He ambled back into the tavern for a moment, and returned. They saw him enter the door and they heard him climbing the staircase.

"Should be good," said a man behind Colon.

After a while the braying stopped.

"Can't turn around, see. Far too narrow," said the elevated-donkey expert. "Can't turn around, won't go backward. Well-known fact."

"There's always a know-all, right, Beti?" said Colon.

"Yeah. Always."

The tower was full of silence. Several members of the crowd found their attention drawn to it.

"I mean, if you could get three or four men up the stairs, which you can't, you could sort of move it a leg at a time, if you didn't mind being kicked and bitten to death . . ."

"All right, all right, back away from the tower, will you?"

The guards were back. One of them was carrying a rolled-up carpet.

"All right, all right, give us room—"

"I can hear hooves," said someone.

"Oh, yeah, like our friend in the fez is getting the donkey down the stairs?"

"Hang on, I can hear them too," said Colon.

Now all eyes stared at the door.

Lord Vetinari emerged, holding a length of rope.

The voice behind Colon said, "All right, it's just a bit of rope. He was probably banging a couple of coconut shells together."

"You mean, ones that he found in the minaret?"

"He had them with him, obviously."

"You mean, he carries coconut shells around?"

"You can't *turn* a donkey round in— All right, that's a fake donkey head . . ."

"It's moving its ears!"

"On a string, on a string—all right, it's a donkey, okay, but it's not the *same* donkey. It's one he had in a hidden pocket . . . well, no need to look at me like that. I've seen them do it with doves . . ."

Then even the unbeliever fell silent.

"Donkey, minaret," said Lord Vetinari. "Minaret, donkey."

"Just like that?" said a guard. "How did you do it? It was a trick, right?"

"Of course it was a trick," said Lord Vetinari.

"I *knew* it was just a trick."

"That's right, it was just a trick," said Lord Vetinari.

"So . . . how did you do it, then?"

"You mean you can't spot it?"

The crowd craned to see.

"Er . . . you had an inflatable donkey—"

"Can you think of any reason why I should go around with an inflatable donkey?"

"Well, you—"

"One that you wouldn't mind explaining to your own dear mother?"

"If you're going to put it like that—"

"'s easy," said Al-jibla. "There's a secret compartment in the minaret. Must be."

"No, you've got it all wrong, it's just an *illusion* of a donkey . . . Well, all right, it's a *good* illusion . . ."

By now half the people were around the donkey and the others were clustered in the doorway of the minaret, looking for secret panels.

"I think, Al and Beti, this is where we walk away," said Lord Vetinari, behind Colon. "Just down this little alley here. And when we turn that corner, we run."

"What've we got to run for?" said Beti.

"Because I've just picked up the magic carpet."

Vimes was already lost. Oh, there was the sun, but that was just a *direction*. He could feel it on the side of his face.

And the camel rocked from side to side. There was no real way of judging distance, except by hemorrhoids.

I'm blindfolded on the back of a camel ridden by a D'reg, who everyone says are the most untrustworthy people in the world. But I'm almost positive he's not going to kill me.

"So," he said, as he rocked gently from side to side, "you may as well tell me. Why 71-hour Ahmed?"

"He killed a man," said Jabbar.

"And D'regs object to a little thing like that?"

"In the man's own tent! When he had been his guest for nearly tree dace! If he had but waited an hour—"

"Oh, I *see*. Definitely bad manners. Had the man done anything to deserve it?"

"Nothing! Although . . ."

"Yes?"

"The man *had* killed El-Ysa." The D'reg's tone suggested that this wasn't much of a mitigating circumstance, but that it ought to be mentioned out of completeness.

"Who was she?"

"El-Ysa was a village. He poisoned a well. There had been a dispute over religion," he added. "One thing led to another . . . but even so, to break the tradition of hospitality . . ."

"Yes, I can see that's a terrible thing. Almost . . . impolite."

"The hour was important. Some things should not be done."

"You're right there, at least."

By mid-afternoon Jabbar let him take off the blindfold. Wind-carved heaps of black rock stood out of the sand. Vimes thought it was the most desolate place he'd ever seen.

"They say once it was green," said Jabbar. "A well watered land."

"What happened?"

"The wind changed."

At sunset they reached a wadi between more wind-scoured rocks, and it was only the length of the shadows, deepening the shallow indentations, that began to give them back an ancient shape.

"They're buildings, aren't they?" said Vimes.

"There was a city here, a long time ago. Did you not know?"

"Why should I know?"

"Your people built it. It was called Tacticum. After a warrior of yours."

Vimes looked at the crumbled walls and fallen pillars.

"He had a city named after him . . ." he said to no one in particular.

Jabbar nudged him. "Ahmed is watching you," he said.

"I can't see him anywhere."

"Of course. Get down. And I hope we meet again in whatever is your paradise."

"Right, right . . ."

Jabbar turned the camel round. It left much faster than it had arrived.

Vimes sat on a rock for a while. There was no sound but the hissing of the wind in the rocks and the cry of some bird, far away.

He thought he could hear his own heart beating.

"Bingeley . . . bingeley . . . beep . . ." The Dis-organizer sounded worried and uncertain.

Vimes sighed. "Yes? Appointment with 71-hour Ahmed, eh?"

"Er . . . no . . ." said the demon. "Er . . . Klatchian fleet sighted . . . er . . ."

"Ships of the desert, eh?"

"Er . . . beep . . . error code 746, divergent temporal instability . . ."

Vimes shook the box. "Something wrong with you?" he demanded. "You're still giving me someone else's appointments, you idiot box!"

"Er . . . the appointments are correct for Commander Samuel Vimes . . ."

"That's me!"

"Which one of you?" said the demon.

"What?"

". . . beep . . ."

It refused to say more. Vimes considered throwing it away, but Sybil would be hurt if she found out. He thrust it back into his pocket and tried to concentrate on the scenery again.

His seat might have been part of a pillar once. Vimes saw other pieces some way away, and then realized that a heap of apparent rubble was a fallen wall. He followed this, his footsteps echoing off the cliffs, and realized that he was walking between old buildings, or where buildings had been. Here was the wreck of some stairs, there the stump of a pillar.

One was a little higher than the others. He pulled himself up and found, on its flat top, two huge feet. A statue must have stood here. It probably stood, if Vimes knew anything about statues, in some kind of noble attitude. Now it had gone, and there were just feet, broken off at the ankles. They weren't exceptionally noble.

As he lowered himself again he saw, protected because this side was out of the wind, some lettering carved deeply into the plinth. He tried to make it out in the fading light:

"AB HOC POSSUM VIDERE DOMUM TUUM"

Well . . . "domum tuum" was "your house," wasn't it? . . . and "videre" was "I see" . . .

"What?" he said aloud. "'I can see your house from up here?' What kind of a noble sentiment is that?"

"I believe it was meant to be a boast and a threat, Sir Samuel," said 71-hour Ahmed. "Somewhat typical of Ankh-Morpork, I've always thought."

Vimes stood very still. The voice had been right behind him.

And it *was* Ahmed's voice. But it lacked that hint of camel spit and gravel that it had possessed in Ankh-Morpork. Now it was the drawl of a gentleman.

"It's the echoes here," Ahmed went on. "I *could* be anywhere. I could have a crossbow aimed at you right *now*."

"You won't fire it, though. We've both got too much at stake."

"Oh, there is honor among thieves, is there?"

"I don't know," said Vimes. Oh, well . . . time to see if he was dead right or just dead. "Is there honor among policemen?"

Sergeant Colon's eyes went big.

"Swing my weight to one side?" he said.

"That's how magic carpets are steered," said Lord Vetinari calmly.

"Yes, but supposing I swing myself off?"

"We'll have a lot more room," said Beti unfeelingly. "C'mon, sarge, you know how to throw your weight around."

"I ain't throwing my weight *anywhere*," said Colon firmly. He was lying full length on the carpet, both hands gripping it as hard as possible. "It's not natural, just a bit of broadloom between you and certain splash."

The Patrician looked down. "We're not over water, sergeant."

"I know what I meant, sir!"

"Can we slow down a bit?" said Beti. "The breeze is invading my privacy, if you get my drift."

Lord Vetinari sighed. "We're not going very fast as it is. I suspect this is a very old carpet."

"There's a frayed bit here," said Beti.

"Shut up," said Colon.

"Look, I can poke my finger right through—"

"Shut up."

"Notice how it kind of wobbles when you move?"

"Shut up."

"Here, look, those palm trees down there look really small."

"Nobby, you're scared of heights," said Colon. "I *know* you're scared of heights."

"That's sexual stereotyping!"

"No, it's not!"

"Yes, it is! You'll be expecting me to break my ankle a lot and scream all the time next! It's my job to prove to you that a woman can be as good as a man!"

"Practically identical in your case, Nobby. You've caught too much sun, that's what it is. You are not female, Nobby!"

Beti sniffed. "That's just the sort of sexist remark I'd expect from you."

"Well, you're not!"

"It's the principle of the thing."

"Well, at least we now have transport," said Lord Vetinari, his tone suggesting that the show was over. "Unfortunately, I had no time to find out where the army is."

"Ah! I can help you there, sir!" Colon tried to salute, and then made a grab for the carpet again. "I found out by cunning, sir!"

"Really?"

"Yessir! It's at a place called . . . er . . . En al Sams la Laisa, sir."

The carpet drifted onward for a moment, in silence.

"'The Place where the Sun Shineth Not'?" said the Patrician.

There was more silence. Colon was trying not to look at anyone.

"Is there a somewhere called Gebra?" said Nobby, sulkily.

"Yes, Be— corporal. There is."

"They've gone there. Of course, you've only got a woman's word for it."

"Well done, corporal. We shall head up the coast."

Lord Vetinari relaxed. In a busy and complex life he'd never met people quite like Nobby and Colon. They talked all the time yet there was something almost . . . *restful* about them.

He watched the dusty horizon carefully as the ancient carpet curved around. Under his arm was the metal cylinder Leonard had made for him.

Drastic times required drastic measures.

"Sir?" said Colon, his voice muffled by the carpet.

"Yes, sergeant?"

"I've got to know . . . How *did* you . . . you know . . . get the donkey down?"

"Persuasion, sergeant."

"What? Just talking?"

"Yes, sergeant. Persuasion. And, admittedly, a sharp stick."

"Ah! I *knew*—"

"The trick of getting donkeys down from minarets," said the

Patrician, as the desert unwound below them, "is always to find that part of the donkey which seriously wishes to get down."

The wind had settled. The bird up on the cliffs had shut down for the night. All Vimes could hear was the sizzle of the little desert creatures.

Then Ahmed's voice said: "I am genuinely impressed, Sir Samuel."

Vimes took a deep breath. "You know, you really fooled me," he said. "'May your loins be full of fruit.' That was a good one. I really thought you were just—" He stopped. But Ahmed continued:

"—just another camel-driver with a towel on his head? Oh, dear. And you'd been doing so well up to now, Sir Samuel. The Prince was very impressed."

"Oh, come *on*. You were all but making suggestive comments about melons. What was I supposed to think?"

"Don't fret, Sir Samuel. I consider it all a compliment. You can turn around. I wouldn't dream of harming you unless you do something . . . foolish."

Vimes turned. He could just make out a shape in the afterglow.

"You were admiring this place," said Ahmed. "Tacticus's men had it built when he tried to conquer Klatch. It's not really a city by today's standards, of course. It was really just making a point. 'Here we are and here we stay,' as it were. And then the wind changed."

"You murdered Snowy Slopes, didn't you?"

"The term is executed. I can show you the confession he signed beforehand."

"Of his own free will?"

"More or less."

"What?"

"Let us say, I pointed out to him the alternatives to signing the confession. I was kind enough to leave you the pad. After all, I wanted to keep your interest. And don't look like that, Sir Samuel. I need you."

"How can you tell how I look?"

"I can guess. The Assassins' Guild had a contract on him in any case. And by a happy chance I *am* a Guild member."

"You?" Vimes tried to bite down on the word. And then: why *not* him? Kids got sent a thousand miles to be taught in the Assassins' Guild school . . .

"Oh, yes. The best years of my life, they tell me. I was in Viper House. Up School! Up School! Right Up School!" He sighed like a prince and spat like a camel driver. "If I shut my eyes I can still recall the taste of that peculiar custard we used to get on Mondays. Dear me, how it all comes back . . . I remember every soggy street. Does Mr. Dibbler still sell his horrible sausages inna bun in Treacle Mine Road?"

"Yes."

"Still the same old Dibbler, eh?"

"Still the same sausages."

"Once tasted, never forgotten."

"True."

"No, don't move too quickly, Sir Samuel. Otherwise I'm afraid I shall be cutting your own throat. You don't trust me, and I don't trust you."

"Why did you drag me here?"

"Drag you? I had to sabotage my own ship so you wouldn't lose me!"

"Yes, but . . . you . . . knew how I'd react." Vimes's heart began to sink. *Everyone* knew how Sam Vimes would react . . .

"Yes. Would you like a cigarette, Sir Samuel?"

"I thought you sucked those damn cloves."

"In Ankh-Morpork, yes. Always be a little bit foreign wherever you are, because everyone knows foreigners are a little bit stupid. Besides, these are rather good."

"Fresh from the desert?"

"Hah! Yes, *everyone* knows Klatchian cigarettes are made from camel dung." A match flared, and for a moment Vimes caught a glimpse of the hooked nose as Ahmed lit the cigarette for him. "That is one area where, I regret to say, prejudice has some evidence on its side. No, these are all the way from Sumtri. An island where, it is said, the women have no souls. Personally, I doubt it."

263

Vimes could make out a hand, holding the packet. Just for a moment he wondered if he could grab and—

"How is your luck?" said Ahmed.

"Running out, I suspect."

"Yes. A man should know the length of his luck. Shall I tell you how I know you are a good man, Sir Samuel?" In the light of the rising moon Vimes saw Ahmed produce a cigarette holder, insert one, and light up almost fastidiously.

"Do tell."

"After the attempt on the Prince's life I suspected *everyone.* But you suspected only your own people. You couldn't bring yourself to think the Klatchians might have done it. Because that'd line you up with the likes of Sergeant Colon and all the rest of the Klatchian-cigarettes-are-made-of-camel-dung brigade."

"Whose policeman are you?"

"I draw my pay, let us say, as the *wali* of Prince Cadram."

"I shouldn't think he's very happy with you right now, then. You were supposed to be guarding his brother, weren't you?" So was I, Vimes thought. But what the hell . . .

"Yes. And we thought the same way, Sir Samuel. You thought it was your people, I thought it was mine. The difference is, I was right. Khufurah's death was plotted in Klatch."

"Oh, really? That's what they *wanted* the Watch to think—"

"*No,* Sir Samuel. The important thing is what someone wanted *you* to think."

"Really? Well, you've got that wrong. All the stuff with the glass and the sand on the floor, I saw through . . . that . . . straight . . . away . . ."

His voice faded into silence.

After a while Ahmed said, almost sympathetically, "Yes, you did."

"Damn."

"Oh, in some ways you were right. Ossie *was* paid in dollars, originally. And then, later on, someone broke in, making sure they dumped *most* of the glass outside, and swapped the money. And distributed the sand. I must say that I thought the sand was going a bit too far, too. No one would be *that* stupid. But they wanted to make sure it looked like a bungled attempt."

"*Who was it?*" said Vimes.

"Oh, a small-time thief. Bob-Bob Hardyoyo. He didn't even know why he was doing it, except that someone was willing to pay him. I commend your city, commander. For enough money, you can find someone to do *anything.*"

"*Someone* must have paid him."

"A man he met in a pub."

Vimes nodded glumly. It was amazing how many people were prepared to do business with a man they'd met in a pub.

"I can believe that," he said.

"You see, if even the redoubtable Commander Vimes, who is known even to some senior Klatchian politicians as an unbendingly honest and thorough man, if somewhat lacking in intelligence . . . if even *he* protested that it was done by his own people—well, the world is watching. The world would soon find out. Starting a war over a rock? Well . . . that sort of thing makes countries uneasy. They've all got rocks off their coast. But starting a war because some foreign dog had killed a man on a mission of peace . . . that, I think, the world would understand."

"Lacking in intelligence?" said Vimes.

"Oh, don't be too depressed, commander. That business with the fire at the embassy. That was sheer bravery."

"It was bloody terror!"

"Well, the dividing line is narrow. That was one thing I hadn't expected."

In the rolling, clicking snooker table of Vimes's mind the black ball hit a pocket.

"You *had* expected the *fire,* then?"

"The building should have been almost empty—"

Vimes moved. Ahmed was lifted off his feet and slammed against a pillar, with both of Vimes's hands around his neck.

"That woman was trapped in there!"

"It . . . was . . . necessary!" said Ahmed hoarsely. "There . . . had . . . to be a . . . diversion! His . . . life was . . . in danger, I had to get him out! I did . . . not know . . . about the . . . woman until too late . . . I give you my word . . ."

Through the red veil of anger Vimes became aware of a prickle in the region of his stomach. He glanced down at the knife that had appeared magically in the other man's hand.

"Listen to me . . ." hissed Ahmed. "Prince Cadram ordered his brother's death . . . What better way to demonstrate the . . . perfidy of the sausage-eaters . . . killing a peace-maker . . ."

"His own brother? You expect me to believe that?"

"Messages were sent to . . . the embassy . . . in code . . ."

"To the old ambassador? I don't believe *that!*"

Ahmed stood quite still for a moment.

"No, you really don't, do you?" he said. "Be generous, Sir Samuel. *Truly* treat all men equally. Allow Klatchians the right to be scheming bastards, hmm? In fact the ambassador is just a pompous idiot. Ankh-Morpork has no monopoly on them. But his deputy sees the messages first. He is . . . a young man of ambition . . ."

Vimes relaxed his grip. "Him? I *thought* he was shifty as soon as I saw him!"

"I suspect that you thought he was Klatchian as soon as you saw him, but I take your point."

"And you could read this code, could you?"

"Oh, come now. Don't you read Vetinari's paperwork upside down when you're standing in front of his desk? Besides, I am Prince Cadram's policeman . . ."

"So he's your boss, right?"

"Who is *your* boss, Sir Samuel? When push comes to shove?"

The two men stood locked together. Ahmed's breath wheezed.

Vimes stood back. "These messages . . . you've got them?"

"Oh, yes. With his seal on them." Ahmed rubbed his neck.

"Good grief. The originals? I'd have thought they'd be under lock and key."

"They were. In the embassy. But in the fire many hands were needed to carry important documents to safety. It was a very . . . *useful* fire."

"A death warrant for his own brother . . . well, you can't argue against that in court . . ."

"What court? The king *is* the law." Ahmed sat down. "We are not like you. You kill kings."

"The word is 'execute.' And we only did it once, and that was a long time ago," said Vimes. "Is *that* why you brought me here? Why all this drama? You could have come to see me in Ankh-Morpork!"

"You are a suspicious man, commander. Would you have believed me? Besides, I had to get Prince Khufurah out of there, before he, ahah, 'died of his wounds.'"

"Where's the Prince now?"

"Close. And safe. He is safer in the desert than he would ever be in Ankh-Morpork, I can assure you."

"And well?"

"Getting better. He is being looked after by an old lady whom I trust."

"Your mother?"

"Ye gods, no! My mother is a D'reg! She'd be terribly offended if I trusted her. She'd say she hadn't brought me up right."

He saw Vimes's expression this time. "You think I am an educated barbarian?"

"Let's just say I'd have given Snowy Slopes a running start."

"Really? Look around you, Sir Samuel. Your . . . beat . . . is a city you can walk across in half an hour. Mine is two million square miles of desert and mountain. My companions are a sword and a camel and, frankly, neither are good conversationalists, believe me. Oh, the towns and cities have their guards, of a sort. They are uncomplicated thinkers. But it is my job to go into the waste places and chase bandits and murderers, five hundred miles from anyone who would be on my side, so I must inspire dread and strike the first blow because I will not have a chance to strike a second one. I am an honest man of a sort, I think. I survive. I survived seven years in an Ankh-Morpork public school patronized by the sons of gentlemen. Compared to that, life among the D'regs holds no terrors, I assure you. And I administer justice swiftly and inexpensively."

"I heard about how you got your name . . ."

Ahmed shrugged. "The man had poisoned the water. The only well for twenty miles. That killed five men, seven women, thirteen children and thirty-one camels. And some of them were very valuable camels, mark you. I had evidence from the man who sold him the poison and a trustworthy witness who had seen him near the well on the fateful night. Once I had testimony from his servant, why wait even an hour?"

"Sometimes we have trials," said Vimes brightly.

"Yes. Your Lord Vetinari decides. Well, five hundred miles from anywhere the law is me." Ahmed waved a hand. "Oh, no doubt the man would suggest there were mitigating circumstances, that he had an unhappy childhood or was driven by Compulsive Well-Poisoning Disorder. But I have a compulsion to behead cowardly murderers."

Vimes gave up. The man had a point. The man had a whole sword.

"Different strokes for different folks," he said.

"I find the one at shoulder height generally suffices," said Ahmed. "Don't grimace, it was a joke. I knew the Prince was plotting and I thought: this is not right. Had he killed some Ankh-Morpork lord, that would just be politics. But this . . . I thought, why do I chase stupid people into the mountains when I am part of a big crime? The Prince wants to unite the whole of Klatch. Personally, I like the little tribes and countries, even their little wars. But I don't mind if they fight Ankh-Morpork because they want to, or because of your horrible personal habits, or your unthinking arrogance . . . there's a lot of reasons for fighting Ankh-Morpork. A lie isn't one of them."

"I know what you mean," said Vimes.

"But what can I do alone? Arrest my Prince? I am his policeman, as you are Vetinari's."

"No. I'm an officer of the law."

"All I know is, there must be a policeman, even for kings."

Vimes looked pensively at the moonlit desert.

Somewhere out there was the Ankh-Morpork army, what there was of it. And somewhere waiting was the Klatchian army. And thousands of men who might have quite liked one another had they met socially would thunder toward one another and start killing, and after that first rush you had all the excuses you needed to do it again and again . . .

He remembered listening, when he was a kid, to old men in his street talking about war. There hadn't been many wars in his time. The city states of the Sto Plains mainly tried to bankrupt one another, or the Assassins' Guild sorted everything out on a one-to-one basis. Most of the time people just bickered, and while that was pretty annoying it was a lot better than having a sword stuck in your liver.

What he remembered most, among the descriptions of puddles filled with blood and the flying limbs, was the time one old man said, "An' if your foot caught in something, it was always best not to look and see what it was, if'n you wanted to hold on to your dinner." He'd never explained what he meant. The other old men seemed to know. Anyway, nothing could have been worse than the explanations Vimes thought of for himself. And he remembered that the three old men who spent most of their days sitting on a bench in the sun had, between them, five arms, five eyes, four and a half legs and two and three-quarter faces. And seventeen ears (Crazy Winston would bring out his collection for a good boy who looked suitably frightened).

"He *wants* to start a war . . ." Vimes had to open his mouth because otherwise there was no room to get his head around such a crazy idea. This man who everyone said was honest, noble and good *wanted* a war.

"Oh, certainly," said Ahmed. "Nothing unites people like a good war."

How could you deal with someone who thought like that? Vimes asked himself. A mere murderer, well, you had a whole range of options. He could deal with a mere murderer. You had criminals and you had policemen, and there was a sort of see-saw there which balanced out in some strange way. But if you took a man who'd sit down and *decide* to start a war, what in the name of seven hells could you balance him with? You'd need a policeman the size of a country.

You couldn't blame the soldiers. They'd just joined up to be pointed in the right direction.

Something clicked against the fallen pillar. Vimes glanced down and pulled the baton out of his pocket. It glinted in the moonlight.

What damn good was something like this? All it really meant was that he was allowed to chase the little criminals, who did the little crimes. There was nothing he could do about the crimes that were so big you couldn't even see them. You *lived* in them. So . . . safer to stick to the little crimes, Sam Vimes.

"ALL RIGHT, MY SONS! LET 'EM HAVE IT RIGHT UP THE JOGRAPHY!"

Figures bounded over the fallen pillars.

There was a metallic whirr as Ahmed unsheathed his sword.

Vimes saw a halberd coming toward him—an Ankh-Morpork halberd!—and street reaction took over. He didn't waste time sneering at someone stupid enough to use a pike on a foot soldier. He dodged the blade, caught the shaft, and pulled it so hard that its owner stumbled right into his upswinging boot.

Then he jerked away, struggling to untangle his sword from the unfamiliar robes. He ducked another shadowy figure's wild slice and managed to make an elbow connect with something painful.

As he rose he looked into the face of a man with an upraised sword—

—there was a silken sound—

—and the man swayed backward, his head looking surprised as it fell away from the body.

Vimes dragged his headdress off.

"I'm from Ankh-Morpork, you stupid sods!"

A huge figure sprang in front of him, a sword in each hand.

"I'LL CUT YER TONKER OFF'F YER YER GREASY— Oh, is that you, Sir Samuel?"

"Huh? Willikins?"

"Indeed, sir." The butler straightened up.

"Willikins?"

"Do excuse me one moment, sir KNOCK IT OFF YOU MOTHERLOVIN SONS OF BITCHES I had no apprehension of your presence, sir."

"This one's fightin' back, sarge!"

Ahmed had his back to a pillar. A man already lay at his feet. Three others were trying to get close enough to the *wali* while staying away from the whirling wall he was creating with his sword.

"Ahmed! These are on our side!" Vimes yelled.

"Oh, really? Pardon *me*."

Ahmed lowered his sword and removed the cigarette holder from his mouth. He nodded at one of the soldiers who had been trying to attack him and said, "Good morning to you."

"'ere, are you one of ours, too?"

"No, I'm one of—"

"He's with me," Vimes snapped. "How come you're here, Willikins? *Sergeant* Willikins, I see."

"We were on patrol, sir, and were attacked by some Klatchian gentlemen. After the ensuing unpleasantness—"

"—you should've seen 'im, sir. 'e bit one bastard's nose right orf!" a soldier supplied.

"It is true that I endeavored to uphold the good name of Ankh-Morpork, sir. Anyway, after we—"

"—and one bloke, sarge, stabbed 'im right in the—"

"Please, Private Bourke, I am apprising Sir Samuel of events," said Willikins.

"Sarge ort to get a medal, sir!"

"Those few of us who survived tried to get back, sir, but we had to conceal ourselves from other patrols and were just considering lying up until dawn in this edifice when we espied you and this gentleman here."

Ahmed was watching him with his mouth open.

"How many were in this Klatchian patrol, sergeant?" he said.

"Nineteen men, sir."

"That's a very precise count, in this light."

"I was able to enumerate them subsequently, sir."

"You mean they were all killed?"

"Yes, sir," said Willikins calmly. "However, we ourselves lost five men, sir. Not including Privates Hobbley and Webb, sir, who regrettably seem to have passed away as a result of this unfortunate misunderstanding. With your permission, sir, I will remove them."

"Poor devils," said Vimes, aware that it was not enough but that nothing else would be, either.

"The fortunes of war, sir. Private Hobbley, Ginger to his friends, was nineteen and lived in Ettercap Street, where until recently he made bootlaces." Willikins took the dead man's arms and pulled. "He was courting a young lady called Grace, a picture of whom he was kind enough to show me last night. A maid at Lady Venturi's, I was given to understand. If you would be good enough to pass me his head, sir, I will get on with things SMUDGER WHO TOLD YOU TO SIT DOWN GET ON YORE

FEET RIGHT NOW GET OUT YORE SHOVEL TAKE OFF YORE HELMET SHOW SOME RESPECT GET DIGGINGHA!"

A cloud of smoke rolled past Vimes's ear.

"I know what you are thinking," said Ahmed. "But this *is* war, Sir Samuel. Wake up and smell the blood."

"But . . . one minute they're alive—"

"Your friend here knows how it works. You don't."

"He's a butler!"

"So? It's kill or be killed, even for butlers. You're not a natural warrior, Sir Samuel."

Vimes thrust the baton in his face.

"I'm not a natural *killer!* See this? See what it says? I'm supposed to keep the peace, I am! If I kill people to do it, I'm reading the wrong manual!"

Willikins appeared silently, hefting the other corpse. "I was not privileged to know much about this young man," he said, as he carried him behind a rock. "We called him Spider, sir," he went on, straightening up. "He played the harmonica rather badly and spoke longingly of home. Will you be taking tea, sir? Private Smith is having a brew-up. Er . . ." The butler coughed politely.

"Yes, Willikins?"

"I hardly like to broach the subject, sir . . ."

"Broach it, man!"

"Do you have such a thing as a biscuit about you, sir? I hesitate to provide tea without biscuits, but we have not eaten for two days."

"But you were on patrol!"

"Forage party, sir." Willikins looked embarrassed.

Vimes was bewildered. "You mean Rust didn't even wait to take on food?"

"Oh, yes, sir. But as it transpired—"

"We knew there was somethin' wrong when the mutton barrels started to explode," muttered Private Bourke. "The biscuits was pretty lively too. Turned out bloody Rust'd bought a lot of stuff even a rag'ead wouldn't eat—"

"And we eat *anything*," said 71-hour Ahmed solemnly.

"PRIVATE BOURKE YOU ORRIBLE MAN SPEAKIN OF YORE COMMANDIN OFFICER LIKE THAT YOU WILL BE

ON A CHARGE I apologize, sir, but we are feeling a little faint."

"Long time between noses, eh?" said 71-hour Ahmed.

"Ahahaha, sir," said Willikins.

Vimes sighed. "Willikins . . . when you've finished, I want you and your men to come with me."

"Very good, sir."

Vimes nodded at Ahmed.

"And you too," he said. "Push has come to shove."

The hot wind flapped the banners. The sunlight sparkled off the spears. Lord Rust surveyed his army and found that it was good. But small.

He leaned toward his adjutant.

"Let us not forget, though, that even General Tacticus was outnumbered ten to one when he took the Pass of Al-Ibi," he said.

"Yes, sir. Although I believe his men were all mounted on elephants, sir," said Lieutenant Hornett. "And had been well provisioned," he added meaningfully.

"Possibly, possibly. But then Lord Pinwoe's cavalry once charged the full might of the Pseudopolitan army and are renowned in song and story."

"But they were all killed, sir!"

"Yes, yes, but it was a famous charge, nevertheless. And every child knows, do they not, the story of the mere one hundred Ephebians who defeated the entire Tsortean army? A total victory, hey? Hey?"

"Yes, sir," said the adjutant glumly.

"Oh, you admit it?"

"Yes, sir. Of course, some commentators believe the earthquake helped."

"At least you will admit that the Seven Heroes of Hergen beat the Big-Footed People although outnumbered by a hundred to one?"

"Yes, sir. That was a nursery story, sir. It never really happened."

"Are you calling my nurse a liar, boy?"

"No, sir," said Lieutenant Hornett hurriedly.

"Then you'll concede that Baron Mimbledrone *single-handedly* beat the armies of the Plum Pudding Country and ate their Sultana?"

"I envy him, sir." The lieutenant looked at the lines again. The men were very hungry, although Rust would probably have called them sleek. Things would have been even worse if it hadn't been for the fortuitous shower of boiled lobsters on the way over. "Er . . . you don't think, sir, since we have a little time in hand, we should look to the disposition of the men, sir?"

"They look well disposed to me. Plucky men, eager to be at the fray!"

"Yes, sir. I meant . . . more . . . well . . . positioned, sir."

"Nothing wrong with 'em, man. Beautifully lined up! Hey? A wall of steel poised to thrust at the black heart of the Klatchian aggressor!"

"Yes, sir. But—and I realize this is a *remote* chance, sir—it might be that while we're thrusting at the heart of the Klatchian aggressor—"

"—black heart—" Rust corrected him.

"—black heart of the Klatchian aggressor, sir, the arms of the Klatchian aggressor, those companies *there* and *there,* sir, will sweep around in the classic pincer movement."

"The thrusting wall of steel served us magnificently in the second war with Quirm!"

"We lost that one, sir."

"But it was a damn close-run thing!"

"We still lost, sir."

"What did you do as a civilian, lieutenant?"

"I was a surveyor, sir, and I can read Klatchian. That's why you made me an officer."

"So you don't know how to fight?"

"Only how to count, sir."

"Pah! Show a little courage, man. Although I'll wager you won't need to. No stomach for a battle, Johnny Klatchian. Once he tastes our steel, he'll be off!"

"I certainly hear what you say, sir," said the adjutant, who had been surveying the Klatchian lines and had formed his own opinion about the matter.

His opinion was this: the main force of the Klatchian army had, in recent years, been fighting everyone. That suggested, to his uncomplicated mind, that by now the surviving soldiers were the ones who were in the habit of being alive at the end of battles. And were also very experienced at facing all kinds of enemies. The stupid ones were dead.

The current Ankh-Morpork army, on the other hand, had never faced an enemy at all, although day-to-day experience of living in the city might count for something there, at least in the rougher areas. He believed, along with General Tacticus, that courage, bravery and the indomitable human spirit were fine things which nevertheless tended to take second place to the *combination* of courage, bravery, the indomitable human spirit *and* a six-to-one superiority of numbers.

It had all sounded straightforward in Ankh-Morpork, he thought. We were going to sail into Klatch and be in Al-Khali by teatime, drinking sherbet with pliant young women in the Rhoxi. The Klatchians would take one look at our weapons and run away.

Well, the Klatchians had taken a good look this morning. So far they hadn't run. They appeared to be sniggering a lot.

Vimes rolled his eyes. It worked . . . but *how* did it work?

He'd heard plenty of good speakers, and Captain Carrot was not among them. He hesitated, lost the thread, repeated himself and in general made a mess of the whole thing.

And yet . . .

And yet . . .

He watched the faces that were watching Carrot. There were the D'regs, and some of the Klatchians who had stayed behind, and Willikins and his reduced company. They were listening.

It was a kind of magic. He told people they were good chaps, and they knew they weren't good chaps, but the way he told it made them believe it for a while. Here was someone who thought you were a noble and worthy person, and somehow it would be unthinkable to disappoint them. It was a mirror of a speech, reflecting back to you what you wanted to hear. And he meant it all.

Even so, men occasionally glanced up at Vimes and Ahmed and

he could see them thinking, in their separate ways, "It must be all right if they're in on it." That, he was ashamed to realize, was one of the advantages of armies. People looked to other people for orders.

"This is a trick?" said Ahmed.

"No. He doesn't know any tricks like that," said Angua. "He really doesn't. Uh-oh . . ."

There was a scuffle in the ranks.

Carrot strode forward and reached down, bringing up Private Bourke and a D'reg, each man held by the collar in one big fist.

"What's going on, you two?"

"He called me the brother of a pig, sir."

"Liar! You called *me* a greasy dishcloth-head!"

Carrot shook his head. "And you were both doing so well, too," he said sadly. "There really is no call for this. Now I want you, Hashel, and *you,* Vincent, to shake hands, right? And apologize, yes? We've all had a rather trying time, but I know you're both fine fellows underneath it all—"

Vimes heard Ahmed murmur. "Oh, well, *now* it's all over . . ."

"—so if you'll just shake hands we'll say no more about it."

Vimes glanced at 71-hour Ahmed. The man was wearing a sort of waxen grin.

The two scufflers very gingerly touched hands, as if they were expecting a spark to leap the gap.

"And now you, Vincent, apologize to Mr. Hashel . . ."

There was a reluctant " 'ry."

"And we're sorry for what?" Carrot prompted.

" . . . sorry for calling him a greasy dishcloth-head . . ."

"Well said. And *you,* Hashel, apologize to Private Bourke."

The D'reg's eyes scurried around their sockets, looking to find a way out that would allow their body to come too. Then he gave up.

" 'ry . . ."

"For . . . ?"

" 'ry for calling him a brother of a pig . . ."

Carrot lowered both men.

"Good! I'm sure you'll get along splendidly once you get to know each other—"

"I didn't just see that, did I?" said Ahmed. "I didn't just see him talk like a little schoolteacher to Hashel who, I happen to know, once hit a man so hard his nose ended up in one of his ears?"

"Yes, you did," said Angua. "And now watch them."

When the rest of the men turned their attention back to Carrot the scufflers looked at one another, as unfortunates who had both been through the same baptism of fiery embarrassment.

Private Bourke gingerly offered Hashel a cigarette.

"It only works around him," said Angua. "But it *does* work."

Let it go on working, Vimes prayed.

Carrot walked over to a kneeling camel and climbed into the saddle.

"That's 'Evil Brother-in-Law of a Jackal,'" said Ahmed. "Jabbar's camel! It bites everyone who tries to ride it!"

"Yes, but this is Carrot."

"It even bites Jabbar!"

"And you notice how he knew how to get on a camel?" said Vimes. "How he wears the robes? He's *fitting in.* The boy was raised in a dwarf mine. It took him about a month to know my own damn city better than I do."

The camel rose. Now the flag, Vimes thought, give him the flag. When you go to war, there's got to be a flag.

On cue, Constable Shoe passed up the spear with the tightly rolled cloth around it. The constable looked proud. He'd stitched the thing in conditions of great secrecy half an hour before. One thing about a zombie, you always knew someone who had a needle and thread.

But don't unfurl it, Vimes thought. Don't let them see it. It's enough for them to know they're marching under a flag.

Carrot brandished the spear.

"And I promise you this," he shouted, "if we succeed, no one will remember. And if we fail, no one will forget!"

Probably one of the worst rallying cries, Vimes thought, since General Pidley's famous "Let's all get our throats cut, boys!" but it got a huge cheer. And once again he speculated that there was magic going on at some bone-deep level. People followed Carrot out of curiosity.

"All right, you've got an army, I suppose," said Ahmed. "And now?"

"I'm a policeman. So are you. There's going to be a crime. Saddle up, Ahmed."

Ahmed salaamed. "I am happy to be led by a white officer, offendi."

"I didn't mean—"

"Have you ever ridden a camel before, Sir Samuel?"

"No!"

"Ah?" Ahmed smiled faintly. "Then just give it a prod to get started. And when you want to stop, hit it very hard with the stick and shout 'Huthuthut!'"

"You hit it with a stick to make it stop?"

"Is there any other way?" said 71-hour Ahmed.

His camel looked at Vimes, and then spat in his eye.

Prince Cadram and his generals surveyed the distant enemy, from horseback. The various Klatchian armies were drawn up in front of Gebra. Compared to them, the Ankh-Morpork regiments looked like a group of tourists who had missed their coach.

"Is that *all?*" he said.

"Yes, sire," said General Ashal. "But, you see, they believe that fortune favors the brave."

"That is a reason to field such a contemptible little army?"

"Ah, sire, but they believe that we will turn and run as soon as we taste some cold steel."

The Prince looked back at the distant banners. "Why?"

"I couldn't say, sire. It appears to be an item of faith."

"Strange." The Prince nodded to one of his bodyguards. "Fetch me some cold steel."

After some hurried discussion a sword was handed up very gingerly, handle first. The prince peered at it, and then licked it with theatrical care. The watching soldiers laughed.

"No," he said at last. "No, I have to say that I don't feel the least apprehensive. Is this as cold as steel gets?"

"Lord Rust was probably being metaphorical, sire."

"Ah. He is the sort who would be. Well, let us go forward and meet him. We must be civilized, after all."

He urged his horse forward. The generals fell in behind him.

The Prince leaned down toward General Ashal again.

"And why are we going out to meet him before battle commences?"

"It's a . . . it's a goodwill gesture, sire. Warriors honoring one another."

"But the man's a complete incompetent!"

"Indeed, sire."

"And we're about to set thousands of our countrymen against one another, aren't we?"

"Indeed, sire."

"So what does the maniac want to do? Tell me there's no hard feelings?"

"Broadly speaking, sire . . . yes. I understand the motto of his old school was 'It matters not that you won or lost, but that you took part.'"

The Prince's lips moved as he tried this out once or twice. Finally he said: "And, knowing this, people still take orders from him?"

"It would seem so, sire."

Prince Cadram shook his head. We can learn from Ankh-Morpork, his father had said. Sometimes we can learn what not to do. And so he'd set out to learn.

First he'd learned that Ankh-Morpork had once ruled quite a slice of Klatch. He'd visited the ruins of one of its colonies. And so he'd found out the name of the man who had been audacious enough to do this, and had got agents in Ankh-Morpork to find out as much about him as possible.

General Tacticus, he'd been called. And Prince Cadram had read a lot and remembered everything, and "tactics" had been very, very useful in the widening of the empire. Of course, this had its own drawbacks. You had a border, and across the border came bandits. So you sent a force to quell the bandits, and in order to stamp them out you had to take over their country, and soon you had another restless little vassal state to rule. And now *that* had a border, over which came, sure as sunrise, a fresh lot of raiders. So your new *tax-paying* subjects were demanding protection from their brother raiders, neglecting to pay their taxes, and doing a little light banditry on the side. And so once again you stretched your forces, whether you wanted to or not . . .

He sighed. For the serious empire-builder there was no such thing as a final frontier. There was only another problem. If only people would understand . . .

Nor was there such a thing as a game of war. General Tacticus knew that. Learn about your opposite number, *yes,* and respect his abilities if he had them, certainly. But never pretend that afterward you were going to meet up for a drink and charge-by-charge replay.

"He could well be insane, sire," the general went on.

"Oh, good."

"However, I'm told that he recently referred to Klatchians as the finest soldiers in the world, sire."

"Really?"

"He added 'when led by white officers,' sire."

"Oh?"

"And we are offering him breakfast, sire. It would be most impolite of him to refuse."

"*What* a good idea. Have we got an adequate supply of sheeps' eyes?"

"I took the liberty of telling the cooks to save some up for this very eventuality, sire."

"Then we must see he gets them. After all, he will be our honored guest. Well, let us do this thing properly. Please try to look as if you hate the taste of cold steel."

The Klatchians had set up an open-sided tent on the sand between the two armies. In the welcome shade a low table had been laid. Lord Rust and his company were already waiting, and had been for more than half an hour.

They stood up and bowed awkwardly as Prince Cadram entered. Around the tent the Klatchian and Ankh-Morpork honor guards eyed one another suspiciously, every man trying to get the drop on the others.

"*Tell me . . . Do any of you gentleman speak Klatchian?*" said Prince Cadram, after the lengthy introductions.

Lord Rust's grin stayed fixed. "Hornett?" he hissed.

"I'm not quite certain what he said, sir," said the lieutenant nervously.

"I thought you knew Klatchian!"

"I can read it, sir. That's not the same . . ."

"Oh, don't worry," said the Prince. "As we say in Klatch, this clown's in charge of an army?"

Around the tent, the Klatchian generals suddenly went poker-faced.

"Hornett?"

"Er . . . something about . . . to own, to control . . . er . . ."

Cadram smiled at Lord Rust. "I'm not entirely familiar with this custom," he said. "You often meet your enemies before battle?"

"It is considered honorable," said Lord Rust. "I believe that on the night before the famous Battle of Pseudopolis officers from both sides attended a ball at Lady Selachii's, for example."

The Prince glanced questioningly at General Ashal, who nodded.

"Really? Obviously we have so much to learn. As the poet Mosheda says, *I can't believe this man.*"

"Ah, yes," said Lord Rust. "Klatchian is a very poetic language."

"Excuse me, sir," said Lieutenant Hornett.

"What is it, man?"

"There's . . . er . . . something going on . . ."

There was a column of dust in the distance. Something was approaching fast.

"One moment," said General Ashal.

He came back from his saddle with an ornate metal tube, covered in the curly Klatchian script. He squinted into one end and pointed the other at the cloud.

"Mounted men," he said. "Camels *and* horses."

"That's a Make-Things-Bigger device, isn't it?" said Lord Rust. "My word, you *are* up to date. They were invented only last year."

"I didn't buy this, my lord. I inherited it from my grandfather—" The general looked through the eyepiece again. "About forty men, I'd say."

"Dear me," murmured Prince Cadram. "Reinforcements, Lord Rust?"

"They've . . . the rider in the lead is holding a . . . a banner, I think, still rolled up—"

"Certainly not, sire!" said Lord Rust. Behind him, Lord Selachii rolled his eyes.

"—ah, now he's unfurling it . . . it's . . . a *white* flag, sire."

"Someone wishes to surrender?"

The general lowered his telescope. "It doesn't . . . I don't . . . they seem to be in a great hurry to do so, sire."

"Send a squad to apprehend them," said Prince Cadram.

"We will do so too," added Lord Rust hurriedly, nodding to the lieutenant.

"Ah, a joint effort," said the Prince.

A few seconds later groups of men detached themselves from each army and rode out on an interception course.

Everyone saw the sudden glints of sunlight from the approaching cloud. Weapons had been drawn.

"Fighting under a flag of surrender? That's . . . *immoral!*" said Lord Rust.

"Novel, certainly," said the Prince.

The three companies would have met, had it not been that even experts find it hard to judge how much ground a running camel can cover. By the time both commanders realized they should start to turn, they should have already been turning.

"It seems your people misjudged things, sire," said Lord Rust.

"I *knew* I should have had them led by white officers," said the Prince. "But . . . oh dear, it seems your men have been equally unlucky—"

He stopped. Some confusion had resulted. The foray parties had their instructions, but no one had told them what to do if they ran into the other foray party. And it was composed, after all, of men they were about to fight, and everyone knew they were treacherous greasy towel heads or perfidious untrustworthy sausage-eating madmen. And this was a battlefield. And everyone was frightened and, therefore, angry. And everyone was armed.

Sam Vimes heard the shouting behind him but had other things on his mind at this point. It is impossible to ride a running camel without concentrating on your liver and kidneys, in the hope that they won't be pounded out of your body.

The thing's legs weren't moving right, he was sure. Nothing on normal legs could be jolting him around so much. The horizon jerked backward and forward and up and down.

What was it Ahmed had said?

Vimes hit the camel hard and yelled, "Huthuthut!"

It accelerated. The jolts ran together, so that his body was no longer being jolted but was in effect in a permanent state of jolt.

Vimes thrashed it again and tried to yell, "Huthuthut!" although the word came out more like "Hngngngn!" In any case, the camel found some extra knees somewhere.

There was more shouting behind him. Turning his head as much as he dared, he saw several of his accompanying D'regs falling behind. He was certain he heard Carrot yell, but he couldn't be certain because of his own screaming.

"Stop, you bastard!" he yelled.

The tent was coming up fast. Vimes slapped the stick down again and hauled on the reins and, clearly now judging with special camel sensitivity that this was the most embarrassing moment to stop, the camel stopped. Vimes slid forward, flung his arms round a neck that was apparently thatched with old doormats, and half fell, half dropped on to the sand.

Other camels were thudding to a halt around him. Carrot grabbed his arm.

"Are you all right, sir? That was amazing! You really impressed the D'regs, screaming defiance like that! And you were still shouting for the camel to go faster when it was already galloping!"

"Gngn?"

The guards around the tent were hesitating, but that wouldn't last long.

The wind caught the white flag on Carrot's lance, making it snap.

"Sir, this *is* all right, isn't it? I mean, usually a white flag—"

"Might as well show what we're fighting for, eh?"

"I suppose so, sir."

D'regs had surrounded the tent. The air was full of dust and screams.

"What happened back there?"

"A bit of a fracas, sir. Our—" Carrot hesitated and then corrected himself. "That is, Ankh-Morpork soldiers and Klatchians have started fighting, sir. And the D'regs are fighting both of them."

"What, before the battle's officially declared? Can't you get disqualified for that?"

Vimes looked back at the guards and pointed to the flag.

"You know what this flag is?" he said. "Well, I want you to—"

"Aren't you Mr. Vimes?" said one of the Morporkians. "And that's Captain Carrot, isn't it?"

"Oh, hello, Mr. Smallplank," said Carrot. "Feeding you well, are they?"

"Yessir!"

Vimes rolled his eyes. That was Carrot again, *knowing* everyone. And the man had called him "sir" . . .

"We just need to go through," said Carrot. "We won't be a minute."

"Well, sir, these tow—" Smallplank hesitated. Certain words didn't come so easily when the subjects were standing very close to you, looking very big and tooled up. "These Klatchians are on guard too, you see—"

A stream of blue smoke was blown past Vimes's ear.

"Good morning, gentlemen," said 71-hour Ahmed. He had a D'reg crossbow in each hand. "You will note that the soldiers behind me are also well armed? Good. My name is 71-hour Ahmed. I will shoot the last man to drop his weapons. You have my word on it."

The Morporkians looked puzzled. The Klatchians began to whisper urgently.

"Put 'em down, boys," said Vimes.

The Morporkians threw their swords down hurriedly. The Klatchians dropped theirs very shortly afterward.

"A tie between the gentleman on the left and the tall one with the squint," said 71-hour Ahmed, raising both crossbows.

"Hey," said Vimes, "you can't—"

The bows twanged. The men dropped, yelling.

"However," said Ahmed, handing the bows to a D'reg behind him, who handed him another loaded one, "out of deference to the sensibilities of Commander Vimes here, I'm settling for one in the thigh and one in the toes. We are, after all, on a mission of peace."

He turned to Vimes. "I'm sorry, Sir Samuel, but it's important that people know where they stand with me."

"These two don't," said Vimes.

"They'll live."

Vimes moved closer to the *wali*.

"*Huthuthut?*" he hissed. "You told me that it meant—"

"I thought it would prove a good example to all if you were in the lead," Ahmed whispered. "The D'regs will always follow a man who is in a hurry for the fray."

Lord Rust stepped out into the sunlight and glared at Vimes.

"Vimes? What the hell are you doing?"

"Not turning a blind eye, my lord."

Vimes pushed past and into the shade. There was Prince Cadram, still seated. And there were a lot of armed men. These, he noted almost in passing, didn't have the look of ordinary soldiers. They had the much tougher look of loyal bodyguards.

"So," said the Prince, "you come in here armed, under a flag of peace?"

"Are you Prince Cadram?" said Vimes.

"And you, too, Ahmed?" said the Prince, ignoring Vimes.

Ahmed nodded, and said nothing.

Oh, not now, thought Vimes. Tough as leather and vicious as a wasp, but now he's in the presence of his king . . .

"You're under arrest," he said.

The Prince made a little sound between a cough and a laugh.

"I'm *what?*"

"I am arresting you for conspiracy to murder your brother. And there may be other charges."

The Prince put his hands over his face for a moment and then pulled them down toward his chin, in the action of a tired man endeavoring to come to grips with a trying situation.

"Mr.—?" he began.

"Sir Samuel Vimes, Ankh-Morpork City Watch," said Vimes.

"Well, Mr. Samuel, when I raise my hand the men behind me will cut you d—"

"I will kill the first man that moves," said Ahmed.

"Then the second man that moves will kill *you*, traitor!" shouted the Prince.

"They'll have to move *very* fast," said Carrot, drawing his sword.

"Any volunteers to be the third man?" said Vimes. "Anyone?"

General Ashal moved, but only very gently, holding up a hand. The bodyguards relaxed slightly.

"What was that . . . *lie* you uttered about a murder?" he said.

"Have you gone mad, Ashal?" said the Prince.

"Oh, sire, before I can disbelieve these pernicious lies, I do need to know what they are."

"Vimes, you *have* gone insane," said Rust. "You can't arrest the commander of an army!"

"Actually, Mr. Vimes, I think we could," said Carrot. "And the army, too. I mean, I don't see why we *can't*. We could charge them with behavior likely to cause a breach of the peace, sir. I mean, that's what warfare *is*."

Vimes's face split in a manic grin. "I *like* it."

"But in fairness our—that is, the Ankh-Morpork army—are also—"

"Then you'd better arrest them too," said Vimes. "Arrest the lot of 'em. Conspiracy to cause an affray," he started to count on his fingers, "going equipped to commit a crime, obstruction, threatening behavior, loitering with intent, loitering *within* tent, hah, traveling for the purposes of committing a crime, malicious lingering and carrying concealed weapons."

"I don't think that one—" Carrot began.

"*I* can't see 'em," said Vimes.

"Vimes, I *order* you to come to your senses this minute!" roared Lord Rust. "Have you been out in the sun?"

"That's one count of offensive behavior to his lordship as well," said Vimes.

The Prince was still staring at Vimes.

"You seriously think that you can *arrest* an army?" he said. "Perhaps you think you have a *bigger* army?"

"Don't need one," said Vimes. "Power at a point, that's what Tacticus says. And here it's the one right on the end of Ahmed's crossbow. That wouldn't frighten a D'reg, but you . . . I reckon you don't think like them. Tell your men to stand down. I want the order to go out right now."

"Even Ahmed would not shoot his prince in cold blood," said Prince Cadram.

Vimes snatched the crossbow. "I wouldn't ask him to!" He took aim. "Give that order!"

The Prince stared at him.

"Count of three!" shouted Vimes.

General Ashal leaned down and whispered something to the Prince. The man's expression stiffened and he glanced back at Vimes again.

"That's right," said Vimes. "It runs in the family."

"It would be murder!"

"Would it? In wartime? I'm from Ankh-Morpork. Aren't I supposed to be at war with you? Can't be murder if there's a war on. That's written down somewhere."

The general leaned down and whispered.

"One," said Vimes.

Now there was a hurried argument.

"Two."

"Myprincewishesmetosay—" the general began.

"All right, slow down," said Vimes.

"If it makes you any happier, I will send out the order," said the general. "Let the messengers leave."

Vimes nodded and lowered the bow. The Prince shifted uneasily.

"And the Ankh-Morpork army will stand down as well," said Vimes.

"But, Vimes, you're on *our* side—" Rust began.

"Bloody hell, I'm going to shoot *someone* today and it could just be you, Rust," Vimes snarled.

"Sir?" Lieutenant Hornett tugged at his commander's jacket. "May I have a word?"

Vimes heard them whispering, and then the young man left.

"All right, we are all disarmed," said Rust. "We are all 'under arrest.' And now, commander?"

"I ought to read them their rights, sir," said Carrot.

"What are you talking about?" said Vimes.

"The men out there, sir."

"Oh. Yeah. Right. Do it, then."

Oh gods, I arrested an entire battlefield, Vimes thought. And you can't *do* that.

But I've *done* it. And we've only got six cells back at the Yard, and we keep the coal in one of them.

You can't *do* it.

Was this the army that invaded your country, ma'am? No, officer, they were taller than that . . .

How about this one? I'm not sure—get them to march up and down a bit . . .

Carrot's voice could be heard outside, slightly muffled:

"Now . . . can you all hear me? You gentlemen in the back there? Anyone who can't hear me, please raise . . . all right, has anyone got a megaphone? Some cardboard I could roll up? In that case I'll shout . . ."

"What now?" said the Prince.

"I'm taking you back to Ankh-Morpork—"

"I don't think so. That would be an act of war."

"You are making a mockery of the whole business, Vimes!" said Lord Rust.

"So long as I'm doing something right, then." Vimes nodded at Ahmed.

"Then you can answer for your crime here, sire," he said.

"In what court?" said the Prince.

Ahmed leaned closer to Vimes. "What was your plan from here on?" he whispered.

"I never thought we'd get this far!"

"Ah. Well . . . it has been interesting, Sir Samuel."

Prince Cadram smiled at Vimes. "Would you like some coffee while you are considering your next move?" he said. He gestured to an ornate silver pot on the table.

"We've got proof." Vimes said. But he could feel the world dropping away. The point about burning your boats is that you shouldn't be standing on them when you drop the match.

"Really? Fascinating. And to whom will you show this proof, Sir Samuel?"

"We'll have to find a court."

"Intriguing. A court in Ankh-Morpork, perhaps? Or a court here?"

"Someone told me that the world watches," said Vimes.

There was silence except for the muffled sounds of Carrot, outside, and the occasional buzz of a fly.

"*. . . bingeley-bingeley beep . . .*" The Dis-organizer's voice had lost its chirpy little edge, and sounded sleepy and bewildered. Heads turned.

"*. . . Seven eh em . . . Organize Defenders at River Gate . . . Seven twenty-five . . . Hand-to-Hand Fighting in Peach Pie Street . . . Seven forty-eight eight eight . . . Rally Survivors in Sator Square . . . Things To Do Today: Build Build Build Barricades . . .*"

He was aware of surreptitious movement behind him, and then slight pressure. Ahmed was standing back to back with him.

"What is that thing talking about?"

"Search me. Sounds like it's in a different world, doesn't it . . . ?"

He could feel events racing toward a distant wall. Sweat filled his eyes. He couldn't remember when he'd last had a proper sleep. His legs twinged. His arms ached, pulled down by the heavy bow.

"*. . . bingeley . . . Eight oh two eh em, Death of Corporal Littlebottombottom . . . Eight oh three eh em . . . Death of Sergeant Detritus . . . Eight oh threethreethree eh em and seven seconds seconds . . . Death of Constable Visit . . . Eight oh three eh em and nineninenine seconds . . . Death of death of death of . . .*"

"They say that in Ankh-Morpork one of your ancestors killed a king," said the Prince. "And he also came to no good end."

Vimes wasn't listening.

"*. . . Death of Constable Dorfl . . . Eight oh three eh em and fourteenteenteen seconds . . .*"

The figure in the throne seemed to take up the whole world.

"*. . . Death of Captain Carrot Ironfoundersson . . . beep . . .*"

And Vimes thought: *I nearly didn't come. I nearly stayed in Ankh-Morpork.*

He had always wondered how Old Stoneface had felt, that frosty morning when he picked up the ax that had no legal blessing because the King wouldn't recognize a court even if a jury could be found, that frosty morning when he prepared to sever what people thought was a link between men and deity—

"*. . . beep . . . Things To Do Today Today Today: Die . . .*"

The sensation flowed into his veins like fresh warm blood. It was the feeling that you got when the law ran out, and you looked into a mocking face on the other side of it and you decided that you couldn't go on living if you did not step over the line and do one clean thing—

There was shouting outside. He blinked away the sweat.

"Ah . . . Commander Vimes . . ." said a voice somewhere back over the border.

He kept his aching gaze sighted along the bow. "Yes?"

A hand darted down and grabbed the arrow out of its groove. Vimes blinked. His finger automatically squeezed the trigger. The string slammed back with a *thunk*. And the look on the Prince's face, he knew, would keep him warm on cold nights, if there were ever cold nights again.

He'd heard them all die. But they *weren't* dead. And yet the damn thing had sounded so . . . accurate . . .

Lord Vetinari dropped the arrow fastidiously, like a society lady who has had to handle something sticky.

"Well done, Vimes. I see you've got the donkey up the minaret. Good morning, gentlemen." He gave the company a happy smile. "I see I am not too late."

"Vetinari?" said Rust, seeming to wake up. "What are you doing here? This is a battlefield—"

"I wonder." The Patrician gave him a very brief smile of his very own. "Outside there seem to be a lot of men sitting around. Many of them seem to be having what I believe is known in military parlance as a brew-up. And Captain Carrot is organizing a football match."

"He's *what?*" said Vimes, lowering the bow. Suddenly the world had to be real again. If Carrot was doing something as dumb as that, things were normal.

"Quite a large number of fouls so far, I'm afraid. But I wouldn't call it a battlefield."

"Who's winning?"

"Ankh-Morpork, I believe. By two hacked shins and a broken nose."

For the first time in ages Vimes felt a little pang of patriotism.

Everything else in life was in the privy, but when it came to gouging and kicking he knew which side he was on.

"Besides," Vetinari went on, "I believe quite a large number of people are technically under arrest. And clearly a state of war is not, in practical fact, in being. It is merely a state of football. Therefore, I believe, I am, shall we say . . . back. Excuse me, sire, but this won't take a moment."

He held up a metal cylinder and began to unscrew the end.

For some reason Vimes felt inclined to take a few steps away from it. "What's that?"

"I thought this might become necessary," said Vetinari. "It took some preparation, but I am certain it will work. I hope they're readable. We did our best to keep the damp off them."

A thick roll of paper dropped out on to the floor.

"Commander, have you nothing you should be doing?" he added. "Refereeing, perhaps?"

Vimes picked up the roll and read the first few lines.

"Whereas . . . heretofore, etc., etc. . . . . City of Ankh-Morpork . . . *Surrender?*"

"What?" said Rust and the Prince together.

"Yes, surrender," said Vetinari cheerfully. "A little piece of paper and it's all over. I think you'll find it all in order."

"You can't—" Rust began.

"You can't—" said the Prince.

"Unconditionally?" said General Ashal sharply.

"Yes, I think so," said Vetinari. "We give up all claim to Leshp in favor of Klatch, we withdraw all troops from Klatch and our citizens from the island, and as for reparations . . . shall we say a quarter of a million dollars? Plus various favorable trade arrangements, most-favored nation status and so on and so on. It's all here. Feel free to read it at your leisure."

He passed the document over the head of the Prince and into the hands of the general, who flicked through the pages.

"But we haven't *got*—" Vimes began. Perhaps I *did* get killed, he thought. I'm on the other side, or someone hit me very hard on the head and this is all some kind of mirage—

"It's a forgery!" snapped the Prince. "It's a trick!"

"Well, sire, this man certainly does appear to be Lord Vetinari and these do seem to be the official seals of Ankh-Morpork," said the general. "'Whereas . . . whereby . . . without prejudice . . . ratification within four days . . . way of trade' . . . yes, this does, I have to say, look genuine."

"I won't accept it!"

"I see, sire. It does, though, appear to cover all the points which in your speech last week you—"

"I *certainly* wouldn't accept it!" Rust shouted. He waved a finger under Vetinari's nose. "You'll be banished for this!"

But we haven't *got* that money, Vimes repeated, but this time to himself. We're a very rich city, but we haven't got any actual money. The wealth of Ankh-Morpork is in its people, we're told. And you couldn't remove it with big pliers.

He felt the wind change.

And Vetinari watching him.

And there was something about General Ashal. A certain hunger . . .

"I agree with Rust," he said. "This is dragging the good name of Ankh-Morpork in the mud." To his mild surprise he managed to say that without smiling.

"We lose nothing, sire," General Ashal insisted. "They withdraw from Klatch and Leshp—"

"Damned if we will!" screamed Lord Rust.

"Right! And have everyone know we've been *beaten?*" said Vimes. *"Outwitted?"*

He looked at the Prince, whose gaze was hunting from man to man, but occasionally staring at nothing, as if he was watching some inner vision.

"A quarter of a million is not enough," the Prince said.

Lord Vetinari shrugged. "We can discuss it."

"There is much that I need to buy."

"Things of a sharp metallic nature, no doubt," said Vetinari. "Of course, if we are talking about goods rather than money, there is room for . . . flexibility . . ."

And now we're going to arm him too, Vimes thought.

"You'll be out of the city in a week!" Rust screamed.

Vimes thought the general smiled briefly. Ankh-Morpork

without Vetinari . . . ruled by people like Rust. His future was looking bright indeed.

"The surrender *will* need to be ratified and formally wit-
nessed, however," said Ashal.

"May I suggest Ankh-Morpork?" said Lord Vetinari.

"No. On neutral territory, of course," said the general.

"But where, between Ankh-Morpork and Klatch, is there such
a thing?" said Vetinari.

"I suppose . . . there *is* Leshp," said the general thoughtfully.

"What a good idea," said the Patrician. "That would not have
occurred to me."

"The place is ours anyway!" snapped the Prince.

"*Will* be, sire. Will be," said the general soothingly. "We will
take possession. Quite legally. While the world watches."

"And that's it? What about my arrest?" said Vimes. "I'm not
going to—"

"These are matters of state," said Vetinari. "And there are . . .
diplomatic considerations. I am afraid the good ordering of international affairs cannot hinge upon your concerns over the doings
of one man."

Once again Vimes felt that the words he was hearing were not
the words that were being said.

"I won't—" he began.

"There are larger issues here."

"But—"

"Sterling work, nevertheless."

"There are big crimes and little crimes, is that it?" said Vimes.

"Why don't you take some well-earned rest, Sir Samuel? You
are," Vetinari flashed one of his lightning-fast smiles, "a man of
action. You deal in swords, and chases, and facts. Now, alas, it is
the time for the men of words, who deal in promises and mistrust
and opinions. For you the war is over. Enjoy the sunshine. I trust
we shall all be returning home shortly. I would like you to stay,
Lord Rust . . ."

Vimes realized that he'd been switched off. He spun round
and marched out of the tent.

Ahmed followed him. "That's your master, is it?"

"No! He's just the man who pays my wages!"

"Often hard to know the difference," said Ahmed sympathetically.

Vimes sat down on the sand. He wasn't certain how he'd been managing to stand up. There was some kind of a future now. He hadn't the faintest idea what was in it, but there *was* one. There hadn't been one five minutes ago. He wanted to talk now. That way, he didn't have to think about the Dis-organizer's death roll. It had sounded so . . . *accurate* . . .

"What's going to happen to you?" he said, to drive the thought out of his mind. "When this is over, I mean. *Your* boss isn't going to be pleased with you."

"Oh, the desert can swallow me."

"He'll send people after you. He looks the type."

"The desert will swallow them."

"Without chewing?"

"Believe it."

"It shouldn't have to be like this!" Vimes shouted, at the sky in general. "You know? Sometimes I *dream* that we could deal with the big crimes, that we could make a law for countries and not just for people, and people like him would have—"

Ahmed pulled him upright and patted him on the shoulder.

"I know how it is," he said. "I dream too."

"You do?"

"Yes. Generally of fish."

There was a roar from the crowd.

"Someone's scored a convincing foul, by the sound of it," said Vimes.

They slid and staggered up the side of a dune, and watched.

Someone broke from the scrum and, punching and kicking, staggered toward the Klatchian goal.

"Isn't that man your butler?" said Ahmed.

"Yes."

"One of your soldiers said he bit a man's nose off."

Vimes shrugged. "He's got a very pointed look if I don't use the sugar tongs, I know that."

A white figure marched authoritatively through the mill of players, blowing a whistle.

"And that man, I believe, is your king."

"No."

"Really? Then I am Queen Punjitrum of Sumtri."

"Carrot's a copper, same as me."

"A man like that could inspire a handful of broken men to conquer a country."

"Fine. Just so long as he does it on his day off."

"And he too takes orders from you? You are a remarkable man, Sir Samuel. But you would not, I think, have killed the Prince."

"No. But you'd have killed me if I had."

"Oh, yes. Flagrant murder in front of witnesses. I am, after all, a copper."

They'd reached the camels. One looked round as Ahmed prepared to mount, thought better of spitting at him, and hit Vimes instead. With great precision.

Ahmed looked back at the footballers.

"Up in Klatchistan the nomads play a game very similar to that," he said. "But on horseback. The aim is to get the object around the goal."

"Object?"

"Probably best just to think of it as an 'object,' Sir Samuel. And now, I think, I shall head that way. There are thieves in the mountains. The air is clear up there. As you know, there is always work for policemen."

"You thinking of returning to Ankh-Morpork at any time?"

"You'd like to see me there, Sir Samuel?"

"It's an open city. But be sure to call in at Pseudopolis Yard when you arrive."

"Ah, and we can reminisce about old times."

"No. So you can hand over that sword. We'd give you a receipt and you can pick it up when you leave."

"I'd take some persuading, Sir Samuel."

"Oh, I think I'd only ask once."

Ahmed laughed, nodded at Vimes and rode away.

For a few minutes he was a shape at the base of a column of dust, and then a shifting dot in the heat haze, and then the desert swallowed him.

* * *

The day wore on. Various Klatchian officials and some of the Ankh-Morpork people were summoned to the tent. Vimes wandered close to it a few times and heard the sound of voices raised in dispute.

Meanwhile, the armies dug in. Someone had already erected a crude signpost, its arms pointing to various soldiers' homes. Since these were all in part of Ankh-Morpork the arms all pointed exactly the same way.

He found most of the Watch sitting out of the wind, while a wizened Klatchian woman cooked quite a complicated meal over a small fire. They all seemed to be fully alive, with the usual slight question mark in the case of Reg Shoe.

"Where've you been, Sergeant Colon?" said Vimes.

"Been sworn to secrecy about that, sir. By his lordship."

"Right." Vimes didn't press the point. Getting information out of Colon was like getting water out of a flannel. It could wait. "And Nobby?"

"Right here, sir!" The wizened woman saluted in a clash of bangles.

"That's *you?*"

"Yessir! Doing the dirty work as per the woman's role in life, sir, despite the fact that there is less senior watchmen present, sir!"

"Now then, Nobby," said Colon. "Cheery can't cook, we can't let Reg do it because bits fall into the pan, and Angua—"

"—doesn't do cookery," said Angua. She was lying back on a rock with her eyes closed. The rock was the slumbering shape of Detritus.

"Anyway, you just started doing the cooking like you was expecting to have to do it," said Colon.

"Kebab, sir?" said Nobby. "There's plenty."

"You certainly got a lot of food from somewhere," said Vimes.

"Klatchian quartermaster, sir," said Nobby, grinning beneath his veil. "Used my sexual wiles on him, sir."

Vimes's kebab stopped halfway to his mouth and dripped lamb fat on to his legs. He saw Angua's eyes slam open and stare in horror at the sky.

"I told him I'd take my clothes off and scream if he didn't give me some grub, sir."

"That'd scare the daylights out of me, sure enough," said Vimes. He saw Angua breathe out again.

"Yeah, I reckon if I played my cards right I could be one of them fatal femmies," said Nobby. "I've only got to wink at a man and he runs a mile. Could be useful, that."

"I *told* him he could change back into his uniform, but he says he feels more comfortable like this," whispered Colon to Vimes. "I'm getting a bit worried, to tell you the truth."

I can't handle this, Vimes thought. This isn't in the book of rules.

"Er . . . how can I explain this . . . ?" he began.

"I don't want any of them in-you-endoes," said Nobby. "It's a good idea to walk a mile in someone else's shoes, that's all I'm saying."

"Well, so long as it's just sh—"

"I've just been gettin' in touch with my softer side, all right? Seein' the other man's point of view, sort of thing, even if he's a woman."

He looked at their faces and waved his hands vaguely. "All right, all right, I'll put my uniform on after I've tidied up around the camp. Will that make you all happy?"

"Something smells nice!"

Carrot ran up, bouncing his football. He'd stripped to his waist. The whistle bounced on its string around his neck.

"I've declared half-time," he said, sitting down. "So I've sent some of the lads into Gebra to get four thousand oranges. Shortly the combined Ankh-Morpork regimental bands will put on a display of counter-marching while playing a selection of military favorites."

"Have they *practiced* counter-marching?" said Angua.

"I don't think so."

"Should be good, then."

"Carrot," said Vimes, "I don't wish to pry, but how, in the middle of a desert, did you find a football?" And the voice in the back of his mind insisted: you heard him die, you heard them all die . . . somewhere else.

"Oh, these days I carry a deflated one in my pack, sir. A very pacifying object, a football. Are you all right, sir?"

"Eh? What? Oh. Yes. Just a bit . . . tired. So who's winning?" Vimes patted his pockets, and found his last cigar.

"It's broadly speaking a tie, sir. I had to send four hundred and seventy-three men off, though. Klatch is now well ahead on fouls, I'm sorry to say."

"Sport as a substitute for war, eh?" said Vimes. He rootled in the ashes of Nobby's fire and pulled out a half-consumed . . . well, it helped to think of it as a desert coal.

Carrot gave him a solemn look. "Yes, sir. No one's using weapons. And have you noticed how the Klatchian army is getting smaller? Some of the chiefs from distant parts are taking their men away. They say there's no point in staying if there's not going to be a war. I don't think they really wanted to be here in any case, to tell you the truth. And I don't think it's going to be easy to get them to come back—"

There was shouting behind them. Men were coming out of the tent, arguing. Lord Rust was among them. He looked around, talking to his companions. Then he spotted Vimes and rocketed furiously toward him.

"Vimes!"

Vimes looked up, hand halfway to his cigar.

"We would have won, you know," growled Rust. "We would have won! But we were betrayed on the brink of success!"

Vimes stared at him.

"And it's *your* fault, Vimes! We'll be the laughingstock of Klatch! You know the value these people put on face, and we won't have any! Vetinari is *finished!* And so are you! And so is your stupid, mongrel, *cowardly* Watch! What do you say to that, Vimes? Eh?"

The watchmen sat like statues, waiting for Vimes to say something. Or even move.

"Eh? Vimes?"

Rust sniffed. "What's that smell?"

Vimes slowly shifted his gaze to his fingers. Smoke was rising. There was a faint sizzling.

He stood up and brought his fingers up in front of Rust's face.

"Take it," he said.

"That's . . . just some trick . . ."

"Take it," said Vimes.

Mesmerized, Rust licked his fingers and gingerly took the ember. "It doesn't hurt—"

"Yes, it does," said Vimes.

"In fact it— Aargh!"

Rust jumped back, dropped the ember and sucked his blistered fingers.

"The trick is not to mind that it hurts," said Vimes. "Now go away."

"You won't last long," Rust sneered. "You wait until we're back in the city. You just wait." He strode off, holding his stricken hand.

Vimes went back and sat down by the fire. After a while he said: "Where's he gone now?"

"Back to the lines, sir. I think he's ordering the men home."

"Can he see us?"

"No."

"You sure?"

"There's too many people in the way, sir."

"You're quite sure?"

"Not unless he can see through camels, sir."

"Good." Vimes stuck his fingers in his mouth. Sweat was pouring down his face. "Damn damn damn! Has anyone got any cold water?"

Captain Jenkins had got his ship afloat again. It had taken a lot of digging, and some careful work with balks of timber and the assistance of a Klatchian captain who had decided not to let patriotism stand in the way of profit.

He and his crew were resting on the shore when a greeting rang out from over them.

He squinted into the sun.

"That . . . that can't be Vimes, can it?"

The crew stared.

"Let's get aboard right *now!*"

A figure started down the face of the dune. It moved very fast, much faster than a man could run on the shifting sand, and moved in a zig-zag fashion. As it drew nearer, it turned out to be a man standing on a shield.

It slid to a halt a few feet away from the astonished Jenkins.

"Good of you to wait, captain!" said Carrot. "Very many thanks! The others will be down in a minute."

Jenkins looked back to the top of the dune. There were other, darker figures there now.

"Those are D'regs!" he shouted.

"Oh, yes. Lovely people. Have you met them at all?"

Jenkins stared at Carrot. "Did you *win*?" he said.

"Oh, yes. On penalties, in the end."

Green-blue light filtered through the tiny windows of the Boat.

Lord Vetinari pulled the steering levers until he was pretty certain that they were heading toward a suitable ship and said:

"What is it I can smell, Sergeant Colon?"

"It's Bet— It's Nobby, sir," said Colon, pedalling industriously.

"Corporal Nobbs?"

Nobby almost blushed. "I bought a bottle of scent, sir. For my young lady."

Lord Vetinari coughed. "What exactly do you mean by 'your young lady'?" he said.

"Well, for when I get one," said Nobby.

"Ah." Even Lord Vetinari sounded relieved.

"On account of I expect I shall now, me having fully explored my sexual nature and now feeling fully comfortable with myself," said Nobby.

"You feel comfortable with yourself?"

"Yessir!" said Nobby happily.

"And when you find this lucky lady, you will give her this bottle of—"

"'s called 'Kasbah Nights,' sir."

"Of course. Very . . . *floral*, isn't it?"

"Yessir. That's 'cos of the jasmine and rare ungulants in it, sir."

"And yet at the same time curiously . . . *penetrative*."

Nobby grinned. "Good value for money, sir. A little goes a long way."

"Not far enough, possibly?"

But Nobby rusted even irony. "I got it in the same shop that sarge got the hump, sir."

"Ah . . . yes."

There wasn't very much space in the Boat, and most of it was taken up with Sergeant Colon's souvenirs. He'd been allowed a brief shopping expedition "to take home something for the wife, sir, otherwise I'll never hear the last of it."

"Mrs. Colon will like a stuffed camel hump, will she, sergeant?" said the Patrician doubtfully.

"Yessir. She can put things on it, sir."

"And the set of nested brass tables?"

"To put things on, sir."

"And the"—there was a clanking—"set of goat bells, ornamental coffee pot, miniature camel saddle and this . . . strange glass tube with little bands of different colored sand in it . . . what are these for?"

"Conversation pieces, sir."

"You mean people will say things like 'What are they for?', do you?"

Sergeant Colon looked pleased with himself.

"See, sir? We're talking about 'em already."

"Remarkable."

Sergeant Colon coughed and indicated with a tilt of his head the hunched figure of Leonard, who was sitting in the stern with his head in his hands.

"He's a bit quiet, sir," he whispered. "Can't seem to get a word out of him."

"He has a lot on his mind," said the Patrician.

The watchmen pedaled onward for a while, but the close confines of the Boat encouraged a confidentiality that would never have been found on land.

"Sorry to hear you're getting the sack, sir," said Colon.

"Really," said Lord Vetinari.

"You'd definitely get my vote, if we had elections."

"Capital."

"I think people *want* the thumbscrew of firm government, myself."

"Good."

"Your predecessor, Lord Snapcase, now he *was* mental. But, like I've always said, people know where they stand with Lord Vetinari . . ."

"Well done."

"They might not *like* where they're standing, of course . . ."

Lord Vetinari looked up. They were under a boat now and it seemed to be going in the right direction. He steered the Boat until he heard the *thunk* of hull hitting hull, and gave the auger a few turns.

"Am I being sacked, sergeant?" he said, sitting back.

"Well, eh, I heard Lord Rust's people say that if you rat . . . rat . . ."

"Ratify," said Lord Vetinari.

"Yeah, if you *ratify* that surrender next week, they'll get you exiled, sir."

"A week is a long time in politics, sergeant."

Colon's face widened in what he thought of as a knowing grin. He tapped the side of his nose.

"Ah, *politics*," he said. "Ah, you should've *said*."

"Yeah, they'll laugh at the other foot then, eh?" said Nobby.

"Got some secret plan, I'll be bound," said Colon. "You know where the chicken is all right."

"I can see there's no fooling such skilled observers of the carnival that is life," said Lord Vetinari. "Yes, indeed, there is something I intend to do."

He adjusted the position of the camel-hump pouffe, which in fact smelled of goat and was beginning to leak sand, and lay back.

"I'm going to do nothing. Wake me up if anything interesting happens."

Nautical things happened. The wind spun about so much that a weathercock might as well be harnessed to grinding corn. At one point there was a fall of anchovies.

And Commander Vimes tried to sleep. Jenkins showed him a hammock, and Vimes realized that this was another sheep's eyeball. No one could possibly sleep in something like that. Sailors probably kept them up for show and had real beds tucked away somewhere.

He tried to make himself comfortable in the hold, and dozed while the others talked in the corner. They were very politely keeping out of his way.

"—ordship wouldn't give the whole thing away, would he? What were we fighting for?"

"He'll have a hard job hanging on to the job after this, that's for sure. It's dragging the good name of Ankh-Morpork in the mud, like Mr. Vimes said."

"For Ankh-Morpork, mud is *up.*" That was Angua.

"On der other han', everyone is still breathin'." That was Detritus.

"That's a vitalist remark—"

"Sorry, Reg. What you scratchin' for?"

"I think I picked up a filthy foreign disease."

"Sorry?" Angua again. "What can a *zombie* catch?"

"Don't like to say . . ."

"You're talking to someone who knows every brand of flea powder they sell in Ankh-Morpork, Reg."

"Oh, if you must know . . . Mice, miss. It's shameful. I keep myself clean, but they just find a way—"

"Have you tried everything?"

"Excepting ferrets."

"If his lordship goes, who'll take over?" That was Cheery. "Lord Rust?"

"He'd last five minutes."

"Maybe the guilds will get together and—"

"They'll fight like—"

"—ferrets," said Reg. "The cure's worse than the disease."

"Cheer up, there'll still be a Watch." That was Carrot.

"Yes, but Mr. Vimes'll be out on his ear. 'cos of politics."

Vimes decided to keep his eyes closed.

A silent crowd was waiting on the quayside when the ship finally docked. They watched Vimes and his men walk down the gangway. There were one or two coughs, and then someone called out:

"Say it ain't so, Mr. Vimes!"

At the foot of the gangplank Constable Dorfl saluted stiffly.

"Lord Rust's Ship Got In This Morning, Sir," the golem said.

"Anyone seen Vetinari?"

"No, Sir."

"Afraid to show his face!" someone shouted.

"Lord Rust Said You Were To Do Your Duty, Damn You," said Dorfl. Golems had a certain literalness of speech.

He handed Vimes a sheet of paper. Vimes grabbed it and read the first few lines.

"What's this? 'Emergency Council?' And this? . . . *Treason?* Against Vetinari? I'm not carrying this out!"

"Can I see, sir?" said Carrot.

It was Angua who noticed the wave, while the others were staring at the warrant. Even in human form a werewolf's ears are pretty sensitive.

She wandered back to the quayside and looked downriver.

A wall of white water a few feet high was running up the Ankh. As it passed, boats were lifted and rocked.

It sloshed by her, sucking at the quay and making Jenkins's boat dance for a moment. There was a crash of crockery somewhere aboard.

Then it was gone, a line of surf heading toward the next bridge. For a moment the air smelled not of the Ankh's *eau de latrine* but of sea winds and salt.

Jenkins appeared out of his cabin and looked over the side.

"What was that? The tide changing?" Angua called up.

"We came up on the tide," said Jenkins. "Beats me. One of those phenomena, I expect."

Angua went back to the group. Vimes was already red in the face.

"It *has* been signed by quite a lot of the major guilds, sir," Carrot was saying. "In fact they're all here except the Beggars and the Seamstresses."

"Really? Well, piss on 'em! Who are they to give *me* an order like *that?*"

Angua saw the look of pain cross Carrot's face.

"Uh . . . *someone* has to give us orders, sir. In a general sort of way. We aren't supposed to make up our own. That's sort of . . . the point."

"Yes . . . but . . . not like . . ."

"And I suppose they represent the will of the people—"

"That bunch? Don't give me that rubbish! We'd have been

slaughtered if we'd fought! And then we'd be in just the same position as we—"

"This does look legal, sir."

"It's . . . ridiculous!"

"It's not as if *we* are accusing him, sir. We just have to make sure he turns up at the Rats Chamber. Look, sir, you've had a very trying time—"

"But . . . arrest Vetinari? I can't—"

Vimes stopped, because his ears had caught up. And because that was the point, wasn't it? If you could arrest anyone, then that's what you had to do. You couldn't turn round and say "but not *him*." Ahmed would snigger. Old Stoneface would turn in all five of his graves.

"I can, can't I?" he said, sadly. "Oh, all right. Put out a description, Dorfl."

"That Will Not Be Necessary, Sir."

The crowds moved aside as Lord Vetinari walked along the quay, with Nobby and Colon behind him. At least, if it wasn't Sergeant Colon it was a very strangely deformed camel.

"I think I caught quite a lot of that, commander," said Lord Vetinari. "Please do your duty."

"All you've got to do is go to the palace, sir. Let's—"

"You're not going to handcuff me?"

Vimes's mouth dropped open. "Why should I do that?"

"Treason is very nearly the ultimate crime, Sir Samuel. I think I should *demand* handcuffs."

"All right, if you insist." Vimes nodded at Dorfl. "Cuff him, then."

"You haven't any shackles, by any chance?" said Lord Vetinari, as Dorfl produced a pair of handcuffs. "We may as well do this thing properly—"

"No. We *don't* have any shackles."

"I was only trying to help, Sir Samuel. Shall we be going?"

The crowd weren't jeering. That was almost frightening. They were just waiting, like an audience watching to see how the trick was going to be done. They parted again as the Patrician headed toward the center of the city. He stopped and turned.

"What was the other thing . . . oh, yes, I don't have to be dragged on a hurdle, do I?"

"Only if you're actually executed, my lord," said Carrot, cheerfully. "Traditionally, traitors are dragged to their place of execution on a hurdle. And then you're hung, drawn and quartered." Carrot looked embarrassed. "I know about the hanging and quartering but I'm not sure how you're drawn, sir."

"Are you any good with a pencil, captain?" said Lord Vetinari innocently.

"No, he's not!" said Vimes.

"Do you actually *have* a hurdle?"

"*No!*" snapped Vimes.

"Oh? Well, I believe there's a sports equipment shop in Sheer Street. Just in case, Sir Samuel."

A figure walked across the trampled sand near Gebra, and paused when a voice very near ground level said, hopefully, "Bingeley-bingeley beep?"

The Dis-organizer felt itself being picked up.

WHAT KIND OF A THING ARE YOU?

"I am the Dis-organizer Mk II, with many handy hard-to-use features, Insert Name Here!"

SUCH AS?

Even the Dis-organizer's tiny mind felt slightly uneasy. The voice it was speaking to didn't sound right.

"I know what time it is everywhere," it ventured.

SO DO I.

"Er . . . I can maintain an up-to-the-minute contacts directory . . ." The Dis-organizer felt movements that suggested the new owner had mounted a horse.

REALLY? I HAVE A GREAT MANY CONTACTS.

"There you are, then," said the demon, trying to hold on to its rapidly draining enthusiasm. "So I make a note of them, and when you want to contact them again—"

THAT IS GENERALLY NOT NECESSARY. MOSTLY, THEY STAY CONTACTED.

"Well . . . do you have many appointments?" There were hoof-beats, and then no sound but rushing wind.

MORE THAN YOU COULD POSSIBLY IMAGINE. NO . . . I THINK, PER-
HAPS, YOUR TALENTS COULD BE BETTER EMPLOYED ELSEWHERE . . .

There was more rushing wind, and then a splash.

The Rats Chamber was crowded. Guild leaders were entitled to
be there, but there were plenty of other people who considered
they had a right to be in at the death, too. There were even some
of the senior wizards. Everyone wanted to be able to say to their
grandchildren "I was there."*

"I feel certain I ought to be wearing more chains," said Vetinari,
as they paused in the doorway and looked at the assembled crowd.

"Are you taking this seriously, sir?" said Vimes.

"Incredibly seriously, commander, I assure you. But if by some
chance I survive, I authorize you to buy some shackles. We must
learn to do this sort of thing properly."

"I shall keep them handy, I assure you."

"Good."

The Patrician nodded at Lord Rust, who was flanked by Mr.
Boggis and Lord Downey.

"Good morning," he said. "Can we make this quick? It's going
to be a busy day."

"It pleases you to *continue* to make Ankh-Morpork a laughingstock," Rust began. His glance flicked to Vimes for a moment, and
wrote him out of the universe. "This is not a formal trial, Lord
Vetinari. It is an arraignment so that the charges may be known. Mr.
Slant tells me that it will be many weeks before a full trial can be
mounted."

"Expensive weeks no doubt. Shall we get on with it?" said
Vetinari.

"Mr. Slant will read the charges," said Rust. "But in a nutshell,
as you are well aware, Havelock, you are charged with treason.
You surrendered most ignobly—"

"—but I did not—"

"—and quite illegally waived all rights to our sovereignty of
the country known as Leshp—"

---

* Although of course wizards aren't allowed to, because they're not supposed to
have grandchildren.

"—but there is no such place."

Lord Rust paused. "Are you quite sane, sir?"

"The surrender terms were to be ratified on the island of Leshp, Lord Rust. There is no such place."

"We *passed* it on the way here, man!"

"Has anyone looked recently?"

Angua tapped Vimes on the shoulder.

"A strange wave came up the river just after we arrived, sir—"

There was some urgent conversation among the wizards, and Archchancellor Ridcully stood up.

"There seems to be a bit of a problem, your lordships. The Dean says it really *isn't* there."

"It's an *island*. Are you suggesting someone's stolen it? Are you sure you know where it is, man?"

"We do know where it is, and it isn't there. There's just a lot of seaweed and wreckage," said the Dean coldly. He stood up, holding a small crystal ball in his hands. "We've been watching it most evenings. For the fights, you know. Of course, the picture is pretty bad at this distance—"

Rust stared at him. But the Dean was too large to be written out of the scene.

"But an entire island can't just vanish," said Rust.

"In theory they can't just appear either, my lord, but this one did."

"Perhaps it's sunk again," said Carrot.

Now Rust glared at Vetinari.

"Did you know about this?" he demanded.

"How could I know something like that?"

Vimes watched the faces around the room.

"You *do* know something about this!" said Rust. He glanced toward Mr. Slant, who was leafing hurriedly through a large volume.

"All I know, my lord, is that Prince Cadram has, at a politically dangerous time for him, given up a huge military advantage in exchange for an island which seems to have sunk under the sea," said Lord Vetinari. "The Klatchians are a proud people. I wonder what they will think?"

And Vimes thought about General Ashal, standing beside

Prince Cadram's throne. Klatchians like successful leaders, he thought. I wonder what happens to the unsuccessful ones? I mean, look at what *we* do when *we* think—

Someone nudged him.

"'s us, sir," said Nobby. "They said they didn't have any hurdles but they do a ping-pong table for ten dollars. There's a small trampoline we could drag him on but sarge thinks that'd be a bit ridiculous."

Vimes walked out of the room, dragging Nobby with him, and pushed the little man against the wall.

"Where did you get to with Vetinari, corporal? And remember I know when you tell me lies. Your lips move."

"We . . . we . . . we . . . just went on a little voyage, sir. He said I wasn't to say we went under the island, sir!"

"So you— *Under* Leshp?"

"Nossir! We didn't go down there! Stinking hole it was, too. Stunk of rotten eggs, the whole bloody cave, and as big as the city, believe me!"

"I bet you're glad you didn't go, then."

Nobby looked relieved. "That's right, sir."

Vimes sniffed. "Are you using some kind of aft—" —he corrected himself— "some kind of insteadofshave, Nobby?"

"No, sir?"

"Something smells of fermented flowers."

"Oh, it's just a souvenir I picked up in foreign parts, sir. It kind of lingers, if you know what I mean."

Vimes shrugged and went back into the Rats Chamber.

"—and I resent most strongly the suggestion that I would have negotiated with His Highness in the knowledge that . . . ah, Sir Samuel. The keys to the handcuffs, please."

"You knew! You knew all the time!" Rust shouted.

"Is Lord Vetinari charged with anything?" said Vimes.

Mr. Slant was scrabbling through another volume. He looked quite flustered, for a zombie. His gray-green shade was distinctly greener.

"Not as such . . ." he muttered.

"But he *will* be!" said Lord Rust.

"Well, when you find out what it is you be sure and let me

309

know, and I'll go and arrest him for it," said Vimes, unlocking the handcuffs.

He was aware of cheering outside. Nothing stayed secret very long in Ankh-Morpork. The damn island wasn't there anymore. And, somehow, it had all worked out.

He met Vetinari's eyes. "Piece of luck for you, eh?" he said.

"Oh, there's always a chicken, Sir Samuel. If you look hard enough."

The day turned out to be nearly as trying as war. At least one carpet made the flight from Klatch, and there was a constant stream of messages between the palace and the embassy. A crowd still hung around outside the palace. Things were happening, and even if they did not know what they were they weren't going to miss them. If any history was going to occur, they wanted to watch it.

Vimes went home. To his amazement, the door was answered by Willikins. He had his sleeves rolled up and was wearing a long green apron.

"You? How the hell did you get back so quickly?" said Vimes. "Sorry. I didn't mean to be impolite—"

"I inveigled myself onto Lord Rust's ship in the general confusion, sir. I did not wish to let things go to rack and ruin here. The silverware is frankly disgusting, I am afraid. The gardener does not have the least idea how to do it. Allow me to apologize in advance for the shocking condition of the cutlery, sir."

"A few days ago you were biting people's noses off!"

"Ah, you must not believe Private Bourke, sir," said the butler, as Vimes stepped in. "It was only one nose."

"And now you've hurried back to polish the silver?"

"It does not do to let standards slip, sir." He stopped. "Sir?"

"Yes?"

"Did we win?"

Vimes looked into the round pink face.

"Er . . . we didn't lose, Willikins," he said.

"We couldn't let a foreign despot raise a hand to Ankh-Morpork, could we, sir?" said the butler. There was a slight tremble in his voice.

"I suppose not . . ."

"So it was right, what we did."

"I suppose so . . ."

"The gardener was saying that Lord Vetinari put one over on the Klatchians, sir . . ."

"I don't see why not. He's done it with everyone else."

"That would be very satisfactory, sir. Lady Sybil is in the Slightly Pink Drawing Room, sir."

She was knitting inexpertly when Vimes came in, but rose and gave him a kiss.

"I heard the news," she said. "Well done." She looked him up and down. As far as she could see, he was all there.

"I'm not sure that we won . . ."

"Getting you back alive counts as a win, Sam. Although of course I wouldn't say that in front of Lady Selachii." Sybil waved the knitting at him. "She's organized a committee to knit socks for our brave lads at the front, but it turns out you're back. And I haven't even worked out how to turn a heel yet. She's probably going to be annoyed."

"Er . . . how long do you think my legs are?"

"Um . . ." She looked at the knitting. "Do you need a scarf?"

He kissed her again.

"I'm going to have a bath and then something to eat," he said.

The water was only lukewarm. Vimes had some hazy idea that Sybil thought that really hot baths might be letting the side down while there was a war on.

He was lying with his nose just above the surface when he heard, with the addition of that special *gloinggloing* sound that comes from listening with your ears underwater, some distant talking. Then the door opened.

"Fred's here. Vetinari wants you," said Sybil.

"Already? But we haven't even *started* dinner."

"I'm coming with you, Sam. He can't keep on calling you out at all hours, you know."

Sam Vimes tried to look as serious as any man can when he's holding a loofah.

"Sybil, I'm the Commander of the Watch and he's the ruler of the city. It's not like going to complain to the teacher because I'm not doing well in geography . . ."

"I said I'm coming with you, Sam."

*   *   *

The Boat slipped down its rails and into the water. A stream of bubbles came up.

Leonard sighed. He had very carefully refrained from putting the cork in. The current might roll it anywhere. He hoped it'd roll to the deepest pit of the ocean, or even right over the Rim.

He walked unnoticed through the crowds until he came to the palace. He let himself into the secret corridor and avoided the various traps without thinking, since he himself had designed them.

He reached the door to his airy room and unlocked it. When he was inside he locked it again, and pushed the key back under the door. And then he sighed.

So that was the world, was it? Clearly a mad place, with madmen in it. Well, from now on he'd be careful. It was clear that some men would try to turn *anything* into a weapon.

He made himself a cup of tea, a process slightly delayed while he designed a better sort of spoon and a small device to improve the circulation of the boiling water.

Then he sat back in his special chair and pulled a lever. Counterweights dropped. Somewhere, water sloshed from one tank to another. Bits of the chair creaked and slid into a comfortable position.

Leonard stared bleakly out of the skylight. A few seabirds turned lazily in the blue square, circling, hardly moving their wings . . .

After a while, his tea growing cold, Leonard began to draw.

"Lady Sybil? This *is* an unexpected surprise," said Lord Vetinari. "Good evening, Sir Samuel, and may I say what a nice scarf you're wearing. And Captain Carrot. Please sit down. We have a lot of business to finish."

They sat.

"Firstly," said Lord Vetinari, "I have just drafted a proclamation for the town criers. The news is good."

"The war *is* officially over, is it?" said Carrot.

"The war, captain, never happened. It was a . . . misunderstanding."

"Never happened?" said Vimes. "People got killed!"

"Quite so," said Lord Vetinari. "And this suggests, does it not, that we should try to understand one another as much as possible?"

"What about the Prince?"

"Oh, I am sure we can do business with him, Vimes."

"I don't think so!"

"Prince Khufurah? I thought you rather liked the man."

"What? What happened to the other one?"

"He appears to have gone on a long visit to the country," said the Patrician. "At some speed."

"You mean the kind of visit where you don't even stop to pack?"

"That kind of visit, yes. He seems to have upset people."

"Do we know which country?" said Vimes.

"Klatchistan, I believe— I'm sorry, did I say something funny?"

"Oh, no. No. Just a thought crossed my mind, that's all."

Vetinari leaned back. "And so once again peace spreads her tranquil blanket."

"I shouldn't think the Klatchians are very happy, though."

"It is in the nature of people to turn on their leaders when they fail to be lucky," Vetinari added, his expression not changing. "Oh, there will no doubt be problems. We will just have to . . . discuss them. Prince Khufurah is an amiable man. Very much like most of his ancestors. A flask of wine, a loaf of bread and thou, or at least a selection of thous, and he'd not be too interested in politics."

"They're as clever as us," said Vimes.

"We just have to stay ahead of them, then," said Vetinari.

"A brain race, sort of," said Vimes.

"Better than an arms race. Cheaper, too," said the Patrician. He flicked through the papers in front of him. "Now then, what was— Oh, yes. The matter of traffic?"

"Traffic?" Vimes's brain tried to do a U-turn.

"Yes. Our ancient streets are becoming very congested these days. I hear there is a carter in Kings' Way who settled down and raised a family while in the queue. And the responsibility for keeping the streets clear is, in fact, one of the most ancient ones incumbent on the Watch."

"Maybe, sir, but these days—"

"So you will set up a department, Vimes, to regulate matters. To deal with things. Stolen carts and so on. And keeping the major crossroads clear. And perhaps to fine carters who park for too long and impede the flow. And so on. Sergeant Colon and Corporal Nobbs would, I think, be eminently fitted for this work which, I suspect, should easily be self-financing. What is your opinion?"

A chance to be "self-financing" and not get shot at, thought Vimes. They'll think they've died and gone to heaven.

"Is this some sort of a reward for them, sir?"

"Let us say, Vimes, that where one finds one has a square peg, one should look for a square hole."

"I suppose that's all right, sir. Of course, that means I'll have to promote someone—"

"I am sure I can leave the details to you. A small bonus for each of them would not be out of order. Ten dollars, say. Oh, there is one other thing, Vimes. And I am particularly glad that Lady Sybil is here to hear this. I am persuaded to change the title of your office."

"Yes?"

"'Commander' is rather a mouthful. So I have been reminded that a word that originally meant *commander* was 'Dux.'"

"Dux Vimes?" said Vimes. He heard Sybil gasp.

He was aware of a waiting hush around him, such as may be found between the lighting of a fuse and the bang. He rolled the word over and over in his mind.

"*Duke?*" he said. "Oh, *no*— Sybil, could you wait outside?"

"Why. Sam?"

"I need to discuss this very personally with his lordship."

"Have a row, you mean?"

"A discussion."

Lady Sybil sighed. "Oh, very well. It's up to you, Sam. You know that."

"There are . . . associated matters," said Lord Vetinari, when the door closed behind her.

"No!"

"Perhaps you should hear them."

"No! You've done this to me before! We've got the Watch set up, we've almost got the numbers, the widows and orphans fund is so big the men are queueing up for the dangerous beats, and the dartboard we've got is nearly new! You can't bribe me into accepting this time! There is *nothing* we want!"

"Stoneface Vimes was a much-maligned man, I've always thought," said Vetinari.

"I'm not accepting— What?" Vimes skidded in mid-anger.

"I've always thought that, too," said Carrot loyally.

Vetinari stood up and went to stand by the window, looking down at Broad Way with his hands behind his back.

"The thought occurs that this might be time for . . . reconsideration of certain ancient assumptions," said Vetinari.

The meaning enveloped Vimes like a chilly mist.

"You're offering to change history?" he said. "Is that it? Rewrite the—"

"Oh, my dear Vimes, history changes all the time. It is constantly being reexamined and reevaluated, otherwise how would we be able to keep historians occupied? We can't possibly allow people with their sort of minds to walk around with time on their hands. The Chairman of the Guild of Historians is in full agreement with me, I know, that the pivotal role of your ancestor in the city's history is ripe for fresh . . . analysis."

"Discussed it with him, have you?" said Vimes.

"Not yet."

Vimes opened and shut his mouth a few times. The Patrician went back to his desk and picked up a sheet of paper.

"And, of course, other details would have to be taken care of . . ." he said.

"Such as?" Vimes croaked.

"The Vimes coat of arms would be resurrected, of course. It would have to be. I know Lady Sybil was extremely upset when she found you weren't entitled to one. And a coronet, I believe, with knobs on—"

"You can take that coronet with the knobs on and—"

"—which I hope you will wear on formal occasions, such as, for example, the unveiling of the statue which has for so long disgraced the city by its absence."

For once, Vimes managed to get ahead of the conversation.

"Old Stoneface again?" he said. "That part of it, is it? A statue to old Stoneface?"

"Well done," said Lord Vetinari. "Not of you, obviously. Putting up a statue to someone who tried to *stop* a war is not very, um, statuesque. Of course, if you had butchered five hundred of your own men out of arrogant carelessness, we'd be melting the bronze already. No. I was thinking of the first Vimes who tried to make a future and merely made history. I thought perhaps somewhere in Peach Pie Street—"

They watched one another like cats, like poker players.

"Top of Broad Way," Vimes said hoarsely. "Right in front of the palace."

The Patrician glanced out of the window. "Agreed. I shall enjoy looking at it."

"And right up close to the wall. Out of the wind."

"Certainly."

Vimes looked nonplussed for a moment. "We lost people—"

"Seventeen, caught in skirmishes of one sort or another," said Lord Vetinari.

"I want—"

"Financial arrangements will be made for widows and dependants."

Vimes gave up.

"Well done, sir!" said Carrot.

The new duke rubbed his chin.

"But that means I'll have to be married to a duchess," he said. "That's a big fat word, *duchess.* And Sybil's never been very interested in that sort of thing."

"I bow to your knowledge of the female psyche," said Vetinari. "I saw her face just now. No doubt when she next takes tea with her friends, who I believe include the Duchess of Quirm and Lady Selachii, she will be entirely unmoved and not faintly smug in any way."

Vimes hesitated. Sybil was an amazingly levelheaded woman, of course, and this sort of thing . . . She'd left it entirely up to him, hadn't she? . . . This sort of thing wouldn't . . . Well, of *course* she wouldn't, she . . . Of course she would, wouldn't she? She wouldn't swank, she'd just be very comfortable knowing that they knew that she knew that they knew . . .

"All right," he said, "but, look, I thought only a king could make someone a duke. It's not like all these knights and barons, that's just, well, political, but something like a duke needs a—"

He looked at Vetinari. And then at Carrot. Vetinari had said that he'd been *reminded* . . .

"I'm sure, if ever there *is* a king in Ankh-Morpork again, he will choose to ratify my decision," said Vetinari smoothly. "And if there never is a king, well, I see no practical problems."

"I'm bought and sold, aren't I?" said Vimes, shaking his head. "Bought and sold."

"Not at all," said Vetinari.

"Yes, I am. We all are. Even Rust. And all those poor buggers who went off to get slaughtered. We're not part of the big picture, right? We're just bought and sold."

Vetinari was suddenly in front of Vimes, his chair hitting the floor behind his desk.

"Really? Men marched away, Vimes. And men marched back. How glorious the battles would have been that they never had to fight!" He hesitated, and then shrugged. "And you say bought and sold? All right. But not, I think, needlessly spent." The Patrician flashed one of those sharp, fleeting little smiles to say that something that wasn't very funny had nevertheless amused him. "*Veni, vici . . .* Vetinari."

Seaweed floated away on aimless currents. Apart from the driftwood, there was nothing to show that Leshp had ever been.

Seabirds wheeled. But their cries were more or less drowned out by the argument going on just above sea level.

"It is entirely our wood, you nodding acquaintance of a dog!"

"Oh? Really? On your side of the island, is it? I don't *think* so!"

"It floated up!"

"How do you know we didn't have some driftwood on our side of the island? Anyway, *we've* still got a barrel of fresh water, camel breath!"

"All right! We'll share! You can have half the raft!"

"Aha! Aha! Want to negotiate, eh, now we've got you over a barrel?"

"Can we just say yes, Dad? I'm fed up with treading water!"

"And you'll have to do your share of the paddling."

"Of course."

The birds glided and turned, white scribbles against the clear blue sky.

"To Ankh-Morpork!"

"To Klatch!"

Down below, as the sunken mountain of Leshp settled further onto the sea bed, the Curious Squid jetted back along its curious streets. They had no idea why, at enormous intervals, their city disappeared up into the sky, but it never went away for very long. It was just one of those things. Things happened, or sometimes they didn't. The Curious Squid just assumed that it all worked out, sooner or later.

A shark swam by. If anyone had risked placing an ear to its side, they would have heard: "Bingeley-bingeley beep! Three pee em . . . Eat, Hunger, Swim. Things To Do Today: Swim, Hunger, Eat. Three oh five pee em: Feeding Frenzy . . ."

It wasn't the most interesting of schedules, but it *was* very easy to organize.

Unusually, Sergeant Colon had put himself on the patrol roster. It was good to get out in the cool air. And also, for some reason, the news had got around that the Watch were somehow bound up with what seemed, in some indefinable way, to have been a victory, which meant that a Watch uniform was probably good for the odd free pint at the back door of the occasional pub.

He patrolled with Corporal Nobbs. They walked with the confident tread of men who had been places and seen things.

With a true copper's instinct, the tread took them past Mundane Meals. Mr. Goriff was cleaning the windows. He stopped when he saw them and darted inside.

"Call that gratitude?" sniffed Colon.

The man reappeared carrying two large packages.

"My wife made this specially for you," he said. He added, "She said she knew you'd be along."

Colon pulled aside the waxed paper.

"My word," he said.

"Special *Ankh-Morpork* curry," said Mr. Goriff. "Containing yellow curry powder, big lumps of swede, green peas and soggy sultanas the—"

"—size of eggs!" said Nobby.

"Thank you very much," said Colon. "How's your lad, then, Mr. Goriff?"

"He says you have set him an example and now he will be a watchman when he grows up."

"Ah, right," said Colon happily. "That'll please Mr. Vimes. You just tell him—"

"In Al-Khali," said Goriff. "He is staying with my brother."

"Oh. Well . . . fair enough, then. Er . . . thanks for the curry, anyway."

"What sort of example do you think he meant?" said Nobby, as they strolled away.

"The good sort, obviously," said Colon, through a mouthful of mildly spiced swede.

"Yeah, right."

Chewing slowly and walking even slower, they headed toward the docks.

"I was gonna write Bana a letter," said Nobby, after a while.

"Yeah, but . . . she thought you was a woman, Nobby."

"Right. So she saw, like, my inner self, shorn of . . ." Nobby's lips moved as he concentrated, "shorn of surface thingy. That's what Angua said. Anyway, then I thought, well, her boyfriend'll be coming back, so I thought I'd be noble about it and give her up."

"'cos he might be a big stroppy bloke, too," said Sergeant Colon.

"I never thought about that, sarge."

They paced for a while.

"It's a far, far better thing I do now than I have ever done before," said Nobby.

"Right," said Sergeant Colon. They walked on in silence for a while and he added: "O'course, that's not difficult."

"I still got the hanky she gave me, look."

"Very nice, Nobby."

"That's genuine Klatchian silk, that is."

"Yeah, it looks very nice."

"I'm never going to wash it, sarge."

"You soppy old thing, Nobby," said Fred Colon.

He watched Corporal Nobbs blow his nose.

"So . . . you're going to stop using it, are you?" he said, doubtfully.

"It still bends, sarge. See?" Nobby demonstrated.

"Yeah, right. Silly of me to ask, really."

Overhead, the weathervanes started to creak round.

"Made me a lot more understanding about women, that experience," said Nobby.

Colon, a much-married man, said nothing.

"I met Verity Pushpram this afternoon," Nobby went on, "and I said how about coming out with me tonight and I don't mind about the squint at all and I've got this expensive exotic perfume which'll totally disguise your smell, and she said bugger off and threw an eel at me."

"Not good, then," said Colon.

"Oh, *yeah,* sarge, 'cos she *used* to just *cuss* when she saw me. And I've still got the eel, and there's a good feed off it, so I look upon it as a very positive step."

"Could be. Could be. Just so long as you give someone that scent soon, eh? Only even the people across the street are starting to complain."

Their feet, moving like bees toward a flower, had found their way to the waterfront. They looked up at the Klatchian's Head, on its spike.

"It's only wooden," said Colon.

Nobby said nothing.

"And it's, like, part of our traditional heritage an' that," Colon went on, but hesitantly, as if he didn't believe his own voice.

Nobby blew his nose again, an exercise which, with all its little arpeggios and flourishes, went on for some time.

The sergeant gave in. Some things didn't seem quite the same anymore, he had to admit. "I've never really liked the place. Let's go to the Bunch of Grapes then, all right?"

Nobby nodded.

"Anyway, the beer here is frankly piss," said Colon.

Lady Sybil held her handkerchief in front of her husband.

"Spit!" she commanded.

Then she carefully cleaned a smut off his cheek.

"There. Now you look very—"

"—ducal," said Vimes gloomily. "I thought I'd done this once already . . ."

"They never actually had the Convivium after all that fuss," said Lady Sybil, picking some microscopic lint off his doublet. "It's got to be held."

"You'd think if I'm a duke I wouldn't have to wear all this damn silly outfit, wouldn't you?"

"Well, I did point out that you could wear the official ducal regalia, dear."

"Yes, I've seen it. White silk stockings are not *me*."

"Well, you've got the calves for them—"

"I think I'll stick with the commander's costume," said Vimes quickly.

Archchancellor Ridcully hurried up. "Ah, we're ready for you now, Lord Vi—"

"Call me Sir Samuel," said Vimes. "I can just about live with that."

"Well, we've found the Bursar in one of the attics, so I think we can make a start. If you'd take your place . . ."

Vimes walked to the head of the procession, feeling every gaze on him, hearing the whispers. Maybe you could get chucked out of the peerage? He'd have to look that up. Although, considering what lords had got up to in the past, it would have to be for something really, really awful.

Still, the drawings of the statue looked good. And he'd seen what was going to go in the history books. Making history, it turned out, was quite easy. It was what got written down. It was as simple as that.

"Jolly good," Ridcully bellowed, above the buzz. "Now, if we all step smartly and follow Lor— Com— Sir Samuel we ought to

321

be back here for lunch no later than half past one. Is the choir ready? No one is treading on anyone else's robes? Then orf we go!"

Vimes set out at the mandatory slow walking pace. He heard the procession start up behind him. There were no doubt problems, as there always are on civic occasions which have to involve the old and deaf and the young and stupid. Several people were probably already walking in the wrong direction.

As he stepped out into Sator Square there were the jeers and various flatulent noises and murmurs of "Oozee then, oozee finkee izz?" that are the traditional crowd responses on these occasions. But there were one or two cheers, too.

He tried to look straight ahead.

Silk stockings. With *garters.* Well, they were out. There were a lot of things he'd do for Sybil, but if garters figured anywhere in the relationship they weren't going to be on him. And everyone said he had to wear a purple robe lined with vermine. They could forget that, too.

He'd spent a desperate hour in the library, and all that stuff about the gold knobs and silk stockings was so much marsh gas. Tradition? He'd show them tradition. What the *original* dukes wore, as far as he could see, was good sensible chain mail with blood on it, preferably other people's—

There was a scream from the crowd. His head jerked round and he saw a stout woman sitting on the ground, waving her arms.

"'e stole my bag! And 'e never showed me 'is Thieves' Guild badge!"

The procession shunted to a halt as Vimes stared at the figure legging it across Sator Square.

"You stop right there, Sidney Pickens!" he yelled, and leapt forward.

And, of course, very few people *do* know how Tradition is supposed to go. There's a certain mysterious ridiculousness about it by its very nature—*once* there was a reason why you had to carry a posy of primroses on Soul Cake Tuesday, but *now* you did it because . . . that's what was Done. Besides, the intelligence of that creature known as a crowd is the square root of the number of people in it.

Vimes was running, so the University choir hurried after him. And the people behind the choir saw the gap opening up and responded to the urge to fill it. And then everyone was just running, because everyone else was running.

There were occasional whimpers from those whose heart, lungs or legs weren't up to this kind of thing, and a bellow from the Archchancellor who had tried to stand firm in the face of the frantic stampede and was now having his head repeatedly trodden into the cobbles.

And apprentice thief Sidney Pickens ran because he'd taken one look over his shoulder and seen the whole of Ankh-Morpork society bearing down on him, and that sort of thing has a terrible effect on a growing lad.

And Sam Vimes ran. He tore off his cloak and whirled away his plumed hat, and he ran and ran.

There would be trouble later on. People would ask questions. But that was later on—for now, gloriously uncomplicated and wonderfully clean, and hopefully with never an end, under a clear sky, in a world untarnished . . . there was only the chase.